Mills & Boon is proud to present
a wonderful selection of novels featuring
her trademark Mediterranean males from
international bestselling author

JACQUELINE BAIRD

Each volume has three terrific, powerful
and passionate stories written by
a queen of the genre.
We know you'll love them…

September 2014

October 2014

November 2014

December 2014

January 2015

February 2015

Mediterranean Tycoons

UNTAMED & UNLEASHED

JACQUELINE BAIRD

MILLS & BOON

Published in Great Britain 2014
by Mills & Boon, an imprint of Harlequin (UK) Limited,
Eton House, 18-24 Paradise Road, Richmond, Surrey, TW9 1SR

ISBN: 978-0-263-25018-3

010-1014

Harlequin (UK) Limited's policy is to use papers that are natural, renewable and recyclable products and made from wood grown in sustainable forests.The logging and manufacturing processes conform to the legalenvironmental regulations of the country of origin.

Printed and bound in Spain
by Blackprint CPI, Barcelona

Jacqueline Baird was born and brought up in Northumbria. She met her husband when she was eighteen. Eight years later, after many adventures around the world, she came home and married him. They still live in Northumbria and now have two grown sons.

Jacqueline's number one passion is writing. She has always been an avid reader and she had her first success as a writer at the age of eleven, when she won first prize in the Nature Diary of the Year competition at school. But she felt a little guilty because her diary was more fiction than fact.

She always loved romance novels and, when her sons went to school all day, she thought she would try writing one. She's been writing for Mills & Boon ever since and she still gets a thrill every time a new book is published.

When Jacqueline is not busy writing, she likes to spend her time travelling, reading and playing cards. She was a keen sailor until a knee injury ended her sailing days, but she still enjoys swimming in the sea when the weather allows.

With a more sedentary lifestyle, she does visit a gym three times a week and has made the surprising discovery that she gets some good ideas while doing the mind-numbingly boring exercises on the cycling and weight machines.

PICTURE OF INNOCENCE

JACQUELINE BAIRD

CHAPTER ONE

LORENZO ZANELLI, owner of the centuries-old Zanelli Merchant Bank, originally bankers to Italian principalities and now a global concern, exited the elevator at his office suite on the top floor of the magnificent old building in the heart of Verona, a frown marring his broad brow.

His business lunch with Manuel Cervantes, the head of an Argentinean conglomerate whose family had been valued clients for years, had gone well, but Lorenzo was not a happy man… His secretary had called to warn him he was going to be late for his next appointment as his lunch had severely overrun—despite the fact that they had completed their business quite quickly.

As soon as work was out of the way Manuel had turned to a more personal topic: the necessity of giving up his career as a mountaineer and keen photographer to take over the running of the company after the death of his father five years ago and his subsequent marriage and two children. Then finally he had shown Lorenzo some shots he had belatedly got around to printing from his last trip to the Alps.

They were pictures taken at the main base camp on Manuel's final expedition to Mont Blanc, and included by sheer chance a few shots of Lorenzo's brother,

Antonio, and Damien Steadman his friend, wearing bright red jackets and even brighter grins, just arriving as Manuel's team were about to start their ascent.

The next morning Manuel's team had been on the last stage of the climb to the summit when he had received news that his father had suffered a heart attack. He'd been airlifted off the mountain by helicopter, and his last shot was a view of the mountain as he was flown down to base camp for the dash back to Argentina to be at his father's bedside. He had heard much later of Antonio's tragic death, and had thought Lorenzo would like to have what were probably the last pictures of his brother. Lorenzo was grateful, but it brought back memories he had spent years trying to forget.

Lorenzo had been looking through the photos as he'd walked back to his offices, taking in the implications of the detail in the landscape shot Manuel had pointed out to him, when he'd literally bumped into an old friend, Olivia Paglia, which had delayed him even further.

His frown deepened as he saw the fair head of a woman seated in the reception area, obviously waiting for him. He had almost forgotten about Miss Steadman, and now was not the best time to deal with her…

'Lucy Steadman?' he queried, casting a dark glance her way. He remembered seeing her years ago when, on a business trip to London, he had called briefly at Antonio's apartment to check in on his little brother. She had been a plump, plain-faced little schoolgirl in a baggy sweater, with long fair pigtails, who had been visiting her brother and was leaving as Lorenzo arrived. Her brother Damien had met Antonio at university in London, and they'd become firm friends and flatmates. A friendship that had ended tragically, and one he certainly did not need reminding of for a second time today…

'Sorry for the delay, but it was unavoidable.' She rose to her feet and he noted she had scarcely changed at all. Small—she barely reached his shoulder—with her hair scraped back in a knot on top of her head, her face free of make-up. The baggy sweater had been replaced with an equally voluminous black suit, with a long skirt that did her no favours at all. Slender ankles, he noted, and tiny feet, but the flat shoes she wore had definitely seen better days. She obviously cared little for her appearance—not a trait he admired in a woman.

Lucy Steadman looked up and up at the man standing in front of her. Antonio had told her once his brother was a lot older than him, and a staid, boring banker who did not know how to enjoy life, amongst other similarly harsh comments, and now she could see what he had meant…

Tall—well over six feet—he was dressed conservatively in a dark suit, a white shirt and plain dark tie. And expensively, she guessed. His broad shoulders were outlined superbly by the well-cut jacket, and she hastily lifted her gaze from where it had drifted down to his hips and thighs to fix on his face. The man was hard and unsmiling, but Antonio had missed one attribute that was immediately obvious to Lucy, even with her limited experience of men.

Lorenzo Zanelli was a truly arresting male, with a subtle aura of animal magnetism about him that any women past puberty could not fail to recognise. Given the severity of his clothes, surprisingly his thick black hair was longer than the current fashion and brushed the white collar of his shirt. The planes of his face were firmly etched , his heavy lidded eyes were brown, almost black, and deep-set beneath thick arched brows his nose large and definitely Roman and his mouth wide and tightly controlled.

'You must be Lorenzo Zanelli,' she said, and held out her hand.

'Correct, Miss Steadman,' he responded, and took her hand.

His clasp was firm and brief, but the sudden ripple of sensation that shot up the length of her arm affected Lucy well after he had dropped her hand, and she simply stared at him. She had the oddest notion he was familiar to her, yet she had no memory of ever having met him before, and he in no way resembled his brother.

He wasn't handsome in the conventional sense, but his face was fascinating. There was strength in his bold features—a powerful character that was undeniable—and the subtle hint of sensuality about his mouth intrigued her. Her gaze lingered on the perfectly chiselled lips, the bottom fuller than the top, and she found herself imagining what his kiss would taste like…sensuous and beguiling. A tiny shudder vibrated through her body and, shocked by her physical response to an uncharacteristic flight of fantasy, she swiftly raised her eyes and ignored her strange reaction to a man she had every reason to dislike.

Lucy excused her totally unprecedented lapse with the wry thought that Lorenzo Zanelli was the sort of man to make anyone look twice. In fact she would like to paint a portrait of him, she mused, slipping back in to her professional comfort zone.

'Miss Steadman, I know why you are here.'

His deep, slightly accented voice cut into her reverie, and she blinked just in time to see his dark eyes flick disdainfully over her. She felt the colour rise in her cheeks with embarrassment at having been caught staring. 'You do?' she murmured inanely. Of course he did—she had written to him...

Her original reason for this trip to Italy was to personally deliver a portrait she had painted of an Italian countess's recently departed husband. The lady had commissioned the painting after walking into Lucy's art and craft gallery with the friend she'd been visiting in England. Lucy had received via the post dozens of photographs of the man, and she had been thrilled that her work was finally going to get some recognition beyond the local scene.

Not that she was seeking fame—realistically, in today's world where a pickled sheep or an unmade-bed made millions—she knew she was never going to get it, but it was nice to feel appreciated for what she did excel at. She had a natural gift for catching the likeness and character of any subject, be it a stuffed dog—her first ever commission!—or a person. Her paintings in oils—full-figure or portrait, large canvas or miniature—were good, even if she did say so herself...

She had confirmed her trip to Verona with the Countess when she had finally managed to get an appointment with Signor Zanelli. After a phone call that had got her nowhere she had written to the Zanelli Bank, asking for its support in staving off the forced buy-out of Steadman Industrial Plastics by Richard Johnson, one of the largest shareholders in her family's firm. She had received a short letter back from some manager, stating that the bank did not discuss its policy on individual investments.

She had very reluctantly, as a last resort, written another letter and marked it 'Personal and Private', addressing it to Lorenzo Zanelli himself. From all she had heard about the man she had formed the opinion he was a typical super-rich alpha male, totally insensitive to other people and with the arrogant conviction that he was always right. He never changed his mind, not even when a formal inquest said otherwise, and she disliked him intensely…

Lorenzo Zanelli had been horrible to Damien after the inquest into the mountaineering accident that had caused Antonio's death, accosting him outside the courthouse and telling him coldly that while legally he might have been found innocent of any fault as far as he was concerned Damien was as guilty as hell, and might as well have cut Antonio's throat instead of the rope. Her brother, devastated by the loss of his friend, had felt badly enough as it was. Lorenzo Zanelli had made him feel a hundred times worse and he had never really recovered.

As far as Lucy was aware there had been no contact between the two families since, and it had come as a shock to her to discover after Damien's death the Zanelli bank was a third silent partner in her family firm. Lorenzo Zanelli was the last man she wanted to ask for a favour but she had no choice. Trying to be positive, she'd told herself maybe she was wrong about Lorenzo—maybe it had been his grief at losing his brother that had made him say horrible things to Damien, and with the passage of time he would have a much more balanced view.

So Lucy had swallowed her pride and written to him, blatantly mentioning her family's friendship with his brother Antonio. She had informed him she was visiting Verona for a day or two, and had almost begged for a few minutes of the man's time before finally being granted an appointment today.

The continuation of Steadman Industrial Plastics as a

family firm was dependent on Lucy persuading Zanelli to agree with her point of view. Not that she had any family left, but to the residents of the small town of Dessington in Norfolk, where she'd been born and had grown up, Steadman's was the main employer, and even though she had not lived there since graduating from college she did still visit occasionally, and she did have a social conscience—which she knew Richard Johnson did not.

She was pinning her hopes on Signor Zanelli. But now, after what she had heard about him and being faced with the man in person, she was having serious doubts.

She had arrived in Verona at ten this morning—well, not exactly *in* Verona. The budget airline she had travelled with had landed at an a airport almost two hours away. She'd just had time to book into her hotel and get here on time, and her flight back was tomorrow evening at eight. On her arrival at his office the great man's secretary had taken her name, made a phone call, and then told her in perfect English that Signor Zanelli was going to be delayed. She had asked her if she would like to reschedule the appointment and, flicking through a diary, had suggested three days' time.

Lucy had countered with a request for the next morning, sacrificing her plan to explore the town and the famed arena. Her appointment with the Contessa was in the afternoon. The secretary had told her it was not possible, but she could wait if she liked. She had had no choice but to agree.

'Miss Steadman?'

He repeated her name and, startled out of her wandering thoughts, she glanced up at him, green eyes clashing with brown. The arch look he gave her was all male arrogance.

'You're a determined little thing, I'll give you that,' he drawled and, turning to his secretary, said something in Italian that sounded like 'ten minutes—then call' before throwing over his shoulder, 'Come, Miss Steadman. This will not take much time.'

Lucy bit back the response that sprang to mind. It had already taken a heck of a lot of her time. Pausing for a moment, she tried to smooth the creased black linen skirt she wore—a pointless exercise—and watched the broad back of the man as he disappeared into his inner sanctum, the door swinging closed behind him. He might be strikingly attractive, but he was certainly no gentleman, and her nerves tightened a notch.

'You'd better go in now,' the secretary said. 'Signor Zanelli does not like to be kept waiting.'

Given how long *she* had been waiting—her appointment had been for two and it was now after three—Zanelli had some nerve, she thought, her temper rising. Dismissing the odd effect he had on her own nerve, she squared her shoulders and, taking a few deep breaths, walked across the room and into the man's office.

He was standing behind a large antique desk, talking rapidly into a telephone which he put down when he saw her.

'Take a seat.' He indicated a chair in front of the desk as he sank into a big black leather one behind it. 'Then say what you have to say, and make it quick—my time is valuable.'

He had not waited for her to sit down. In fact he was well on the way to being the rudest man she had ever met, and she had been right to dislike him sight unseen, Lucy decided, her green eyes sparking angrily.

She said without thinking, 'I can't believe you are Antonio's brother.'

Antonio had been handsome and lovable, and her brother Damien's best friend at university. Lucy had been fourteen when her brother had brought Antonio home the first time for the mid-term break, and she had developed a terrific crush on the young Italian—so besotted she had actually started taking Italian language lessons at school. Antonio, only four years older, but a decade older in experience, had not taken advantage—quite the opposite. He had treated her as a friend and had not made her feel foolish at all. Unlike this hard-faced man, looking at her across the wide expanse of the desk with cold eyes and without a tender bone in his body, she was sure.

'You are nothing like him. You *look* nothing like him.'

Lorenzo was surprised. Lucy Steadman had spirit. Her face had flushed with colour, highlighting the delicate bone structure. She wasn't plain as he had thought, but she *was* angry. His mouth tightened. He did not want to fight with her, he simply wanted her out of his sight as quickly as possible—before his anger got the better of him and he told her in return exactly what he thought of *her* brother…

'You are right. My younger brother was the beautiful one, both inside and out, whereas I—so Antonio used to tell me—am a serious, hard-headed banker with ice in his veins who should lighten up and enjoy life. Not that it did Antonio much good,' he said starkly.

For a moment Lucy thought she saw pain shadow his eyes as he spoke. She had been tactless, letting her dislike of the man show, and politely offered her sympathy. 'I am sorry…so sorry,' she murmured, as the memory of the tragic accident that had killed his brother and which she felt had been instrumental in the death of hers filled her mind. 'I understand how you feel,' she said, and began telling him about her brother.

'Damien never really got over losing his best friend.' She did not add *thanks in part to you,* but she thought it. 'He was never well afterwards. I was finishing my second year at college and tried to help, but it was no good in the end,' she admitted. 'Though he did begin working with my father in the business his heart wasn't in it. Then, when my father died the following year, it was another blow to him. With my father gone Damien could not manage everything, so he decided to hire a manager to oversee the running of the business and within a year everything seemed to be getting better. Then last year Damien went on holiday to Thailand and died there.' He had recklessly stopped taking his medication, and it still hurt Lucy to think of him. 'So I really do know how you feel.'

Lorenzo doubted that Lucy Steadman had an inkling of his real feelings, and he wasn't about to tell her. 'I'm sorry for your loss,' he said coolly. 'But now can we get down to business—the proposed sale of Steadman's, I believe?'

Lucy had almost forgotten the reason she was there as images of the past and this man filled her mind. Suddenly it hit her that she had not made a very good start, and the speech she had prepared had gone clean out of her head.

'Yes—no. Not a sale—I mean, let me explain…'

One devilish brow arched sardonically in her direction. 'I will give you five minutes,' he said, and looked pointedly at his wristwatch.

He had fine black hairs on his wrist, she noted, and

shook her head. What was she thinking…? *Concentrate,* she told herself.

'When my father died, in accordance with his will Damien inherited the family home in Dessington and seventy-five percent of the business. I had the other twenty-five and the holiday house in Cornwall. My father was not big on equality of the sexes.'

'I don't need your opinions—just facts.' Though he knew most of them. The manager in charge of the bank's small investments had kept him informed of any development at Steadman's over the years, but common courtesy decreed he listen to her. But now he realised the reason for the woman's unvarnished looks and clothes. Lorenzo was all for equality of the sexes, and made a point of employing and promoting intelligent women in his organisation, but he had no time for a latter-day women's libber who thought the world owed her a living without her having the requisite skills to earn one, and his patience was fast running out.

Lucy took a deep breath. 'After Damien died I inherited all that was left… Manufacturing plastics is not my thing, so I was quite happy to leave the running of the place to the manager while the lawyer dealt with probate. Unfortunately it was only when the lawyer finalised everything a couple of months ago, and called me in to explain my inheritance, that I discovered my father—with Damien's agreement—had seven years earlier made Antonio a partner in the business by selling him forty percent of the firm. I was still at boarding school at the time, and knew nothing about it, but apparently it was agreed between them all that Damien and Antonio were going to be partners in the business and run it between them when my father retired. Unfortunately Antonio died, so it was never to be.' She sighed, and then chewed nervously on her bottom lip. This was the hard part.

She raised a hand and counted off the fingers of the other hand to help her concentrate. 'So, after my father died I did not *actually* inherit twenty-five percent of the business.' She counted off a second finger. 'It was twenty-five percent of what was only sixty percent.' She counted a third finger. 'So that was twenty…no, wait… fift—'

'*Basta!* Enough.'

Lucy raised her head, her green eyes clashing with his 'You've put me off now,' she declared, waving her hands out wide.

'I'm a banker—I can do the maths. A word of advice—never go into business.' And she could have sworn she saw a hint of amusement in his dark eyes before the shutters came down and his hard, expressionless gaze fixed on her.

'Your time has run out, so I will put you out of your misery. Your brother—who was obviously quite keen on partners,' he said, with a hint of sarcasm in his tone, 'took on another partner eighteen months ago, selling fifteen percent of his share to Richard Johnson, who as it turns out is a property developer. Now your brother has died he wants to buy out the other two partners, demolish the factory and build a block of apartments on the land. You are six percent short of a majority on your own, and you want my bank, which now controls Antonio's investment, to side with you to stop the development.'

In that moment Lorenzo, who had been ambivalent over what action to take—a rare occurrence for him—made up his mind. He had toyed with the idea of supporting Miss Steadman—the monetary aspect was next to nothing to the bank, and it also meant he could avoid discussing with his mother a subject that would reignite the pain of her losing Antonio.

He was intensely protective of his mother—had been since his father's death, and even more so since the death of Antonio. She was a tender-hearted, compassionate woman, who had accepted the inquest result as gospel, and he had taken immense care to ensure she never found out about his confrontation outside the courthouse with Damien. He had paid off the reporter who had caught the declaration of his true view on the case.

But Lucy Steadman was not a good investment. She had been quite happy to let her father and brother keep her in comfort while spouting off about equality of the sexes, and frankly, after what he had learnt earlier today, any thought of assisting a Steadman in any way was anathema to him.

'Yes, that is exactly right—otherwise the factory will close and a lot of people will lose their jobs. That would be a devastating blow to Dessington, the town I grew up in, and I can't let that happen.'

'You have little choice. The factory just about breaks even, but makes very little profit for its partners and consequently is of no interest to this bank. We will be selling to Mr Johnson, who is offering a good return on our original investment.' He could not resist turning the screw a little. 'Bottom line—unless you can come up with a higher figure than that currently on offer to buy out my bank's interest in the next couple of weeks the sale will go through.'

'But I can't—I only have my shares.'

'And two houses, apparently. You could possibly raise money on those with your bank.'

'No—just one and a half. Damien mortgaged his,' Lucy murmured to herself. That was something else she had not known.

'Somehow that does not surprise me,' he drawled cynically and, rising to his feet, walked around the desk to stop in front of her. 'Take my advice, Miss Steadman, and sell out. As you said yourself, you have no interest in plastics, and neither does this bank.'

She glanced up the long, lithe length of him, her green eyes clashing with hard black.

'How old are you? Twenty—twenty-one?' he asked.

'Twenty-four,' she snapped. At five feet two and with youthful appearance, it had been the bane of her life at college, when she'd continually been asked for proof of her age. Even now she still had to carry identification if she wanted to enter licensed premises.

'Twenty-four is still young. Do as your brother did and have fun. Allow me to show you out.'

Throw her out, more like, Lucy thought, and panicked. 'Is that it?' She leapt to her feet and grasped his arm as he turned towards the door. 'No discussion? At the very least give me more time to try and raise the money. I'll do anything I can to save the factory.'

Lorenzo looked down into her eyes. They were an amazing green, he realised, big and pleading. He lost his train of thought for a moment…

He could do without Lucy Steadman and her persistence. He had known of her initial call to the bank, and that she had been sent the bank's standard response. When he'd received her personal letter informing him she was visiting Verona he had told his secretary to arrange a meeting for two reasons. Firstly out of respect for his mother's feelings, because she was the one who had given Antonio the money to buy his share in

Steadman's in the first place, without Lorenzo or the bank's knowledge, and it seemed she had a sentimental attachment to the investment.

It had only been after Antonio's death and the inquest, when Lorenzo had got around to dealing with his brother's personal estate, that he'd actually discovered his brother was a partner in Steadman's. He had queried his mother about the investment because the transaction had not been made through the Zanelli Bank but the Bank of Rome, and had suggested she sell. Her reply had astounded him.

Her own mother's advice when she'd married had been to always keep a separate account that one's husband knew nothing about, as it gave a wife a sense of independence. Obviously her account could not be at the Zanelli Bank, hence it was at the Bank of Rome. As for selling, she hadn't been sure—because it still gave her great comfort to know that Antonio had not been the lightweight people had thought, but had made plans for the future and intended being a successful businessman in his own right.

Lorenzo didn't agree. On finishing university Antonio and Damien had taken a gap year together, to travel around the world. That had spread into a second year, until their last mountaineering escapade that had seen Antonio dead at twenty-three. He doubted if either of them would have settled down to run a plastics factory… But he hadn't argued with his mother, and she had agreed to his suggestion that he buy the investment from her and bring it under the control of the Zanelli Bank.

The other reason he had agreed to meet Lucy Steadman was in memory of his brother. Because if he was honest he felt guilty. He had been so involved with work and his own business affairs that he had not paid as much attention to Antonio as he should have done. He had loved his brother from the moment he was born, but Antonio had been only eight when Lorenzo had left home for university, and holidays aside he had never returned, going straight to America after graduating. When he did return on the death of his father, to take over the bank, Antonio had been a happy-go-lucky teenager with his own group of friends. At eighteen he'd gone to live in London, so they'd never spent much time together as adults. But he remembered Antonio had mentioned Lucy a few times and had thought her a delightful child. So, although he despised her brother, he had agreed to see her. But after what he had learned over lunch today any fleeting compassion for a member of the Steadman family was non-existent.

Suddenly the frustration that had simmered inside him since speaking with Manuel exploded inside him, and the woman hanging on to his arm was the last straw. Abruptly he hauled her against him, covered her softly pleading lips, and kissed her with all the angry frustrated feelings riding him.

Lucy did not know what had hit her. Suddenly she was held against a hard body, and his mouth slammed down on hers. For a moment she froze in shock. Then she became aware of the movement of his firm lips, the subtle male scent of him, and excitement sizzled though her heating her blood and melting her bones. She had been kissed before, but never like this. He fascinated, thrilled and overwhelmed her every sense. When he abruptly thrust her away she was stunned by the immediacy of her response, and stood in a daze simply staring at him.

Lorenzo never lost control and was shocked by what

he had done—even more shocked by the sudden tightening in his groin. He looked down at the poorly dressed girl gazing at him and noticed the telltale darkening of the pupils in her big green eyes, the flush in her cheeks, the pulse that beat frantically in her throat. He realised she was his for the taking. He also realised he had definitely been too long without a woman to actually consider seducing this one.

'No, there is nothing you can do to make me change my mind. You are not my type,' he said, more harshly than was warranted.

Lucy blinked, snapping out of the sexual fog that held her immobile, and really looked at him. She saw the hard, cynical smile and realised he had actually thought she was offering him her body. Having kissed her, he wasn't impressed, and humiliation laced with a rising anger flooded through her.

'To be brutally frank, Miss Steadman, neither I nor the bank have any wish to continue doing business with a Steadman. You have wasted your time coming to Verona and I suggest you take the next flight out. Is that clear enough for you?'

Lucy saw the determination in his cold black eyes and knew he meant every word. She had the fleeting notion this was personal, and yet he didn't know her. But then again she'd disliked him without knowing him. Antonio had told her his brother was known as a brilliant financier and ruthless at negotiating with a hint of pride in his tone.

He'd been absolutely right, but she doubted he would have been proud of his brother had he lived to see this day. Antonio had been a gentle soul, whereas the man before her did not have one…

'Perfectly,' she said flatly.

Lucy was an artist, but she was also a realist. Her mother had died when she was twelve, and her father had never recovered from the loss of the love of his life. And then her brother last November. Lucy had learnt the hard way there was no point fighting against fate.

She stepped back, straightened her shoulders and, willing her legs to support her, walked past Lorenzo to the door and opened it. She turned and let her gaze sweep over him from head to toe. Big, dark and as immovable as a rock, she thought, and had to accept that short of a miracle she had little to no chance of saving Steadman Industrial Plastics.

'I can't say it was a pleasure meeting you, but just so you know I am in town for another day. You never know—you might change your mind.' She said it simply to goad the man—he was such a superior devil he needed someone to deflate his ego.

'Not this particular part of town. Security will have strict instructions not to allow you access. I want nothing to do with your business or you. Plump, brainless, badly dressed and mousy women have no appeal to me.'

'You really are the arrogant, opinionated, ruthless bastard Antonio said you were.' She shook her head in disgust, and left.

CHAPTER TWO

SHOCKED rigid, Lorenzo stood for a moment, her words ringing in his ears. Her last comment had hit a nerve. Was that what Antonio had really thought of him? Not that it mattered now his brother was dead, but it was the way he had died that still rankled, and the photographs given to him today had not helped.

At the inquest Damien Steadman had been called to give evidence, along with the rescue service personnel who had found Antonio's body too late to save him. Damien had been the lead climber, and had reached the top of a forty-foot cliff-face when Antonio had lost his footing and been left suspended in mid-air. Damien had tried to pull him up, but had finally cut the rope binding them together, letting Antonio fall.

A few years earlier, after a television documentary about a similar incident where both men had ultimately survived, the mountaineering community had concluded cutting the rope was the correct action to take, as it enabled the lead climber to try and seek help for his companion. The same conclusion had been reached at Antonio's inquest. Damien Steadman had been exonerated of any fault—which had enraged Lorenzo. His mother, devastated by grief, had been too ill to attend, but he had sat through the entire proceedings and not been impressed by Damien's vague account. When Damien had had the nerve to approach him after the inquest, to offer his sympathy on the death of his brother, Lorenzo had lost it. He had told the young man as far as he was concerned he was as guilty as hell, he hoped he rotted in hell, and a lot more besides before walking away.

Five years later, with the grief and rage dimmed, he could look at the tragedy with some perspective, but it still did not sit easy with Lorenzo. He doubted he would have cut a rope on his friend, but then he had never been in that position—and Damien Steadman *had* eventually raised the alarm.

It was the *eventually* that disturbed him more now—that and the lingering taste of Lucy Steadman's lush mouth beneath his. Where the hell had *that* thought come from? he wondered. She was far too young, never mind the rest of her faults.

His decision to sell the Steadman's shares was the right one. His last connection to the Steadman family would be finally cut. He'd explain it to his mother somehow, and thankfully would never see Lucy Steadman again.

Banishing her from his mind, he sat down at his desk, clicked on the computer and called his secretary.

The following afternoon, after a restless night in the strange hotel bed, during which a large dark man who looked suspiciously like Lorenzo Zanelli had seemed to slip in and out of her dreams with a surprisingly erotic frequency, and a morning spent exploring Verona, Lucy exited the taxi outside a magnificent old building, feeling excited, if a little hot. But then almost every building in Verona was fabulous and old, she thought wryly.

She carefully placed her leather satchel holding the portrait on the desk in the foyer of the most luxurious apartment building in the city, according to the taxi driver who had brought her here. Looking around, she believed him as she handed her passport to the concierge at his request for identification.

She reached a hand around to rub her lower back. Carrying the satchel around all morning had not been a great idea, but she had not wanted to waste time returning to the hotel.

'The Contessa della Scala is at home, *signorina.* Number three—the third floor. But first I must call and tell her you have arrived.' He handed her passport back and, placing it back in her satchel, she glanced around the elegant foyer towards the elevator.

The doors opened and a man walked out—and her mouth fell open in shock as what felt like a hundred butterflies took flight in her stomach.

Dark eyes clashed with green. 'You!' he exclaimed, and in two lithe strides Lorenzo Zanelli was at her side. 'What do you think you are doing, following me around?' he demanded and grabbed her arm.

'Following you around? You must be joking,' Lucy jeered, the butterflies dying a sudden death at his arrogant assumption. She tried to shake off his hand, but with no luck. 'Oh, for heaven's sake, get over yourself and let go of me.'

'How did you get in here? This is a secure building.'

'Through the door. How do you think?' she snapped.

'And that is the way you are going out, right now—after I have had words with the incompetent concierge who allowed you to enter.'

At that moment the concierge put down the telephone

and turned back to smile at Lucy. But before he could speak Lorenzo Zanelli launched a torrent of Italian at the poor man.

Lucy's Italian lessons had not been completely wasted, but she could only understand Italian rather than speak the language, so she didn't try now. She watched with interest as Lorenzo's voice slowly faded as the concierge responded. She noted the slow dark flush crawl up the tanned olive-toned face and almost laughed out loud. The superior devil was totally embarrassed, and suddenly she was free.

Lorenzo Zanelli looked down at Lucy and saw the amusement in her green eyes, and for the first time since he was a teenager he felt like a prize idiot. What on earth had possessed him to think she was following him? Probably the same irrational urge that had made him kiss her yesterday. He was acting totally out of character—usually he was the most controlled of men—and it had to stop. But she *had* told him she was going to be in town another day and suggested he might change his mind, so his assumption was not that ridiculous. Obviously he realised she had been winding him up, but however he tried to justify his behaviour he still felt like a fool.

'I owe you an apology, Miss Steadman,' he admitted curtly. 'I am sorry; it seems you have every right to be here.'

'Apology accepted—but I bet it nearly choked you,' Lucy prompted with an irrepressible grin. There was something very satisfying in seeing the stiff-necked arrogant banker made to look a fool.

'Not quite, but close,' he said, his lips quirking at the corners in a self deprecating smile. 'So how do you know the Countess della Scala?' he asked.

His smile—the first she had seen from him—made her heart turn over. But, remembering their last meeting and what he was really like, she stiffened. 'Mind your own business,' she said bluntly. 'As I recall you told me quite succinctly yesterday you wanted nothing to do with mine.' And, brushing past him, she walked to the elevator and stepped inside.

The petite, elegant Countess was an absolute delight, Lucy thought ten minutes later, sitting in a comfortable chair and watching the elderly lady reclining on a sofa and examining the eighteen-by-twelve portrait of her husband that her manservant held a few feet away from her.

'I love it—absolutely love it,' she said, then instructed the manservant to place it on the table while she decided where to hang it. She turned back to Lucy. 'You have captured my beloved husband perfectly. All my friends will be green with envy, and I can see a lot more commissions coming your way and a great future ahead of you.'

'I hope so.' Lucy grinned. 'But thank you. I'm glad you like it, because it was a real pleasure to do—he was a very handsome man.'

'Oh, he was—and so jolly. Nothing like Lorenzo Zanelli. The nerve of the man, trying to have you thrown out of the building. Are you sure you are all right.'

'How on earth did you know about that?' Lucy asked in surprise.

'The concierge is a good friend of mine and keeps me informed of everything. Zanelli's behaviour was disgraceful—I can't imagine what he was thinking.'

'I had a brief meeting with him yesterday over something his bank has an interest in, and he jumped to the conclusion I was following him,' Lucy said with a grin. 'He obviously has an overblown sense of his attraction to women, or he is just paranoid. I had no idea he lived here.'

'Ah, my dear—Lorenzo Zanelli doesn't live here, but friends of his, Fedrico and Olivia Paglia, have an apartment here. Unfortunately Federico was injured in a hunting accident in January and has been in a rehabilitation clinic ever since. There has been the occasional rumour circulating about Lorenzo Zanelli's involvement with the poor man's wife, because he has visited Olivia a few times, though I can't see it myself. He is much more likely to be taking care of her husband's business affairs than *her*.' She chuckled. 'Zanelli has the reputation of being a loner, a very private man and a workaholic. Olivia Paglia is a real social butterfly—which is why I can't see the two of them together. They are like chalk and cheese.'

'They say opposites attract,' Lucy inserted, fascinated by the Contessa's conversation.

'Personally I don't believe it. But enough gossip. When we first met I was struck by how bright you looked, wearing a brilliant blue top and white tailored trousers. Now, I hope you won't take this the wrong way, my dear, but that black suit is ill fitting and absolutely dreadful.'

Lucy burst out laughing. 'I know—it's terrible. I borrowed it from a friend because turning up in jeans and a top or a colourful kaftan, which is pretty much all I own, didn't seem very businesslike. Plus, even though I had the portrait packaged I did not want to put it in the cargo hold. It took up most of my hand luggage, and I just managed to squeeze in a spare blouse and underwear.'

An hour later, against all her attempts to refuse, Lucy left with a vintage designer dress courtesy of the Contessa, and shoes to match.

She boarded the plane back to England with a spring in her step. She might not be able to save the family firm, but at least she had a nice cheque in her purse that would help, and a dress to wear for her friend Samantha's hen party this weekend. The following weekend was the wedding, and Lucy was to be the chief and only bridesmaid.

Lorenzo Zanelli viewed the procession down the aisle through cynical eyes. The bride, tall and attractive, looked virginal in white, with the extravagantly layered skirt of her gown cleverly concealing the fact she was pregnant. Another good man bites the dust! he thought, and wondered how James, an international lawyer and partner in his father's London law firm, had allowed himself to be caught so easily.

He had known James for years. His father was English and his mother Italian—her family home was on the shores of Lake Garda, near the Zanelli family home. He had met James as a teenager in the summer holidays at a local sailing club, and they had been friends ever since.

Usually Lorenzo avoided weddings like the plague, but now he was grateful he had accepted James's invitation—it could not have come at a better time. The past two weeks had seen his perfectly contented and well-ordered life severely disrupted.

First the photographs from Manuel had disturbed him so much he'd been angry on meeting Lucy Steadman, and behaved with less than his usual iron control. And then her expectation that he would agree to help her keep a business she had no interest in and that made little money had infuriated him still further. Kissing her had been a bad mistake, but how like a woman to expect a man to bail her out…

Then there was the complete and utter fool he had made of himself the next day. Instantly assuming the green-eyed little witch was following him. He still could not believe he had actually tried to have her thrown out of the building. For some reason her laughing eyes had featured in his dreams ever since, and why a plump little woman dressed not much better than a bag lady was disturbing his sleep he had no idea.

Maybe he was having a midlife crisis… His usual taste in women veered towards tall elegant brunettes, well groomed, immaculately dressed, and preferably with a brain…

The dinner party last Saturday with a few friends should have put him back on an even keel, but it had turned out to be a surprise birthday party arranged by Olivia Paglia—as if he needed reminding he was thirty-eight. His luck had continued its downward spiral when on Monday a photograph of him, with Olivia wrapped around him as they exited the supper club at two on Sunday morning, had appeared in the press, with an article full of innuendo.

The following day had brought a summons from his mother—the one woman in the world whose opinion actually mattered to him. His father had died when he was twenty-six, and he had been head of the family ever since—though he only occasionally stayed at the family home. He had various properties of his own that he used. Seeing the disappointment and anger in her eyes when she'd demanded an explanation for his behaviour with a married woman had bothered him.

Astonishingly, his mother had confided in him that she had always known her husband had kept a mistress. She had not liked it, but had accepted it. But even his father, for all his faults, would never have taken a married woman to his bed—and certainly not his best friend's wife…

Lorenzo could have told her his father had not had *one* mistress but two when he died. He knew because he had paid them off—plus he had known since he was a teenager of others, which had caused a rift between him and his father and was the reason he had gone to America to make his own way in the world. On his return he had discovered three more were on the books—his father had actually pensioned them off! Instead he'd bitten his tongue and listened as she berated him.

A Zanelli had never before been the subject of the tabloid press—he had disgraced the name. And then she'd got on to her favourite subject: it was past time he found a wife and settled down to produce a grandchild—an heir to the Zanelli name. Then, with tears in her eyes, she reminded him he was the only son left.

He had consoled himself that with luck, by the time he returned to Italy, the gossip started by the newspaper report would have blown over, and hopefully his mother would have forgotten as well. On flying into Exeter airport he had rented a car, and had driven down to Cornwall last night. He had booked into a country house hotel for the weekend, and would be flying out of London on Monday to New York for a week or two…

Much as he loved his own country, given the traditional position he had to uphold in Verona, he preferred the vitality of New York, where he usually had a lover. The women tended to be career-orientated, smart and sexy, and while his business affairs often appeared in the financial press his private affairs rarely registered on the press radar there. Whereas, given the status of the Zanelli name, in Verona, his every move was scrutinised by the gossip columns.

The bride passed by, and he caught sight of the single bridesmaid. For a moment he thought he was hallucinating.

Lucy Steadman... It couldn't be?

Her mousy hair was not mousy at all, but a kaleidoscope of colour, with hints of red and gold, swept up at the sides and held with a garland of rosebuds on the crown of her head, revealing her delicate features and then falling in soft silken waves down her back.

His dark eyes moved slowly in stunned amazement over her shapely body. The strapless sea-green dress she wore enhanced the creamy smoothness of her skin and clung lovingly to her full firm breasts, a handspan waist and slim hips. How had he ever imagined she was fat? he asked himself, and could not take his eyes off her.

She had the most supple, sexiest body he had ever seen, and he felt an instant stirring in his own as she glided down the aisle. The natural sway of her pert derrière forced him to adjust his pants. And this was the woman he had told he never wanted to see again...

Though on the plus side he suddenly realised his sexual antennae hadn't been at fault after all, but working perfectly when he had kissed her—which put paid to his mid-life crisis theory...

He had parted with his last lover Madeleine, a New York accountant, at New Year, because unfortunately she had begun to hint at commitment...something he was averse to.

But he definitely *did* need a woman—and a weekend affair with the luscious Lucy would suit him perfectly on so many levels. She lived in England—he divided his time mostly between Italy and New York. He could sate himself in her sexy little body with no danger of ever having to see her again. Unworthy of him, he knew, but he couldn't help thinking there would be a satisfying kind of justice in bedding Damien Steadman's sister and walking away…

Seated on the bride's side of the church, a misty-eyed Lucy watched as her friend Samantha and James Morgan, with eyes only for each other, took their wedding vows. No one could doubt the deep love they shared, and if ever a girl deserved happiness it was Sam, she thought.

Lucy had arrived at Samantha's parents' house, set on the cliffs above Looe, at eight that morning. They had all had breakfast together, and the rest of the time Lucy had spent in a kind of controlled chaos, getting dressed with the hairdresser and make-up artist fussing around her, while trying to keep Samantha calm and getting her ready for the service at two-thirty.

An hour ago Lucy had left for the church with the pageboy in a limousine, and—apart from having to take the little boy around the back of the old church for a pee—so far everything was going like a dream for her best friend.

Lucy had first met Samantha as a child, when she had spent every summer with her parents at their holiday home in Looe. They had both attended the children's Holiday Club and become friends. But after her mother died her father had refused to holiday in Cornwall any more, and consequently Lucy had lost touch with Samantha. It had only been after she had finished art college and inherited the family holiday home in Looe, setting up house and her own business there, that they had renewed their friendship.

Samantha had been one of the first customers in her art and craft gallery, and they had instantly recognised each other. They had both had troubled teen years—Lucy had lost both her parents, and Samantha had been diagnosed with leukaemia at the age of thirteen and fought a five-year-long battle to full recovery. Lucy knew that was the reason Samantha had got pregnant within two months of meeting James. Convinced her leukaemia treatment had left her infertile, she had never considered contraception necessary.

Lucy sighed. She was a romantic at heart. After all, Samantha had suffered before meeting James and falling in love. Getting married with a baby on the way was the perfect happy ending.

'Lucy, time to sign the register.' The best man, Tom, took her arm.

Ten minutes later the church bells began to peal, and the bride and groom walked back down the aisle as man and wife.

Lucy followed behind with Tom. She had met him at the rehearsal on Thursday night—he was James's best friend and a banker in the City. But nothing like the hateful, hard-faced banker she had met in Verona: Lorenzo Zanelli. Tom was fun.

The ceremony over, feeling totally relaxed, she glanced around the colourful congregation.

'You look beautiful, Lucy,' a deep, slightly accented voice drawled, and she almost dropped her posy of roses at the sight of the man sitting in the pew, his dark head tilted back, watching her.

She looked down into a pair of mocking eyes, her

mouth hanging open in shock. 'What are you doing here?'

'I was invited.'

'Move, Lucy—we are holding up the traffic.' She shut her mouth and was grateful for Tom's hand at her back, urging her on down the aisle.

Lorenzo Zanelli at Samantha's wedding—it wasn't possible.

Unfortunately it was, she realised as she spent the next half-hour at the bidding of the photographer as the wedding photos were taken. Somehow every time she looked up Zanelli seemed to be in her line of vision. Not surprising, she told herself. At over six feet, with broad shoulders and bold features, he had a presence about him that made him stand out in any crowd, and the superbly tailored silver-grey suit he wore with easy elegance simply enhanced his magnificent physique.

Seated at the top table at the wedding reception, Lucy tried to dismiss Zanelli's presence from her mind and give all her attention to Tom. He was easy to talk to, and when the meal was over and the speeches began his was one of the best.

The bride and groom opened the dancing, and then everyone else joined in. Tom turned out to be a good dancer and he made her laugh. When the music ended he led her to the side of the dance floor and said, 'Do you mind if I rescue my girlfriend now? She's bound to be feeling lonely, seated with strangers. I'll take you back to the table first.'

'Not necessary.' She smiled. 'I am going to find the powder room.'

'Okay!'

But Tom had barely been gone two seconds before Lorenzo Zanelli appeared at her side.

'Lucy, this *is* a pleasant surprise—can I have this dance?'

She tilted her head back to look a long way up into his harshly attractive face. 'I seem to recall you never wanted to see me again,' she said bluntly. 'So why bother?'

'Ah! Because I have never really seen you until now...' He stepped back and deliberately let his dark gaze roam over her, from head to toe and back up, to linger for a moment on the soft curve of her breasts revealed by the strapless dress, before his dark eyes lifted to capture hers with an unmistakable sensual gleam in their black depths.

Lucy fought down the blush that rose up her throat, but she could do nothing about the sudden hardening of her nipples against the soft silk of her gown.

'What is your English saying, Lucy? To hide one's light under a bushel?' His deep, melodious voice made his accent more pronounced. 'I never knew what a bushel was, but now thanks to you I do—a big, black shapeless garment.' One black brow rose enquiringly. 'I am right, yes?'

'No.' But she could not help her lips twitching. Even the Contessa had remarked on the ill-fitting suit.

'So I ask again—dance with me?' And before she knew it he had caught her hand in his.

The same tingling feeling affected her arm, and she burst into speech. 'How do you know James Morgan?' she demanded, slightly breathless, Lorenzo was not as staid as she had thought—he could turn on the charm like a tap—but she did not want to dance with him. She didn't like the man, and he had made it plain what he thought of her: nothing... But her own innate honesty forced her to admit she didn't trust herself up close to him. Tentatively she tried to ease her hand from his, but with no success. His long fingers tightened around hers.

'His mother is Italian and her parents' home is on the shores of Lake Garda. James and I met as teenagers when he visited with his family in the summer, and now whenever I need an international lawyer James is the man I call.' Reaching out, he slid his arm around her waist and drew her towards him.

Suddenly Lucy was aware of the warmth of his long body, the slight scent of his cologne, the masculine strength of him, in a purely carnal way that stunned her. She could not tear her eyes away from the mobile mouth, suddenly recalling the heart-stopping feel of lips that had once kissed hers as he continued speaking.

'I've never actually met the bride before, but that is not surprising. James has only known her eight months, and it is out of necessity a bit of a rushed affair, I believe?'

Charming, but definitely arrogant and opinionated, Lucy thought, no longer having any trouble raising her fascinated gaze from his mouth to look up into his dark eyes. Her own sparked with anger at his slur on Samantha.

'That is an unkind comment to make on what is a very happy day. Samantha is my friend, and for your information I happen to know it was love at first sight for both of them. Plus, James asked her to marry him *before* she knew she was pregnant.'

'You are a loyal little thing—and, I think, a hopeless romantic. But I bow to your superior knowledge and apologise for my thoughtless comment. Now, let's dance,' he ended with a grin.

His rueful grin and the proximity of his big body

were having a disastrous effect on her thought process. Biting back the yes that sprang to her lips, she stiffened in his hold. 'Why would I want to dance with a man who has sold my family business out from under me?'

The only place Lorenzo wanted the delectable Lucy was under *him,* and he saw his opportunity. 'There you are mistaken. The deadline is next week and I have not given the final go-ahead yet. It has occurred to me that if the land is valuable in the middle of a recession it will be a lot more valuable in the future.'

Lucy's eyes widened in surprise on his hard attractive face. Had he just said what she thought he had? 'You mean you are actually reconsidering your decision?' He lifted her hand and placed it against his chest, and she was instantly aware of the beat of his heart beneath her palm. Her own heart began to race. 'The factory could stay open for a while longer?' she prompted, a sudden huskiness affecting her vocal cords.

'It is a possibility to consider,' Lorenzo murmured, squeezing her hand and drawing her closer, well aware of how he affected her. 'But, as you said, this is a wedding and a happy occasion, so let us forget about business for now and enjoy the party.'

Against her better judgment, surprisingly Lucy did. Lorenzo was a superb dancer, she realised as they moved around the floor in perfect harmony. His hand on her back was firm and controlling, guiding her effortlessly to the music, and a long leg slid between hers as he spun her around. The only problem was her rapid pulse and the growing warmth spreading from her belly to every sensory nerve in her body. She glanced up at him, and her breath caught at the slumbering passion in the dark eyes that met hers.

She amended her earlier assessment. He certainly wasn't old. He was a superbly fit, incredibly attractive man, and her mouth went dry as another part of her anatomy shockingly did the opposite. Her lips parted slightly, the tip of her tongue circling them. She wasn't aware the music had stopped until Lorenzo briefly squeezed the hand he held against his chest and let it go.

He had damn near kissed Lucy on the dance floor, Lorenzo realised with a sense of shock, but she had given him plenty of provocation. Her sexy little body had moved against his with a sensuality that instantly aroused him. The scent of her, fresh and light, had filled his nostrils, and the soft silken smoothness of her skin beneath his palm, the gentle brush of her glorious hair against his hand on her back as they danced, had been a constant caress. Then she'd licked her lips, and he had been in imminent danger of embarrassing himself and her in front of everyone. He needed to get her alone…

Taking a step back, but keeping an arm lightly around her waist, he quipped, 'I think you deliberately hide your light under a bushel, Lucy—you have great rhythm.' And he was supremely confident he could induce her into being even more rhythmic in bed. Her fabulous body was made for sex. Looking down into the slightly dazed eyes of the woman curved in the crook of his arm, he added, 'But now I think a glass of champagne and some fresh air is needed.'

'Lorenzo?'

He heard his name called, but ignoring it, he attempted to steer Lucy away.

She looked over his shoulder. 'I think the man at the

table behind you is trying to get your attention…' she said, and he silently groaned.

'Come have a drink with us, Lorenzo!' the accented voice demanded.

CHAPTER THREE

LORENZO recognised the voice, and good manners dictated it was a request he could not ignore. With his hand on Lucy's waist, he reluctantly turned.

A moment later Lucy, with Lorenzo's arm still around her waist and a glass of champagne in her hand, was being introduced to Aldo Lanza, the bridegroom's uncle from Italy, his wife Teresa, their two sons and their wives, and four grandchildren.

'Trust Lorenzo to grab the beautiful bridesmaid before anyone else had a chance,' Aldo said as he kissed Lucy's hand. Casting a knowing glance at the man holding her, he added, 'Don't be fooled by his easy charm—he can be a hard devil when you get to know him.' And he winked…

'I already gathered that,' Lucy said with a grin, enjoying Aldo's easy banter and putting her glass down on the table. 'We have met before.'

'Ah—you have visited Verona, perhaps? A beautiful city, no?'

'Yes, I have, and the architecture *is* stunning. The arena is amazing, too, but I did not have much time to look around as I was there on business.'

'Beautiful and clever. What line of business are you in?' he asked.

'Enough questions, Aldo,' Lorenzo interrupted. 'I'm sure Lucy does not want to discuss business at a wedding.' He had introduced Lucy without mentioning her surname, thinking the less Aldo knew the better—because his wife Teresa was the biggest gossip in Verona.

'No, really—I don't mind,' Lucy said swiftly. The arrogance of Lorenzo speaking on her behalf had touched a nerve. Her father and brother, much as she had loved them, had had a habit of doing the same. Which was partly the reason she had decided to move to Cornwall after her father's death, although Damien had been nothing but encouraging about her setting up her own business in Looe.

'I own an art and craft gallery here in the town. But I specialise in painting portraits, and was in Verona to deliver a completed commission to my client—a charming Italian lady. You may know her—the Contessa della Scala? In fact, I met Lorenzo in the foyer of her apartment block,' she said, giving Lorenzo a saccharine-sweet smile, reminding him he was not always as invincible as he thought…

Lorenzo's dark eyes narrowed angrily on her mocking green. It was the worst thing she could have said, given his recent appearance in the gossip columns. The Lanzas knew Olivia Paglia had an apartment in the same building.

Suddenly Lucy was aware of a pause in the conversation, and she wondered if she had gone too far. Then Aldo said something in Italian to his wife, and Teresa frowned. Looking at Lorenzo, she spoke equally swiftly.

Lucy looked on in amazement as the conversation became animated between the three, with much waving of hands. She barely caught a sentence, but was enthralled by Lorenzo's deep husky voice—and then she heard Aldo repeat the words 'Contessa della Scala' and all eyes turned on her.

'You know the Contessa della Scala well?' Teresa asked in English.

'I wouldn't say well, but I have met her couple of times and spoken to her on the phone. She is a lovely lady, and a delight to talk to.'

'Oh, so clever and *bella signorina*...' Teresa switched back into Italian, and the conversation went right over Lucy's head again.

Lorenzo's hand slowly tightened around Lucy's waist. He thought he had covered well by telling them they had met a couple of times and he had known Lucy for a while—which wasn't an outright lie. But then he'd had to field a dozen questions about his 'artist friend' and he'd realised he actually knew next to nothing about Lucy and had jumped to the assumption she did nothing. He also realised he had made an even bigger fool of himself than he had imagined, presuming Lucy had come to Verona specifically to see him about the Steadman deal when her main priority had obviously been her own business.

The chatter that had broken out at her comment and Lorenzo's fingers biting into her waist surprised Lucy. His dark head was bent towards her, and he spoke softly against her ear.

'You could have told me you are an artist, Lucy.'

His warm breath and the way he said her name did funny things to her tummy, and she wriggled out of his hold just as James appeared and saved her from answering.

'I see you have met the Italian side of my family,

Lucy—and now it is my turn to dance with the bridesmaid, according to my wife Samantha.' He said *wife* with such pride Lucy smiled. And, glad of the reprieve from Lorenzo's constant presence, she let James lead her on to the floor.

'They can be a bit overwhelming *en masse,* and Sam thought you might need rescuing.'

'Not really—they all seem charming, if a little intimidating.'

She danced with James, and then threw herself into circulating and lost count of the number of men she danced with. With relief she accepted when Samantha asked her to accompany her back to the house and help her get changed into her honeymoon outfit. Her wedding dress, though fabulous, was killing her, she said, and as Lucy had stitched her into it in the first place, when a seam had split, she knew just what she meant.

Half an hour later she lined up with most of the guests along the drive as Samantha and James drove away in his treasured vintage green e-type Jaguar sports car.

Waving with one hand, Lucy wiped a few tears of joy for her friend from her cheek with the other.

'Proof positive of my suspicion that you are a hopeless romantic.' A long arm wrapped around her waist and she was spun round against a hard male body. 'Here—use this.' Lorenzo handed her a pristine white handkerchief.

'It's not necessary.' She placed her hands on his chest and pushed herself free of his hold. 'But thank you,' she said politely.

She had been carefully avoiding him for ages, and if their eyes had met accidentally she had quickly glanced away. But she hadn't been able to help noticing he'd had no shortage of dance partners all night. Not that she had been looking! And now he had caught up with her…

Lorenzo slipped the hanky in his jacket pocket and, taking her hand in his, said, 'Walk with me, Lucy. I don't feel like returning to the party just yet, and as Samantha's friend you must know these gardens well. You can lead me around.'

In more ways than one, Lorenzo acknowledged wryly. He couldn't remember the last time he had been so physically attracted to a woman he'd had to make a determined effort to prevent his body betraying him every time he looked at her.

Lucy was about to refuse when suddenly she remembered he had held out some hope for Steadman Industrial Plastics and agreed. Maybe she could talk to him sensibly and get him to agree to keep the factory open. The only slight problem with that idea was she simply had to look at Lorenzo for every sensible thought in her head to vanish. And the warmth of his hand holding hers seemed so right, so natural, she had no desire or will to break free.

They strolled down to where the garden ended at the cliff-edge, and looked out over the sea. The sun was just beginning to set over the far side of the bay.

'Do you realise the twenty-first of June is the longest and lightest day of the year in the northern hemisphere—the ideal day for a wedding? And at midnight there is going to be a magnificent fireworks display.' She was babbling, but Lorenzo made her nervous—and a lot of other things she wasn't ready to face just yet.

She didn't like the man. He was arrogant and rude, and a staid, boring banker was not high on her checklist of what she looked for in a man. Then again, she had never found *any* man who ticked her boxes… In fact after her one attempt at sex she had decided she was probably frigid and could happily stay celibate. But somehow Lorenzo Zanelli had the power to drive her senseless with only a kiss. She had dated a few men, but none had turned her legs to jelly the way Lorenzo did by simply holding her, and it frightened her.

'Why didn't you tell me you were an artist when we met?'

'You never asked.'

'I did ask why you were at the Contessa's—you could have told me then.'

'I could—but as you had just tried to have me thrown out of the building and called me a plump, brainless, badly dressed and mousy woman the day before, I didn't think you deserved an answer.'

'I'm sorry. I want to apologise for that day in my office. My comment was totally uncalled-for. I had a picture of you in my mind from the first time I saw you at my brother's apartment in London. You were a schoolgirl in a baggy sweater and pigtails, and I didn't really look past that.'

'I *thought* there was something familiar about you!' Lucy exclaimed, a long-forgotten memory surfacing of a big, dark frowning man in a dark suit once arriving at Antonio's apartment as she was leaving.

'Yes, well—now I know my view of you was totally false,' he said, with a self-derisory smile. 'But you caught me on a really bad day. My business lunch had gone on for far longer than it should have and I was badly delayed. I was running hopelessly late—unheard of for me. I'm not usually so…'

'Insufferably arrogant? Opinionated? Superior?' she offered cheekily. 'I may not be a whiz with numbers, like you, but when it comes to physical figures I am really good.'

One look at her walking down the aisle of the church had told Lorenzo *that,* but he bit back the sexual innuendo that sprang to mind. 'I really am sorry for my boorish behaviour.' He gently squeezed her hand. 'Please can we forget our first meeting and begin again?'

It was the *please* that did it. His apology sounded genuine, and Lucy glanced back up at him and was lost in the warmth of the sincerity in his deep brown eyes. 'Yes, okay,' she agreed, and suddenly shivered.

'Here—take my jacket,' Lorenzo offered, letting go of her hand to open his jacket.

'No, really—I'm fine.'

His lips twisted in a slow smile and, catching her hand again, lacing his fingers through hers, he cradled her hand on his chest. His other arm encircled her waist to pull her pliant body into the warmth of his. 'Then let me warm you…'

His dark head bent, and Lucy knew he was going to kiss her. When his lips brushed lightly against hers she felt her heart turn over. Never in her life had she experienced the dizzying sensations swirling around inside her that his kiss evoked. Her lips parted beneath his and the subtle invasion of his tongue into the moist heat of her mouth had her closing her eyes. Her free hand reached up to clasp his broad shoulders and cling as he folded her closer still. The blood bubbled in her veins and she was wildly, gloriously aware of sensations she had never experienced before. When she felt his hand stroking up her spine, finding her bare back under the tumbling mass of her hair, she trembled.

'Ah, Lucy!' He sighed, and broke the kiss, his dark eyes gleaming down into hers. He dropped soft kisses on her brow, her glowing cheeks, and then bent his dark head to say huskily against her ear, 'This is the time, but not the place. I think—'

Lucy never did hear what he thought, as they were once more interrupted by the booming voice of Aldo Lanza, calling out his name.

'I think I could kill that man,' Lorenzo ground out, but straightening up, held her lightly against his side as he responded.

The rest of the evening took on a dream-like quality. At Aldo's insistence they rejoined his party in the marquee. Lorenzo swirled her around the dance floor in his arms and she felt as if she was floating on air. Between dances he told her he had an apartment in Verona and one in New York, and he split his time between the two. His mother lived in the family home on Lake Garda, and he visited as often as work allowed. Apparently she suffered from angina and was quite frail. Lucy told him about art college in London and starting her business here in Looe, and how much she loved being her own boss.

For Lucy the night took on a magic all of its own as Lorenzo, holding her to his side, took her to gather with all the other guests in the garden to watch the fireworks display on the stroke of midnight.

How had she ever thought she disliked him without knowing him? So Lorenzo had lost his temper with Damien after the inquest? In fairness, it had to have been a traumatic time for him, and she could not really blame Lorenzo for Damien going off the rails afterwards. Lucy had sacrificed a lot for Damien, given him much more help than most sisters ever did, and yet his reckless behaviour had negated her help and ultimately led to his tragic death.

And how had she ever thought Lorenzo was boring? she wondered as he laughed and joked with the other guests as they said their goodbyes. She was totally captivated, her eyes shining like stars as she looked up at him as he turned back to her.

'The party is almost over, Lucy. Can I take you home now?' he asked, and the question in the glittering dark eyes said so much more.

'I am staying here tonight—to help with the clearing up,' she said reluctantly.

'Do you have to?' His long fingers curled about her wrist, his thumb carelessly caressing the soft underside, sending shivers of awareness through her body. 'I could tell our hostess you are too tired and I'm taking you home for some much needed rest.'

Her eyes locked with his, and the sexual tension that had sparked between them all evening heightened almost to breaking point. They both knew it was not a rest he was suggesting. Lucy's pounding heart wanted to say yes, but her head and her conscience was telling her to say no. She couldn't—she had promised. And then Samantha's mum interrupted them.

'There you are, Lucy. I was looking for you.'

Ten minutes later Lucy was seated in the passenger seat of Lorenzo's car on the way home, not sure how it had happened.

Lorenzo walked around the bonnet of the top-of-the-range BMW he'd rented and opened the passenger door. Reaching for her hand, he helped her out of the vehicle. He had sensed Lucy mentally pulling away from him as they had made the short journey to the outskirts of the town, and he needed to keep physical contact with her.

He wasn't about to strike out now. It had occurred

to him, as the evening wore on and he'd watched her dance, smile and flirt with a variety of men, that far from being too young and not possessing the traits he looked for in a lover—as he had thought when they'd met in Verona—the opposite was true. She was the perfect sexual partner for a weekend.

Lucy Steadman was no ordinary little small-town girl but an artist, accustomed to a bohemian lifestyle from her years at art college in London, and now living in Cornwall—the most popular county in England for artists and latter-day hippies. She was a free spirit and, judging by her response when he held and kissed her, and her body that oozed sex appeal, she had to be a woman well-versed in the pleasures of the flesh.

'Here—let me take the key.' He took the key she had taken from her purse and opened the door.

Lucy turned to close the door and found Lorenzo doing it for her. 'Would you like a coffee?' she asked, glancing up at him.

Slowly he shook his head and reached out one long finger, stroking her cheek in an intimate gesture.

'You know what I want—what we both want—and it isn't coffee,' he husked. 'I've been aching to do this again for hours.' And his arm wrapped around her waist, his mouth found hers, and she was lost in the wonder of his kiss.

Her mouth was warm and eager for his, and it never occurred to Lucy to resist. Her purse fell unnoticed to the floor as she reached for him, her hands clinging to his broad shoulders, her lips parting to the probing demand of his tongue, and she closed her eyes and gave herself up to the exciting sensations rioting around her body.

'The bedroom,' he groaned, and she indicated the

stairs with her hand. He swept her up in his arms and with unerring accuracy found her bedroom.

He lowered her down onto the white coverlet of the queen-sized bed and straightened up, swiftly shrugging off his jacket and removing something from the pocket. He dropped it on the side table as his jacket fell to the floor, followed by the rest of his clothes.

Lucy's eyes widened in awe as, lit by the light of the moon shining through the window, she saw his magnificent body naked.

She had seen naked men before, in life class at college, but the models had been mostly grey-haired elderly men, carefully posed. And she had made love once with a boy—Philip, who had shared an apartment with her and two other girls at college. It had been the same night that she'd seen a newsflash on the television about two climbers in an accident on Mont Blanc, giving Damien and Antonio's names. One had been thought seriously injured but it hadn't been stipulated which. She had been terrified for both of them. Philip had tried to find out more, without any success, and then taken her in his arms to soothe her fears. They had ended up making love. With hindsight it had been comfort sex, with both of them half clothed and he as inexperienced as her. She had been thoroughly ashamed afterwards, and wary of men ever since.

But nothing had prepared her for Lorenzo, standing boldly in the flesh… She could not take her eyes off him. His shoulders were wide, his chest broad, with a shadow of black body hair that tapered down to a narrow waist, flat stomach, lean hips and long legs. He was also mightily aroused, and she swallowed hard suddenly, slightly afraid.

'Are you waiting for me to undress you or admiring

the view?' he asked, with the confident grin of a man totally at ease in his naked masculinity. Not waiting for an answer, he knelt on the bed and pressed fervent little kisses on her face, her throat, while his hands, with a deftness she could only wonder at, removed her dress.

Beneath, she was wearing only white lace briefs, and a thousand nerve-endings sprang to life as he hooked his fingers in the lace and slowly pulled them down her legs.

'You are beautiful—so beautiful, Lucy.' He dropped a kiss on her stomach and she trembled in helpless response as his hands palmed her breasts, his thumbs gently grazing the burgeoning nipples, bringing them to rigid points of aching pleasure.

Lucy's response was a low moan as quivering arrows of sensation shot from her breasts to her pelvis.

'Perfect,' he murmured, and his mouth closed over a pert nipple, his tongue licking and suckling.

Her back arched involuntarily, and little whimpering sounds of pleasure escaped her as with frightening expertise Lorenzo delivered the same erotic torment to the other breast, before he found her mouth again and kissed her long and deep as his hands caressed her skin, shaping her waist, her hips, her thighs…

She reached for him, her small hands clasping his shoulders, stroking around his neck, holding him closer, her fingers raking through the thick black hair of his head, desperate for more.

Suddenly he reared back. 'I want you, Lucy. *Dio,* how I want you.' He groaned and nudged her legs apart, to settle between her thighs, and she could feel the hard pressure of his erection against her pelvis as he pinned her to the bed, kissing her with a deep, demanding passion that aroused an answering passion in her—a need, a longing that banished any faint doubt from her mind.

The rough hair of his chest rubbed against her swollen breasts, and her body felt electrified by the heat, the power of him. He kissed her throat, her shoulders, his mouth hard, and one hand curved under her hips to lift her slightly.

His mouth found the rigid tips of her breasts again, suckling first one and then the other, while his other hand dipped between her thighs, his long fingers exploring the hot moist centre of her with devastating skill.

She writhed achingly beneath him, her nails digging into the satin-smooth skin of his shoulders. She was white-hot with wanting, her need for him shuddering through her, the emotion so intense it was almost pain.

He lifted her hips higher, her legs involuntarily parted wider—and he was there, where she ached for him. She groaned as she felt him ease into her. There was the slightest twinge of pain as her moist sheath stretched to accommodate him, then exquisite hot, pulsating power as Lorenzo thrust slowly deeper and then withdrew.

Her body screamed with tension and she locked her legs around him, frantic for him to continue. He thrust again, deeper and faster, possessing her completely, and she cried out as her body convulsed in a million explosive sensations so intense her breath actually stopped with the sheer ecstasy of it all. She was aware of one last mighty thrust as her internal muscles still convulsed around him, and gloried in the great shudders that racked Lorenzo's huge frame. She was filled with a sense of oneness, a completion she had never imagined existed.

Lorenzo rolled off Lucy, his breathing ragged, his

heart pounding and his head spinning. She was everything he had expected and much more. She was so responsive… He couldn't remember losing control so completely ever before in his life. Of course he *had* been without a woman for a while, he rationalised, and, turning, he looped an arm around her shoulders and tucked her pliant body against his side.

'Are you okay? I didn't hurt you?' he asked. She was so small, so tight, that for a fleeting moment he had wondered if she was a virgin, but had quickly dismissed the thought. Lucy was obviously a woman of the world.

'No—quite the reverse,' she murmured softly, in a voice full of emotion at the wonder of him. She laid her hand on his broad chest. 'I am better than okay—sublime.' Rising up on one elbow, she leant over him and pressed a kiss on his chin—the highest she could reach. 'You, Lorenzo, are nothing like the staid banker I thought.' She looked up at him, her green eyes dazed with love, and gave him a languorous smile. 'You're brilliant, the most perfect lover in the…' She was about to say *world,* but a wide yawn stopped her.

'Glad to be of service,' he said softly. Running his hand through the tumbled mass of her hair, he smoothed it from her face and dropped a gentle kiss on her brow before folding his arms around her.

Lucy buried her head on his chest and, safe in the cradle of his arm, fell asleep.

Lucy slowly opened her eyes and blinked as the early-morning rays of the sun shining through the window dazzled her. For a moment she was disorientated and, yawning, stretched her slender body. She felt aches in places she had never felt before and, dreamlike, the events of the night fluttered through her mind.

She glanced across the bed and saw the indentation in the pillow and realised it wasn't a dream but reality. She had made love with Lorenzo Zanelli not once but twice… The first time had been incredible, and she'd thought nothing in the world could be better, but Lorenzo had proved her mistaken.

She had fallen asleep, exhausted, and it might have been minutes or an hour later when she'd awoke to find the bedside light on—just as a naked Lorenzo had strolled out of her *en suite* bathroom. What had followed had been a revelation in eroticism.

With a skill and an expertise she could only marvel at he had kissed and caressed her, encouraging her to do the same to him, and she had in the process discovered a sensual side of her nature she had never known she possessed. Finally Lorenzo had made long, slow love to her, almost driving her out of her mind as he'd taken her to the brink of paradise over and over again, until in the end she'd been begging for the release that only he could give her.

She looked around the room. No sign of his clothes—he was gone…

She closed her eyes and groaned, blushing at the thought of how wantonly she had behaved. Lorenzo probably thought she behaved that way with any man and considered her nothing more than a one-night stand. Mortified, she pulled the coverlet up over her naked body.

'A little late for modesty,' a deep, dark voice drawled, and she opened her eyes to see Lorenzo walking towards her.

'I thought you had gone,' she blurted, pulling herself up into a sitting position and tucking the coverlet under her arms while her eyes drank in the sight of him. He was dressed in the same grey suit, slightly crumpled now, and his white shirt was open at the neck, revealing the slightest glimpse of his dark chest hair. In his hand he held a mug of coffee.

'As if I would, after what we shared and I hope we can share again,' he prompted and, crossing to the side of the bed, deposited the mug of coffee on the bedside table. 'For you—I thought you might need the caffeine.' And he gave her a wicked smile that made her blush.

'Thank you,' she said, and picked up the mug and took a long drink of coffee. Lorenzo hadn't walked out on her, and he obviously did *not* think of her as a one-night stand. He wanted to see her again—he had said so—and his words warmed her heart and squashed all her doubts. 'You are right—I did need that.' She grinned up at him. 'But you should have woken me. You're the guest—I should have made it for you.'

He sat down on the bed and, leaning forward, lightly brushed her lips with his. 'No, it was my pleasure, Lucy. You are one very sexy lady. And you had a long day yesterday and an even longer night.'

His dark gaze met hers and she could not look away. The latent sensuality in his eyes was mesmerising her. A heated blush coloured her cheeks, and other parts of her were equally warm. 'Even so…'

'No, don't argue. I thought you needed to sleep, but then I remembered you told me Sunday was one of your busiest days in the tourist season, and you open at ten. So I decided to leave before anyone turns up.'

'What time is it?' Lucy demanded, panicking. Her head had cleared of the sensual haze Lorenzo's presence seemed to cause.

'Nine—you have plenty of time.' And, standing up, he looked down at her, his expression suddenly serious.

'I hope you don't mind but I had a look around. It is a nice place you have here—living accommodation upstairs and the gallery on the ground floor. But I couldn't help noticing you only have one lock on the front door. Your security is very poor—especially for a woman living on her own.'

Lucy drained her mug of coffee and placed it on the table. There was nothing wrong with her security, but she was thrilled by the thought that he was concerned for her safety. It had to mean he cared. She glanced up at him, her eyes sparkling with humour. 'Lorenzo, you are beginning to sound like a stuffy banker again.'

'If we had time I would show you I am not.' He chuckled, and reached down to clasp her head between his strong hands and kiss her senseless. 'Unfortunately we don't have time.' He straightened up. 'But I'll come back this evening and take you out to dinner. What time do you close?'

Breathless, Lucy said, 'I close at four—but if we are going out…'

'I'll see you at seven,' he husked and, planting a swift kiss on her head, he left.

Lucy watched him leave with a beaming smile on her face. Lorenzo didn't just want sex. He was actually taking her on a date. That had to be a good sign…

CHAPTER FOUR

THE doorbell rang, and Lucy, with one last glance at her reflection in the mirror, adjusted the spaghetti straps of the bright blue summer dress she wore, picked up her purse and ran downstairs to open the door.

'You look fabulous,' Lorenzo said, and Lucy simply looked.

She had never seen him wear anything but a perfectly tailored suit—the uniform of choice for a seriously powerful conservative male. But now, casually dressed in pale trousers and a white shirt, with a cashmere sweater draped across his wide shoulders, his black hair dishevelled by the breeze and with a smile of wickedly masculine appreciation curving his lips, he could have been a latter-day pirate. She tilted back her head to look into his eyes and saw banked-down desire in the dark depths. Her own widened in instant response.

'Don't look at me like that, Lucy, or we will never get to dinner,' he said ruefully and, slipping an arm around her waist, he lowered his mouth down to hers as though he could not help himself.

At the first gentle brush of his lips Lucy's parted eagerly beneath his and she melted against him, her knees going weak as he kissed her with a subtle promise of passion.

'We have to go now,' he said huskily, and, keeping a hand on her back, took her key and urged her out of the house, locking the door behind them.

Right at that moment Lucy realised she would quite happily go to the end of the earth with Lorenzo, and suddenly the confusion, the butterflies in her stomach whenever she saw him, and the incredible joy she had felt when they made love all made sense. For the first time in her adult life she was experiencing the magic of overwhelming sexual attraction to a man. She had only ever read about it before, and never been able even to imagine it, but now she could—and maybe more!

Later, sitting opposite him at the table in dining room of the country house hotel where he was staying, she fell even deeper under his spell if that was possible.

Over the meal, with some prompting from him, she told him more about her business and the three fellow artists who displayed their wares in her gallery. Leon was a brilliant woodcarver, Sid was a potter, and his wife Elaine—who worked in the gallery on a permanent basis—had a talent for tapestry and quilting. She was also the owner of the big black linen suit…

Lorenzo seemed impressed, and told her a little more about himself. He was an amusing and informative conversationalist. She learnt he worked between Italy and New York and occasionally London, where the bank kept an office dedicated to the UK stock market. He owned a villa in Santa Margherita, and liked to spend his leisure time sailing his yacht around the Mediterranean.

'I'm sorry, Lucy, I must be boring you. Would you like to go on somewhere else? A club or casino maybe?' he said earnestly.

'You could never bore me, and I don't think there is either of those around here,' she informed him wryly.

And a casino wasn't exactly where she had imagined their evening would end.

A vivid image of his naked body gloriously entwined with her own made a blush rise up her throat, and she glanced across at him. He read her mind, and a knowing sensual smile curved his firm lips. Their eyes met, and the air between them was suddenly heavy with sexual tension.

'Let's get out of here.' Lorenzo abruptly stood up and, moving around the table, took her hand. He helped her to her feet and quickly out of the dining room, his hand gripping hers as he led her up the grand staircase to his first-floor suite.

She glanced around as he closed the door behind them. It was a sitting room with a fireplace—and she never saw the rest as Lorenzo swept her up in his arms…

Covering her mouth with his, kissing her with a hungry, driven passion, he carried her through to the bedroom. They fell on the bed in a tangle of arms and legs, mouths and hands. Lorenzo quickly divested her of the blue sundress she wore, and Lucy was no slouch in tearing at his shirt buttons. Within seconds they were both naked. There was no foreplay, just a frantic coupling, and they came together in an explosion of raw passion.

'I needed that,' Lorenzo groaned, and curved her into the hard heat of his body.

What followed was a lazy love-fest as he kissed her gently and explored every inch of her. Between talking nonsense and laughing, he trailed tender kisses down the length of her spine, asking about the scar he found there. Lucy chuckled, telling him it was just a cut, and then, turning, explored equally thoroughly down the front of *his* great torso. The end result was ecstasy…

'Wake up, Lucy.'

She opened her eyes and snuggled closer to his strong body. 'You are insatiable,' she murmured, wrapping her arm around his waist and lightly kissing his chest. They had made love twice already, but even so, pressed against him flesh on flesh, she felt the familiar quiver of desire snake through her body.

'Sorry, Lucy, I hate to disappoint you, but it really is time I took you home. I have to leave at dawn to drive to London—I'm flying out to New York about noon.' And, rolling off the bed, he shot her a brief smile and strolled across to the bathroom.

Lucy watched him go, admiring his bronzed body—the broad back, elegant spine, the firm buttocks and long legs—and feeling slightly disappointed. Silly, she knew, but she couldn't help wondering if this was it.

She slid out of bed and, gathering up her underwear and dress from the floor, slipped them on. Her sandals were by the door, where they had fallen along with her purse, and after slipping her feet into the high heels she straightened up. She caught sight of her face in the dresser mirror and almost groaned. No make-up, and her hair all over the place. Taking a comb from her purse, she mechanically ran it through her hair, sweeping the long mass behind her ears. She didn't want to think of Lorenzo's departure…

He reappeared from the bathroom, wearing boxer shorts, and as she watched he slipped on trousers and pulled a sweater over his head. Then, glancing at her, he quipped, 'You look ready for more…' with a devilishly suggestive arch of a black eyebrow. 'Come on—before I change my mind.'

Not sure if that was a compliment or not, she smiled and they left.

Sitting in the car five minutes later, as he drove in silence through the country lanes, Lucy cast him a sidelong glance. She tried to tell herself she was worrying over nothing—Lorenzo was a busy man and of course he had to leave—it didn't mean she would not see him again. She looked at him. His attention was centred on the road ahead, his hands resting lightly on the steering wheel as he manoeuvred the car through the narrow roads with ease and speed. At this rate she would be home in a few minutes, she realised.

'So, when will I see you again?' she asked, and without thinking rested her hand on his leg.

Lorenzo tensed. Originally he'd had no intention of seeing Lucy again. But as he looked down at her hand, her small soft fingers, then lower to her shapely legs curved towards him, suddenly a picture of those same legs locked around him and her cries of pleasure as he thrust into her hot, tight little body filled his mind. Somehow the weekend affair he had planned didn't seem such a great idea after all…

He had been without a woman for months, he was a free agent, and the two nights he had spent with Lucy had been incredible. He could not remember ever having such great sex or such fun with a woman, and he was reluctant to give her up. In fact, he mused, keeping Lucy as a lover, quietly tucked away in a corner of England, held a lot of appeal. He visited London occasionally, usually flying in and out in a day, but that could be altered.

He decided to leave his options open.

'Soon, I hope. But, like you, I do have to work, I'll try and get back next weekend—if not the week after. But I'll give you a call.'

Lucy sighed with relief as Lorenzo stopped the car and after walking around the bonnet helped her out. The summer dress she wore was no protection against the cool night air and she shivered. Lorenzo looped an arm around her shoulders and walked her to the front door. Taking the key from her purse she looked up at him. 'Would you like to come in for a nightcap?' she asked hopefully, reluctant to see him go.

'I won't, if you don't mind,' he said with a rueful smile. 'Because if I do I'll kiss you, and it won't stop there.'

'No…I don't mind now I know you are coming back again,' Lucy responded blithely.

'Good.' Dropping a brief kiss on the top of her head—he didn't dare do anything more—he said, 'Now, lock the door behind you.'

Lorenzo's arm fell from her shoulders and she turned and put the key in the lock. Then she suddenly remembered why she had met him in the first place, and spun back.

'Wait a minute, Lorenzo—we never got around to discussing Steadman's, and we need to before Tuesday.' Then she remembered something else. 'You don't have my number. I'll give—'

'No need. The bank will have it,' Lorenzo stated.

Her words were a timely reminder. He had her number in more ways than one, he thought, his dark eyes narrowing cynically on her face. Her head was turned towards him, her green eyes incredibly large and luminous, the light of the moon making her pale skin almost translucent. Her long hair, swept back behind her small ears, seemed to fall in a shimmering mass down her back. Beautiful, and temptation personified, but not to him…not any more.

'Oh, yes—of course.' She turned completely around and smiled up at him. 'But about the factory…Tuesday is the deadline, and I need to know before I speak to my lawyer if you are going to reject the offer to sell and keep the factory open. Maybe later, if we ever do decide to redevelop,' she continued, warming to her theme, 'perhaps it could be shops and a recreation centre—something that could provide other work in the community. Dessington is in a pretty part of Norfolk—not far from the coast—and it could bring in tourists much like here.'

Lorenzo listened to her with deepening distaste as she rambled on about what 'they' might do if the factory eventually did close. Enthralled by her lush body, he had almost forgotten her hated name, and the business that had brought them together. But—typical female—Lucy had not, and though she took the high moral ground, wanting to save the workers, basically she was out for every penny she could get. He had learned his lesson years ago, when he'd lived in America and found the girl he had been going to surprise with an engagement ring in bed with another man—a man she'd imagined was wealthier than him—and it was not one he would ever forget.

Women always had an agenda, and Lucy was no exception. There was no denying sex with her was incredible, though she was not as adventurous as some women he had known—sometimes even seeming shocked—and she did have a tendency to blush, which was amazing given her lifestyle. Or maybe it was just a ploy to give the impression of innocence. He didn't care, because her last appeal had confirmed his original decision. The weekend affair was over, and he had no intention of seeing her again.

'Your ideas sound admirable, Lucy, but totally misguided. There is no *we,*' he said with brutal frankness. 'I told you the first time you asked I had no intention of doing business with a Steadman again, and that has not changed.'

Lucy couldn't believe what she was hearing. She stared at him, tall, dark and remote, his eyes cold and hard, and felt as if she was looking at a stranger. 'But you said…' She stopped. It had been his suggestion they might keep the factory… She didn't understand what was happening—didn't want to. 'I thought…' What did she think? That they were friends? More than friends…? 'We made love—'

'We had sex,' Lorenzo cut in, and she was silenced by his statement. 'Something I consider more pleasure than business, but if you want to mix the two fair enough,' he drawled with a shrug of his broad shoulders. 'I will postpone selling for a month, to give you time to make other arrangements if you can.' The light, conversational tone of his voice belied the cold black eyes looking down at her, devoid of any glimmer of light.

'You will?' she murmured, but inside her heart shrivelled as the import of his words sank in. To Lorenzo they'd had sex, nothing more. Whereas she, in her inexperience, had begun to imagine it was a whole lot more—something very special—and she was halfway to falling in love with him. How could she have been so wrong?

'Yes. I don't like weddings, and avoid them whenever possible, but thanks in the most part to you, Lucy, I have rather enjoyed the weekend. In fact I'll delay the sale of Steadman's for *two* months,' he offered. 'You were really good, and cheap at the price.'

Lucy stared at him with wide, wounded eyes and dragged in a deep, agonising breath. His words sliced at her heart. She had never been so insulted in her life, and she fought back the pain that threatened to double her over. That he could actually think she had made love to him simply to get him to agree a deal over Steadman's horrified her—but then she recalled Lorenzo had thought the same the first time he had kissed her in his office. His mindset had never altered. He was still a power-wielding, cynical banker, to whom money was everything and everything had a price—including her. His insinuation that he might hang onto the factory had been nothing more than a ploy to soften her up and get her into bed, but if he thought she would be grateful that he was postponing the sale he had got the wrong girl.

When not blinded by love—no, not love, *sex,* Lucy amended, she was a bright, intelligent woman. Suddenly the pain gave way to fury, and she started to raise her hand, wanting to lash out at him, then stopped. Violence was never an answer, but his insinuation that he was paying for her services had cut her to the bone. Lorenzo had used her, but it was her own dumb fault for letting him. He actually *was* the ruthless devil his brother had said, and yet she still could not quite believe it.

'Why?' Lucy asked. 'Why are you behaving like an immoral jerk?'

'Oh, please—don't pretend you are Miss Morality, Lucy. You enjoyed the sex as much as I did,' he informed her, with an arrogantly inclined head, his glittering dark eyes looking down at her contemptuously. 'You are exactly like your brother—up for anything at any cost. And *your* brother cost mine his life.'

'But it was an accident,' she said, confused by the change of subject.

'So the coroner said—but I believe what your brother did was contemptible…tantamount to manslaughter,' Lorenzo stated, but he saw no reason to prolong the conversation by getting into the details with Lucy. It was over and done with, and he was finished with her. 'So now you know why I have no desire to do business with Steadman's. I will *never* forgive and forget—is that plain enough for you?'

Lucy was stunned by the antagonism in his voice. She had not been mistaken when they'd met in his office and she had the thought his refusal was personal…it *had* been. Her face paled as the full weight of his contempt hit her, and anger almost choked her.

'Yes,' she said coldly. 'I always knew, but I forgot for a while.' Her slender hands clenched at her sides to prevent the urge to claw his devious eyes out. She'd had no chance from the start, she realised bitterly. If the only reason Lorenzo had had sex with her was some perverted form of revenge or payback for her brother's perceived behaviour, she didn't know—and cared less. All she *did* know was she was not taking it lying down.

'Damien told me what you said to him after the inquest, blaming him for what happened, but foolishly—knowing how it feels to lose someone you love—when I met you I decided anger and grief had maybe made you act out of character. I gave you the benefit of the doubt, but now I see how wrong I was. You really are a ruthless devil. But I *am* holding you to your promise of two months' reprieve. As you so succinctly put it, I have paid for it—with sex.' And, spinning on her heel, she walked into the house, slamming the door behind her.

Lorenzo was stunned for a moment. The fact she

knew about his confrontation with her brother had shocked him—though it was not really so surprising when he thought about it. Not that it mattered any more. He was never going to see her again. He got in the car and left.

Quivering with rage and humiliation, Lucy threw her keys down on the table in the entrance hall and dashed up the stairs to her flat, trying to ignore Lorenzo's hateful insults. But every time she thought of him—thought of what she had done with him—she felt cheap and dirty.

She ripped off her clothes and headed straight for the shower, ashamed and angry. Lorenzo had as good as called her a whore, and she wanted to wash every trace of him off her body. But perversely that same body remembered every touch, every caress.

Maybe she was fated to be ashamed every time she had sex, she thought hysterically, and finally she crawled into bed and let the tears fall, crying until she had no tears left.

Monday morning Lucy woke from a brief tormented sleep, hugging her pillow. For a second she inhaled the scent of Lorenzo, and smiled. Then reality hit, and she dragged herself out of bed, telling herself she must change the sheets. She staggered into the bathroom and groaned when she looked in the mirror. Her eyes were red and swollen from the tears she had shed over Lorenzo Zanelli, and however much she tried to convince herself he wasn't worth a second thought her body ached for him with every breath she took.

Showered, and dressed in cotton pants and a tee shirt, she stood in the gallery, a cup of coffee in her hand, and glanced around. Usually it gave her pleasure, looking over her little kingdom before anyone arrived. She was proud of what she had accomplished. But today she didn't get the same thrill.

'Hi, Lucy.'

Lucy drained her coffee cup and tried to smile as Elaine walked in with a spring in her step, ready to start the working week—before she took in her friend's face.

'My God, that must have been some night. I know you rarely drink, but you look like you have a one hell of a hangover.'

'No, nothing like that,' Lucy said. 'Much worse.'

'Do tell all.' Elaine tilted Lucy's head up with a finger and really stared at her. 'You look different, and you have been crying. That can only mean one thing—man trouble. I thought yesterday you looked remarkably happy, but we were so busy I never got to ask you why. What happened last night? Discovered he was married, did you?'

'Discovered he was only interested in a dirty weekend,' Lucy said bitterly, but couldn't bring herself to tell Elaine the whole story.

'Lucy, you are far too naïve where men are concerned. Stop beating yourself up because you were finally tempted by sex—you've never had a lover as long as I've known you, and it was way past time you did. Put it down to experience and get over it. You are not the first and won't be the last. Weddings are notorious for causing brief affairs. Too much champagne and the best man gets off with the bridesmaid, the guests get off with each other. One wedding Sid and I went to the *bridegroom* actually got off with the bridesmaid—needless to say the marriage only lasted the length of the honeymoon, when the happy couple returned home and the bride found out.'

'I don't believe it.' Lucy actually managed a weak smile.

'Ask Sid—the groom was an acquaintance of his. He told me the man was a serial womaniser and I didn't believe him, but he was right.'

'Okay, you've made your point. Actually, when I first met Lorenzo I didn't like him, and my original impression was he was no gentleman. I should have trusted my instincts and steered clear. He certainly proved me right.'

'Good—you are seeing him for the rat he obviously is, and that is the first step to recovery. Now, put the experience behind you and get on with your life. I'll take over here and you can spend the day in your studio, creating your next great masterpiece or making a start on your latest commission. If you stay here you will scare the customers.'

Lucy agreed—not that she felt like painting. All she wanted to do was forget the weekend had ever happened. She took out her sketchbook and began to draw, but to her dismay found the small boy's face she was copying had morphed into a remarkable likeness of Lorenzo.

She looked at it for a long time and then, turning the page of her sketchpad, began again. Art had always been her release valve from any pressure in life, and before long she was totally immersed in her work.

The next day her lawyer called and confirmed that the sale of Steadman's had been postponed for two months. So Lorenzo had done what he promised. He was a cynical devil to pay for her favours in such a way, but at least it gave her some time to figure something out for the factory. On the sketch she had started yesterday she coloured the eyes red and added horns, whiskers and a tail…

Somehow it was cathartic, thinking of him that way. Whenever Lucy felt really down, her body hot and aching, her mind tormented by images of him making love to her, she would only have to look at the sketch to remind herself what a devil…a love-rat…he really was.

'At last you look more like yourself,' Elaine declared, walking into the gallery on Saturday morning three weeks later and eyeing Lucy up and down. 'That turquoise dress Leon brought back from India is gorgeous—the colour really suits you, and the beading is perfect. But go upstairs and take that braid out of your hair and leave it loose. Remember you are a beautiful, highly talented artist, and when you try you can sell anything and everything. I have a feeling we are going to have a great day today.'

Lucy laughed. 'I'm not sure that is a compliment to my paintings.' But she did as Elaine said, and went upstairs and unbraided her hair. She stood in front of the mirror, brushing her hair back from her brow and fastening it with a silver clip, then brushed the long length down to tumble over her shoulders in gentle waves. Slowly it dawned on her that Elaine was right. The pale, sad-eyed reflection of the last few weeks was gradually fading.

Last night she had taken a walk down into the centre of Looe, and as she'd strolled along the harbour through the crowd of happy holidaymakers she'd been reminded of how much she had loved the place from the very first time her parents had brought her here. How much she still loved the place. She'd felt her heart lift a little.

This morning, on a whim, she had put on the brightly coloured dress, and she looked more like her old self again. Picking up a lipstick, she applied it to her full lips and, smiling, added a touch of mascara to her long lashes and clipped on an earring. Business was going well, and she had enough commissions to keep her busy for a while. Life was good.

Even the trip two weeks ago she had been dreading, to clear out the family home in Dessington before putting the house on the market, had turned out to be inspirational.

Meeting old friends from school, visiting the factory and talking to the workers, being greeted by shopkeepers and reminded how much everyone had respected her grandfather, who had started the business, and her parents, who had been socially active in the town until her mum died, had all reminded Lucy what a happy childhood she had.

The memories had helped concentrate her mind on the problem of the factory, and standing looking around the huge garden of her family home she'd had a *eureka* moment… She had come up with a brilliant idea that could save the factory and help the community.

She had spoken to her lawyer, arranging to meet Richard Johnson—the third partner in Steadman's—and had pitched her proposition to him. He was not the ogre she had imagined, and after a productive meeting with him and his architect, and subject to the approval of the town council, they had agreed on a very different deal. Lucy had made the necessary arrangements with her bank, and also a telephone call from her new partner yesterday it was virtually a done deal. What gave her the most satisfaction was the fact she had achieved everything without any help from the despicable Zanelli.

Deep down Lucy had always known Lorenzo was not for her. In every respect they were poles apart—in temperament and aspiration, and in culture… He was a billionaire banker, devoted to making more money, with centuries of tradition behind him making him the arrogant, cynical man he was. Her life was her art and her friends. Money didn't bother her so long as the bills were paid and her conscience was clear.

Unlike Lorenzo, who didn't *have* a conscience, she thought. And later she was to be proved absolutely right…

CHAPTER FIVE

LORENZO had extended his stay in New York to three weeks, and had on his return to Italy last night found, as expected, the Olivia Paglia rumours had faded away—problem solved. This morning he had agreed to his mother's request to have dinner with her tonight, as he had not visited in over a month. And now he had an even bigger problem that was a hell of a lot harder to solve.

He glanced at his mother across the dining table. He hadn't seen her so animated in years, but the reason for it exasperated him. He glanced down again at the handful of photographs spread on the table. Teresa Lanza had presented them to his mother, along with the information that the girl in the picture was none other than Lucy Steadman. How had he hoped to keep that quiet, with the Lanza family in attendance? He must have been out of his mind.

'Why did you not tell me, Lorenzo? You let me scold you about that Paglia woman and all this time you had a lovely girlfriend—a talented artist, no less. Was it because you thought I might be upset because of her relationship to Damien? You need not have worried. I remember Antonio telling me about Damien's sister—he thought she was a lovely girl. Antonio and Damien were such great friends, and I never blamed Damien for the tragic accident. As the coroner said, he did the right thing to try and save Antonio's life.' She sighed. 'It was just a pity the rescue services were too late.'

Lorenzo stiffened in his chair, his lips twisting in a cynical smile. He didn't agree, but there was no point arguing so he ignored her last comment. 'I do not have girlfriends, Mother. I have female partners occasionally, and Lucy Steadman is neither. I barely know her, so drop the subject.'

'Oh, dear!' she said, and he caught a slightly guilty look on her face before she continued. 'Well, that is not the impression Teresa got. She showed me all the photos they took of you and Lucy together at the wedding, and it was very good of her to make these copies for me. Teresa said you seemed very close, and you told her you had known Lucy for quite a while. She also told me that Lucy has no family left—her father died, and then her brother last year. She is all alone in the world. You could have told me, Lorenzo.'

He picked up his wine glass and drained it in one gulp. 'I did not know myself until recently,' he said, appalled at the way the conversation was going. 'As for Teresa Lanza, she must have misunderstood me. I never said I had known Lucy for quite a while. I said I had known *of her* for a while. I have met her twice—once at the wedding, and once before that on business.' Thinking fast, he saw an opportunity to rid himself of at least one problem and explain to his mother why it made sense to sell the shares in Steadman's.

'As you apparently know, Lucy Steadman is an artist. She has no interest in plastics whatsoever. She was in Verona recently, to deliver a painting, and at her request we had a meeting at the bank to discuss the sale of Steadman Industrial Plastics. I didn't mention it to you in case it upset you. I know how pleased you were about Antonio investing in the firm, planning for the future, and you may have wanted the bank to hang on to Steadman's for sentimental reasons that make no financial sense to the other partners.'

'Oh! You're right—I would have liked to keep the link to Antonio, so I can understand your reasoning. But I see now selling is the obvious thing to do. Tying an artist to a plastics factory is laughable. In fact I want you to ask her here for a visit.'

Lorenzo could not believe what he was hearing. 'Why on earth would you want to do that?' he asked, barely hiding his astonishment.

'Why—to offer her my condolences on the loss of her brother and father, of course. I should have done it long ago. Besides which, if I met Lucy I could commission her to paint a portrait of Antonio. By all accounts the portrait she has done of the Contessa della Scala's husband is wonderful. So you will ask her for me?'

It was more of a command than a request, but one he had no intention of fulfilling.

'As I said, Mamma, I hardly know the girl. But what I do know is she is dedicated to her work and runs an art and craft gallery in Cornwall. The summer is her busiest period, so she could not get away even if she wanted. And I don't know her well enough to ask.'

'Lorenzo, I am not so old I can't recognise a lover's kiss—and if you don't ask her I will. I'll ring her. You must have her phone number…or the bank will.'

The hell of it was his mother would. She might be frail, but she had a stubborn streak. Suddenly Lorenzo realised his weekend affair was in danger of becoming a millstone around his neck, and he had no one to blame but himself… He had been so intent on getting Lucy into bed all his thinking had been concentrated below the belt. His innate control and common sense had flown out of the window.

Silently he cursed. It had never entered his head that the Lanzas would take pictures of the wedding guests. There was one of him with his arm lodged firmly around Lucy's waist while they talked, and the most damning of all had to be Aldo's work—it was him kissing Lucy in the garden, just before the man had interrupted them…

'We were not lovers. It was too much champagne and a friendly kiss—that is all. But all right…I'll call Lucy,' he conceded, and left shortly after.

Back in his apartment, Lorenzo stood by the window, looking out over the city without actually seeing it, a glass of whisky in his hand. Antonio, as the baby of the family, had been his mother's favourite, though she had tried not to show it, and with hindsight Lorenzo recognised Antonio had been indulged by all of them. He knew his mother was not likely to give up on the idea of meeting Lucy and commissioning a portrait of Antonio any time soon… He crossed the room and flopped down on the sofa, draining his glass and putting it on the table. Whisky was not the answer.

The hell of it was Lorenzo could not see a way out of the situation without involving Lucy Steadman.

Basically he had two options. He could do as his mother asked and mention commissioning a portrait of Antonio to Lucy, invite her to visit his mother. The big flaw in that scenario was that Lucy knew of his run-in with Damien, which he wished to keep from his mother. She had been hurt enough, and didn't need bitterness added to her memories. The whole idea was a non-starter as far as he was concerned.

He had cut Lucy out of his life and wanted it to stay that way—and after the brutal way he had left her he was sure she would refuse any invitation from him point-blank. But if by some fluke Lucy *did* accept, he had no doubt as a woman scorned she would take great delight in telling his mother of his run-in with Damien just to spite him. A ruthless gleam sparked in his dark eyes. That was never going to happen—because Lucy wasn't going to get the chance.

The second option—the one that appealed to his cynical mind and which, with his experience of women, he knew would succeed—was the only option. He would offer Lucy a big fat bribe. He would give her the bank's shares in Steadman's in return for her refusing any overtures his mother might make and for her silence on the accident if she did contact her.

Lucy had disturbed his peace of mind long enough. He had taken an old girlfriend out to dinner in New York and given her only a goodnight kiss when she had been expecting a whole lot more—as had he until he'd realised he felt no inclination to take the stunning brunette back to his apartment or anywhere else.

Lucy had wanted him to vote with her on the Steadman's deal. Well, this way she could have the shares outright and do what the hell she liked with them. The money was nothing to him, and he had wasted far too much of his time dwelling on Lucy Steadman as it was. Finally all connection with the despised family would be severed for good.

He flicked on his cell phone to dial Lucy's number, having got it from the bank and entered it in his speed dial, and then stopped. She would certainly hang up on him. Better to catch her by surprise, even though it meant he would have to see her again. Definitely for the last time, he told himself, and ignored the stirring in his body at the thought…

Instead he rang his lawyer, and told him what he needed by morning.

'Lucy!' Elaine cried, and dashed into the small kitchen at the back of the gallery, where Lucy was standing with the teapot in her hand, about to pour out a couple of much needed cups of tea, after a very successful day's trading, to enjoy while they closed up.

'What's the panic? A late influx of customers?' Lucy queried.

'No—just one. A man asking for you. I can see now why you were so upset over the Lorenzo guy. Scumbag he may be, but he is here—and what a hunk. I bet he is great in bed. Not that I'm suggesting you should make the same mistake again.'

Lucy paled, then blushed, then paled again, her stomach churning at the thought of seeing Lorenzo again.

'Go,' Elaine said, taking the teapot from her hand and pushing her towards the hall. 'Get rid of him—and if you need help call me.'

She didn't need help—not any more, not on any level. She was over him. But that didn't stop the painful details of the last time they'd been together flashing through her mind. Why he was back she didn't know—and didn't want to know. He could not have made it plainer: he'd used her, paid her, and despised her simply for who she was.

Straightening her shoulders and flicking her hair back from her face, Lucy walked down the hall, determination in every step she took. She would not allow any man to use her and walk over her ever again…

Lorenzo appeared in the open doorway of the gallery

and her heart lurched at the sight of him. She hesitated. He was casually dressed, in a white linen shirt open at the throat and washed denim jeans that hung low on his hips and clung to his muscular thighs like a second skin—designer, no doubt, she thought, and glanced up. Her green eyes clashed with deep brown, and it took every ounce of will-power she possessed to hold his gaze as her traitorous heart pounded like a drum in her chest.

'Lucy.' He said her name, and smiled the same slightly rueful but sensual smile that had seduced her before. But she was wiser now, and wasn't fooled.

'Mr Zanelli,' she responded, walking forward. He was so confident she would fall into his arms—she could see it in his eyes, in the arrogant tilt of his head, and felt anger stir deep within her…along with a more basic emotion which she battled to ignore. 'This is a surprise. I never expected to see you again. Come to buy a painting?' she suggested facetiously.

'No, I've come to see you. We need to talk.'

'No, we don't. I have no interest in anything you say.'

'Not even if it means saving Steadman's?' Lorenzo prompted, sure that would tempt her. But he was sorely tempted himself, and the sudden tightening in his groin was a reminder of how much.

He had flown into Newquay Airport, barely an hour's drive away, and he had every intention of returning to Italy tonight. The sooner the better. He hadn't slept with a woman since Lucy, and the strain was getting to him.

Every time he saw her she was different—from bag lady to gowned elegance to young and sexy in a skimpy summer dress. Today she was an exotic vision in a plunging necked shimmering turquoise silk eastern thing, with a beaded band beneath her high firm breasts and a skirt that swirled around her feet. Some of her glorious hair was swept back in a clip on top of her head, and the rest fell in a silken mass down over her shoulders. In one ear she was wearing the most amazing huge silver spiderweb earring, with long white feathers attached that floated down against the curve of a breast. As for her mouth—her lips were painted a vibrant pink, and so full and sensually promising he ached to taste them and a whole lot more. Never, even as a teenager with rampant hormones, had he ever felt such a need to kiss a woman.

'No, thank you.' Lucy said bluntly.

Dragging his gaze from her lips, Lorenzo saw the anger in her eyes and realised what she had said. 'A polite refusal, but not a very sensible one—or business-like,' he prompted, and moved closer. He could see the pulse beating in her slender neck. She was not as cool as she would have him believe.

'You once told me I should stay out of business and you were right. The way you do business is despicable and the cost far too high for any self-respecting person. Now, I must ask you to leave—we are about to close.' Lucy walked to the front door and flipping the sign to 'Closed', held the door open. 'This is the way out.'

She glanced back at Lorenzo. He stood where she had left him, his dark eyes narrowed angrily on her face, then in two lithe strides he was beside her. His hand reached out to circle her throat and he tipped her head back. Shocked, she grasped his wrist with her free hand to pull his hand away.

'You didn't find me despicable when you were naked beneath me on the bed, moaning my name.' He brushed his lips lightly against hers and laid his other hand over her breast. To her shame, her lips stung and her nipple tightened beneath his palm. 'And it wouldn't take me five minutes to get you that way again, Lucy,' he taunted her softly.

Lorenzo was so damned arrogant—and yet possessed of a vibrant sexuality that could heat up a room and every woman in it, Lucy thought helplessly. He was almost irresistible, but resist him she did, her pulse-rate rising with her anger at the insult. She dug her nails hard into his wrist and he let go of her throat. She let go of the door and did what she should have done weeks ago. Bringing her hand up, she struck him as hard as she could across the face, catching him unawares. Her hand cracked against his cheek and rocked him back on his heels. The heavy door caught his shoulder.

Lucy, chest heaving in outrage, stepped back into the hall and spun round to face him. 'You have a mind like a sewer. Sex and money is all you think about!' she yelled, her green eyes spitting with rage. 'That is exactly what I would expect from you and you got exactly what you deserved.'

'Hey, Lucy?' Elaine called out as she appeared in the hall. 'Is everything okay?'

Appalled by her loss of temper, Lucy stared at Lorenzo's cheek, with the imprint of her fingers clearly visible, and then at Elaine. 'Yes, it's fine,' she said, and took a deep steadying breath, forcing a smile to her lips. She did not want to involve Elaine. 'Mr Zanelli and I had a discussion, that is all.'

'We still are, Lucy,' Lorenzo inserted, reining in the furious impulse to shake her till she rattled. What was it about this witch of a woman that made him lose his legendary control? He was here for one reason only, he reminded himself. He could fob his mother off for a while, but he was taking no chances—and he needed Lucy to agree to have nothing to do with his mother if she *did* call. Especially if she tried to commission a painting that would keep Lucy Steadman on the periphery of his life for heaven knew how long.

But holding her by the throat was no way to go about it.

He turned to the other woman, slightly taller and a lot wider than Lucy. 'Elaine, isn't it?' he said smoothly, his razor-sharp brain quickly recalling Lucy's explanation that Elaine, who did tapestries, also helped out at the shop. 'Don't concern yourself. Lucy and I got our wires crossed—I believe that is the English expression—but it is nothing we cannot put right, I assure you.'

'That does not look like a wire that crossed your face,' Elaine quipped. 'More like a hand—and it serves you right. A married man should know better than to mess around with a single woman.'

Elaine's witty comment in rushing to her defence cooled Lucy's anger—then she realised she had by omission misled her friend.

Lorenzo's cheek was stinging, and he had probably bruised his shoulder, but he could have sworn his head was clear and he was in control. Yet these two women were intent on driving him crazy—and who the hell was the married man?

'What married man?' he asked, his dark gaze skimming from Elaine to settle on Lucy and catch the guilty look on her expressive face.

Surely she had not taken up with another man already? A married one at that? Not that he cared—he was here for the express purpose of getting Lucy Steadman out of his life for good, and was prepared to pay to do so. His one regret was that he hadn't cut the Steadmans out of his family's life years ago, before her brother had talked Antonio into the reckless lifestyle that had got him killed. As for Lucy—he knew exactly what type of woman she was and yet the thought of her with another man did nothing to help his self-control.

'You, of course,' Elaine answered. 'Lucy told me all about you.'

'Did she, now?' Lorenzo said, never taking his eyes off Lucy. He saw her nervously chew her bottom lip and she would not look him in the eye. 'I'm surprised at you, Lucy. You know perfectly well I am not married—never have been, and never likely to be. Which makes me wonder what other fairytales you have told your friend,' he drawled, shaking his head mockingly. 'We really do need to talk.'

'He is *not* married?' Elaine queried, and looked at Lucy.

Lucy finally met her friend's puzzled gaze. 'Not to my knowledge—and if you recall I never said he was, Elaine. I think you must have jumped to the wrong conclusion after giving me the benefit of your own dubious wedding experiences.'

Elaine looked from Lucy to Lorenzo and back again. 'Ah, well, that is different.' She chuckled, obviously amused. 'Well, good luck, Lucy, in sorting out your problems. I'll just get my bag and leave.' And she disappeared down the hall, to reappear a minute later, with a cheery wave and a goodbye as she closed the door and left.

There was silence. Lucy glanced up and found Lorenzo's gleaming dark eyes resting on her. Something in his look made her stomach curl and she flushed hotly.

'Time for you to leave, Mr Zanelli,' she said curtly. 'We have nothing more to discuss and I need to lock up.' She glanced back at him. 'I don't want any more customers *or* uninvited visitors.'

He did not respond—didn't move. He was towering over her, intimidating her with his presence, and suddenly the hall seemed smaller. Lucy had had enough. 'Goodnight, and good riddance. Is that plain enough for you?' she mocked, parroting the words he had said to her the last time she had seen him, and she reached for the handle to open the door again.

But Lorenzo was quicker, and before she could react a strong hand had clamped around her waist and pulled her hard against his body, trapping her arm against her side while the other hand slid beneath the heavy fall of her hair to tug her head back. Deliberately he bent and pressed his mouth against the pulse that beat erratically in her throat, and she felt it like a flame.

'Don't,' she gasped, and pushed against his chest with her hand while his mouth seared up her slender neck. 'Let go of me, you great brute. I *hate* you,' she flung at him savagely.

'No, you don't.' His head came up. His eyes were black in his hard, masculine face, and Lucy could not control the slight tremor in her limbs. 'You want me. But then women like you can't help themselves,' he said contemptuously.

She punched his chest with a curled fist, but it was like hitting a brick wall. She lifted her knee and suddenly he whirled her round, making her head spin. Before she could draw breath, let alone find her feet, his head lowered, and she moaned in protest as his mouth came down hard and ruthless against her lips, forcibly parting them, demanding her surrender.

For a moment she made herself stay rigid in his arms, but then her mouth trembled in helpless response and she succumbed to the powerful passion of his kiss. When he finally released her she stumbled back and deliberately wiped her hand across her mouth, but to her shame she could not wipe away so easily the warring sensations inside her.

'You should not have done that, Mr Zanelli,' she snapped.

Lorenzo stared down at her, his broad shoulders tense, his face expressionless. 'Maybe not, but you provoked me—and if I have succeeded in shutting you up long enough to listen it was well worth it. And you can drop the "Mr Zanelli"—you know my name and you have used it too intimately to pretend otherwise. Now, we can go up to your apartment and I'll tell you why I am here.'

Lucy looked at him warily, silently conceding it *was* a bit childish calling him Mr Zanelli. Her real problem was that she didn't trust him, but short of throwing him out—which was a physical impossibility—she hadn't much choice but to listen to what he had to say.

'And it isn't what you are thinking,' he drawled, with a sardonic lift of one ebony brow. Though his body was telling him different…

'I'll listen, but not here,' Lucy conceded. 'I usually go into town on Saturday evening to eat. You can come with me.' She wanted Lorenzo out of her home and among other people—simply because her own innate honesty forced her to admit she didn't trust herself alone with him.

'My car or yours?' Lorenzo asked as, after locking up the gallery, they walked out into the front yard that doubled as a car park.

'Neither.' Lucy flicked a glance up at him. 'We can walk down the hill—it is not far.'

Stepping onto the grass verge that ran down the side of the road and Lorenzo joined her, but didn't look too comfortable when a Jeep whizzed past with a group of four young men on board.

'Hi, Lucy!' they all yelled, and waved. Lucy waved back.

'Friends of yours?' Lorenzo asked.

'Yes—students in my weekly art class at the high school. Now, why don't you start talking? I'm listening.'

Another car went by and tooted its horn, and Lucy waved again.

'No. I'd prefer to wait until we reach the restaurant,' Lorenzo said, adding, 'Less interruptions.' And more time for him to regain his self-control.

He'd had no idea she taught art—but then he did not really know her except in the biblical sense. And he didn't want to. Lucy Steadman infuriated him, enraged him and aroused him, and he did not like it—did not like *her.* But he did need her silence, and in his experience the best way to get anything from a woman was to humour her for a while—let her think she was in control…

Lucy hid a smile. He was in for a rude awakening if he was expecting a restaurant…

Lorenzo looked around with interest when they reached the main road. Set in a narrow valley, Looe was very picturesque, with a stone bridge that spanned the tidal river to the other side of town. Lucy led him down the main street that wound its way alongside the harbour and the river to the beach. He couldn't believe the number of tourists around, or the amount of people that Lucy knew. Every few yards someone stopped her to say hello.

He wasn't really surprised. With her long hair flowing over her shoulders, the feather-laden earring fluttering in the breeze and her brilliant smile she looked like some rare exotic butterfly. But there was no mistaking she was a woman, and the pressure in his groin that had plagued him from the minute he set eyes on her was becoming a problem again…

Ten minutes later, sitting on the harbour wall, Lorenzo glanced warily down at the box Lucy handed him, and then at her.

'I got you pizza because you're Italian. The fish and chip shop sells all sorts,' she said, opening the carton containing her fish and chips.

'Thanks.' Lorenzo opened the box. 'I think…' he drawled, eyeing what passed for a pizza in an English holiday town with some trepidation. He didn't want to know what the assorted toppings and cheeses were, but it was nothing like any pizza *he* had ever seen.

'I am ready to listen, so fire away,' Lucy said, shooting Lorenzo a sidelong glance, secretly amused. He was eyeing the pizza as if it was going to jump up and bite him, not the other way around. How were the mighty fallen… He must want something from her pretty badly to lower himself to sitting on a harbour wall and eating a takeaway pizza.

'We have a problem, Lucy.'

There is no we were the words that sprang to mind, but Lucy resisted the urge to taunt him with the words he had used the last time they were together. Let him hang himself, she thought. There was something immensely satisfying in knowing that whatever Lorenzo was after he was not going to get it. Instead she picked up a chip and ate it.

'We do?' she queried. Stringing the superior devil along was going to be fun. Breaking off a piece of battered cod, she popped it in her mouth and glanced up at him with fake concern, licking her lips.

'Yes.' Lorenzo tore his gaze away from the small pink tongue running along her top lip. 'Remember the wedding?' She arched a delicate brow in his direction. Stupid question—of course she did. 'Unfortunately Teresa Lanza called in to my mother to fill her in about the wedding—including the fact that Lucy Steadman was the bridesmaid. Then she showed her the photographs she had taken—quite a few of you and I.'

'Is this story going anywhere?' Lucy cut in. She had finished her fish and chips, and she had finished with Lorenzo, but sitting close to him on the wall, with the brush of his thigh against her own, was testing her resolve to the limit. Stringing him along had lost its appeal.

'The upshot is that my mother wants me to invite you to visit her in Italy. She also wants to commission a portrait of Antonio. Obviously I don't want you anywhere near her. I can put her off for a while, but unfortunately she is determined lady. If I don't ask you she says she will ask you herself. If she does, you are to refuse any offer she makes.'

'Don't worry—I will. I'm not a masochist. Listening to *you* denigrating my brother and I was more than enough,' Lucy said and, standing up, walked along the harbour to the nearest littler bin and deposited the carton in it.

Lorenzo followed her. She noted he hadn't eaten even half the pizza as he tipped it in the bin, and wasn't surprised. But she *was* surprised he had come all this way to tell her not to speak to his mother. That hurt. As if she needed telling again how low he thought her…

She walked on.

'Wait, Lucy.' He grasped her upper arm. 'I have not finished.'

'I have,' she said flatly, glancing up at him and doing her best to ignore the warmth of his hand around her arm. 'I've got the message loud and clear. I am not usually impolite, but if by any remote chance your mother calls me I will make an exception and tell her to get lost. As you said, no contact of any kind ever again between a Steadman and a Zanelli can only be a good thing—and you can start by letting go of my arm and getting out of my life for good.'

His face darkened, and if she wasn't mistaken he looked almost embarrassed, but he did let go of her arm and she carried on walking back the way they'd come.

'I don't want you to be rude to her,' he said, walking along beside her. 'My mother does not know what I know about Damien. She believes your brother did his best to try and save Antonio, and I don't want her disillusioned and hurt again. You must make no reference whatsoever to my argument with Damien. Total silence on the subject—do you understand?'

He glanced down at her, and Lucy had the spiteful thought that he had had no problem disillusioning *her* when she had for a moment imagined herself falling in love with him, or hurting *her* feelings. Why should his mother be exempt?

'Okay, I'll let her down gently but firmly and keep silent about you,' she said, with a hint of sarcasm in her tone that went straight over his arrogant head.

'Good. I propose that you regretfully suggest any

reminder of Damien and Antonio upsets you so much you could not possibly face the prospect of bringing it all back—something along those lines. I'll leave the excuses up to you—women are good at dissembling—and in return I will give you the bank's holding in Steadman's. Naturally my lawyer has drawn up a confidentiality agreement that will be binding on both sides. I have it in the car. All I need is for you to sign and it is a done deal.'

Lorenzo obviously adored his mother, and wanted to protect her, but he was just as controlling with the frail little woman as he was with everything else, Lucy thought. For a second she had been sympathetic to his predicament of trying to save his mother from any hurt, even though she knew he was wrong about Damien, but his insulting comment that women were basically good at lying, and his offer to buy her off with his bank's share of Steadman's, had killed any sympathy she felt stone-dead.

'I'll think about your offer as we walk back,' she said noncommittally. But inside she was seething. He had no qualms about deceiving his mother, albeit he believed it to be for her own good. But that he had the arrogance—the gall—to ask Lucy to do the same, and say that he would pay her for her trouble, was beyond belief. The man thought he could buy anyone and anything, from sex to silence. She almost said no. But a grain of caution—not something she was known for—told her that just in case anything went wrong with her plan to save the factory she should say yes…

Lucy didn't speak to him or look at him again, but she could feel his eyes on her—could sense the growing tension in him with every step she took until they finally reached her home.

'So, Lucy, do your agree?' he asked, stopping by his car.

'Yes. But with one proviso…no, two,' she amended. 'If your mother calls I will not lie to her—though I will remain silent about you and Damien and refuse any invitation she may make politely and finally.'

'Excellent.' Lorenzo smiled cynically. Money never failed. He opened the car door to get the briefcase containing the documents.

Lucy wasn't finished. 'But as far as the confidentiality agreement goes—forget it. You will have to take my word. And as for commissioning a painting…wait here a minute.'

And while Lorenzo was hastily extracting himself from the car, with a resounding bump on his proud forehead, Lucy ducked inside the house, locking the door behind her.

She made straight for her studio at the rear of the gallery, ignoring the hammering on the front door. When she found what she was looking for among the stack of paintings she looked at it for a long moment, a sad, reflective smile on her face, before picking it up. About to leave, she hesitated. Finding her sketch of Lorenzo, she took that as well.

If Lucy had learnt anything over the last twelve years it was not to dwell on the past and what might have been but to cut her losses and get on with living. Straightening her shoulders, the painting and the sketch under her arm, she retraced her steps. She opened the door to see Lorenzo bristling with anger, his fist raised and ready to knock again.

'I had not finished,' he snapped. 'Let me make it perfectly clear it is my way or no way and your proviso is not acceptable. The confidentiality agreement is a must, and non-negotiable.'

'Then forget it. I'm not interested in your seedy idea, and I am finished with you *and* your family.' Anger taking over her common sense, Lucy shoved the painting and the sketch at him. 'Here—take these and your mother won't need to call.' He was so surprised he took them. 'I don't need them or you any more. I have another partner—an honourable man.' And she slipped back in the house, slamming and locking the door behind her.

Lorenzo barely registered what she'd said. He was transfixed by the painting. It was of his brother Antonio, and it was stunning. Lucy had captured the very essence of him—the black curling hair, the sparkling eyes and the smile playing around his mouth. He looked so alive, so happy with life. It was uncanny. Lorenzo realised something else. For Lucy—who could only have been a teenager at the time—to have painted this, she must have been half in love with her subject.

Then he turned the sketch over, and stilled. The painting was all light and warmth, but the sketch was the opposite—dark and red-eyed. There was no mistaking the facial likeness to him, and the little witch had added horns above the ears, and a tail. The tail was long and a given—because the sketch was a caricature of Lorenzo as a huge black rat…

Certainly not one for the family gallery or his mother…but under the circumstances it was amusing, he conceded wryly. Then her parting comment registered, and all trace of amusement faded as a cold dark fury consumed him.

Lorenzo glanced at the house, his eyes hard as jet, and debated trying again. No, next time he would be better prepared—and there would *be* a next time…

Never mind the fact he could not trust Lucy, or that she had slapped him, or that she had insulted him with the sketch. What really enraged him was that she actually had the colossal nerve to think for a second she could outsmart him in a business deal.

He needed to know the identity of this *honourable man*—the mystery benefactor who had obviously convinced Lucy he could help her save Steadman's. So much so she had turned down *his* offer with a spectacularly original gesture. He would make damn sure she lived to regret it.

Lorenzo spent the Sunday at his villa at Santa Margherita and went sailing for a few hours, having assured his mother over the phone that he had spoken to Lucy but she was too busy to visit. He said he was sure he could persuade her to do the portrait if she left it with him.

Relaxed and feeling much more like his usual self, he flew out to New York on Monday, having set in motion his investigation into the Steadman's deal, but no longer sure he was going to do anything about it.

He would sell the shares on the allotted date, as planned, and give his mother the painting in a few weeks. That would satisfy her and put an end to the whole affair.

He returned two weeks later. On entering the outer office he saw his secretary smiling widely. She presented him with the new edition of a monthly society magazine, opened at the centre page.

'Nice wedding. I recognised the bridesmaid—your new girlfriend, apparently—but I never would have suspected what was under that black suit. What a body—

lucky you!' She grinned. 'And the report you requested is on your desk.'

'What the hell?' He swore and grabbed the magazine, groaning at the headline: 'English wedding for Signor Aldo Lanza's nephew, James Morgan.' Then there were two pages of pictures of the bridal party, including Lucy, smiling broadly, and all the Italian guests, with accompanying names and captions. In one, Lucy was pinned to his side. She looked stunning, smiling up at him with her small hand resting on his shirt-front, and he was grinning down at her. The intimacy of the shot was undeniable, and the caption read: 'Lorenzo Zanelli with the bridesmaid, a long-time friend and companion.'

He read some more, then stormed into his office, slamming the door behind him.

He sat down behind his desk, fuming. The brief scandal of being linked to Olivia, a married woman, paled into nothing compared to this. Of course they had connected Lucy to her brother and resurrected the tragic accident in detail. As if he needed reminding of it…

It was all the fault of Teresa Lanza, but there was not a damn thing he could do about it. Now he knew why his mother had looked so guilty. She must have known this was coming out. The wedding had been too late in June to make the July edition, but it had certainly made the August one.

He threw it to one side and picked up the report on Steadman's. By the time he'd read it he was so enraged he slammed down the document and leapt to his feet, the deadly light of battle in his eyes. This was no longer anything to do with business or family, but strictly personal…

If there was one thing Lorenzo revelled in it was a challenge—be it at sea, sailing his yacht, or in the world of high finance—and now Lucy had become a real challenge. Pacing the floor, he realised he had seriously underestimated her. Far from being not cut out for business, she had come up with a plan to save Steadman's—and it was very imaginative and economically sound. Any bank—including his—would judge it a decent investment and back the venture.

To be beaten by a slip of a woman was unthinkable to him. Lucy had effectively sidelined him as a partner in Steadman's, and the factory was to stay open. The housing development and much more was to be built at the opposite side of town, in seven acres taken from the eight-acre river frontage garden of the house Lucy owned, in a deal she had made with Richard Johnson the property developer and third partner in Steadman's. Between them, they had the majority.

Whether she had slept with the man or not he didn't know—and didn't care. She was clever—he'd give her that—but better men and women than her had tried and failed to outsmart him, and there was no way she was getting away with it.

A few telephone calls later Lorenzo had left the bank and boarded his private Lear jet to Newquay Airport, a ruthless gleam of triumph in his dark eyes. A car and driver waited for him when his plane landed. He was back in his normal ruthless business mode, and about to make Lucy an offer she could not refuse…

CHAPTER SIX

LUCY put down the telephone and walked slowly back into the gallery, her mind in turmoil. The call had been from Mr Johnson, her partner in the development deal. He had pulled out. No real explanation had been given—just a terse comment that he was not interested in doing business with her any more and then he'd hung up. She'd tried to ring back but the cell had gone directly to messages.

Monday was usually a slow day, and she was on her own. Much as she wanted to go upstairs and scream at the devastating news she had received she couldn't.

In between serving customers she racked her brains, trying to find a solution. She called her lawyer, who was as shocked at the news as she was, but told her he would make some enquiries and find out exactly what had happened and get back to her. She called her bank and they were no help—other than to remind her she now had to pay the mortgage on two properties.

By five-thirty Lucy had run out of ideas…

A little old lady was wandering around the pottery exhibits, and Lucy made herself walk across and ask if she could help. Five minutes later she had wrapped a hand-painted vase and taken the money, and watched as the lady left. Wearily she rubbed her back and, head spinning, sank down on the seat behind the till. Automatically she began to count the day's takings.

Now what was she going to do? she asked herself, eying the cash. Ordinarily she would have considered it a good day, but as she had taken a mortgage out on the gallery, because the bank had insisted on her having capital available up-front before considering the development loan, she was now in serious trouble.

She heard the sound of footsteps on the polished wood floor and her head whipped up. When she saw who it was all the breath was sucked from her body, her pulse racing almost as much as her mind.

'You!' she exclaimed, rising to her feet, unable to tear her eyes away from the man walking towards her. Lorenzo. There was nothing casual about him today. He was wearing an expertly tailored navy suit, and she knew by his hard, expressionless face that there was nothing casual about his visit.

Inexplicably a shiver of fear snaked down her spine.

'Lucy.' He said her name and his eyes looked straight into hers. She saw the glint of triumph in the dark depths and she knew…

'It was you,' she said, her lips twisting bitterly, anger nearly choking her. 'You got to Mr Johnson didn't you? You bastard…'

'Such language, Lucy. Really, that is no way to do business—your customers would be horrified. I told you once before business is not your thing, but I have to concede you gave it a damn good try. Your plan was excellent, but did you really think for one minute I would allow you to get the better of me?' he demanded, with an arrogant arch of one dark eyebrow.

'You *admit* it was you?' she said, horrified and furious.

'Yes. I made your new partner an offer he could not refuse,' he said, and turned round to stroll to the front door. She thought he was leaving, but instead he locked the door and turned back, staring at her with narrowed eyes, his expression unreadable. 'I've warned you before about security. You really should not sit counting money on your own. Any sneak thief could come in and rob you.'

'Like you,' she spat. 'Robbing me of Steadman's.'

Her anger drained away as the enormity of her predicament hit her. Lorenzo must have bought out Richard Johnson, so he was now the major shareholder in Steadman's and he would certainly close the factory.

'But why?' she asked, shaking her head. 'We were still going to buy you out on the agreed date, at a profit you told me yourself was good. You'd have been finished with Steadman's for ever—just what you always wanted.' She didn't understand...

'Not quite.' His eyes scanned provocatively down her shapely body, making her remember things she had fought hard to forget without much success. Colour rose in her cheeks as he walked towards her. 'I want more, Lucy.' His smile was chilling.

'More money?' she asked. 'But that does not make any sense. Buying out Mr Johnson must have cost you money, and you wanted to sell to make more money—or so you told me to up the offer the first time we met.' Lucy was no financial genius, as Lorenzo purportedly was, but even she could see the huge flaw in his deal.

'No, not money,' he said, his dark eyes fixed intently on her flushed face. 'A drink will do for a start. But upstairs—in comfort.' He made a sweeping gesture with his hand. 'After you,' he said, mocking her.

'No,' she said defiantly. 'I can find another partner...'

Even as she said the words she knew it was futile. Lorenzo now held all the cards.

'You already have, Lucy—me. I told you once before it was my way or no way. You obviously didn't listen.'

She didn't bother to answer. There was no point.

She turned back to the till, suddenly bone-weary, all the fight draining out of her, and mechanically finished cashing up. She locked the till and with the money in her hand walked past Lorenzo and upstairs to her apartment. She went straight to the bookcase that held the safe and put the cash inside, aware that he had followed her but helpless to do anything about it.

'Not much of a safe,' Lorenzo said as she locked it and, straightening up, turned back towards him.

Lucy drove him crazy. He had felt his body react the moment he'd walked in the door and seen her wearing a pair of denim shorts and a red open-necked shirt. Try as he might to control himself, seeing Lucy bending over the damn safe had almost crippled him. She had caused him more trouble than any woman he had ever known, had got under his skin for far too long, and yet he still lusted after her. He could not leave her alone, and now he was no longer going to try.

'It suits me,' Lucy responded. The security or otherwise of her house was the least of her problems under the circumstances. The immediate threat to her safety being Lorenzo. 'Take a seat. I'll get you some tea or coffee—I have nothing stronger.'

'Wait,' Lorenzo snapped and, grasping her shoulders, yanked her hard against him.

She looked up at him, and her eyes widened when they met his. What she saw in the black depths made her shiver with fear—she hoped it was fear… She tried to struggle free, but with insulting ease a strong arm swept around her back and his hand grasped her waist, holding her tight as his long fingers threaded through her hair to grip the back of her head in the palm of his hand.

A shocked gasp escaped her as she caught a glimpse of the naked desire in his dark eyes, then his mouth crashed down on hers. She raised her hands to push him away, but it was a useless gesture. His chest was as hard as marble—but a lot warmer, she realised without wanting to. She couldn't move, couldn't think. All she could do was feel as he kissed her with a demanding passion that ignited a spark deep in her belly.

Suddenly it burst into flame and her traitorous body was suffused with heat. Involuntarily she parted her lips to the hungry demand of his, her hands stroking over his chest and her body swaying into his in willing surrender. It had been so long, too long, and she could deny it no longer. She wanted Lorenzo—wanted him totally…

He lifted his head and stepped back. His hands fell from her and she was free.

'The chemistry is still there, as electric as ever, and that is all I needed to know.' She heard his deep voice as if from a distance—heard the hint of mockery as he added, 'I'll have that coffee now.'

Shamed by her body's betrayal, she closed her eyes for a moment as the heat drained out of her. When she opened them she looked at Lorenzo. His expression was hard and uncompromising. She was tempted to ask him why he was really here, but she didn't really want to know the answer because she had a horrible suspicion she would not like it.

'Okay,' she murmured, too shaken to argue, and, turning on her heel, she headed for the kitchen.

Making the coffee gave her a chance to recover from the body shock that had made her melt in his arms. She tried to tell herself her resistance was low because she was tired and Lorenzo had caught her off guard, it would never happen again, but not with any great conviction.

She returned to the living room five minutes later, a mug of instant coffee in each hand. Lorenzo had removed his jacket and tie and opened the top few buttons of his shirt. He was lounging back on her one and only sofa, looking as if he owned the place.

He glanced at her as she walked towards him, and reached out to take the coffee mug in his hand without saying a word.

It occurred to Lucy that tipping it over his head might give her some satisfaction, but resisted the urge and handed it to him. Her impulsive ideas had got her into more than enough trouble over the years, but her leap into property development had to be the biggest doozy yet. If only the bank had not been quite so briskly efficient in giving her a mortgage on this place. If only she had not been so quick to transfer the cash to the partnership to secure the development deal. Then it wouldn't be so bad.

If only were the saddest words in the world…

She crossed to sit down in a battered old Art Deco-style chair she had been going to re-cover for ages but never got round to, and, taking a sip of her coffee, glanced around her home. But for how much longer?

Lorenzo was right about the factory. It only just about broke even, and after the taxes were paid there was little or no profit. So basically the only income she had was from the gallery, which barely covered the two mortgages she'd have to pay until she sold the house in

Dessington. Any delay in selling and she'd very quickly go bust, she knew.

A frustrated sigh escaped her.

'That was a big sigh, Lucy. Something troubling you?'

She cast Lorenzo, her nemesis, a furious look. Lost in her troubled thoughts, she had not realised his heavy-lidded eyes were narrowed, assessing her much like a spider studied a fly caught in its web, she thought, as he smiled.

'I suppose you find it amusing, trying to wreck my plans. Excuse me if I do not.'

'Not trying—I have done,' he said, draining his coffee and cup and placing it on the occasional table. He straightened up. 'Fifty five percent of Steadman's now belongs to me. I can keep it open or shut it down. The decision is mine. As for your aspirations to develop the land adjacent to your old home—that depends on me also. Apparently your friendly lawyer called a town meeting to reassure the people and the workers you and Johnson had agreed not to close the factory. He went on to explain how a new development had been proposed and it was going to be sited in some of the eight acres of garden at your family home, donated very generously by you. That was a big mistake, Lucy.'

'I don't think so,' she muttered.

'Ah, Lucy—you should stick to art. Trust me, finance is really not your thing,' he said bluntly. 'Have you heard the term "asset-rich but cash-poor"? That is now you—because you have two mortgaged properties and a factory that makes little money and you cannot sell. The land you own could have been sold or even leased, but instead you've given away your only asset,' he drawled mockingly, casting a blatantly suggestive glance over her body before continuing. 'The outlined plan is for luxury housing, shops, a swimming pool and sports centre, and some less expensive housing to be available only for locals to purchase. The development to be named the Delia Steadman Park in honour of your mother. The whole town was delighted, apparently.'

'How on earth do you know all this?' Lucy asked.

'I made it my business to know,' he said, rising to his feet and pacing the length of the room. He turned and stopped beside her chair, staring down at her.

Refusing to be cowed, she met his dark eyes head-on. They were unreadable, and she placed her coffee mug on the floor as an excuse to look away from his harshly attractive face.

'I also know that—unlike when *I* asked you, Lucy—this time you *did* sign a legally drawn-up partnership agreement with your developer friend. But your small-town lawyer—who is, by the way, really more interested in his position as town mayor than lawyer—omitted to make it non-negotiable, and Johnson sold out to me. I am now your partner in everything except the mortgaged house in Dessington and this gallery, which you have also foolishly mortgaged. By my reckoning you won't have this much longer.'

It was worse than she'd thought, and she looked up at him again. A cruel, sardonic smile twisted his mouth.

'I'm sure I don't have to spell it out to a woman like you what that means. I own you—for as long as I want.'

A woman like her… Was there no end to his insults? Her shocked glance saw his eyes were no longer unreadable. She recognised all too well the emotion that now blazed in them: dark desire, barely leashed.

'And I *do* want you, Lucy,' he said, and she could not

suppress the shiver of revulsion his comment caused. An imp of devilment in her head defied her to name it for what it really was—excitement, desire, anticipation…

He stared down into her face, reading her reaction, and his hands reached for her, sliding under her arms. He lifted her bodily out of the chair, holding her high, her feet not touching the ground, and involuntarily she clutched at his shoulders to steady herself.

His smile was cruel. 'Ah, that's better,' he said, putting her down and moving his hands around her back, drawing her closer.

The layer of fabric between them was no protection against the shower of electric sensations that tumbled through her at the feel of his warm muscular chest against her breasts, his flat stomach and muscular thighs as he slowly lowered her down his long body to her feet. Aware of his arousal, she gasped and tried to wriggle free. But his hands tightened on her hips in a grip of iron and hauled her hard against him.

'Feel what you do to me and know what you are going to do for me.' He deliberately ground his hips against her, enflaming her senses, but she made her hands fall to her sides rather than touch him as they ached to do, all her will-power going into fighting her own rising need.

His hands lifted from her hips to link lightly around her back, and she managed to draw away a little from the seductive warmth of his great body—but not free. She had a sinking sensation she might never be free of him…

He watched her. She could feel the intensity of his dark eyes even though she'd averted her face. And then he resumed speaking in a clipped tone, as though addressing some underling.

'You, Lucy, will be my lover whenever I want you. And you will do exactly as I tell you on the single occasion you will visit my mother.'

'Visit? Why? I gave you the painting—surely that is enough?'

'I have not given it to her yet. I realised she would insist on thanking you personally. If you recall, before you shoved the painting in my hands I had offered you a very good deal to refuse all contact with her—which you turned down spectacularly.'

Lucy couldn't believe her momentary loss of temper had led to this. 'What if I change my mind and agree now?' she asked.

'Too late, Lucy. The circumstances have changed. Thanks to Teresa Lanza, the August edition of a popular Verona society magazine has a full-page spread of her nephew's wedding—including pictures of you and I and an article about our tragically linked family histories. The so-called accident being once again in the press necessitates a change of plan. You and I will visit my mother as a couple, and you will present the painting to her as a personal gift. She will be delighted, and any speculation on the accident will fade away. Then, after a suitable period, when I tell my mother we are no longer an item she will understand the reason for no further contact and we need never meet again. In return Steadman's will be yours, and as for the rest I'll find you another partner.'

She looked up at him with horrified eyes. 'You can't possibly mean what I think you mean.'

'To qualify—I mean a partner in the building development,' he drawled sardonically, and she saw the way he was looking at her, his eyes running over her in an insolent masculine fashion that insulted rather than approved. 'I am well aware you are more than capable of finding another sexual partner, but for as long as you are with me I insist on exclusivity. Don't worry, it is not a long-term commitment. I have never kept a woman I liked for more than six months. With a woman like you it will probably be a lot less, and you will be free and clear.'

'You really are a first-class despicable bastard.' Her eyes flashed her contempt at him. 'You must be out of your tiny mind to think for a second I'd agree to such a proposition.'

Lorenzo shrugged. 'Take it or leave it,' he said, his hands dropping from her waist. 'I can stand the heat. I doubt if you can. But if you don't mind going bankrupt and losing everything, do what you like.' He glanced around the room. 'This is a nice set-up you have here, and I doubt your artist friends will be happy to see it close.'

Lucy was free, but frozen to the spot. 'You can't possibly do that.'

'Yes, I can. I can close the factory, for a start. I'm a wealthy man, and its monetary loss is negligible to me. And every attempt you make to move on with the housing development I can block for as long as I choose—certainly long enough to see you go broke. Lucky for you,' he drawled mockingly, 'I choose to have you in my bed.'

Colour ran up her neck and face, and her eyes sparked with frustrated rage. But he was right, damn him. Lorenzo was a powerful banker with contacts all over the world. He could pull any strings he liked and make strong men quake. What chance did she have against him? Virtually none…

She looked at him with hatred, and yet she knew deep

down she was going to accept his offer. The factory, the development plan—all that she worked for—was out of her hands. He could wreck everything—even cause her to lose her home, her gallery and the friends that were her life…a life she loved…

'So what's it to be, Lucy? As if I need to ask.' His sardonic eyes took in her small taut figure with mocking amusement. 'You know you are going to agree.'

'Yes, but first I want a binding contract with—'

'Oh, no,' he cut in. 'This is strictly between you and I, and—as you once so memorably said—you will have to take me on trust. But we can shake on it in the English way.' And he held out his hand.

She looked at his strong tanned hand, the long elegant fingers, and then up at his hard, expressionless face. She had the strangest notion he was not as sure of himself as he appeared. She lowered her eyes, her lashes sweeping her pale cheeks, and called herself a fool for trying to read more into his offer than what it was—sex for money, but on a large scale—and reluctantly placed her hand in his.

'So polite, so prim, so British,' he mocked as his hand tightened around hers, pulling her closer. She tried to pull away but he wrapped her hand behind her back, jerking her hard against him. 'That's better,' he said, his free hand unfastening the buttons of her shirt.

'Why are you doing this?' she asked helplessly. The brush of his fingers in the valley of her breasts as he deftly opened her shirt aroused a pulsating sensation deep inside her that she fought to control. 'I won't enjoy it, and you will get no pleasure from me.'

'Oh, I will, Lucy.'

He stared down at her, reading her reaction as he trailed long fingers over the curve of her breasts, dipping beneath the lace of her bra to graze a nipple. She gasped.

'You see, sweetheart?' He mocked her with the endearment as he teased a taut nipple between his long fingers. 'Your pleasure is my pleasure.' His mouth lowered to hers. The burning pressure of his kiss ignited her fiercely controlled feelings and she trembled helplessly. 'I am *so* going to pleasure you, Lucy,' he murmured against her mouth. 'What we had before will seem like a mere taste, and you will be begging me for more.'

'Never!' she cried, but her body seemed to have a will of its own, and she had a terrible desire to touch him, to surrender herself to the sweet agony of his kiss, his caress…

He slipped the shirt from her shoulder along with her bra strap, so he could bend his head to kiss the curve of her neck. She swayed, whimpering in protest, but as he lowered his head further, peeling down her bra to tongue her hardening nipples, the whimper changed to a moan of pleasure.

He lifted his head and she stared up at him, her eyes fixed on his hard, irresistible mouth.

'Still think you won't enjoy it?' he prompted and, dropping his hand, he removed her shirt and bra completely. His black eyes flicked over her from her pink lips, swollen from his kisses, over her slender shoulders to her breasts and the pale rose nipples betraying her arousal. 'Your body is telling me otherwise.'

Naked to the waist, and shamed by her own weakness, Lucy made an attempt to fold her arms in front of her. But he caught her hands and held them at her sides, bent his head, his mouth finding hers again.

The slow, seductive pressure of the kiss coaxing her lips apart was irresistible, and she could feel herself weakening, responding, wanting him—and suddenly she was transported back to the first time they'd made love…the heady excitement…the swirling senses…the exquisite delight of his touch.

Without removing his lips from hers, he swung her up in his arms. With a sense of *déjà vu* she grasped his shoulder, her hand curving around his neck to touch his hair. Her tongue was curling with his, and any lingering thought of resistance was swept away by the flood of desire raging through her.

He carried her into the bedroom and lowered her on to the bed, removing her shorts and briefs in one deft movement. He straightened up, staring down at her with hot hard eyes as he shed his clothes, letting them fall in a heap on the floor.

Lucy did not move. She was mesmerised at the sight of him. It was still daylight outside, and every muscle, every sinew of his great body was perfectly defined. But his facial muscles were tense, his strong jaw clenched as if to control some strong reaction. She had no time to wonder why as he joined her on the bed. The press of his hard body against her, the heat and the strength of him, made her tremble. Leaning over her, he brushed his lips against her brow, the curve of her cheek, and finally her mouth, to kiss her with an oddly gentle passion that was utterly beguiling.

He moved and laid his head against her breasts, turning his face to nuzzle their creamy fullness, suckling and licking the pouting tips as his hands stroked and caressed the quivering flesh down her hips, her thighs, and between her trembling legs. Every nerve in her body was screaming with tension almost to breaking point. Perspiration broke out on her brow, her body, and her small hands clutched at his biceps, his shoulders, roaming restlessly.

Suddenly Lorenzo rolled over onto his back, lifting her over him, his strong hands grasping the top of her legs. With one mighty thrust he impaled her on the rock-hard length of him, and stilled.

'I want to watch you fall apart,' he grated.

Eyes wild, she looked down and saw the molten passion in the black depths of his.

She splayed her hands on his chest and tried to move, his thickness filling her. She needed to move. But a finger slid between the velvet lips where their bodies joined and her head fell back, a long groan escaping her as he delicately massaged the swelling point of pleasure until she shattered into a million pieces. His grip tightened, holding her firm as she convulsed around him in a mind-blowing orgasm.

Only then did he move his hand to her waist and lift her. Rocking his pelvis, he plunged up deeper into her, over and over again, holding her fast until her shaking body trembled on the brink again. Then he spun her beneath him and his mouth covered hers, catching her desperate whimpering moans before he thrust into her with one fierce lunge that seemed to touch her womb and his great body joined hers in a shuddering climax that went on and on in mindless ecstasy.

Lucy fought for breath her internal muscles still quivering in the aftermath of release, her heart pounding. She was conscious of the heavy beat of Lorenzo's heart against her chest as he lay sprawled across her, his head buried in the pillow over her shoulder. How long she lay in mindless awe at what had happened she had no idea, but finally she lifted an arm to wrap it around him, then stopped and let it fall back on the bed.

In contrast to her body, hot and wet with sweat, her heart was suddenly as cold as ice. This was lust, not love, and she must never forget that… Last time when they had made love— There she was, doing it again… When they had had sex, she amended, Lorenzo had disillusioned her so brutally she had felt ashamed, cheap and dirty…

Well, not any more… It was way past time she toughened up—forgot about love and marriage and being the hopeless romantic Lorenzo had called her at Samantha's wedding. Equality of the sexes and all that—not that she had seen much of it so far in her life. But if Lorenzo could enjoy sex for sex's sake then so could she. Her morals were still intact—just in abeyance for a while. The fact that he had none wasn't her problem. And if it suited the swine to pay for the pleasure, then let him.

Ever the fatalist, she knew she'd have to be an idiot to turn down the deal he was offering. Anyway, she didn't have a choice—unless she wrecked a host of other people's lives, and that she could not do. On the plus side, she had no doubt he would soon tire of her, and then she could forget he'd ever existed and get on with her life the way she wanted to.

'I'm too heavy for you, and I need the bathroom,' Lorenzo said practically, and disappeared into the bathroom. Of course he never forgot protection—which was good in the circumstances. But then a man like Lorenzo—powerful and a control freak—had had plenty of practice…

He practised a lot more when he came back to join her on the bed, and when he finally slid off the bed and dressed he stared down at her for a moment. 'Sort out tomorrow when you can take three days off—preferably within the coming month.'

'I can't possibly. I have a business to run…'

'Yes, you can. Your friends will be out of work if you don't.'

'Only Elaine works for me, and she can't run the place on her own. Sid and Leon just display their work here, and I get ten percent of their sales.'

'Ten?' He shook his head. 'It should be much more than that.' And, bending over her, he dropped a kiss on her nose, a sensual gleam in his dark eyes. 'You have many good points, Lucy, that I am well acquainted with.' He smiled. 'But at the risk of sounding repetitive, trust me—business really isn't one of them.' He chuckled, and left.

Lucy lay where he'd left her. She knew she should be furious—and she would be later—but right at this moment all she felt was a languorous sense of physical satisfaction, and she fell into a deep sleep.

CHAPTER SEVEN

THE tourist trade fell off as children returned to school. The summer was virtually over and Lucy was in a plane flying to Italy, trying to come to grips with the course her life had taken. It wasn't easy. She looked out of the window and below her could see the snow-covered peaks of the Alps, sparkling in the sun. Their beauty was lost on her. She was, for want of a better description, Lorenzo's mistress. She had become accustomed to travelling in a chauffeured car and a private jet…how bizarre was that…?

Lorenzo, after that fatal night when he had given her no choice but to become his lover, had virtually taken over her life, and the following morning had charmed Elaine into believing he was genuinely interested in Lucy. Obviously she could not deny it, and it had left her playing the part of his girlfriend all day, every day. The strain was beginning to tell.

That first day Lorenzo had whisked her away for dinner at the luxury country house hotel he had stayed at before, and the pattern had been set. Sometimes he would arrive and take her to the hotel—other times he'd send a car to take her to Newquay or Exeter Airport and the short flight to London, where Lorenzo kept a hotel suite when he was working in the city—which he had been doing a lot lately. Though now she had not seen him for five days—the longest they had been apart. Maybe it was not coincidence. He had stipulated at the beginning that she was to visit Italy in a month. It was exactly a month today. She had a growing feeling this visit would be the conclusion of their relationship. He had got what he wanted. As for Lucy, she was not sure what *she* wanted any more...

Lorenzo was a highly-sexed man, and they rarely got further than the bed—though a desk and the shower and on one memorable occasion a chair outside on the balcony had all figured in their sex-life.

Yet Lucy knew him little better now than she had the first time they'd met. He was for the most part a reserved, emotionless man, who gave little away except in the bedroom, where sometimes, with his dry wit and humour, he made her laugh. Other times he could be incredibly tender, and kiss and caress her as though he adored her. He always called her to arrange their meetings, but occasionally he called just to talk, and she could almost believe they were a normal couple. But maybe that was just wishful thinking on her part. Alone in her own bed at night, aching for him deep down, she knew for her it was more than just sex.

One thing she had learned about him and liked best was that he wore gold-rimmed glasses when working. Somehow they made him look younger and even more attractive, softening his hard face.

Well, maybe not *best*—because she could not deny the sex was fantastic. He had, with skill and eroticism, taught her more about the sensual side of her nature than she had imagined possible. She no longer made any attempt to resist, but welcomed him with open arms, and she knew when it was over between them there would be no other man for her. She could not imagine doing with any man what she did with Lorenzo…didn't want to…

The flight attendant—a handsome young man about her age—appeared, and offered to fasten her seat belt as they were about to begin their descent to the airport. She refused and fastened it herself, because there was something about the way he looked at her she didn't like. But then he was probably accustomed to ferrying women around the world to meet up with his boss, so she could hardly blame him for thinking the worst.

Lucy walked down the steps from the plane, blinking in the bright light, and smoothed the skirt of the red suit she wore down over her hips. A suit Lorenzo had bought for her the one day he had taken her out for lunch in London on what could pass for a date. Afterwards he had insisted on taking her shopping in Bond Street. She had tried to refuse, but he'd reminded her he was the boss and he wanted to see her in fine clothes and lingerie.

She looked up to see Lorenzo striding towards her, as immaculately dressed as ever in a grey suit, his hair as black as a raven's wing gleaming in the midday sun. Her heart turned over. He stopped in front of her and she glanced up through the thick fringe of her lashes, suddenly feeling too warm.

'Good—you made it,' he said coolly and, taking her arm, added, 'This is a private airfield and Customs are a mere formality.' He led her across the tarmac.

No greeting or kiss, Lucy noted. But then sadly they did not have that kind of relationship.

Ten minutes later she was sitting in the back of another chauffeured car, her nerves jangling as Lorenzo slid in beside her, his muscular thigh lightly brushing hers. She could sense the tension mounting in the close confines of the car as the silence lengthened, and finally found her voice. 'How long does it take to get to Lake Garda?'

He turned his head, his dark eyes meeting hers. 'We are going to my apartment in Verona first.'

Lifting a hand, he swept a tendril of hair that had escaped from her severely styled chignon behind her ear, and she felt the touch of his fingers down to her toes, a flush of heat staining her cheeks.

'I think you need to relax before travelling further. I know *I* do,' he said with a predatory smile that left her in no doubt as to what he had in mind.

To her shame, she felt an immediate physical response. Hastily she looked away, and heard him chuckle.

Lorenzo's apartment was a shock. Lucy stood in the huge living room, eyes wide in surprise. She had expected something formal—and it was. Elegant blue and cream drapes hung at the tall windows of the main reception room, and two huge blue silk-covered sofas flanked a white-veined marble fireplace. The bookshelves either side were stuffed with books—hardback and paperback, shoved in haphazardly—and in front stood a big leather captain chair in *scarlet!* A large low glass table had papers and magazines scattered all over it. The room was a bit of a mess…

But a fabulously expensive mess, she realised. An antique bureau had a bronze statue of a naked lady—pure Art Deco—standing on it, along with an incredible yellow and blue glass sculpture of a fish and a carved wooden statue of what looked like a Native American Indian. But it was the walls that really captured her attention. She recognised a Picasso from his Blue Period, a Matisse, and what she was sure was a Gauguin, along with some delicate watercolours and a huge Jackson Pollock that almost filled one wall.

She turned to Lorenzo and saw he had shed his jacket and had tugged his tie loose so the knot fell low on his chest. 'This is nothing like I imagined.' She waved her hand around, grinning delightedly.

'I know it looks a bit untidy, but Diego, my houseman, is on holiday, and I am not in the least domesticated,' he said wryly.

'I had noticed,' Lucy quipped, recalling the way he stripped off and dropped his ruinously expensive clothes anywhere, without a second thought, every time they met. 'But what I meant was I *love* the room—it is so colourful, and the art work is incredible. Some of it I would never have expected you to like.'

He reached for her then, his dark eyes holding hers and his hands closing over her shoulders 'Not quite such a staid old banker as you thought?' he queried, his hands slipping beneath the lapels of her jacket to peel it off her shoulders and drop it on the back of the sofa.

'I never think of you as old,' Lucy murmured, and the tension between them thickened the air as a different silent conversation took place. She was braless, and the white camisole she wore suddenly felt like a strait-jacket.

He glanced down at her breasts, knowing he would see her nipples jutting against the silk. He raised his eyes, reaching for her hair and pulling out the pins. 'I love...your hair.' He ran his long fingers through the silken length. 'The colour is incredible—tawny like a lion is as near as I can get,' he murmured, and closed his arms around her. His dark head bent and the smouldering flame of desire glittered in his eyes as he touched his mouth gently against hers.

It was what Lucy had been waiting for from the moment she had stepped off the plane, if she was honest. The moment she'd set eyes on him he had excited her like no other man ever had or ever would. One look, one touch, and she wanted him—craved him with an intensity of emotion she could not deny. And the more she saw him the worse it got. He filled her every sense until nothing else existed but the consuming need to feel him take her to that magical place where for a few incredible moments they became one explosive entity. However much she tried to pretend it was just sex, deep down she knew she had fallen in love with Lorenzo.

His mouth was like silk, his tongue teasing and easing between her eagerly parted lips, but the gentleness swiftly gave way to a kiss of mutual desperate passion. His hands reached down to the hem of her skirt and tugged it up over her hips. Lucy grasped his shoulders as she felt his long fingers slip between her thighs and rip the lace briefs from her body and she didn't care. She was lost to everything but her hunger, her need for him.

He lifted his head, his face flushed and his black eyes holding hers as he zipped open his pants. 'I want you now,' he grated, and found her mouth again.

Lucy met and matched his demand instantly, totally, pushing her hands beneath his shirt, digging her fingers into the muscles of his back as he gripped her hips and lifted her. Wantonly she gave herself up to the fierce desire driving her, locking her legs around him. His tongue stoked deeper into her mouth and she cried out as he thrust up into the slick, heated centre of her.

The incredible tension tightened as he stretched her, filled her with deep plunging strokes, twisting, thrusting faster, building into an incredible climax that sent her mindless into a shuddering, shimmering wave of endless satisfaction. Then against her mouth Lorenzo groaned her name as he plunged one last time, his heart pounding out of control against hers, his great body shaking.

The silence afterwards was not restful but strained, Lucy slowly realised, shakily dropping her legs from his body, letting her hands fall from his shoulders. He stepped back and zipped up his trousers, and she smoothed her skirt down over her hips. She spied her ripped briefs on the floor. She glanced up at Lorenzo. He was watching her, and had seen the direction of her gaze. Then he spoke.

'Your briefs are finished, Lucy, and your luggage has already gone on to the house. You will have to go commando for a while—but that is probably nothing new for you,' he said with the arch of a brow, before adding, 'I could use a coffee—how about you?'

Lucy nodded her head. 'Yes,' she murmured, and he turned and disappeared through the door to the hall. His 'commando' comment told her everything she needed to know. He had no respect for her at all…never had and never would…

She spotted a few pins on the floor and, picking them up, clipped back her hair. She took her jacket off the back of the sofa and slipped it on, fastened it with a slightly unsteady hand. She was still wearing her high-heeled sandals, and wished viciously she had stabbed him in the back with them five minutes ago.

Still trembling inside, she walked across to the window and looked down at the street below, drawing in a few deep, calming breaths. A steady flow of cars drove along the road, and the pavements were full of people of all ages—some single, some couples and families—all chattering and laughing, going about their daily life as she'd used to do.

So what had happened to her? Lorenzo had happened, and she didn't know herself any more. Worse, she no longer liked herself. She had become one of those weak-willed women she normally pitied—a slave to her senses because of a man. In that moment Lucy knew she could not go on like this. She straightened her slender shoulders and folded her arms across her body, her mind made up. When this visit was over, so was her relationship with Lorenzo—whether he liked it or not. He could do his damnedest, but to save herself she could no longer afford to care.

In trying to be responsible and help other people she had given in to what amounted to blackmail. If she was brutally honest she had not fought very hard to avoid it, and in the process had lost all her self-respect.

She should have known from the start. She had tried before to be responsible for another, to help Damien, and it had ended in tragedy anyway. If Steadman's closed and the development never took place, so be it—at least the town had the seven acres of land she had donated. As for the family home, she would do as the estate agent had suggested weeks ago, when he'd told her that after twelve years of neglect the house badly needed updating and with the smaller garden the best option now was to put it up for auction and sell it for whatever she could get in the current market. She would, and then hopefully she could keep the gallery—probably still mortgaged, but at least she would own it.

'Coffee's ready.'

She turned around. Lorenzo was placing a tray on the glass table and trying to nudge papers out of the way. He sank down on the sofa and, picking up the coffee pot, filled two cups, then glanced across at her. 'Do you take milk and sugar?'

He didn't even know that much about her, she thought bitterly, and it simply reinforced her decision to end things.

'No, thanks. I need the bathroom—where is it?'

'There is one off my bedroom—I'll follow you through. Coffee in bed quite appeals,' he said, with a smile that was a blatant invitation.

'Not to me, it doesn't,' Lucy said coolly. 'Just tell me where the bathroom is. After all, I am here to visit your mother, and it is bad manners to keep her waiting.' She saw the flash of surprise in his eyes and watched them narrow, and felt a chill go through her.

Lorenzo was not accustomed to being denied, and his expression hardened as he looked at Lucy. She had pinned back her hair, replaced her jacket and fastened it, and was now standing stiffly, her arms folded in front of her, defiance in every line of her seductive body. He could make her do as he wanted—but suddenly he no longer had the stomach for it.

'In the hall—second on the left.' He gestured with his hand at the door he had just come through. Lucy was right. It was time they left.

He had shocked himself earlier, taking her without a second thought over the back of the sofa, totally out of control. This could not go on. The ice-cold anger and rage that had consumed him when he'd discovered Lucy had done a deal behind his back had cooled down, and he wasn't proud of the way he had behaved.

With the benefit of hindsight he should have agreed with Lucy the day she'd come to his office—agreed to support the status quo, leaving the running of Steadman's in the hands of the employee who had been dealing with it for the last five years. Instead he had let his anger over his brother's death be stirred up by his lunch with

Manuel and reacted badly. He had made his decision in anger instead of with his usual cool control. And getting involved with Lucy was another crazy mistake. In fact, he realised most of the summer had been one of crazy decisions on his part.

He was a normal, intelligent, healthy man, who enjoyed an active sex-life, but with Lucy he was in danger of allowing sex to take over his life to the detriment of his work and his leisure. He could not allow it to continue.

Since the day he had met her he had slept only one single night at his villa in Santa Margherita and only half a day sailing. And it was well over a month since he had been to New York. Instead he had spent most of his time in England, flying back and forth from Italy, and it had to stop. He still lusted after Lucy, but that was all it was—lust. Without conceit he knew that with his power and wealth he could take his pick of women, and occasionally had in the past. He would again.

His decision made, he rose to his feet and buttoned his shirt. The solution was simple: he just needed to get through the next three days, finish things with Lucy, then move on to a woman more his type who would not disturb the smooth running of his life.

His picked his jacket off the floor and slipped it on, then tightened his tie. When Lucy reappeared he moved towards her. 'Ready to go?'

Lucy glanced at him. 'Yes,' she said, equally direct.

Taking her elbow, he ushered her out of the apartment and down onto the street. 'Get in,' Lorenzo said, holding open the passenger door of a low-slung, lethal-looking yellow sports car.

Lucy did, and quickly fastened the seat belt. She didn't feel safe in this monster of a car, even when it was stationary. She glanced at Lorenzo as he slid into the driving seat and was about to ask what make the car was. But one look at the determined set of his jaw made her change her mind.

There was no other way to describe it—the man drove as if he had a death wish, Lucy thought. The countryside flashed past them in a whirl, and she caught her breath as the car swung around corners.

'Do you *have* to drive so fast?' she finally demanded.

He cast her a sidelong glance and said nothing, but she noticed he did slow down a little, and she could breathe easily again.

Her first glance of Lake Garda made her catch her breath again, and as Lorenzo drove along the one road that ran around the lake she was captivated by the small villages they passed. Eventually he guided the car between two stone towers that supported massive iron gates. The drive wound steeply up through a forest of trees and then veered right. Suddenly the forest ended, and Lucy simply stared in awe at the view before her.

The house was built in pale stone, beautifully proportioned, with circular turrets on all corners and with the forest as a backdrop. The gardens swooped down in lawns and terraces to the edge of the lake, where a wooden boat house was just visible by the trees. A small boat with its sails furled was tied up at the jetty. The overall view was idyllic, and incredible to her artistic eye. Someone had planned the garden skilfully. A pergola, a summerhouse and fountains were all strategically placed to draw the eye to a perfect flow of colour and symmetry.

'Lucy?'

It was the first word Lorenzo had spoken since they'd left Verona, and she glanced at her wristwatch. Well over an hour ago. She realised he had stopped the car. She looked out of the window, her eyes widening in admiration on the portico, a graceful structure with elegant arches and roof supported by four columns.

'Before we go in, a word of warning.'

She turned her head and looked at him. 'What? No stealing the silver?' she quipped.

He didn't so much as smile, just gave her a sardonic glance. 'That is an example of what I am afraid of. You are too impulsive, Lucy—you say everything that enters your head without a second thought.'

Not everything, Lucy thought. Even locked in his arms, in the throes of passion, she resisted the impulse to tell him she loved him.

'When you meet my mother you will be friendly and polite—no going over the top with hugs or confidences. I have the painting in the boot of the car. You will give it to her as a gift and she will be delighted. As for you and I—as far as my mother and the staff are concerned we will behave as close friends, though obviously we will not share a room. It is enough that I have brought you to the family home. Not something I ever do with the women in my life. That, along with an occasional arm around you, will confirm my mother's opinion—thanks to the Lanza woman—that we are a couple. When I tell her it is over between us you will have an excellent reason for no further contact that she will readily accept. Understand?'

'Perfectly. Machiavelli could not have come up with a better plan.'

The arrogance of the man confounded her. When he dumped her she was supposedly going to be so broken-hearted she would cut off all contact with the Zanelli family. The sad thing was she realised he was probably right—though he did not know it.

Forcing a smile to her face, she added, 'You mean pretend we are lovers but no mention of casual sex? I get it.'

'Lucy, cut out the flippant remarks. This is very straightforward. All you have to do is behave yourself in a restrained manner for a couple of days.'

'Yes, I see.'

And she *did* see—all too clearly. It was in his dark, impersonal eyes, in the hard face. He could not have made it clearer that when this visit was over so was she, as far as he was concerned. She turned her head away. It was what she wanted—to be free of him, she told herself, and tried to open the car door.

Before she could, it was swung open by a man Lorenzo introduced as Gianni—the butler!

Lucy stood in the grand hall, two storeys high, with a central staircase that split into two halfway up and ended in a circular balcony. Her green eyes fixed on the lady descending the marble stairs.

His mother was nothing like she'd expected, and when Lorenzo introduced her unexpectedly Lucy was hugged and kissed on both cheeks by the elegant woman. Lorenzo should have warned his mother not to go over the top, she thought. She'd been led to believe she was a frail little woman, but nothing could be further from the truth. Anna, as she insisted Lucy call her, was about five feet six, with thick curling white hair and sparkling brown eyes, and looked a heck of a lot fitter than Lucy felt.

Fifteen minutes later Lucy sat on a satin-covered chair in the most beautifully furnished room she had ever seen, with a glass of champagne in her hand, listening to Anna thanking her for what felt like the hundredth time for the portrait of Antonio.

She had always known Lorenzo was wealthy, but this house was more like a palace—and it seemed it was staffed like one. The butler had reappeared five minutes after they'd entered the room with the painting—gift-wrapped, Lucy had noted, probably down to Lorenzo.

She cast him a glance. He was lounging back on an exquisite antique gilt wooden-edged pink satin sofa, and he gave her the briefest of smiles that did not reach his eyes. If that was his idea of what would pass for 'close friendship' then heaven help him, she thought sadly.

The butler had appeared once more with the champagne, and a maid with a plate of tiny cakes.

To say his mother was ecstatic with her gift was an understatement. 'I can't thank you enough, Lucy.' Anna smiled across at her. The painting was now propped on top of the magnificent fireplace, half covering a picture of a stern-looking gentleman who looked remarkably like an older version of Lorenzo. 'You have captured my Antonio perfectly—but you knew him, and must have lots of photographs from the past. When did you paint it?'

'Well, it was in the March of my second year at college. Antonio and Damien had just come back from their round-the-world tour, and they were staying in the house I shared in London with two other students while they planned their mountaineering trip. I needed a model for a portrait as part of my end-of-year exam, and Antonio offered. Mind you, I had to bribe him to sit still with a constant supply of chocolate-covered Turkish delight, which he adored. Actually, it was good fun,' she said, smiling reminiscently. 'Though now I am older and more experienced I could probably do better.'

'Oh, no!' Anna declared. 'It is beautiful the way it is. It never occurred to me that Antonio had actually sat for you, but of course I can see it now. How else could you have caught him in that perfect moment in time, when he was at his best—healthy, happy and with friends? It is in his eyes, his smile, and it makes your gift doubly precious to me.'

'I'm glad you like it,' Lucy said inadequately, noting the shimmer of tears in Anna's eyes.

'I love it. And now a toast to my Antonio.' She raised her glass.

Lucy lifted hers to her mouth but only wet her lips. The little cake she had eaten had been sickly sweet, and what she could really do with was a cup of tea and something else to eat.

She looked at Lorenzo. He had drained his glass and was looking at his mother with such care and tenderness in his eyes it made her ache. He had never looked at *her* like that, and never would. She tore her gaze away and replaced her glass on the table, shifting restlessly in her chair.

'Champagne not to your taste, Lucy?' Lorenzo queried politely.

She glanced back at him. He was frowning at her—no tenderness in his eyes now, just black ice. She realised if she didn't get out of there soon she was going to scream—definitely not on Lorenzo's list of acceptable behaviour during the visit.

She was sitting there minus her briefs, needing to go to the bathroom, with a nice woman almost in tears and a man who hated her.

'Yes, it is fine,' she said, her green eyes filling with mockery. 'But if you will both excuse me?' She stood up. 'I have been travelling since eight this morning, and I would like to go and freshen up, please.'

'Of course, my dear. Where are my manners? I was so overcome…'

'Hush, Mother.' Lorenzo rose to his feet. 'I'll show Lucy to her room.' And, slipping an arm around her waist, he led her to the door. His mother smiled on benignly.

As soon as they were in the hall Lucy shrugged out of his hold. 'No audience now,' she sniped.

Lorenzo raised an eyebrow and said, 'Follow me.'

She did—up the elegant staircase to where Lorenzo turned right around the galleried landing to the front of the house, then along a corridor. He opened the second door on the left.

'My mother has the master suite next door, so you will be perfectly safe.'

Safe from what or who? Lucy wondered, and followed Lorenzo into the room. She gasped. The décor was all ivory and gold—the bed covered in the finest ivory satin and lace. Next to the fireplace was a *chaise-longue,* and a beautiful occasional table inlaid with hand-painted roses and humming birds. The whole effect was very feminine.

'The bathroom and dressing room are through there.' Lorenzo indicated a door at the opposite end. 'I believe the maid has unpacked your clothes. If there is anything else you need you have only to ring.'

She actually felt like wringing his neck. He was standing there so cool, so remote, when only hours ago he'd been ripping off her briefs. No—best not to go there…

'What I really need is a cup of tea and a sandwich.

Apart from that tiny cake I've had nothing to eat since I left home this morning, and I'm starving.'

'Surely you were offered lunch on the flight? It was all arranged.'

'I *was* offered lunch, but I refused because I got the impression the dashing young flight attendant was offering more.'

'What?' The polite mask had slipped to one of outrage. 'You should have told me—I will dismiss him immediately.'

'No—not on my account. His attitude is not surprising, really. He is probably used to flying loose women out to wherever you happen to be,' she said scathingly, and saw his jaw tighten, a flash of anger in his dark eyes.

Quickly stepping past him, she headed for the bathroom. She heard the bedroom door slam behind her and wasn't surprised.

CHAPTER EIGHT

THE bathroom, like the rest of the house, was perfect. All pale marble, with a big raised bath and a very modern double shower. The vanity unit contained every possible bathroom accessory known to a man—and, she noted, her own modest toilet bag.

Spying a shower cap, she could not resist. She pulled it over her hair and picked up a top designer shower gel. Stripping off her clothes, she stepped into the shower and turned the water on, relishing the soothing spray as she used the heavenly scented gel to wash her body.

Finally she stepped out of the shower and, picking a large white towel off the pile stacked on a shelf, dried herself. Taking another one, she wrapped it sarong-style around her body. Then she took her hairbrush from her toilet bag and brushed her hair.

Lucy walked back into the bedroom feeling refreshed, and saw a tray holding tea and sandwiches on the table by the *chaise-longue*. Lorenzo had done as she'd asked, but she had no doubt the maid had delivered them. She flopped down on the *chaise-longue* and poured a cup of tea, then ate an Italian-style sandwich made with crusty bread and filled with cheese, tomato and something spicy Lucy didn't recognise. It was delicious.

* * *

'Lucy? Lucy…'

Lorenzo didn't want to touch her—he was hard just looking at her. She was stretched out on the *chaise-longue* asleep, her hair tumbled over her shoulders and with one arm above her head, the other across her stomach. A towel that was wrapped around her had slipped to reveal one rose-tipped creamy breast. She was enough to tempt a saint. Yet in sleep, with her long lashes curled against her cheek, she had a look of innocence about her that twisted something inside him.

Slowly Lucy opened her eyes and yawned. She saw the tray with the tea and sandwiches, and realised she must have dozed off.

'Good—you are awake at last.'

At the sound of Lorenzo's voice she glanced up. He had changed into another suit, she noted—then she saw where his eyes rested and blushed scarlet. Quickly she sat up, pulling the towel over her chest.

He looked down at her, his dark eyes mocking. 'Nothing I have not seen before… But that is not what I came for. Dinner is at eight—you have half an hour to get ready. Before I go I should warn you my mother has arranged a party for Wednesday evening—she wants to introduce you to her friends. So you will not be able to leave until Thursday.'

'Well, you can just *un*arrange it,' Lucy said, knotting the towel firmly under her arm. She stood up, feeling vulnerable wearing just a towel when Lorenzo towered over her, his virile masculinity evident in every line of his long lean body, undisguised by the conventional dark suit he wore. With her temper and shamefully her pulse rising at the sight of him, she added, ' You will have to—because I told Elaine I would be back by

Wednesday night at the latest and she is taking Thursday morning off.'

'I knew nothing about the party until this evening. If I had I would have discouraged my mother. The whole point of this visit was to get you out of her life, not more involved.' Even as he said it Lorenzo realised it had been a crazy idea in the first place. What had he been thinking of? One glance at Lucy wearing a towel and he had his answer. She addled his brain without even trying, and the solution was to keep out of her way.

Lucy knew the purpose of this trip was to remove her from his mother's life, but it still stung to be reminded. Flashing him an angry glance, she saw the strong jaw clench as if to control some unwanted reaction, but a moment later she knew she had been mistaken.

'Anyway, it has nothing to do with me now,' he said with a negligent shrug of his broad shoulders. 'But do feel free to tell my mother to cancel.' A mocking smile curved his mouth. 'Rather you than me.'

Silently fuming, ten minutes later Lucy finally found her underwear, neatly packed away in drawers in the dressing room. She picked out a black dress from the few clothes she had brought with her, hanging forlornly in an enormous bank of empty wardrobes.

She had no time to fix up her hair, and had to be content with brushing it back behind her ears and fastening it with a silver slide at the nape of her neck. She used moisturiser on her face, and after a touch of mascara to her long lashes and an application of lipstick to her lips she slipped her feet into a pair of high-heeled sandals and was ready.

Finally she fastened a diamond-studded platinum watch on her wrist. It had been her mother's, and was her most treasured possession. She only wore it on special occasions. Though this wasn't a special occasion so much as a nightmare.

She had argued with Lorenzo that it was up to him to cancel the party, but he had shrugged her off. He had said it was up to her, as the party was basically for her benefit and if she insisted on going home on Wednesday, as planned, the party would not take place. He'd actually had the audacity to say that of course his mother would probably never speak to her again, which was a good result as far as he was concerned, and then walked out.

He knew damn fine, Lucy thought, walking down the grand staircase at a minute to eight, that it wasn't in her nature to be so appallingly bad-mannered. But then again maybe he *didn't* know—he thought she was little better than a street walker anyway.

She hesitated in the hall and adjusted the thin straps of the classic short black fitted dress she wore—another of Lorenzo's purchases. Her thinking was that she might as well wear them in his company, because once this charade was over they were going to a charity shop. She looked around. The walls were lined with what she guessed were family portraits, because the men all had a look of Lorenzo about them—though not quite as striking—and the women were all beautiful. Suddenly she didn't know what she was doing here, and was tempted to run back up the stairs.

But Gianni the butler appeared, and offered to escort her to the dining room. Smiling, she thanked him, her moment of panic over. Then her high heels slipped on the marble floor and she grabbed his arm, laughing with him as they entered the room, where Lorenzo and his mother were chatting quietly.

Both heads turned, and the butler quietly withdrew as Anna smiled and stepped forward. 'Lucy, I hope you are rested. I was so overcome by your gift I forgot you had been travelling all day and forgot my manners, I'm afraid,' she said disarmingly.

Lucy smiled. Anna was a delightful lady—a pity about her son, she thought, glancing at Lorenzo. He was lounging against the fireplace, a glass of what looked like whisky in his hand.

'Shall we sit down, ladies?' he suggested, straightening up and crossing to the long dining table perfectly set with silver and crystal. He pulled out a chair for his mother and Anna sat down. Then, crossing to the other side of the table, his dark eyes resting on her, he drawled softly, 'Lucy, *cara*. Be seated,' and gave her a smile, acting the perfect gentleman.

But Lucy knew otherwise, and realised immediately the endearment was for his mother's benefit. She returned his smile with a false one of her own and took the seat he offered.

After a rocky start, the dinner was not the ordeal Lucy had expected.

Anna insisted she try the red wine she'd had the butler open in her honour—an especially good one from a renowned Tuscan vineyard—and Lorenzo sat at the head of the table, with Lucy and his mother either side of him, which meant the two women could talk easily across the table.

The first thing Anna said, after the wine glasses were filled and the wine tasted, was, 'Lucy, dear, I know it was presumptuous of me to arrange a party for Wednesday evening, but I didn't realise your time was so limited and you were going home that day until Lorenzo told me earlier. He suggested it might be difficult for you to stay longer, as you have a business to run, but I do hope you can. All my friends are invited, and the Contessa della Scala is coming—she is really looking forward to seeing you again. Now, with the portrait, the party will be even better. You will make an old woman very happy, plus you and Lorenzo can spend more time together.' She beamed.

Emotional blackmail at its finest. Maybe it ran in the family? Lucy thought cynically. Lifting her chin, she looked at Lorenzo and caught the taunting gleam in his black eyes. She forced a slow smile to her lips. 'Your concern for my business is touching, Lorenzo, darling.' She baited him with an endearment of her own, and turned back to Anna as the first course was presented.

'Unfortunately my friend Elaine, who is taking care of the gallery, is expecting me back by Wednesday evening because she has a dental appointment on Thursday morning. But it is not an insurmountable problem. I can ring her tomorrow and tell her not to bother opening on Thursday. I can be back before Friday.'

'No, I would not think of putting you out that way,' Anna said immediately. 'Why should you lose business? Lorenzo can find someone to take care of your gallery for you, no trouble at all. In fact you could stay for the rest of the week. After visiting the dentist your friend would probably appreciate having the whole day off and more.'

Lucy had to bite her lip to stop herself laughing at the expression on Lorenzo's face as he looked at his mother in astonishment—horror quickly masked.

'You can do that, can't you, Lorenzo?' his mother queried.

Briefly he flicked Lucy a threatening glance, and

she knew he saw the amusement in her eyes before he looked back at Anna.

'Yes, of course I can, Mother—if Lucy agrees.' His gaze was on her again. 'I can probably arrange to get someone there by Wednesday afternoon, so Elaine can show them the ropes.' An eyebrow rose as he asked innocently, 'One day or two, Lucy?'

'One will be fine,' she said, knowing it was the answer he wanted. What was the point in defying him? She hadn't wanted to stay longer in the first place, so why prolong the agony? 'I must be home by Thursday night.'

'Good, then that is settled,' Anna said, and they finished their first course of risotto with red wine and porcini mushrooms.

The butler offered more wine and Lucy agreed, surprised to see she had finished the glass. But it was really nice, and very mellow.

Anna could certainly talk, Lucy thought as the plates were cleared by the maid. Mostly about Antonio—while Lorenzo sat looking on, his face a blank mask, adding very little to the conversation.

'According to the doctor Antonio was a miracle child. He was very ill when he was born, and it was touch and go for a while, but he made a complete recovery and was soon running all over the place like any other child. I did sometimes wonder if it was because I was a lot older when he was born that he had problems—it was ten years after I had Lorenzo. But he grew up to be a wonderful young man. I only wish I had kept him longer…'

It occurred to Lucy that if Anna had always been so loquacious about her youngest son it might go some way to explain why Lorenzo had grown into the hard, apparently emotionless man he was.

The conversation stopped as the main course was served—veal escalope Marsala—and Lucy tried to change the subject.

'You have a beautiful home, Anna. My bedroom is delightful, and the view from the window is lovely. I could not help noticing when I arrived that the gardens are magnificent, and so cleverly designed—whichever way one looks everything flows together perfectly. Someone at some time must have been a keen landscape gardener.'

'Gardening is my passion,' Anna said, obviously delighted by Lucy's interest. 'When Lorenzo started school my husband gave me permission to have the whole grounds redesigned. It was a huge project, and I spent three years deciding on and finding the flowers, the shrubs, the trees, the fountains—everything. Sometimes Lorenzo would come with me on my search for all the specimens I wanted. Mind you...' she looked lovingly at Lorenzo '...his taste ran to the most vibrant colours, which was odd given his serious nature.'

Lucy did not find it odd at all, having seen his apartment, but she could sense Lorenzo almost squirming in his chair, and cast him a sidelong glance. Not a muscle moved in his darkly attractive face, but when he noticed her looking he lifted a negligent brow and turned back to his mother.

'Lorenzo was a genius at mathematics at a very young age—my husband used to worry he might think he was too clever to settle for the role tradition demanded of him. But his skill was invaluable to me when it came to the design. He was only nine but he worked out all the angles, the lengths of the terraces and the paths where the fountains had to be placed for optimum effect, and made a complete plan for me. All the builder and gardeners had to do was the manual work.'

'That is amazing!' Lucy could not help exclaiming.

'Not really.' Lorenzo finally spoke. 'My mother is prone to exaggeration,' he said coolly, but tempered it with a smile.

The maid arrived and conversation ceased as the plates were cleared again. Dessert was brought in, and talk turned to the planned party.

Finally the butler suggested serving coffee, and Anna got to her feet and said, 'I never drink coffee at night, but you go ahead. I know you will be glad of some time on your own,' she prompted with a smile. 'I have had the most marvellous day I can remember in years, and I'm going to bed now.'

Lorenzo got to his feet to help her, but she refused and patted his cheek, so he bent to kiss hers and she left.

The silence was deafening.

'That went well,' Lorenzo finally said. 'My mother is happy and convinced we are close. Make sure you keep it that way until we leave on Thursday and everything you want is yours.'

Lucy looked up at him, her eyes tracing the hard bones of his face, the cool, steady eyes, the powerful jaw and mobile mouth. He had no idea what she really wanted, she thought sadly and, pushing back her chair, stood up.

'I will,' she said. 'Unlike you, I don't like deceiving your mother, and this can't be over quickly enough for me.' She turned towards the door, adding quietly, 'if you don't mind, I'll forgo the coffee.'

He moved quickly, his hand catching hers, and kissed

her palm. 'I don't mind anything you want, *cara*,' he husked, and her eyes widened in shock.

Her hand trembled in his grasp—and then she realised it was for the benefit of the butler, who had entered the room with the coffee tray. Pulling her hand free, she patted Lorenzo's cheek with more force than necessary and saw his lips tighten. 'You enjoy your coffee.'

Swiftly an arm closed around her waist, his dark head dipped, and he kissed her cheek, his warm breath caressing her ear. 'Not an option,' he murmured. 'Remember our deal? Everyone has to be convinced.' And, raising his head, he said, 'Take the coffee to the lounge, please, Gianni.'

Then his head bent again and his mouth closed possessively over hers, parting her lips. The prolonged assault on her senses swept away all her resistance. His hand moved sensually over her back to press her closer and she arched into him, her eyes closing in abandon.

Suddenly he lifted his head. 'Gianni has gone.'

Her eyes flew open as his comment registered. 'What did you do that for?'

'I saw the way Gianni looked at you, laughed with you when you entered the dining room with your body blatantly on display in that dress. He is a red-blooded man and he is not going to believe for a minute that holding your hand or a kiss on the cheek would satisfy me or any man. Now he will be convinced, and if he is the rest of the staff will be also.'

For a moment Lucy had the odd idea he was jealous of the butler. 'Does your brain ever stop working and planning your next move?'

'I've never really thought about it, but probably not—except perhaps in a moment of intense sexual relief,' he drawled, and ushered her out of the dining room and into the lounge, where the coffee was set on a low table in front of a sofa.

Lucy twisted out of his arm and sat down on the sofa, the colour in her face matching the pink satin, and leant forward to pour out a cup of coffee she did not want simply to hide her blush.

Lorenzo laughed and sat down beside her. 'You know, Lucy, for an experienced woman it never ceases to amaze me how easily you blush—how do you do it?'

She was tempted to tell him then how little experience she really had, but bit her lip and drank the coffee. He would never believe her. He had formed his opinion of her, coloured by his distorted perception of her brother and the ease with which she had fallen into bed with him the first time. By accepting his deal she had reinforced that low opinion, and nothing she could do would ever make him change his mind.

'Practice—just practice,' she said, telling Lorenzo what he wanted to hear.

'Did you practise with Antonio?' he asked. 'You have painted him with a happy smile on his face—did you sleep with him?'

Lucy's eyes widened to their fullest extent on his unsmiling countenance. He couldn't be serious, she thought. But he was, she realised—and suddenly she was furious.

Before she said something she knew she would regret, she got to her feet. 'No,' she said coldly. 'Unlike you, he was a gentleman. Now, if you are satisfied I have played my part as required, I am going to bed. And before you get up—don't bother. There is no one here to see you *playing* the gentleman.'

And she turned away and walked to the door,

leaving him to follow her or not…amazed by his cruel insensitivity…

She looked around the bedroom; someone had laid her nightdress on the bed and turned down the covers. Service at its best, she thought with a wry smile twisting her lips as she entered the bathroom, stripped off her clothes and put them away. She washed her face, cleaned her teeth and, naked, returned to the bedroom. Picking the nightdress off the bed, she slipped it over her head and crawled into the big bed.

She didn't expect to sleep, but surprisingly she did… She stirred once, at the tail-end of a dream of a shadowy figure of a man standing over her, but went straight back to sleep.

The next morning she awoke to the overpowering smell of strong coffee, and, easing herself up the bed, saw the maid approach with a tray which she placed on the bedside table.

'*Buongiorno, signorina.* The *Signora* say to bring coffee,' she said in fractured English, 'Breakfast in one hour.'

'Grazie!' Lucy said. *'Scusi—'* She sprang out of bed and dashed to the bathroom. When she returned, after having been sick, the maid was still there.

'Signorina? Come stai?'

Lucy saw the worried frown on her face and knew enough Italian to reassure her she was fine. The maid left.

It was probably the wine she'd drunk last night, Lucy thought. She was not accustomed to fine red wine—or any wine, for that matter. She poured out a cup of hot milk, with the merest dash of coffee, and standing looking out of the window sipped it slowly.

The view really was breathtaking… And then she

saw the yellow sports car shoot off down the drive. Good—Lorenzo had gone out. With no fear of him appearing, she relaxed a little.

She took a leisurely shower and wondered what to wear. It was a sunny day, and she wanted to have a look around the gardens. With that in mind she decided on a pair of soft denim jeans and bright flowing top. She tied her hair back in a ponytail and finally ventured out of the bedroom.

She did not need to look for the breakfast room. As soon as she reached the foot of the grand staircase Gianni appeared as if by magic and showed her to yet another room—not as large as the others she had seen, but just as elegant, and somehow more homely. Anna was already seated at the table, and looked up as she entered.

'How are you, Lucy? Maria told me you were a little unwell.' She frowned. 'Please sit down, my dear. My doctor calls to see me most days at noon—if you like you could see him as well.'

Lucy smiled and took a seat. 'No, that is not necessary. I am fine—just too much wine, I think,' she said with a rueful smile. 'But I wouldn't mind a walk in the gardens after breakfast. The fresh air will do me good.'

'Well, if you are sure, I will give you a guided tour,' Anna offered. 'Really it should be Lorenzo, but he has gone to the bank. I told him to take the day off, but he takes no notice of me. He works far too hard—always has. When my husband died—good man though he was—the bank was left in a poor condition. Lorenzo took over and soon put everything right, expanding all over the world, but sometimes I do wish he would slow down a little. Which is why I am so pleased he has found *you,* Lucy—you are just what he needs.'

'Oh, I wouldn't say that.' Lucy finally got a word in. 'We are close friends, but realistically we have very little in common.' And with a quick change of subject she added, 'Before I forget, I must call Elaine and tell her of the change of plan.'

Elaine was surprised but happy to agree to the new arrangement of taking Thursday off while the shop was looked after by a temp.

Lucy, on the other hand, was stressed to bits.

Oddly enough, once outside, with the scent of pine trees and perfumed flowers mingling in the warm morning air, Lucy felt better. Meandering with Anna along the paths and terraces of the glorious garden was relaxing. She learnt from Anna the names of dozens of plants, and when they got to the lake learnt the sailing boat had been Lorenzo's when he was a teenager, and he still used it occasionally.

According to Anna he was still a keen sailor, and spent most of his leisure time at Santa Margherita, where he had a villa. He kept a larger racing yacht at the marina, and sailed it very successfully in quite a few races round the Mediterranean.

Lucy was surprised. When Lorenzo had told her he had a yacht she had assumed he meant some big luxury motorised ship. A smile quirked her lips. She did think he looked like a pirate sometimes, so she should not be surprised, she told herself as they walked back to the house.

Lunch was served, and Anna's doctor, who was a widower, joined them at the table. He was a distinguished-looking, charming man, and Lucy warmed to him immediately. She had a sneaky suspicion his interest in Anna was more than medical…

Then the butler appeared, and Lucy was surprised when he informed her Lorenzo was on the private line and wishing to speak to her. He escorted her to the rear of the house, into what was obviously a study, and handed her the telephone.

'Hello?' she said. She could hear voices in the background, one a woman's—probably his secretary.

'Ah, at last.' Lorenzo's deep dark voice echoed in her ear. 'Are you getting along all right on your own, Lucy? No slip-ups?'

'Yes. And if by that you mean have I told your mother that her brilliant saintly son is really a rat? No, I have not.'

'Sarcasm does not become you. Do I detect a bit of frustration there? Missing me already?' he drawled throatily.

'Like a hole in the head,' she snapped, and heard him chuckle.

'No chance I would be given an opportunity to miss your smart mouth—you really know how to dent a man's ego.'

'Not yours, that's for sure.' Her pounding heart was telling her she was more disturbed by his flirtatious tone than she dared admit, but knowing it must be for his secretary's benefit she said, 'Cut the pretence and just tell me what you want. I am in the middle of lunch.'

'Right.' His voice was brusque. 'I have arranged with an English agency for a Miss Carr who lives in Cornwall to help at the gallery. She will call in tomorrow afternoon at three to arrange the details with Elaine. Tell my mother I have back-to-back meetings all day and

I'm staying in Verona tonight. I will be back tomorrow evening for the party. Can you do that?'

'Yes. If that is all, I am going back to finish my lunch.'

Lorenzo was deliberately staying away—or he might even have another woman lined up for tonight, Lucy thought. As if she needed any more proof it was over between them!

'Enjoy your meal,' he said, and hung up.

Lucy relayed the conversation when she got back to the table. Anna did not look happy, but accepted the news with grace.

CHAPTER NINE

FOR some reason Lucy hadn't been able to enjoy her lunch—in fact she'd hardly eaten anything. The doctor, noticing, had mentioned that Anna had told him Lucy had been sick that morning and enquired if she still felt unwell.

Unthinkingly Lucy had told him she thought it was the red wine, because she didn't usually drink, and then added that she was not used to eating such rich food so late.

The doctor had agreed that might be true, but then mentioned the possibilities of gastro enteritis or food poisoning. Anna had looked mortified, and that was why Lucy was now lying on her bed, having submitted to numerous tests.

Lucy liked the elderly man, and at his enquiries had told the doctor about her medical history—including an operation she had undergone a few years earlier, which was one of the reasons she was careful what she ate and rarely drank, and probably why wine affected her so quickly. He had nodded his head and agreed with her.

Her lips twitched and parted in a grin, and she chuckled—then laughed out loud. She was the guest from hell…who had unwittingly implied her hostess had poisoned her. At least Lorenzo would be happy, because when Lucy left there was not the slightest fear of Anna wanting her to visit again.

On the contrary, Anna appeared to be quite happy when Lucy went back downstairs. Dinner was arranged for seven in Anna's favourite garden room at the side of the house, where a small table was set for the two of them. The meal was light and delicious, and Anna confessed she usually ate there, only using the formal dining room when Lorenzo was home—which Lucy gathered was not very often.

Wednesday was chaotic. The huge house was a hive of activity as caterers, florists and extra staff bustled around the place.

The doctor came early—he was staying the night—and after lunch, when Anna had retired to her room to rest, told Lucy her blood tests were clear. It was probably, as she'd thought, the wine—or maybe the stress of visiting Lorenzo's home and mother. He remembered when he'd met his late wife's parents for the first time he'd been sick with nerves before he even got to their house.

Lucy tried to laugh, thanked him, and followed Anna upstairs.

She had a leisurely soak in the huge bath before washing her hair, and then, not feeling in the least tired, decided to go out into the garden and let her hair dry naturally in the fresh air, as she did at home. She pulled on jeans and a light blue sweater and, slipping her feet into soft ballet shoes, she stuck a comb in her pocket and left the house. There were so many people running around she would not be missed.

It was another sunny afternoon, with a slight breeze

rustling the trees, and she wandered down the garden until the noise from the house faded away. Finally she stopped on one of the terraces. A circular fountain stood there, with water cascading down from a fifteen-feet-high centrepiece into a big pool, where koi carp in various shades of gold and yellow were swimming lazily around.

She sat down on a seat conveniently placed, and taking the comb from her pocket pulled it through her hair. It was half dry already. With a sigh she closed her eyes and turned her face up to the sun. Bliss, she told herself. Just one more day and then no more Lorenzo. She would have her life back. But the pain in her heart told her she lied.

'Lucy—I have been looking all over for you.'

For a second she thought she had conjured his voice up in her mind, then her eyes flew open. Lorenzo was standing a foot away, his dark gaze fixed on her face.

'What are you doing out here?'

'Nothing,' she muttered. He was wearing a suit, but his jacket and tie were loose, his black hair dishevelled, and he was looking grimly at her, as if she had committed a cardinal sin. Even so she felt herself tense in instinctive awareness of the magnetic attraction of his big body. 'I didn't realise I had to ask permission,' she said sarcastically, to hide her involuntary reaction to him.

'You don't. But I rang before lunch and spoke to my mother. She told me you were sick and you saw her doctor—are you all right?'

'You are a day late. That was yesterday, and I am fine.'

His apparent concern was too little, too late, and she wasn't fooled by it for a second. It was over. He had made that plain on Monday and they both recognised it—which was why she had not seen him since.

'I guess she told you I think it was the wine and the food. Sorry about that. But, hey—look on the bright side, Lorenzo. She must think I am the guest from hell, accusing her of poisoning me. She will *never* invite me back.'

He didn't so much as crack a smile. If anything, he looked even grimmer.

'No, she hinted you might be pregnant. Very clever, Lucy, but no way will you catch me in *that* trap.' His lips twisted in a sneer. 'If you are pregnant try your last partner—because it has nothing to do with me. I was meticulous with contraception, as you well know, *cara*.'

Only Lorenzo could make an endearment sound like an insult, Lucy thought sourly. If she had ever had the slightest glimmer of hope that he might care for her it was snuffed out in that moment.

Flushed and angry now, she rose to her feet. Tilting back her head, she let her green eyes mock him. 'I'm not pregnant, but thank you for that. It confirmed my sketch of you was spot-on.'

She turned to leave, but he caught her wrist.

His dark eyes flicked over her, from the striking mass of her hair to her pink lips and the curve of her breasts, making her wince at the mixture of contempt and desire she saw in his eyes as they finally met hers.

'This changes nothing. You will behave yourself tonight, stay silent on your brother and the accident, and I will put you on the plane myself tomorrow—is that understood?'

'Yes. Message well and truly received,' she said bitterly, and all the anger and resentment she had bottled up for so long came pouring out. 'For your information, I loved my brother, and I believe he did his best on that mountain—unlike you, who would believe the worst of anyone without a second thought. Antonio said you were a ruthless bastard admiringly, almost with pride, but I bet he never realised you actually are. You hate my brother because of the accident. But Damien did what the experts and the coroner all agreed was the correct thing to do in the circumstances. He cut the rope to go and get help for Antonio and he succeeded. The fact that rescue was too late was nobody's fault—just fate…'

She paused for a moment, remembering. 'But that was not good enough for *you*. With your arrogance and superior intellect you decided they were all wrong. And you couldn't resist taking a bit of revenge out on me, because I'm Damien's sister.' She shook her head in disgust, her hair flying wildly around her shoulders. 'The irony of it is, if I was the one hanging over a cliff tied to you I'd bet my last cent you would cut the rope without hesitation. You make me *sick*,' she said contemptuously.

Lorenzo reached out and, catching her shoulders, jerked her forward, crushing her against him. Ruthlessly his mouth ground down on hers, and he kissed her with an angry passion that had nothing to do with love—only dominance. She struggled to push him away, but her hands were trapped between their bodies. And to her self-disgust even now she could sense herself weakening, responding. In a desperate effort of self-preservation she kicked out with her foot and caught his shinbone, and suddenly she was free.

If she had hurt him Lucy was glad. He deserved a hell of a lot more than a kick in the shin for what he had done to her.

'You are coming with me,' he said and, catching her

wrist, pulled her forward. 'As for cutting the rope—I would never tie myself to *you* in the first place,' he said scathingly, his eyes deadly. 'Cutting the rope is not why I despise your brother. It is because I have proof that he could have saved Antonio and chose not to.'

Lucy drew in a sharp breath. 'That is a horrible thing to say and I don't believe you,' she lashed back at him. 'Maybe it is your own guilty conscience looking for a scapegoat. According to Antonio you spent most of your time in America with a string of different women and he rarely saw you.'

'That's it,' he snarled. 'I will show you the evidence and that will be the end.' And he almost frogmarched her back to the house.

Oblivious to the surprised looks from the dozens of people in the hall, he marched her to the rear of the house, pushed open a door, and led her into the study.

'Sit,' he instructed, and shoved her onto a well-worn black leather sofa. He walked over to a large desk and, opening a drawer, withdrew something, then walked back to stand towering over her.

'You need proof of what an apology for a man your brother was?' He flung a handful of photographs down on the low table in front of her. 'These are pictures taken on the day of the so-called accident that killed Antonio. Look at them.'

He leant over and spread them out in front of her. The first he pointed to was of Antonio and Damien, their faces almost as red as the jackets they wore, laughing. Moisture glazed Lucy's eyes as she stared at the picture. They both looked so young, so vibrant, so full of life—and now they were both dead.

'That is the pair of them arriving at the base camp to

prepare for the climb the next morning. Note the date and time on all of them.'

Lucy didn't see the point. The date of the accident was imprinted on her mind for all time. But she did as he said. Three more were general shots the same day, and within the same hour. Only the fifth—a landscape shot—was of the following day, at two in the afternoon.

'So they look happy?' She brushed a tear from her eye. 'What am I supposed to see?'

'See the small figure in red on the landscape shot that is your brother. These photographs were given to me by a friend, Manuel, who is an expert climber. Damien and Antonio were not at his level, but were experienced climbers. They joined the climbing club together at university, climbed regularly in Britain, in the Alps, and on other continents when they toured the world.' He looked down at her, his black eyes blazing with anger. 'According to Manuel, from the position of your brother on the mountain at that time any reasonably experienced climber could have made it to the base camp in three hours—four at the very most. But it was dark when your brother called the rescue service—*seven hours* after that photograph was taken—too dark to start the search. A complete novice could have got down faster. He let Antonio die.'

Lucy looked up at him. For a second she thought she saw a glimmer of anguish in his eyes, and then it was gone, and he was watching her, waiting, supremely confident in his belief, his dark gaze challenging her to deny the evidence he was presenting her with.

Should she bother? Lucy asked herself. She knew Lorenzo. When he made up his mind about something nothing changed it. He was always right. He had decided she was a promiscuous woman the first time she went to bed with him for no other reason than that she had… He looked at a few photographs and decided they were proof her brother was a murderer, though he had not used that term…

'You really believe that?' Lucy said quietly.

'Yes—the proof is in front of you. Antonio is dead. I lost a brother, and Damien cost my mother her son and devastated her life.'

Lucy's eyes widened. She'd been devastated at Antonio's death, maybe, but Anna still had Lorenzo—her life was hardly over. And she was fed up with being the bad guy—or girl, in her case.

'It didn't do a lot for my life, either, or I would not be sitting here listening to this,' she said sarcastically. 'I have finally realised everything is black and white with you, Lorenzo. Good or bad—no in between. You are always right. Does it ever occur to you not everyone is as strong as you are? Perhaps after hanging onto Antonio for over an hour Damien was weak? Perhaps he passed out and didn't remember? Or maybe the clock was wrong?' she ended facetiously.

'No, there can be no other explanation, Lucy. The evidence is all there in the coroner's report. Your brother said he thought it had taken him four hours to reach the camp, not seven. The coroner's report states Antonio had died not of his injuries but of hypothermia, after spending the night on the mountain, only one or two hours before he was found. He could have lived if it wasn't for your damned brother. So now you have seen the proof, and now you know why Steadman is a dirty word to me.'

Lucy thought of arguing and looked at him. His face was set hard and she shivered. What was the point?

Lorenzo was a strong man—not the type to accept weakness in others.

'Have you nothing to say?' he asked, his dark gaze resting on her.

'Thank you for showing me the photos.' She stood up. 'Can I go now?'

Lorenzo watched her. Damn it, she looked like a schoolgirl in her flat shoes—but he knew she wasn't. Her head was slightly bowed, her beautiful face pale, her expressive eyes guarded. Her hair was falling in a tangle of waves around her shoulders, and she was wearing denim jeans and a soft blue sweater that clung to her every curve. He felt his body stir, and he hated himself and her for his weakness. With a supreme effort of will he forced himself to relax. It was almost over. After tonight he would be free of Lucy and would never have to see her again. So why was he not relieved?

His mouth hardened along with his resolve. 'Yes, go,' he snapped. 'I'll see you in the hall at seven—and wear something appropriate. The black you wore the other night will do.' And, picking up the photos, he strolled over to the desk and returned them to the drawer.

What did he think she would do? Lucy wondered. Turn up in a pair of shorts and a shirt? For a second she was tempted, but quickly dismissed the idea and walked out of the study. She owed it to herself not to disgrace the Steadman name.

Contrary to what Lorenzo seemed to think, she had been well brought up. She had attended a prestigious boarding school and art college. Her family had been reasonably wealthy by any standards, and their home—while not as spectacular as this—lovely. Not overflowing with staff, but there had been a housekeeper who'd arrived at eight every morning and left at four.

Her husband had been the gardener, and the acres of grounds had been well tended. When her parents had entertained extra staff had been hired. Her mother had been a beautiful, loving and elegant lady, whom everyone had adored—especially Lucy. But everything had changed after her mother died.

No, she wasn't going to dwell in the past—she had done too much of that already. And, flicking her wayward hair back, she ran up the stairs to her room.

Lucy stopped at the top of the stairs and drew in a long, steadying breath. The huge hall looked more like a ballroom, with exquisite floral arrangements and a small raised platform at one side, where a quartet were arranging their music. Already quite a few guests had arrived, the men all wearing tuxedos and the woman glamorous in designer gowns, some short, some long, and all probably costing a fortune.

Suddenly Lucy was really glad that she had at the last minute packed the dress the Contessa had given her. It was perfectly appropriate for this sophisticated party. And no way was she wearing the black dress Lorenzo had suggested. After this afternoon, she was never doing anything he said again.

The dress was by an Italian designer, and a classic mini from the nineteen-sixties. Not too short, ending two inches above her knees, it had a curved neckline that revealed the upper swell of her breasts and skimmed perfectly over her hips and thighs. But it was the fabric that made it sensational—a fine silk jersey almost completely covered in white sequins from neck to hem, except for the dazzling psychedelic pattern of silver sequins down the front. On her feet she wore high-heeled sequined shoes.

Lucy made it down the stairs without stumbling, and heaved a sigh of relief when she got to the bottom safely and glanced around. Lorenzo was walking towards her, his dark eyes blazing. Whether he was angry or something else, she didn't know. She had seen him conservatively and casually dressed, but wearing a black tuxedo, a white dress shirt and bow-tie he looked more stunningly attractive than any man had a right to, she thought helplessly, unable to take her eyes off him.

'You are late,' Lorenzo said.

He had watched Lucy walk down the stairs, a shimmering vision in white and silver, and she took his breath away. Her hair was swept up into a swirl on top of her head, with a few long tendrils left to fall down the back of her neck and either side of her face. She was wearing make-up, understated but perfect, and her big green eyes fringed with thick curling lashes looked even larger somehow. Her lips were a glossy deep pink that made him want to taste them—taste her. *No, not any more,* he reminded himself.

'Sorry,' Lucy murmured, and raised her eyes to his. She saw the desire, the hunger he could not disguise, and knew hers were conveying the same emotion. She caught the hint of regret before the shutters came down and Lorenzo spoke.

'Very eye-catching dress, but what happened to the black I suggested?' he demanded, and offered her his arm.

Consigned to the bin, along with all her foolish hopes, Lucy thought bitterly, and took his arm, thankful that tonight was the last act of this ridiculous drama.

They joined his mother, Anna hugged and kissed her, and Lucy lost count of the number of people she was introduced to. Teresa Lanza almost squeezed the air out of her and most of the other guests seemed very pleasant.

Then suddenly there was a hush, and Lucy watched as a stunning, tall and dark-haired woman in red on the arm of a much younger man made an entrance, pausing and looking haughtily around for a second or two.

Lucy felt Lorenzo tense beside her, and caught the slight frown on Anna's face as the couple walked over.

Anna introduced the pair of them to Lucy. 'Signora Olivia Paglia and her son Paolo.'

With the briefest of acknowledgments in her direction, Olivia wrapped her arms around Lorenzo's neck and kissed him on both cheeks. It would have been his mouth if he had not moved his head, Lucy thought, her gaze flickering between the two of them as the woman began speaking.

She gathered from her limited understanding of Italian that Olivia was reminding him of his friend, and how much her poor disabled Fedrico would have loved to be here. It was not possible any more, and it was hard for her on her own, but how grateful she was for Lorenzo's support.

Was Lorenzo really that clueless about what Olivia was doing? Lucy wondered. The only person Olivia was interested in was Lorenzo. It was blindingly obvious. She was playing on his sympathy for his friend with the hope of moving on to him. Or maybe she already had, if the rumoured affair the Contessa had told her of was to be believed. Well, they looked about the same age, and they obviously knew each other very well—they certainly had plenty to say to each other.

As if she wasn't hurting enough already, another thought struck her. Maybe the reason for Lorenzo insisting she meet his mother and play the lover had nothing to do with his fear of Anna contacting her but was a deliberate ploy to use Lucy as a smokescreen to deflect talk of his affair with his friend's wife. She wouldn't put anything past him, and it would explain why except for one lapse he wanted nothing to do with Lucy now she was in Italy.

She glanced at Anna, who was greeting someone else, and then back at Lorenzo and Olivia, who were still talking. She moved to one side, totally disgusted. Then she caught sight of the latest arrival, and a genuine smile slowly curved her lips as she walked forward to meet her.

'Contessa,' she said, and was greeted with a delighted laugh.

'Lucy!' The Contessa put her arms around her and kissed her on both cheeks, then stepped back. 'Let me look at you.'

Grinning, Lucy gave a twirl. 'What do you think? Does it suit me?'

'Perfectly—as I knew it would. You look lovely and it brings back so many happy memories for me. I was nineteen, and wore it the night I first met my husband. Now,' she said, taking Lucy's arm, 'come and show me this painting I've heard about.'

Lucy was happy and relieved to go along with the Contessa. 'It is on an easel in the lounge, I believe.' Arm in arm, they started to walk.

'Good—and later you can tell me what on earth you are doing with Lorenzo Zanelli. He is far too serious for you—though to be fair there is no doubting he is a very attractive man, and definitely all male. But be warned—he is the type of man a woman can enjoy making love with, but to talk with, to really know—never. He has too much pride and passion in his work. Everything else is on the periphery of his life, especially his women—and there must have been a few.'

'I guess so,' Lucy said. 'But I am not doing anything with him. I am going home tomorrow,' she stated as they approached the double doors. And if the Contessa noticed the hint of bitterness in her tone she did not remark on it.

Before they could walk through into the lounge, Lorenzo appeared.

'Contessa…' He spoke to her in Italian.

But she answered in English, with a mischievous glance at Lucy. 'No need to apologise, Lorenzo, for not greeting me on arrival. I could see you were occupied with Signora Paglia, and Lucy more than made up for your lapse.' As a put-down it was brilliant and she smiled at Lucy, her sparkling eyes brimming with merriment. 'Lucy is going to show me her latest work of art—shall we, dear?'

Lorenzo stood frozen to the spot and watched as the two petite women—one old, one young—both beauties, walked into the lounge, the sound of their laughter floating back to him. He had never been so elegantly dismissed in his life.

He was about to follow them when Olivia caught his arm again.

'Lorenzo, you never told me your little friend was an artist and had painted a portrait of your brother—how sweet. And she looks very sweet in that vintage dress. But secondhand clothes have never appealed to me—I prefer new.'

He looked at the tall brunette hanging on his arm. 'What do you mean?'

'Didn't you know? The Contessa gave Lucy the dress

she is wearing. Teresa Lanza overheard them talking, and apparently the Contessa wore it the first time she met her husband. Heaven knows how many years ago *that* was, but at least it saved you having to buy one for your mother's little *protégée.* She probably had nothing suitable for an occasion like this.'

Olivia really was a bitch, Lorenzo finally realised, and from now on Fedrico was going to have to look after his own business affairs. Disabled or not, there was nothing wrong with the man's brain.

Shrugging off her arm, he said, 'Excuse me,' and strode into the lounge.

He spotted Lucy with the Contessa, sitting on a sofa with a group of people standing around them. Lucy was laughing at something young Paolo Paglia had said. Lorenzo took a glass of champagne from a passing waiter and walked over to the group.

'Champagne, Lucy?'

Lucy heard Lorenzo's voice, though she had not seen him approach, and her smile dimmed as she looked up at him and took the glass he offered. If his interest in her had been genuine, and he'd seen her as more than just a body in his bed, he might have noticed she never drank the stuff.

She listened as he effortlessly joined the conversation. But his very presence so close was affecting her hard-won poise—and it was getting worse.

For a man who could hardly wait to get rid of her, and was prepared to pay to do so, he had an odd way of showing it, Lucy thought two hours later. Lorenzo had insisted on sticking with the Contessa and Lucy. He had totally charmed the Contessa, and kept touching Lucy—her arm, her waist. She knew it was just for show, but by the time he escorted them to the buffet laid out in the dining room she was beginning to wonder…

The Contessa left after the buffet, and the band began to play.

Lorenzo led Lucy on to the dance floor and took her in his arms. For a moment it was like the first time they'd danced together—a perfect fit. Held close against his long body, Lucy stopped wondering, and her soft heart began to hope…

Then Lorenzo burst her bubble by speaking.

'Did you hope to insult me by wearing the gown the Contessa gave you?'

It was like a douche of ice water over her head.

'Did I succeed?' Lucy asked, stiffening in his arms.

His dark eyes clashed with hers, something moving in the inky depths. 'Not really—it looks beautiful. But if you wanted a new dress you had only to ask. I would have bought you as many as you like.'

'I think you have paid quite enough already to get me here,' she said. 'As have I. And isn't it time you mingled with your other guests?'

'You are right,' he agreed. 'Maybe I *have* been a little neglectful.' And he led her off the dance floor and through into the lounge, where Anna sat with a few friends.

'Watch what you say,' Lorenzo murmured as he led her over and she sat down beside Anna on the sofa.

The doctor made way for her with a smile and, perching on the cushioned arm. Lorenzo said a few words to the small group which made them smile.

Lucy managed not to flinch as he finally glanced down at her and she recognised the familiar ruthlessness in the tight line of his mouth.

'I'll see you later, *cara*.'

The indifference in his eyes chilled her to the bone. She watched as he walked back into the hall and saw he was quickly surrounded by a crowd of sophisticated friends, all laughing and talking—including Olivia Paglia, competing with the rest for Lorenzo's attention. She looked as if she was winning.

Lucy turned her head away and, pinning a smile on her face, listened as Anna introduced her to Luigi, a small dark man, obviously Italian, but whose English was faultless—as was almost everyone's here, she thought. But then at this level of society that was probably to be expected.

'My congratulations, Lucy. Your portrait of Antonio is amazing—especially for someone so young,' said Luigi.

'Thank you.' She smiled, and when he said he was an art historian the conversation flowed.

For the remainder of the evening Lucy stayed where she was, only moving after Luigi rose to take his leave, kissing both Lucy and Anna goodnight. Then Anna excused herself, as it was nearly midnight and time for her to retire. The rest of the group stood up.

Anna kissed Lucy on the cheek. 'It was good of you, my dear, to spend so much time with us oldies. Now, come—I will find that formidable son of mine and tell him he has played host long enough. I will say goodnight, then you two can enjoy yourselves.'

Lucy didn't think so, but she had no choice but to follow Anna into the grand hall. Lorenzo's dark head bent towards his mother as they said goodnight and then Anna moved towards the stairs.

Lucy was left standing like a lemon, wishing she was

anywhere else but here. She could feel Lorenzo looking down at her, and reluctantly glanced up.

'Are you enjoying the party, Lucy?' he asked, but his eyes were still dark pools, no glimmer of interest in their depths. 'You seem to have been a big hit with everyone—especially Luigi…a good man to know in your line of work.'

Then just behind her she heard a young man's voice.

'At last the lovely Lucy has joined the dance.'

She felt an arm slip around her waist, and quickly pulled away. Another arm wrapped around her—this time Lorenzo's—and she heard the laughter of the people around, and a mocking, 'Well held, Lorenzo.'

'Careful, *cara*.' He smiled. 'Paolo is only a boy.'

But there was no amusement in the dark eyes staring coldly down into hers.

'I can see that,' said Lucy, her cheeks burning and her green eyes sparkling up at him 'Excuse me a moment.'

She spun out of Lorenzo's grasp and swiftly moved through the crowd, making her way upstairs without a backward glance. She had been ignored, laughed at and mocked, and she had finally had enough of the injustice of it all.

Kicking off her shoes, she picked them up and made her way to the bathroom. She stripped off her clothes and washed her face and unpinned her hair. Then, wrapping a towel around her body, she crossed to the dressing room and found her suitcase. She began to pack.

Carefully she wrapped the dress she had worn for the party in tissue. It was a beautiful gift from a lovely lady, though Lucy doubted she would ever wear it again. She left out jeans and a sweater to wear when she left.

She wanted nothing and no one to delay her departure, and if she didn't meet the usual designer-clad elegant standard of the ladies Lorenzo usually transported in his private jet, she didn't give a damn!

She walked back into the bedroom and, switching on the bedside light clicked off the main one. Dropping the towel, she climbed wearily onto the big bed. She pulled the satin and lace cover over her and laid her head down on the plump pillows. It was comfortable, and she heaved a deep, heartfelt sigh. This time tomorrow she would be at home in her own bed, all her problems solved, financially solvent, and free…

She should be ecstatic, so why did she feel so hurt, so defeated? She knew the answer. After Lorenzo's outburst this afternoon she had recognised at last the implacability of his contempt for her. Was it possible to desire someone and hate them at the same time? Yes, she thought bitterly. Lorenzo could.

From the very beginning when she had felt they'd made love Lorenzo had felt…nothing… She moved her hand slowly over her naked body, remembering. Not strictly true… She thought of the dark desire, the passion in his black eyes, the need he could not hide when buried deep inside her.

Then she remembered his comment on Monday night. The only time his brain stopped working and planning was in a moment of intense sexual relief… The only time he stopped despising her… And then she knew she didn't care what proof he thought he had. She had suffered enough pain to last a lifetime because of him.

Her eyes filled with moisture; in a house full of people she had never felt so alone in her life.

Turning, she buried her face in the pillow and gave way to grief for all those she had loved and lost, letting the tears fall. For her mother, her father, her brother—but most of all for the love she had never had and never would have from Lorenzo.

CHAPTER TEN

LORENZO had watched Lucy ascend the stairs. He had been watching her all evening. It was crazy, he knew, and he had to stop. Even if she had not been the sister of a man he despised she was still not for him. She was too young. Paolo was nearer her age, but he'd had some nerve, trying to put his arm around her. For a second he had wanted to knock the cheeky young devil down.

He glanced around the room. The crowd was thinning fast—time to do his duty as host and see them all out. He was not a lover of parties at the best of times—especially in his home—but at least his mother had enjoyed herself.

Gianni was on hand to round up the stragglers, and an hour later only the doctor was still in the lounge, as he was staying the night.

He glanced around the empty hall and saw again in his mind's eye Lucy descending the stairs earlier, a vision in silver and white. Damn it! She was in his head again. She had been in his head for the best part of three months, and it had to stop. He had to forget her exquisite little body was curled up in bed a few metres above his head, despite the frustration coursing through him. The woman was driving him mad. The sooner he could stick her on the plane in the morning and forget he'd ever known her the better.

With the last guest gone, he strode into the salon. He was too tense to sleep, and spotted the doctor still seated on a sofa. He shrugged off his jacket and pulled off the bow-tie, crossing to the drinks cabinet and pouring cognac into two glasses. He handed one to the doctor and sat down in a chair opposite.

'Brilliant party, my boy.'

Lorenzo agreed, and automatically asked him about his mother's health.

'Nothing to worry about. Her blood pressure is fine, and Anna is better than she has been in years. Lucy has given her a new lease on life. You as well, Lorenzo, I shouldn't wonder. You are a very lucky man.' He beamed at him, sipping his glass of cognac, more than slightly drunk. 'That young woman of yours is a true gem—beautiful and talented, with a heart as big as a lion, loving and compassionate…maybe too compassionate for her own good. If I had been her doctor I don't think I'd have advised a teenager to do it.'

'Do what?' Lorenzo asked, draining his glass. He placed it on the low table and reclined back in his chair. Had Lucy had an abortion? he wondered cynically, knowing how the doctor felt about such a procedure, being deeply religious.

'Why—give one of her kidneys to her brother, of course.'

A rushing noise filled Lorenzo's head. The colour leached from his face, and he sat up straight and stared at the doctor with horrified eyes. 'Lucy did what? When?' he demanded in a hoarse voice.

'Surely you must know? When her brother returned to England—after the climbing accident. Apparently the Swiss clinic he spent a day in said he was naturally a bit exhausted, but fine, and discharged him. A couple of weeks later his own doctor and local hospital weren't much better, and three months later he ended up in the Hospital for Tropical Diseases in London. They finally diagnosed him as having a rare disease, probably picked up in South America at the beginning of the year, that attacked the kidneys. The only solution was a transplant. Lucy was a perfect match—not that it did much good. She told me her brother died last year.'

'Lucy…' Lorenzo groaned her name as the enormity of what she had done hit him. 'Will she be all right?' he asked, terrified of the answer.

'Yes, she is fine—very fit. One kidney is almost as good as two. I got her blood results this morning. No food poisoning—nothing wrong at all. Probably, as she said, the wine and too much rich food. She is a very sensible girl, who rarely drinks and watches what she eats. I think Anna was hoping Lucy might be pregnant, but she isn't—and she is not on the pill, either. Doesn't believe in putting anything in her body that is not necessary to her health—very wise.' He suddenly stopped and added belatedly, 'But I should not have told you—doctor-patient confidentiality and all that.' Rising to his feet, he said, 'Time I went to bed. Goodnight, Lorenzo.'

But Lorenzo didn't hear. He was fighting to breathe, his heart pounding in his chest as the full weight of what the doctor had revealed exploded in his mind. Lucy—his Lucy—with the laughing eyes and the brilliant smile. It would kill him if anything happened to her. And in that instant he knew he loved her—probably had from the day she'd walked into his office and he had kissed her.

A host of other memories flooded though his mind: their first night together, when he'd carried her upstairs and she'd given herself to him so willingly. For the first time in his life he'd lost control. He should have known then he loved her.

He remembered kissing the scar at the base of her spine and asking her how she'd got it the second night they were together—when, after the first rush of passion, they had made long, slow love…caressing, exploring and having fun together. She had said it was just a cut, and, so engrossed in what she was doing to him by then, he'd never queried her answer. Later that night he had delivered a cruel cut of his own, and he couldn't bear to think how brutal he had been.

He had actually accused her brother of manslaughter and ended their weekend affair with a ruthlessness as insulting to her as it was shaming to him. Groaning, he buried his head in his hands.

Lucy was never going to forgive him—how could she? He was the staid, arrogant banker she'd called him, who thought he was always right. She had tried to tell him this afternoon, when he'd shoved his so-called proof at her. She had accused him of seeing things in black and white and suggested her brother might have been weakened or passed out. But had he listened? No…

Lorenzo had no idea how long he sat there with every day of the last few months he'd spent with Lucy replaying in his mind—every word, every action. He had read somewhere that love was a kind of madness and, given the crazy way he had behaved since he'd met Lucy, he could believe it.

Finally he got to his feet, and with a steely glint of determination in his eyes walked upstairs. He hesitated for a second outside her bedroom, then opened the door and walked in.

He crossed to the bedside and stared down at where

she lay on her back, her beautiful face illuminated by the bedside light, her eyes closed peacefully in sleep. His conscience told him the way he had behaved towards her was despicable and he should leave now. Let her go home as planned, and get on with her life without him. But he was not that altruistic. What he wanted he fought tooth and nail to get—and he wanted her with a passion, a depth of love, he had never imagined possible. Just the thought of never seeing her again tore him apart.

She stirred slightly.

'Lucy.' He said her name and sat down on the side of the bed. 'Lucy…' he said again, and raised his hand to rest it on her shoulder.

Somewhere in her dreams Lucy heard Lorenzo call her name, and her eyelashes fluttered. She moaned a soft, low sound—'Lorenzo…' Her lips parting in the beginning of a smile. Then she heard it again, louder, and blinked. 'Lorenzo?' she repeated, and felt his touch. She opened her eyes. This was no dream—he was sitting on her bed. 'What are you doing here?' she demanded, knocking his hand away and scrambling back against the pillows, tugging the coverlet to her neck and suddenly very aware of her naked state.

'I had to see you—to talk to you—make sure—'

'Are you out of your mind?' she cried. 'It's the middle of the night.'

'Yes—out of my mind with loving you.'

Loving her…

Her green eyes opened wide. She had to be still dreaming. But, no—Lorenzo was there, larger than life, minus his jacket, his shirt open at the neck. His black hair looked as if he had run his hands through it a hundred times, and his face was grey, but it was the pain in his eyes that shocked her most.

'You look more like a man on death row than a man in love,' she tried to joke. She could not—would not—believe what he had said…

'Oh, Lucy,' he groaned. 'I might as well be if you don't believe me. I love you—it is not a joke.' And, reaching out, he curved his hands around her shoulders. 'The only joke is on me, for not realising sooner,' he said, staring down at her with haunted eyes. '*Dio,* I hope I am not too late.'

Lucy hung on to the coverlet as if her life depended on it and looked at him. This was a Lorenzo she had never seen before. Gone was the hard, emotionless man. She could see the desperation in his eyes, feel it in the unsteady hands that held her, and she could feel herself weakening, beginning to believe him… Her pulses were beating erratically beneath her skin, her heart pounding…

'I have sat downstairs for ages, wondering how to explain my actions…the appalling way I have behaved towards you since the day we met…and the only explanation I have is because I love you.'

Her heart squeezed inside her. 'That has to be the dumbest reason I have ever heard for declaring you love someone.' She wanted to believe him, but with a cynicism she had never had until she'd met him she said, 'What is this? Some ploy to get a farewell lay? Well, you are wasting your time. I know exactly how contemptuous you think I am—a promiscuous, greedy woman who can't help herself around men and who you can pay off. But you're wrong.'

She was angry—at herself for her body's instant response to his closeness, and at Lorenzo for doing this to her now, when she had finally resigned herself to their parting.

'I only ever had sex once in my life before you. As for your paying me off—that convoluted deal was all *your* doing. All I ever asked from you was for you to vote with me and not sell your shares to save my family firm. I ended up blackmailed into your bed. So excuse me if I don't believe you love me. Just leave me alone. I am packed and ready go.' And then she added, 'Try Olivia. I'm sure she will oblige—probably already has, according to rumour.'

He looked stunned. 'Rumour is completely unfounded. My relationship with Olivia Paglia is strictly business, and I will sue anyone who dares repeat it.' He sounded genuinely affronted. 'How the hell did *you* find out about the rumours?'

'I met you coming out of her apartment building, remember? The Contessa told me.'

'I thought better of the Contessa—she is not known as a gossip,' he said, and she saw disillusion in his dark eyes.

'In fairness,' Lucy began, 'the Contessa did not believe them—and now I think you should leave.'

Suddenly he pushed her back against the pillows and leaned over her, his face only inches away. She heard the heavy pounding of his heart—or was it hers?

'Damn it, Lucy, I don't care what you heard. I can't leave you alone, and you are not going anywhere. I know I don't deserve you, but I love you—I want you and I need you…' he stated, staring into her eyes and seeing the darkening pupils. 'Though you don't love me, you *do* want me,' he said, with some of his usual arrogance returning.

She stared back, her mouth going dry, her body heating beneath the pressure of his.

'No, I don't,' she lied, still afraid to believe his sudden avowal of love. 'I don't really know you and I don't trust you.'

'Lucy, you know me better than anyone—but I can't blame you for not trusting me.' He leant back a little, resting his forearms either side of her shoulders. 'I admit I was determined to think the worst of you, and sure I was right about your brother. I didn't know until the doctor told me tonight what you had done for him—donating a kidney. Have you any idea what that did to me?' he demanded his face grim. 'All I could think of was you on an operating table, risking your life for someone else, and it ripped my guts out. I have never been so afraid in my life for another person. I asked the doctor if you were all right. Because in that moment l knew I would not want to live in a world without you. I knew I loved you.' He lowered his head and brushed his lips against hers, and she saw the vulnerability in his dark eyes. 'You have got to believe me—listen to me. Lucy, please give me a chance.'

'All right,' she murmured—not that she had a choice, trapped in the cage formed by his broad chest and arms, but the *please* helped.

'I think I have loved you from the day you walked into my office wearing that horrible suit with your hair scraped back in a pleat. I kissed you—totally out of character for me. With hindsight I can see it was unfortunate that Manuel was the man I'd lunched with that day. He gave me the photographs I showed you this afternoon, and his opinion on the timescale, and I accepted his conclusion. He is a strong man, and like me has not much time for weakness, but now I don't know and I no longer care. The past is past. You say you don't know me, but you do, Lucy. I am the arrogant bastard you called me, and I very rarely change my mind, but

I did that day. I was considering voting with you on the deal, but I was so angry I changed my mind. Then, when I kissed you, I was so overwhelmingly attracted to you I nearly lost control and was embarrassed by it. I lashed out at you.' He laughed—a hollow sound.

'I actually thought I was having a mid-life crisis… But it wasn't—it was you. And I have been lashing out at you ever since. I used my perception of your brother as an excuse to believe you were as bad as I thought him to be in a crazy attempt to deny what was staring me in the face. I love you.'

Deep inside, Lucy felt the dead embers of hope burst into flame. She could see the sincerity in his eyes—hear it in every word he spoke.

'I swore I never wanted to see you again, and yet I came up with reasons to visit you—each one crazier than the last. I was jealous of my dead brother because it was obvious you'd liked him. I was even jealous of Gianni, the butler, when you walked into the dining room with him laughing. I've never seen Gianni laugh like that in his life. And tonight I could have knocked young Paolo down when he laid his hands on you. I was so jealous.' He ran a finger down her cheek. 'I know it is a lot to ask, but can you ever forgive me for the way I have treated you? At least try and forget? Forget the argument over our brothers and business? Forget everything that has happened these past months and give me a chance to prove I love you?'

Lucy looked at him. Lorenzo was jealous. She had not been mistaken. But he was better than most at hiding his feelings. She thought of how on that first night, when he had remonstrated with her about her security, it had given her hope at the time, and of other instances when he'd been protective of her. He said he didn't care what her brother might have done. Later she would tell him how her brother had passed out when he returned home, and the rest—but for now she decided to take a chance, a leap of faith, and believe him.

Her green eyes sparkled and a smile curved her lips. 'I'll give you a chance, but I don't want to forget *everything,* Lorenzo. Some parts were memorable and should be repeated,' she said, with a wriggle against him and a teasing flicker of her lashes. Lifting her hand, she swept back the hair from his brow.

He caught her wrist, his eyes tender and passionate as they met hers. 'Oh, I think I can arrange that,' he said, knowing exactly what she meant. 'But first there is something else,' he said in a husky, unsteady tone.

Lucy tensed, wondering what was coming next.

'I don't expect you to love me, but I want to take care of you—keep you. I know I can make you happy in bed, and maybe in time you will grow to love me if only you will let me try. Lucy, will you marry me?'

Lucy felt her heart swell to overflowing. She saw the vulnerability in his eyes as he waited for her answer—her proud, arrogant lover was unsure…nervous. Taking a deep breath, she said, 'You won't have to try—I do love you.' She saw the confusion, then the growing hope in his eyes. 'I have from the first time we made love. And, yes—I will marry you.'

'You do? You will?' Lorenzo looked shocked, then his dark eyes blazed with emotion and a hint of tears as he wrapped his arms around her, crushing her against his broad chest, and buried his face in the fragrant silken mass of her hair. 'You are sure?' he queried, and then his lips sought hers and he kissed her with achingly sweet tenderness and a love that stole her breath away.

He lifted his head. 'When?' he asked, and his dark eyes watched warily as he waited for her answer.

She realised her confident, powerful man was still uncertain. 'Whenever you like.' She smiled, all the love in her heart shining in her brilliant green eyes. 'The sooner the better,' she said, and finally let go of the coverlet and looped her arm around his neck. 'Do we *have* to wait for the wedding?' she teased.

'*Dio,* no—I can't wait,' Lorenzo groaned, his voice thick with emotion and a hunger that Lucy felt herself.

Taking her arm from his neck, he stripped off his shirt, his pants. Lucy's eyes followed his every move. This was what she wanted—what she yearned for—and as he gathered her in his arms she met the smouldering darkness of his gaze and arched into the hard warmth of his great body, her small hands caressing, her lips parting.

They melded together—heart to heart, mouth to mouth—in a kiss like no other, full of tenderness and longing, passion and love.

'Lorenzo…' she breathed, as his hands slid sensuously over her body and her own caressed his satin smooth skin. He filled up her senses, and with murmured words of love and groans of fervent need their bodies joined in the primeval dance of love, finally fusing together in surge after surge of pure ecstasy, two halves of a whole in perfect love.

'I can't find the words to tell you how you make me feel,' Lorenzo husked as they lay satiated in each other's arms. But he tried, with softly whispered endearments. He eased his weight away, but held her close to his long body, his hands gently stroking her back. 'I don't deserve you, Lucy, but I will never let you go—you are the colour in my life. You are beautiful inside and out.'

A long finger found the scar near the base of her spine. 'I can't believe you did this for your brother.'

'Yes, you can,' Lucy murmured. 'You would have done the same for yours if he'd needed it,' she said lazily as she surfaced from the sensual haze that surrounded her.

'You have more faith in me than I do myself.'

'Ah, but then I love you.' She pressed a kiss on his chest and he rolled over on his back, carrying her with him. And as the dawn of the new day crept through the windows the dance of love started all over again…

'What the hell?' Lorenzo swore as a loud crashing noise woke him. Keeping Lucy safe in the curve of his arm, he sat up.

The maid was standing three feet into the room, and she had dropped the coffee tray she had been carrying. Her face was scarlet, and Lorenzo could understand why as Lucy opened her eyes and smiled up at him, stroking her small hand across his stomach.

'I just need to feel you are real, Lorenzo, and know I wasn't dreaming last night.'

Then to add to the confusion his mother appeared in the doorway, fully dressed.

'What on earth has happened?' she demanded of the maid, and then looked across at the bed. 'Oh, Lorenzo—how could you?'

Lucy heard the voice and snatched her hand away from his stomach, blushing redder than the maid and trying to burrow down beneath the coverlet.

Lorenzo pulled her gently back up. 'Trust me, Lucy—that will look worse.' He grinned and tucked the coverlet under her, putting his arm around her shoulders before looking back across the room.

'Good morning, Mother,' he said, with all the confidence and panache a thirty-eight-year-old man could muster when for the first time in his life he had been caught in bed with a woman by his *mother*... 'I want you to be the first to know Lucy and I are getting married.'

His mother gasped, and then smiled, and was about to rush over.

'But can you save the congratulations and the clean-up until later? Lucy is a little shy right now.'

'Yes—yes, of course.'

The two women backed out of the room.

'As embarrassing moments go, that has to be the worst,' Lucy said.

'Not really. I should have expected something like that. From being a highly successful, staid and arrogant banker, in control of billions, who has never had any trouble with women in his life, this summer has seen women running rings around me. But, on the plus side, I have found the love of my life.' And, laughing out loud, he tipped Lucy back in his arms and kissed her soundly.

EPILOGUE

LORENZO guided the car through the gates and up the drive, a smile on his face. Lucy had married him in the cathedral in Verona on a fine October day—a vision in white and a picture he would carry in his mind for ever. And eight months later their son Antonio had been born—conceived, Lucy was sure, on the night he'd proposed to her. Lorenzo had his doubts, but didn't argue with his wife. She had filled his life with laughter and love, and she collected friends as other people collected stamps. Last week had been Antonio's first birthday, and they had thrown a party for their friends, and his little friends and their families, with a funfair set up in the garden.

Today was Lorenzo's birthday. He had spent the last four days in New York and could not wait to get home and get Lucy alone. He loved his family, but sometimes a man just needed his wife—and he was hard with anticipation. He had it all planned. He was going to surprise Lucy and fly her to Venice, take her to the Hotel Cipriani, where he had booked a suite for the night. They could share an intimate dinner…just the two of them…

* * *

Lucy combed Antonio's soft black hair. He had woken from his afternoon nap an hour ago, and was now dressed and ready for the party. She kissed his cheek and handed him to the nanny to take downstairs. She had not wanted a nanny but Lorenzo had insisted, saying if she wanted to continue with her art it made sense.

He was right. He had arranged for one of the tower rooms to be converted into a studio for her, but she still had the gallery and visited regularly and showed her work there. Elaine now ran it, with Miss Carr the temp—who, having gone full-time, had ended up marrying the woodcarver in residence, confirmed bachelor Leon. In fact all four of them were here now, and downstairs with Anna.

Lucy walked along to the master suite and quickly showered and dressed. Sometimes she had to pinch herself to believe how lucky she was. Lorenzo had made her the happiest woman in the world. She knew he loved her—he showed it in myriad ways—and he had given her a wonderful son she worshipped and adored. He was a great father. How she had ever thought he was staid and boring was inconceivable to her now.

When they'd married he had asked her where she wanted to live, saying he would buy or build her a house anywhere she chose. She'd chosen to live in the house by the lake with his mother. He'd been surprised, but had agreed. They stayed at the villa in Santa Margherita a lot of weekends, and already he was trying to teach Antonio to sail on a specially built boat in the swimming pool. She'd told him he was crazy—the baby had only just learnt to walk—but he'd just laughed and made love to her by the pool.

He still worked hard, and commuted to Verona daily. Sometimes he drove, but he had a new toy—a helicopter which he piloted himself. Tonight he was driving home, thank heaven, otherwise he would be back too soon and ruin her surprise.

Three months ago he had surprised *her*. They had gone to Dessington for the grand opening of the new development, and she had discovered he had bought her old home. She had auctioned it off and converted it into a hotel with James Morgan. Not an ordinary hotel, but a centre where cancer sufferers and their families could have a holiday. Lorenzo knew her mum had died of cancer, and James had done it for Samantha.

They two were arriving any minute, with their son Thomas, and with one last look at her reflection in the mirror Lucy dashed downstairs just in time to welcome them.

Lorenzo stopped the car under the portico, leapt out and dashed into the house—and stopped dead. A huge banner was strung around the balcony, with 'Happy Fortieth Birthday' written on it, and the hall was full of people. His dark eyes went unerringly to Lucy.

She was walking towards him, a brilliant smile on her face, her eyes sparkling with love and laughter. The gown she wore should have been censored, was his second thought. His first was *wow*... A shimmering gold, the dress had a halter-neck and no back, he noted, as she turned for a second to speak to someone, and the bodice plunged between her breasts—slightly larger now, since she had breastfed their son. It nipped in at her tiny waist, then fell smoothly over hips to her feet. And he was in danger of embarrassing himself—but then Lucy always had that effect on him.

She reached up and looped her arms around his

neck. 'Surprise, surprise—happy birthday, Lorenzo darling.'

He wrapped his arms around her and kissed her as the crowd started cheering. 'You will pay for this,' he murmured in her ear. 'I had plans for an intimate dinner for two in Venice. We have to communicate better—starting now.'

And then Antonio came, hurtling to his feet, and he picked his son up and spun him around, and kissed his mother on the cheek. Then he was shaking hands and greeting people, but he put a hand around Lucy's waist and kept her by his side as he made for the stairs, telling Gianni and various others that he needed to get changed. And huskily telling Lucy *she* was going to help him.

'Lorenzo, we can't,' Lucy said, eyeing him with loving amusement as he shed his suit and shirt, dropping them on the bed room floor as usual.

Wearing only boxers, he caught her to him. 'Yes, we can, Lucy. I love you more and more each day. You have given me a wonderful son and you have made me the happiest man in the world. But it has been four days, and right now I ache to be inside you.' And gathering her close, a hand curving around her nape, he kissed her long and deep, his fingers deftly loosening the halter-top.

Lucy closed her eyes. He was right. She could feel the passion, the desire vibrating between them, and when he slipped her dress down to pool at her feet and carried her to the bed she wanted him with a hunger that could not be denied. She always did and always would.

Later, she slipped off the bed and told Lorenzo to wait. She crossed to the dressing room and, taking the parcel she had hidden there, returned to the bed. 'Happy birthday,' she said, and handed him her gift.

Grinning, he ripped off the paper—and stopped, his dark eyes fixed on the painting. He stared for so long in silence, she began to worry.

'I thought it was time there was a portrait of you above the fireplace in the lounge, and your father's was relegated to the hall,' she said. 'But if it's not good enough…'

He turned his head, and she saw the moisture in his eyes. 'Good enough? It is magnificent—the best gift, after our son, you could possibly give me. The days… the hours you must have spent… I am humbled and flattered that you see me so well.' And, slipping the painting gently to the floor, he reached for her.

Lorenzo Zanelli's surprise fortieth birthday party was talked about for months afterwards in the homes of Verona—mainly because it had taken him three hours to get changed for the party, particularly as his wife was helping him!

UNTAMED ITALIAN, BLACKMAILED INNOCENT

JACQUELINE BAIRD

CHAPTER ONE

Zac Delucca stepped out of the chauffeur-driven limousine and glanced up at the four-storeyed Georgian-style building in front of him: the head office of Westwold Components, a company he had finally acquired two weeks ago. He had left Raffe, his top man, in charge of the changeover, so he had not expected to be needed in London in June, and he was not pleased....

He was ruggedly attractive, with black hair and shrewd dark eyes, and the navy silk and mohair suit he wore was a testament to the expertise of his tailor. The jacket stretched taut across shoulders as wide as a barn door, and at six feet five he was a powerful, impressive figure of a man in every respect. Not a man anyone could overlook, though the fierce frown at present marring his bold features would scare all but the bravest into glancing the other way.

Orphaned at a year old by the tragic death of his young parents in a car crash, Zac Delucca had spent his early years in a children's home in Rome. He had left at fifteen, with nothing but the clothes he stood up in and a burning ambition to become a success in life.

Tall, and looking older than his years, he had by sheer guts, determination and keen intelligence dragged himself up from the gutter that beckoned. He had studied by day and used his physical strength in the testosterone-fuelled world of the fighting game at night to earn money and build up a stake to set up his own company: Delucca Holdings.

He had fought masked, under an assumed name, because he'd had total belief in his ability, mentally and physically, to be a winner in life. From a young age he had known he was destined to succeed on a worldwide scale…never mind in a canvas ring…

His first purchase at the age of twenty had been a rundown farm in southern Italy that had included three cottages, a large farmhouse and a thousand acres of neglected land. A few weeks later the government had bought a chunk of the acreage to build a new runway to expand a local airport for the increasing tourist trade.

Some people said he'd had inside information. He had said nothing and recouped the money he had invested and more besides. He'd converted the farm house, which was situated on the coast at the southernmost tip of Italy, with stunning views over the sea, and kept it for his own use.

The remaining land had included an overgrown olive grove he had tried to cultivate himself, but he had quickly realised agriculture was not for him and finally hired an expert in the field to restore, enlarge and manage the farm, while converting the cottages for the staff. Eventually he'd marketed the produce as Delucca Extra Fine Virgin Olive Oil, and Delucca Oil was today the choice of the connoisseur and priced accordingly…

It was the first business Zac had bought and kept.

Now, fifteen years later, Delucca Holdings was an international conglomerate that owned a vast array of companies, including mines, manufacturers, properties and oil of the petroleum variety as well as from the olive tree. Nothing was out of Delucca's grasp.

Ruthless, arrogant, and merciless were some of the terms used by his enemies, but none in the business world friend or enemy could deny he was a financial wizard, and basically honest… A master of the universe who went after what he wanted and always succeeded.

'Are you sure about this, Raffe?' Zac demanded of the man who had exited the car to join him on the pavement.

Raffe Costa was his right-hand man and his friend. They had met over a decade ago, when Zac had applied for funding for a deal from a bank in Naples, where Raffe had been working in the commercial loan office. The pair had hit it off immediately, and two years later Raffe had joined Zac's swiftly expanding company as an accountant-cum-PA. The title was not important. Zac trusted him completely, and knew him to be shrewd and rarely wrong.

'Sure…?' Raffe responded slowly. 'No, I am not absolutely sure, but enough to want you to check it out,' he qualified as they walked towards the entrance. 'It wasn't noticed in the due diligence we conducted before buying, because the siphoning off of funds—if that is what it is—has been done very cleverly, and been deeply hidden in the accounts for years.'

'You'd better be right. Because I had plans to take a holiday, and I did not intend it to be in London,' Zac said dryly, flicking his friend a glance as they entered the building. 'I had a hot climate and a hot woman in mind.'

Zac Delucca was not a happy man. He had no trouble in thinking on several levels at the same time, and right now, while smiling at the security guard as Raffe introduced him, another part of his mind was wondering how quickly—if Raffe's suspicions were correct—he could sort out the problem and leave…

He had, after months of prolonged negotiation, finalised

this deal. Coincidentally it had been the following morning, standing in the shower, that he realised he had been celibate for almost a year. Ten months since he had parted with his last lady, because she was becoming too proprietorial and the *M* word had surfaced more than once.

Amazed at his own restraint, he had swiftly decided to rectify the situation by arranging a couple of dates with a rather striking model from Milan. He had planned to take her out on his yacht for the day and make her his mistress. If they proved to be compatible he had actually considered breaking the habit of a lifetime and allowing her to accompany him on a cruise around the Caribbean for a few weeks.

He had never taken more than a week's holiday in years, but just lately he'd found himself questioning if work was the be-all and end-all of life. Unusual for him. He was not usually given to bouts of introspection and immediately he had decided to do something about it—hence Lisa the Milan model…

Unfortunately, the call last night from Raffe, voicing some concern over the recent acquisition of Westwold Components, looked like scuppering his plan.

He signed the log-in book where the security guard indicated—a formality, but no doubt the man wanted to impress—and was then introduced to the receptionist: Melanie.

'I'm sure Mr Costa will have told you,' the girl simpered, while hanging on to Zac's hand like a leech. 'We are all really happy to become part of Delucca Holdings, and if there is anything I personally can do…' The busty blonde fluttered her eyelashes at him. 'Just ask.'

The woman gushed and pouted at the same time, which was quite a feat, Zac thought cynically.

'Thank you,' he replied smoothly, and, disentangling his hand from the receptionist's grasp, he turned. 'Come on,

Raffe, let's get—' And he stopped, his dark eyes instinctively flaring in primitive masculine appreciation of the woman walking into the building.

'Exquisite,' he murmured under his breath, his stunned gaze roaming over her. She had the face of an angel, and a body to tempt any man with blood in his veins…

Big, misty-blue eyes, pale, almost translucent skin, a small nose and a wide mouth with full lips that begged to be kissed. Long ruby-red hair fell in soft curls around her slender shoulders, and the elegant white obviously designer dress she wore caressed every curve of her slender body. Sleeveless, with a low square neck and a broad white belt circling her tiny waist, it accentuated her high full breasts.

She looked bridal… The unbidden thought flashed in his mind. But the evocative tap of high-heeled shoes on the marble floor knocked it straight out as his gaze lowered to where the hem of the skirt ended on her knees. The red stiletto sandals she wore screamed sex.

His heart almost stopped. She had legs to die for… A mental image of them clamped around his waist had his body hardening instantly.

'Who is that?' he demanded of Raffe.

'I have no idea, but she is gorgeous.'

Zac looked at his friend and saw he was watching the girl as she drew nearer. He had to bite his lip to stop himself saying, *Take your eyes off her. She is mine.*

In that instant he came to a decision. Admittedly she was not his usual type. Tall, elegant brunettes had been his preference up until now. This woman was average height, with that long, red hair, but for some inexplicable reason he wanted her with a hunger he had not felt in a long time. He decided he was going to have her…

His firm lips parted in a loaded smile aimed directly at her, but amazingly the girl walked straight past him with a dismissive shake of her head…

Sally Paxton strode across the foyer of Westwold Components, determination in every step. She flicked a glance at the group of people at the reception desk and caught a brilliant smile from the tallest man in the group. Her heart missed a beat and she felt her shoulders stiffen with tension. She had to appear confident, as if she belonged here. Maybe he was someone she should recognise… She gave a brief nod of her head in acknowledgment.

Sally Paxton was a woman on a mission…and nothing and no one was going to stop her…

Her blue eyes fixed with a determined light on the two elevators situated to the rear of the elegant foyer. One elevator she knew was for general use; the other—the one she wanted—went directly to the top floor, where her father's office was situated.

Zac Delucca, for the first time in his adult life, had been virtually overlooked by a woman, and for a moment it left him dumbfounded.

Recovering, he demanded of the receptionist, 'Who is that girl, and what department does she work in?'

'I don't know. I've never seen her before.'

'Security,' he said, alerting the guard standing nearby, but he was already calling out.

'Stop, miss, you have to sign in!'

Sally stopped in front of the elevator and jabbed at the button, lost in her own angry thoughts. The one and only time she had visited her dad's London office had been over seven years ago. She had been eighteen and had called in unannounced one Wednesday afternoon, after watching her beloved mother open a birthday card from her husband that morning.

Sally had been hoping to persuade her dad to return with her that evening to their home in Bournemouth, rather than waiting until the weekend. It was her mum's birthday, for heaven's sake… At least he had remembered to post a card… But as her mother had recently been discharged from hospital after a mastectomy, Sally had been determined to make him see that his wife needed his support.

The success of the surprise dinner party Sally had planned for the evening had depended on her father's presence.

Her lips tightened in disgust, and briefly she closed her eyes. Even now the scene that had met her eyes was still scorched into her brain, and made her simmer with rage…

Nigel Paxton's secretary had not been in the outer office, so Sally had knocked on her father's door. When no one had answered she had opened it and walked in.

It had not been a pretty sight… There was her dad, leaning over his desk with his half-naked secretary, half his age, sprawled across the desk beneath him.

No wonder they hadn't heard her knock…

Her father…the slick seducer…the serial adulterer…the slimy lying toad…the man her mother loved and thought could do no wrong—the man Sally had slowly grown to despise.

The elevator arrived and she stepped in and pressed the button. Leaning back against the wall, she closed her eyes.

As a young child she supposed she had loved her father, even though he hadn't been around a lot. Their home in Bournemouth had been a large detached Victorian house overlooking the sea. But her father, as chief accountant for

Westwolds Components, was based in the London headquarters of the company, and kept a studio apartment in the city where he stayed during the week.

As an idealistic teenager, anti-war of any kind, she had been horrified when she'd realised the firm her dad worked for manufactured essential parts for weapons. She had announced that it was morally wrong to work in the arms industry, and he had told her she was a silly girl, and to stick to looking good and leave the running of the world to men.

To call him a male chauvinist pig was to insult pigs! Dark haired, handsome and charming to those who did not know him, her father was at the top of his game in the accountancy stakes—but in Sally's book he was a spineless apology for a man.

Well, today he was going to hear just what she thought of him—yet again, and demand he accompany her to visit her mother in the private nursing home in Devon that had been her mum's home for almost two years.

It was over six weeks since her father had shown his face, and she blinked tears from her eyes as she pictured again the look on her mum's face every time Sally arrived to visit. The gleam of hope that faded as she realised her latest visitor was not her husband yet again. Sally's excuse for her dad that 'pressure of work' kept him in London was wearing very thin.

Her mother knew about his affairs, because Sally at eighteen had blurted out what she had seen. And her mother had admitted she had always known about her husband's other women—in the *plural*!

Sally had been horrified when her mother had actually made excuses for him. Explaining how it was difficult for him as a virile man, because she had not been a very able wife in the bedroom department for quite some time even before she had been diagnosed with breast cancer, and that he was a good and generous husband and father and she loved him.

Nothing Sally said had affected her mother's opinion or her love for her husband, and, not wanting to upset her mother, she had been forced to drop the subject.

As for her father—she'd told him exactly what she thought of him, and he had simply responded with the usual: that she was a silly girl who knew nothing of the wants and needs of adults, and that she should mind her own business and concentrate on her studies, because he was paying enough for them...

Immediately, she had wanted to give up her place at Exeter University, where she'd been in her first year studying Ancient History, but her mother would not hear of it. Reluctantly, Sally had to agree, but she could barely bring herself to be civil to her father when he did occasionally return home the same weekend as her.

As it happened, her mother had been right to insist on her continuing her education, because her mum had recovered from the breast cancer remarkably well. Sally had watched her slowly begin to grow in confidence and hope as test after test had come back with positive results.

When her mum had reached the five-year point and still been in the clear she had told Sally it was time for her to spread her wings a little and strike out on her own. After graduating Sally had initially worked at a small local museum near home. But after her mother's encouragement she had applied and secured a job as a researcher at the British Museum in London.

Sally had loved her new job—and the fully furnished one-bedroom apartment she had rented over a bakery in the city. For the first six months life had been good. Her mum had been well, and had occasionally visited her in London. Sally had gone home most weekends, and, excluding her dad, the future had looked rosy. Then the horrendous tragedy of her mum's accident had destroyed their fragile happiness.

Even now Sally could not get her head around how fate could be so cruel… She shook her head as a huge black cloud of sadness enveloped her. It was so unfair. After five years her mum had virtually recovered from the cancer. Only to be knocked down by a car as she walked out behind the bus she had taken to the centre of Bournemouth to shop. After months of treatment she had been left a paraplegic, with no hope of further improvement.

Now every weekend Sally travelled down to Devon, where she stayed in a small hotel near the nursing home so she could spend as much time with her mother as possible. Last Saturday evening Sally had been sitting with her mother and had watched her face light up at the sound of her husband's voice on the telephone, had seen in her eyes the pain and sadness she'd tried to hide as she replaced the receiver, and had listened with growing anger as her mother repeated the conversation.

Apparently her father had called to tell her he could not make it on Sunday, nor the next weekend… His excuse was that with the takeover of the company by the Italian firm Delucca Holdings, he was up to his ears in work.

Sally opened her eyes and took a deep breath. She needed to calm down, and she needed to plan what she was going to say to her father. Yelling at him would be futile. For her mother's sake she needed him to go to the nursing home with her willingly, for once in his selfish life, to act the part of loving husband.

God knew it wasn't as if he was going to have to do it for long… If the consultant was to be believed, her mother's life expectancy was limited.

On her last visit the doctor had called Sally into his consulting room and informed her that her mother's heart was weakened beyond repair, probably as a result of the cancer treatment she had undergone combined with the accident that had followed. He was sorry, but there was nothing more that could be done, and in his opinion her mother had maybe a year at best. But in reality she could go at any time.

The doors opened and Sally exited the elevator. Her dad's office was at the far end of the corridor, and, squaring her shoulders, she tightened her grip on her red clutch purse and made straight for his door.

Zac Delucca crossed to where the security guard stood, pressing the button for the elevator.

'Sorry, sir, she got away. But this elevator only goes to the top floor, where the boardroom and Mr Costa's office is situated. The only other office is Mr Paxton's, the company accountant, but that wasn't his girlfriend—secretary,' he quickly corrected himself. 'Maybe the lady is looking for you?' he suggested, trying to sound positive after having failed in his duty to register all visitors.

So the accountant was having an affair… Zac filed the information away. 'Do not worry, Joe,' he said, glancing at the name tag on his uniform. 'You were distracted—and if what you say is true the lady is not going anywhere. I suggest you get back to you desk.'

The elevator doors glided open, and Zac and Raffe entered.

'Is the lady *likely* to be looking for you?' Raffe asked with a grin. 'Or should I say chasing?'

'I should be so lucky,' Zac drawled, though it was a common occurrence for women to chase him. He was an incredibly wealthy man and, as one reporter had once written, with his kind of wealth, good looks and height—a broken nose notwithstanding—he was a magnet for women the world over. Not that he thought of himself as such…

Concentrating on the task at hand, he asked, 'It is the accountant whom you suspect of fraud, is it not, Raffe?'

'Yes.'

'I take it he is a married man?'

'Yes—married with one child, I believe.'

'And apparently this man has a mistress, and they do not come cheap. Your suspicions are looking well founded, Raffe.'

Sally walked straight into her father's office and stopped. He was sitting behind his desk, his head in his hands, a picture of misery. Maybe she had misjudged him… Maybe he was more upset over his wife's diagnosis than he showed.

'Dad?' she called softly, and he lifted his head.

'Oh, it's you.' He straightened up, frowning. 'What are you doing here? No, don't tell me.' He raised his hand. 'You are on a holier-than-thou mission and want me to go and visit your mum, right?'

He wasn't upset. He was the same selfish bastard he had always been.

'Silly me.' Sally shook her head in disgust. 'For a moment there I thought you were thinking of your wife…' She glanced around the large room and through the open door to the secretary's office beyond, which was empty, and then back to her dad. 'Well, I have had enough of your lies and deceit, and for once in your life you are going to do the decent thing and come with me tonight.'

'Not now, darling,' he snapped, and stood up, straightening his tie.

Zac Delucca had heard the woman's demand that Paxton

go with her as he entered the office, and he did not miss the *darling*, or the sardonic curl of the woman's lips as she responded.

'What's the matter? Your latest Girl Friday deserted you? And I use the word *girl* deliberately,' Sally goaded. And she must have hit the nail on the head as the colour seemed to drain from her dad's face. Then she realised he was looking straight past her. The smile on his face did not reach the eyes that for an instant flickered with fear, quickly masked.

Inexplicably, Sally shivered, despite the slight stuffiness of the office on the hot summer's day, and she felt the hairs on the back of her neck stand on end. Someone else had entered the room, probably his secretary, and she was now shooting daggers at her back, having overheard her comment. Not that Sally gave a damn about upsetting her dad's latest mistress…

'Mr Costa, I was not expecting you back again so soon.'

Sally stiffened as her dad spoke and then stepped forward, ignoring her. Then she heard the Costa man introduce a Signor Delucca.

'Mr Delucca, this is an unexpected pleasure. I am delighted to meet you.'

Her father's hearty greeting rang a little false to Sally. She knew every intonation of his voice, and he did not sound delighted. She certainly was not. His secretary she could handle, but she stiffened as she recognised the name Delucca.

After her father had stated the man was taking over the company Sally had read an article about him in the business section of a newspaper. He was an Italian tycoon, incredibly wealthy, and renowned as the takeover king. His latest acquisition was Westwold. In a footnote to the article, it said that apparently he kept his private life very private, but it was known that he had escorted numerous statuesque models in his time.

Unbelievable… Sally fumed silently. For years she had for her mum's benefit kept the peace with her father, even if it had been mostly by ignoring him. But today, for the first time in years, she had decided to challenge him and demand he cut out the lies and the girlfriend for the weekend and do the right thing by his wife. Instead, for once it seemed he might have been telling the truth. The new owner Delucca was here. Perhaps her dad did intend working the weekend…

But not if she could help it…

CHAPTER TWO

ZAC DELUCCA walked forward and briefly shook the hand Nigel Paxton held out to him. 'The pleasure is mine,' he said suavely, and, turning, shifted his attention to the stunning woman.

He studied her intently for a long moment. Her gaze was fixed on Paxton and never wavered. She did not even glance at Zac, and he was intrigued. Could this gorgeous woman actually be Paxton's lover? Or maybe, by the sound of the conversation he had overheard, a discarded lover? Both scenarios he found very hard to believe. Firstly, she was too young for Paxton, and secondly, any man who had such a female in his bed would be a fool to let her go. With a face and figure like hers she could take her pick of the male population and probably did, he concluded as he noted the banked-down fire in her ice-blue eyes that to a man with his expert knowledge of women denoted a passionate nature.

'Sorry to intrude. I was not aware you had company,' he continued, turning his attention back to the accountant—the possible thief, he reminded himself. 'You must introduce me to your charming friend, Paxton,' he commanded, and waited, his dark eyes once again roaming over the woman's lovely face and exquisite body.

Sally barely registered the stranger's smooth tones as her dad made the introduction.

'Oh, she is not my friend,' her father chuckled, and beamed down at her. He had got that right, she thought cynically. 'This is my daughter, Sally.'

She turned slightly and looked up, and up again, at a positive giant of a man—with black hair and black eyes, and no doubt a black heart, if his unashamed masculine scrutiny of her body was anything to go by.

'Sally… May I call you Sally?' he asked politely, then went on, 'You are a beautiful young woman. Your father must be a very proud man.'

Why did she get the feeling there was an underlying cynicism in his tone? Not that she cared. Overblown words of flattery from a man with a sexually explicit invitation in the dark eyes that met hers did not impress her, and she refused to be intimidated. Her mother was her only concern, and she shrugged off the unfamiliar tremor that slid down her spine.

Straightening her slender shoulders, she held out her hand politely, and it was immediately engulfed in his much larger one. 'Nice to meet you,' she said flatly, and looked back at her father again. At the same time she attempted to slip her hand from Delucca's, but outrageously his thumb slowly stroked the length of her palm and her fingers before setting her free.

How predictable—another one like her dad, she thought bitterly.

Zac Delucca did not miss the flash of distaste in her brilliant blue eyes as he finally let go of her hand. Maybe caressing her palm had been a little juvenile, but he had been unable to resist the temptation to test the softness of her skin against his. For a moment he imagined the brush of every inch of her skin against his naked body, and had to fight to control the surge of arousal the thought induced.

He had definitely been too long without a woman, but now he knew it was not Lisa in Milan or any other woman he wanted. It was *this* woman he wanted, and he resolved to have her. He had no doubt he would succeed—he always did. It was simply a matter of negotiating the when and where, sooner rather than later, if his neglected libido had any say in the matter.

Her voice was low, and ever so slightly husky. Her brilliant blue eyes had been cool as she glanced up at him and swiftly back to her father. Never had a woman so instantly dismissed him. Usually *they* hung on to *his* hand… Yet this beauty had done it twice. Her indifference rankled, and he was all the more determined to make her aware of him…

He watched as her father introduced her to Raffe. She gave him an equally brief smile and turned back to her father yet again. But as she continued speaking, Zac sensed it was not so much that she was ignoring him, but that she was disappointed in her father for some reason. He noted the dark flush that stained the older man's face and he felt the tension between them.

Thinking fast, Sally spoke. 'I hope you don't mind, Mr Delucca,' she said without actually looking at the man, her hard blue eyes fixed on the reprobate that was her father. 'I called round to persuade my father to take me out to lunch. I am always telling him he works far too many hours. Isn't that right, Dad?' she prompted sweetly.

She did not want to reveal her mother's poor health to two virtual strangers, but she did need to get her dad by himself and extract a promise from him to go with her—if not tonight, then in the morning—to visit his wife. He was not fobbing her off again.

'Yes, but you are a little late. I had a sandwich earlier, as I am rather busy, and as you can see, Mr Delucca, the new owner of the company, has just arrived. I can't possibly take you to lunch today. Why don't you run along and I will ring you this evening?'

Next he would be patting her on the head, like the silly girl he thought she was, Sally thought angrily. She knew perfectly well he would not call her tonight. She knew every lying tone of his voice. But she also realised there was not much she could do about it. Not with two strange men standing listening to the exchange.

She stared at her father for a moment. He was smiling his usual charming smile, and yet there was something… She could hear the underlying strain in his voice. Whether it was because she had turned up or because of his new boss's presence she wasn't sure, but before she could decide she felt the brief brush of long male fingers on her forearm—apparently to get her attention. Involuntarily she tensed at the touch, and glanced up in surprise, her blue eyes clashing with black.

'Your father is right, Sally. He is going to be occupied for the rest of the day with Raffe, my accountant.'

For some inexplicable reason, Sally was paralysed by the dark eyes holding hers. They were not actually black, more a deep dark brown, with the faintest tinge of gold, and framed by the longest, thickest, sootiest eyelashes she had ever seen on a man.

What on earth was she doing? She tried to look away. Her mother was her only concern. But somehow her gaze lingered for a moment on his striking face. He wasn't handsome, she decided. At some time his nose had been broken, and had healed, leaving a slight bump, and above one arched black eyebrow there was an inch-long scar.

'But I could not possibly allow a young lady to lunch alone.'

Still studying his face, she was only half registering his words. Then with a jolt she swiftly lowered her gaze as she suddenly had a good idea where his statement was going. She glanced back up to see Delucca turn his attention to her dad.

'If you have no objection, Paxton, I will take your daughter to lunch. Raffe is more than capable of explaining the business we need to discuss, and I will see you later.'

Sally was too stunned by the turn of events to object immediately. Instead she glanced from one man to the other, and caught the hardest look pass between them, and then her father responded—at his jovial best.

'That is extremely kind of you, Mr Delucca. Problem solved. Sally, darling, Mr Delucca will take you to lunch—isn't that good of him?'

Sally looked from her dad up to the man towering over her, his dark eyes gleaming with sardonic amusement and something more she did not want to recognise. She shivered and did not bother to answer her dad. Good…? There was nothing good about this man. Of that she was sure…

Ten minutes later Sally was sitting in the back of a limousine, Zac Delucca seated beside her, on her way to a lunch she did not really want.

'Comfortable, Sally?'

'Fine,' she responded automatically. How the hell had this happened? she asked herself for the umpteenth time.

'The restaurant is about twenty minutes away—a favourite of mine when I am in London.'

'Fine,' she murmured, rerunning in her head the conversation in the office.

When she had finally found her voice she had tried to get

out of going to lunch with the excuse that she wasn't that hungry and she was sure Mr Delucca was far too busy to waste time with her.

Delucca had silkily stated that time was never wasted with a beautiful woman. She had noted the devilish humour in his dark eyes, and just known he was laughing at her. He was the kind of man who always won, and she had wanted to slap him.

He'd known that as well, she was sure.

Then there was her dad, who for some reason had seemed very keen for her to go out with the man. In fact, he had practically insisted. With the two of them ganging up on her, she'd never had a chance.

Still, how bad could it be? she asked herself. A quick meal and then she could leave Delucca at the restaurant and grab a cab home. She gazed out of the car window and idly wondered how they made the tinted glass that looked black from the outside of the car, but from the inside was clear, allowing her to see everything outside.

She felt the brush of a hard masculine thigh against her own and moved slightly. If Delucca was coming on to her he was wasting his time. She wasn't interested. She ignored the sudden warmth in her thigh…

Men did not interest her. Men in general did not figure large in her life, and with her father as an example it was hardly surprising. What with caring and worrying about her mother's health for most of her adult life—because her father certainly did not—she had never had the time for a boyfriend since she'd left school, even if she had wanted one. If her mother's doctor was right, she might soon have all the time in the world, and the knowledge made her want to weep. With sightless eyes she stared out of the window, a deep sigh escaping her.

Zac Delucca, for the first time in years, was stumped by a

woman. The woman at his side was barely aware of his existence. Her uninterested responses to any attempt at conversation were monosyllabic, and it irritated the hell out of him.

He had even resorted to allowing his thigh to brush against hers, and while it had done dangerous things to his libido she had dismissed the contact without a glance. He was definitely losing his touch, he thought, a wry grin twisting his firm lips.

'That was a big sigh. Is my company so boring?' He prompted sardonically.

The deep, dark tone of his voice reminded Sally where she was, and she turned her head to look at him. 'Not at all, Mr Delucca,' she replied coolly, and watched as he squared his impressively broad shoulders and casually stretched a long arm across the back of the seat behind her. Not touching, but somehow enclosing her. She drew in a shaky breath, not liking the unfamiliar weak sensation that he somehow aroused in her.

'Then please call me Zac,' he invited smoothly. Her face was a perfect social mask, but he had sensed her unease when he had moved closer. She was not as unaware of him as she appeared, and at last he had got her attention. 'I want there to be no formality between us, Sally,' he told her huskily.

In fact, he wanted nothing at all between them—not a stitch of clothing, just flesh on flesh. He had never felt so fiercely attracted to a woman in his life, and he watched her reaction as, unable to resist touching her, he allowed his long fingers to slide down and caress her shoulder.

She jumped like a scalded cat and shot back. 'I don't want anything at all between us.'

He could not prevent a chuckle as she verbalised his thought exactly, but he was pretty sure she was not thinking along the same lines as him.

'I'm glad you find me amusing,' she snapped, looking anything but amused. 'And take your hand off me.' She leant forward, shrugging her shoulder to dislodge his hand.

Zac let her, and settled back in the seat. Maybe he had made a mistake. Did he have the time to pursue her, and did he really want to? She was just another typical high-maintenance little rich girl, with her nose put out of joint because the doting father who kept her in comfort had refused to jump to her bidding.

The irony did not escape him. If Raffe's suspicions were correct, he had already paid for Sally Paxton's lifestyle without any of the benefits of keeping a beautiful woman.

He studied her for a long moment. She was incredibly lovely. Maybe he could make time. Her hands were folded in her lap, the soft swell of her breasts was just visible above the square-cut neckline of her dress, and her face was hauntingly beautiful but somehow sad. The end of an affair maybe… Easier for him if she was unattached…

'Not so amusing. More intriguing,' Zac finally responded, suddenly needing to know. 'Tell me—do you have a man in your life?'

Sally had heard the question countless times before. While she did not bother with men, quite a few bothered her, and she had developed a surefire way to cool their interest.

'No. Do you have a wife?' she retorted, glancing at him. He was still too close for her liking, his hard bicep touching her shoulder. Perhaps it wasn't deliberate—he was a big man, with an even bigger ego to match, she surmised, and put her plan into action. 'Because I never go out with married men.'

'No wife.' He smiled a hunter's smile, Sally thought. 'Nor do I want one,' he confirmed. Lifting one long finger, he swept a stray tendril of her hair around her ear and stroked down her cheek to tip her chin towards him. 'And no significant woman at the moment. So there isn't anything to prevent us getting together. I am a very generous lover, in bed and out. Trust me—I promise you will not be disappointed.'

The sheer arrogance of the man astounded Sally. She had only met him half an hour ago. Yet already he had told her he wasn't into commitment but was looking for an affair. Bottom line, she amended, he was looking for sex. Nothing more. Just like her dad.

She fought her instinctive reflex to knock his finger from her chin, and instead lifted wide blue eyes to his. They were dark and gleaming with masculine confidence. Well, not for long, she determined.

'Oh, I don't know, Zac,' she said huskily, and finally deliberately used his name. 'I am almost twenty-six, and I *do* want a husband—just not someone else's.' His finger fell from her chin. She caught the flicker of wariness in his dark eyes and wasn't surprised. Typical male reaction…

She gave him a wry smile. 'I too think it is good to be honest about one's intentions, as you so obviously are, Zac.' Sally doubted he noticed the underlying sarcasm in her tone. 'Therefore I feel I should do the same. Ideally, I would like to have three children, while I am young enough to enjoy them, so basically I do not have time to waste on an affair with you, even if I wanted to.'

The expression on his face was comical. From confident, ardent suitor to wary and outraged male in less than sixty seconds.

'I can assure you no woman has ever found an affair with me a waste of time,' he declared arrogantly, and she almost laughed out loud.

Unable to help herself, she expanded on the theme.

'If you say so.' She shrugged her shoulders. 'Then again, you must be—what? Thirty-six, seven…'

'Thirty-five,' he snapped.

He didn't like that, and Sally stifled a grin. 'Still, you're not getting any younger either. Maybe you will change your mind about marriage. You will certainly make someone a wonderful husband,' she complimented him, and was actually beginning to enjoy herself. He moved slightly, his arm no longer touching her shoulder, and for the first time since meeting him she actually gave him her whole attention.

She turned her back half against the window in order to face him, and deliberately let her big blue eyes roam slowly over him. His hair was silky black, with a tendency to curl, obviously controlled by superb styling. His eyes were heavy lidded, and at the moment narrowed, hiding his expression. His features were big: large nose, a wide mouth with perfectly chiselled lips, the bottom one slightly fuller, and a square jaw with a delightful indentation in his chin.

Actually, he was very attractive, Sally acknowledged. His shoulders were wide, his chest broad and his muscled thighs were stretching the fabric of his trousers, she noted as he moved further away and crossed the leg nearest to her over his other knee.

A student of body language would probably say that was a sign of rejection… Her ploy had worked, Sally thought. But to make sure, she added, 'You do have all the attributes to make a good husband—you're a fine figure of a man, fit and filthy rich.'

Zac had listened with growing disquiet as she spoke. The woman was after a husband—a rich husband. She was the same as all the rest of her species. Her saving grace, if one could call it that, was that at least she had put all her cards on the table up front.

Getting into anything with her would be a huge mistake, his inbuilt sense of survival screamed at him. But, when she had barely looked at him since they met, feeling her gorgeous blue eyes examining every inch of him had been the most erotic experience he had known in ages. Out of necessity he had crossed one leg over the other knee, to hide the wayward reaction of his body.

Thank the Lord the car was slowing down. In a minute they would be at the restaurant. A swift meal and a polite goodbye, and the fact he had trouble keeping his hands off this woman he would put down to his lengthy celibacy. His common sense was telling him this lady was dangerous to his peace of mind. Time to walk away.

He glanced at Sally. She was sitting back in the seat again, but her eyes were no longer cold. They were sparkling. He caught the glint of feline satisfaction in the blue depths, and her soft mouth quirked at the corners in a barely concealed grin.

The little devil! Had she been teasing him? Deliberately trying to put him off? He wasn't sure, and that was another first for him. Usually he could read a woman like a book, but this one had him tied in knots.

Warning bells rang loud and clear in his head, but he ignored them. He needed to delve a little deeper to discover what really made her tick. He had sensed her sadness and disappointment earlier—at her father or men in general he wasn't sure. She had done her best to ignore him, but then she had examined him with blatant female thoroughness and he knew she liked what she saw.

He was not a fool. He had felt her reaction the moment he had put a finger on her arm in the office, and again when he touched her cheek. She was not immune to him. But was she really looking for a wealthy husband?

Did he care? He had escaped that trap all his life, and he was smart enough to continue to do so. But he enjoyed a challenge, and Sally Paxton was definitely a challenge—one that he was determined to pursue and conquer.

She was an adult woman, not some shy young virgin, and he did not have to deprive his body of the pleasure of hers simply because she was looking for a husband, he concluded—to his own satisfaction.

CHAPTER THREE

THE restaurant was one of the best in London, and as they were led to their table by the *maître d'*, with Delucca's hand firmly in the small of her back, Sally began to wonder if she had been as clever as she thought at discouraging him.

Something had gone wrong. His hand was like a brand, burning through the raw silk of her dress, and if his reaction as he had helped her from the limousine was anything to go by she was in deep trouble. He had declared that now they knew where they stood they could get better acquainted over lunch.

He certainly didn't believe in wasting time, and she certainly did not want to get better acquainted with the man, she thought as her chair was held out for her and she sat down at the table. Briefly she looked around. There were more people leaving than arriving, and she glanced at the slim gold watch on her wrist. Not surprising, as it was two in the afternoon.

Suddenly, she was tired. She had been working all week, helping set up the latest exhibition to be staged at the museum. This morning the opening for the press and dignitaries had taken place, and she had attended at the request of her boss to answer any questions about the historical provenance of the exhibits. Usually she went to work in neat skirts and tops, but today she had dressed more smartly for the occasion. For months now she had been researching the history of the different exhibits, some of which had been brought up from the vast storage cellars and never been shown before.

Her boss knew of her mum's condition and had kindly allowed her to slip away at one o'clock. Almost two years of faithfully visiting her mother every weekend plus holidays, not to mention the constant worry, had taken their toll and she felt completely washed out.

The last thing she needed was to fight off the attentions of a predatory male. What she really needed was her bed…alone….

'Madam?'

She looked up. 'Sorry,' she murmured to the hovering *maître d'*, and took the menu.

'Perhaps you would prefer I order for you?'

There it was, that deep accented voice again, intruding on her thoughts. Reluctantly, Sally glanced across the table at her companion. For a moment their eyes met, and she recognised the challenging gleam in the depths of his before glancing down at the menu in her hand.

He was sitting there, all arrogant, powerful male, and she was about to refuse when she thought, why bother? The quicker he ordered, the quicker they ate, and the quicker she could get away from his disturbing presence. Because, being brutally honest, she recognised he *did* disturb her, in a way she had never felt before. But then he probably had the same effect on every woman on the planet. He was one hundred percent macho male, and then some…

No wonder he wasn't into commitment. Why would he settle for one woman when he had the pick of the best, according to the article she had read about him. It had extolled his brilliant business acumen and ended mentioning his preference for model girlfriends.

She certainly wasn't in his league, and nor did she want to be, she concluded firmly.

'Fine,' she said, and handed the menu back to the *maître d'*, and let her hand drop on the table, her fingers idly playing with a fork. She wasn't hungry—what did it matter what the man ordered?

'They do a very good steak here, and I can recommend the sea bass, but everything they serve is excellent.'

'The fish will be fine.'

'Fine,' Zac drawled with biting sarcasm. She was back to uninterested again. Grim-faced, he relayed the order to the *maître d'*, including a bottle of rather good wine. But inside he was seething.

Fine, she agreed when he mentioned the wine, without even looking at him. He had seen her glance at her watch as they arrived. He had never known any woman to be interested in the time when with him. Now she was sitting there, head bent, fiddling with a fork. Nobody ignored him—and certainly not a woman whose father had embezzled money out of a business of his. No matter how beautiful she was.

'Tell me, Sally, what do you do when you are not pressuring your father to take you to lunch?' he began silkily. 'Do you fill your days with shopping and visiting the beautician? Not that you need to…' He reached across and caught her hand in his, turning it over to examine the smooth palm. 'Does this soft hand actually do any work, or does Daddy keep you?'

Sally's head shot up as a tingling sensation snaked through her arm, and swiftly she pulled her hand free. Suddenly, she was intensely aware of Zac Delucca, in more ways than one. She was intelligent enough to know when she had been insulted. How typical of a super-rich tycoon like him to automatically think that simply because she had one Friday afternoon free her father supported her financially. Well, she was damned if she was going enlighten him. Let him keep his sexist attitude—she didn't care…

'I do shop—doesn't everyone?' she said nonchalantly. It was the truth. 'And I visit the hairdresser sometimes.' Again it was the truth. 'The rest of the time I read a lot.' Also the truth.

The food and wine arrived, interrupting the exchange, and Sally was grateful. She really wasn't up to sparring with the man any more. She had a feeling he was far too intelligent to be deceived by anything anyone said for long.

Zac filled her wine glass, although she had refused a drink. He insisted she try it. He offered her a piece of his steak on his fork, and she was so surprised by the intimacy of the gesture she actually took it.

He asked what her favourite film was. She said *Casablanca*, and he told her she was a hopeless romantic, then added that if he had been in Humphrey Bogart's position he would have taken the woman and run, which made her smile but somehow did not surprise her… His favourite film was *Cape Fear*, which she did find odd—until they got around to discussing books.

She told him she liked to read history and biographies, as well as being partial to the occasional murder story. And she discovered he spent most of his time reading financial journals and reports, but he did confess to reading the occasional thriller when he had time. Which figured, given *Cape Fear* was his first choice of film.

Sally sat back in her chair, replacing her knife and fork on the plate, surprised to note she had emptied her plate without realising. Against all expectations the lunch had been quite pleasant. Zac was a witty conversationalist, and he had made her smile—quite an accomplishment in her present state of mind.

She refused Zac's suggestion of a dessert and agreed to a coffee. He placed the order with the waiter, and Sally glanced around the restaurant again. The furnishings were elegant, the staff discreet, and it was obviously very expensive. Luckily, she was dressed for the occasion—not that she had expected to be here. The clientele were mostly wealthy, high-powered business people, she surmised. Of the few that were left she recognised a famous female presenter from the television and a well-known comedian.

'Sally Salmacis, as I live and breathe,' a voice called out.

Sally's eyes widened, and she pushed back her chair and leapt to her feet as six feet of shockingly ginger-haired male came striding towards her.

'Algernon!' she laughed.

Blue eyes met blue, and they grinned at each other, sharing a long-standing joke. Then she was swept up in a bear hug and kissed briefly on the lips, before being held at arm's length.

'Let me look at you. Gosh, you are more gorgeous than ever, Sally. How long has it been since I saw you? Two, three years?'

'About that,' she agreed. 'But what are you doing here?' she asked. 'I thought you were still collecting butterflies in the Amazon. I had visions of you being eaten alive by mosquitoes.'

'Yes, well, not quite—but not far off. You know me. I never could stand the heat.'

'Hardly surprising.' She arched one delicate eyebrow. 'I did warn you, Al.' His complexion, if anything, was even fairer than hers.

They had met at primary school, two redheads with unusual names, and had naturally gravitated towards each other as protection against the bullies. Al was the only person who dared to use her given name. She had demanded even her parents must call her Sally after her first year at school, and

Algernon had done the same, demanding his parents call him Al. As teenagers they had planned on taking a year off after university to go around the world together, starting with South America—Al for the butterflies, and Sally to see the ruins of Machu Picchu. Her mum's illness had put an end to Sally's dream, but she still lived with the faint hope that she would do it one day.

'So what are you up to?' she queried, delighted to see him again.

'Working in the family firm with Dad. We had just finished lunch, and I was following him out when I spotted you. But what about you? Still studying the Ancients?' he prompted with a grin.

'Yes.' She grinned back.

'I have to dash, but give me your new number. I tried your old with no joy.' He took his cell phone out of his pocket and entered the number as Sally told him.

Zac Delucca had seen and heard enough. The telephone number was the final straw. For a woman with no man in her life, this guy, if not now, obviously had been. He had never seen Sally so animated—certainly not with him. When he had heard the younger man speak to her, then seen him take her in his arms and kiss her, he had been blinded by a red tide of sheer male jealousy—not an emotion he was familiar with, and it had stunned him for a moment. But not any more…

'Sally, darling.' He rose to his feet and crossed to her side. 'You must introduce me to your friend,' he demanded, fixing the young man with a gimlet-eyed stare.

Suddenly remembering where she was and who she was with, Sally swiftly made the introduction. She saw Al flinch as Zac shook his hand. The man was demonstrating his superior strength like a rutting bull, she though disgustedly. And where did he get off, calling her darling?

Al, ever the gentleman, responded politely. 'Pleased to meet you Mr Delucca. A shame our meeting has to be so brief.' He gave Sally an apologetic glance. 'Sorry, Sally, I can't stay and talk. You know Dad, he will be waiting outside. champing at the bit to get back to work. I'm going to a house party this weekend, but I will call you next week and we can have dinner and catch up. What do you say?'

It took a brave man to stand up to Delucca, but Al refused to be intimidated and Sally gave her old friend a gentle smile.

'Yes, that would be lovely,' she said, and watched him walk out.

She resumed her seat as the waiter arrived with their coffee, her eyes misty with memories of a happier time. Al had never teased her about the stutter she had developed as a child after the death of her grandmother, who had lived with them. He had been her staunch defender and best friend all through her school years. He had attended every birthday party she had, and been a frequent visitor to her home. And she had spent countless summer days playing around the swimming pool at his home, a magnificent thirties-style Art Deco house situated in Sandbanks, overlooking Poole Harbour.

He had been the first boy to kiss her, and he had been as shy as her. The sex side of things had not progressed much further than a few tentative gropes which had made them giggle, and they'd realised they were more brother and sister than lovers.

They had drifted apart since leaving school. She had gone to university in Exeter, while Al had gone to Oxford to study botany, much against his father's wishes. They had kept in touch, and met up in the holidays occasionally, but with her mum's illness, gradually their only contact had become the occasional telephone call or chance meeting, like today.

The last time she had seen him had been when they had bumped into each other in Bournemouth and gone for a drink. Al had been all fired up with the Amazon trip he was about to embark on, and had asked Sally to go with him. She had reluctantly refused, explaining that her mum was in the clear, but that she, Sally, was about to start a great new job in London.

It seemed a lifetime ago now…

'Very touching.' A deep, mocking voice cut into her memories. 'Al is an old friend, I take it? Or should I say lover?'

She looked across at Zac, caught the latent anger in his eyes, and realised that beneath the cool, sophisticated exterior he was not pleased. Well, she was not a happy bunny either. She had not wanted to go to lunch with the man in the first place.

'Say what you like. It is no business of yours.'

'It is my business. When I take a lady out to lunch I expect her to behave like a lady, not leap up into another man's arms—a man who yells her name, *Sally!*—and when he demands "*Sal my kiss*" proceeds to kiss him.'

Sally was puzzled for a moment, then her blue eyes widened in understanding. Her lips twitched and, unable to help herself, she burst out laughing. Of all the nicknames she had been called at school—*salami*, or simply *sausage* being the favourites—no one had ever put *that* interpretation on her birth name.

'I'm glad you found it amusing because I didn't.' His accent had thickened and the anger in the black eyes that blazed into hers was all too real.

If that was what he had thought, in a way she could see his point, and she decided to tell him the truth.

'You were mistaken. Al did not ask me for a kiss.' She grinned. 'My first name is not Sally but Salmacis.' She gave him the proper pronunciation, a syllable at a time. *'Sal-ma-sis.'* And saw disbelief, puzzlement and finally curiosity in his dark eyes.

Zac didn't know whether to believe her. Salmacis was not a name he had ever heard in any language, and he knew half a dozen. If it was an excuse it was a hell of a good one. Yet she looked sincere, and English was not his first language, he could have been mistaken.

'Salmacis.' He rolled the name off his tongue and rather liked it. 'What kind of name is that?'

'It is Greek. When my mum was pregnant with me she spent the last four months of her pregnancy on bedrest. She got hooked on reading Greek mythology.'

Then Sally told him the legend. 'Apparently Salmacis was the nymph of a fountain near Halicarnassus in Asia Minor. She became one with the youth Hermaphroditos. And before you ask, no, I am not a hermaphrodite—but I believe that is the origin of the word.'

'It never entered my head.' Zac chuckled. 'What possessed your mother to give you such a peculiar though rather lovely name?' he demanded, still smiling broadly. 'You have to admit it is extremely unusual.'

For a moment Sally was stunned, her heart racing out of control as she met his enquiring gaze. His dark eyes danced with golden lights, his hard face was transformed into a softer, younger version by the brilliance of his smile, and she could not help smiling back at him.

'I think it was the last fable she read before going into labour, and unfortunately for me it stuck in her mind,' she said wryly.

'No, not unfortunate. You are far too exotic—no, that isn't the word.' Zac shook his dark head, searching his brain for the English equivalent of what he wanted to say. 'Your beauty is too unique. No—too mystical for a Sally,' he declared with satisfaction. 'Salmacis suits you much better.' He saw the humour in her expressive eyes. How had he ever thought they were cold?

'I much prefer Sally—in fact, I insist on it. So be warned—call me Salmacis and I will ignore you.'

'Okay—Sally,' he conceded, and added, 'But I am a little surprised she persuaded your father to agree to such an unusual name. Accountants are not known for their flights of fancy.'

The sparkle vanished from her eyes like a light being switched off, to be replaced with a familiar blank look.

'She didn't have to. My dad married Mum because he got her pregnant when she was eighteen and he was thirty-five,' Sally told Zac. It was the truth. Exhaustion from her hectic work schedule and from worrying about her mother overtook her, and she could not be bothered to dissemble.

'Apparently, he was so upset when the doctor told him she would not have any more children, no future son, he didn't much care what name I was given.'

Appalled by Sally's matter-of-fact revelation, Zac realised her father's attitude must have hurt her. To actually let the child know how he'd felt was a disgraceful thing to do. But then Nigel Paxton was almost certainly a thief and an unfaithful husband: sensitivity was obviously not his strong point.

'I think we should leave now.' Her voice intruded on his thoughts. 'We are the only couple left.'

Zac had not noticed, but glancing around the room he saw she was right.

When was the last time a woman had held his attention to the exclusion of everything else around him? he asked himself. Never. The realisation shocked him rigid. In that moment he determined there was no way he was going to let it happen again. Sally was as dangerous as she was beautiful, and she was not for him…

'Finish your coffee and we will go,' he agreed, and beckoned the *maître d'*. He handed him a credit card and a bundle of notes for a tip, and after draining his coffee cup stood up.

The meal had turned out okay, despite its difficult start, and he had learnt a lot about Salmacis—too much, he thought wryly. From what he had overheard earlier, Sally obviously knew about her father's infidelity and resented the fact he had more time for a girlfriend than he had for her. Hence turning up at the office today and demanding her father lunch with her.

Money obviously was not enough for the lovely Salmacis; she was the type who craved attention from the men in her life. Given the reaction of her father to her name, he could understand why she behaved the way she did. But clinging, needy women did not appeal to him, he rationalised, confirming his decision not to see her again.

He glanced down at her. She looked fragile and, act or not, he couldn't prevent himself from slipping an arm around her waist as he led her out of the restaurant. She made no attempt to pull away, another first, but leant against him as they walked to where the limo was parked a few yards away.

He let the chauffeur help her inside.

She was magic to hold, he thought ruefully as he slipped into the back seat beside her, but every male instinct he possessed told him this was one woman he was going to pass on—for his own preservation.

'Where would you like us to drop you off?' he asked. 'Bond Street? Harrods?' he suggested, with an edge of cynicism in his tone.

'Harrods is fine.'

He'd thought as much. A bit of retail therapy was all any woman needed to keep her happy.

She looked up at him with soft blue eyes, and he could not resist. He wrapped an arm around her waist and slid his hand through the silken tumble of her hair to tip up her face.

'What are you doing?' she murmured.

'Oh, I think you know,' he drawled huskily, and covered her lush lips with his own.

He could not let her go without kissing and tasting her just once, he told himself…

CHAPTER FOUR

STARTLED out of her lethargy as a strong arm slipped around her waist, Sally arched back in instinctive denial of the intimacy he was seeking. She glanced up at his darkly attractive face and recognised the sensual intent in his eyes. She was stunned by the sudden flash of awareness that heated her whole body. He was going to kiss her…

Her pulse began to race, and as his dark head bent she could almost feel the virile power emanating from his mighty frame. For a second she was tempted to abandon herself to what he was offering. But she knew it would be a disastrous mistake. She had no time in her life for an affair with Zac or any other man, even if she wanted one. She put her hands up to push him away, but too late…

Zac's warm mouth claimed hers with a soft sensuality that totally confused and captivated her. She closed her eyes, her lips involuntarily parting to accept the subtle intrusion of his tongue as he deepened the kiss with a skilful, seductive passion that blew all thought of resistance from her mind.

Sally had never experienced a kiss like it. Dizzy with a sensual excitement she had never known before, she let her mouth cling to his, and eagerly, if a little inexpertly, returned the passion. Suddenly he broke the kiss, and tiny moans of regret escaped her, quickly followed by a gasp of pleasure as he trailed kisses down her throat and lower, to trace with his tongue the gentle curve of her breasts revealed by the neckline of her dress.

His hand dropped to slip beneath the fabric, long fingers edging beneath the delicate lace of her bra to cup her naked breast, a thumb teasing the burgeoning tip to send rivers of unbelievable sensation flowing through her body. His mouth returned to hers, and she was enthralled by his taste, his touch, drowning in the sea of erotic pleasure his kisses and caresses evoked. She felt the heat of his palm on her bare leg, his hand stroking up her thigh, and she trembled, the blood pulsing thick and fast through her veins. She was ablaze with sensuous hunger, with a need she didn't understand but knew she wanted fulfilled badly.

So this was what she had been missing—this was the reason people loved sex, she thought wonderingly, and curved her hand around his neck to mesh her fingers in the silken hair of his head.

Abruptly he pulled away, and without his support Sally flopped back against the seat. Lost in a haze of sexual arousal, she murmured, 'What happened?'

'We have arrived at your destination. Harrods.'

His deep accented voice speared like an icicle through the emotional fog clouding her brain. She was mortified. She had not noticed the car had stopped. She glanced down and, horrified, adjusted the bodice of her dress. She looked out of the window—anywhere but at the man next to her. Finally, as the silence lengthened, reluctantly she looked back at Zac Delucca.

He was watching her, his eyes as dark as night, the remnants of desire swirling in the liquid depths.

'Shame, I know, Sally.' His lips quirked at the corners in

the beginnings of a smile. 'But we can continue this later. Have dinner with me tonight.'

'No,' she said abruptly. Sally had never felt so embarrassed and ashamed in her life. Noting her skirt had hitched up around her thighs, she swiftly smoothed it down with trembling hands. Never in all her life had a man kissed and touched her so intimately. And she couldn't understand what had come over her.

'Tomorrow night, then,' he prompted.

How the hell had it happened? Sally asked herself for the second time today in the luxury of his limousine. This time it was much worse, and it was Zac Delucca's fault again. When he had spoken of his skills as a lover she had never dreamt he meant to try and prove his statement with such explicit speed that the defensive wall she had built around herself would crumble with just one kiss…

'Sorry, no. I am going away for the weekend.'

'Cancel and spent the weekend with me,' he demanded arrogantly.

Staring at him, her blue eyes widening, Sally unconsciously ran the tip of her tongue over her slightly swollen lips, where the taste of Zac still lingered. It would be so easy to say yes to a weekend of mindless pleasure instead of sadness, and suddenly she was afraid of the speed with which he had turned her life upside down. Then she realised he had been nowhere near as affected by the passionate interlude as she had been, and, given the churning in her stomach, still was!

He probably seduced women in his limo on a regular basis, and she had very nearly been his latest conquest…

She thought of her mother, who really needed her, as opposed to a man like Delucca, who certainly did not—except in the shallowest way. Zac was undoubtedly a formidable man, used to getting whatever and whoever he wanted, and he was her father's new boss.

But then again, Sally thought, she didn't give a fig for her father. If she offended his boss, so what?

'That's an outrageous suggestion and not one I would ever consider,' she said bluntly. 'And I promised my mother.'

'Loyalty to your mother is an admirable trait. We can make it dinner on Monday night.'

Not only was he arrogant, he was also pig-headed, and she did not bother to reply as, to her relief, the chauffeur opened the car door. She needed to get as far away from Zac Delucca as she could, and, swinging her legs out of the car, she stood up. She hesitated and glanced back at Zac. Good manners were ingrained in her.

'Thank you for lunch, Mr Delucca, and the lift,' she said formally. 'Goodbye.' And, turning, she hurried along the street.

She did not go into the store, Zac noted as he watched her walk along the pavement. Her rear view was as enticing as the rest of her, and the reason he had eschewed good manners and not helped her out of the limousine was still causing him a problem.

'Drive on,' he ordered the chauffeur. Sally—or Salmacis, he smiled to himself—intrigued and also confused him.

By nature he was a decisive man. Once he decided on a course of action in both the business world and his private life he never changed his mind. Yet a certain red-haired woman had him changing his mind over and over again.

Needy was a no-no; husband-hunting was a no-no; idle little rich girl was a no-no—and he did not believe for a minute that she was spending the weekend with her mother. Partying was more her style, if the slight violet shadows under her beautiful eyes were anything to go by. He would bet on it… She wasn't his usual type at all.

Yet, against all that, after deciding to kiss her goodbye he had changed his mind again.

As soon as their lips had met she had caught fire in his arms, melting against him, running her fingers through his hair, inflaming him further. She was the most incredibly responsive woman he had ever met, and there was no way he was walking away.

He strolled back into Paxton's office and glanced at Raffe, who shook his head slightly. So Paxton did not know yet they were on to him. Good.

'Your daughter and I had a pleasant lunch, Paxton. She asked to be dropped off at Harrods, though I noticed she didn't go in the store.'

'You know what young women are like—always changing their minds,' he said with an ingratiating smile. 'I gave her a studio apartment in Kensington and it is not far from Harrods. She probably decided to walk home.'

Zac knew enough about property in London to know that an apartment in the Royal Borough of Kensington did not come cheap. Sally was a lucky girl, and Paxton was looking guiltier by the minute.

Sally drove into the car park of the nursing home and cut the engine. She glanced up at the mellow stone, half covered by the rampant scarlet Virginia creeper. The sun was shinning, it was a glorious June day, and yet she felt none of the joy such a beautiful day should bring. For a moment she folded her arms across the steering wheel and let her head drop. She had to smile for her mother, even though her heart felt like lead in her chest. It was hard…so very hard… Even more so now she knew the doctor's prognosis…

As she had guessed, her father had not rung her last night, and she had had no luck in getting in touch with him until this morning, when he'd informed her that because Delucca was there he could not possibly get away this weekend.

For once Sally believed him. After yesterday's lunch with the man, she knew no one could refuse him—herself included. She still cringed when she thought of the way she had reacted to his kiss and, worse, the way she had spent a restless night trying to banish him from her mind—without much success.

Lifting her head, she drew in a deep, steadying breath and brushed a stray drop of moisture from her eye. At least today she would not have to lie to her mother. Her dad *was* tied up with business.

Five minutes later, forcing a smile to her face, Sally breezed into her mother's room with a cheerful hello.

She was sitting in her wheelchair, an expectant smile on her face—a still lovely face, although now it was deeply lined with pain. Her hair was no longer the soft red Sally remembered. After her chemo it had grown back a mousy brown, and was now streaked with grey.

Yet her mum had not given up, Sally thought as she walked towards her. She had still applied her make-up—and even if the foundation was a bit streaky and the lipstick not perfect she had tried… Probably because she expected her husband. But she was destined to be disappointed yet again.

Sally swallowed the lump that formed in her throat, and dropped a soft kiss on her lined cheek.

The nurse had dressed her mum in the pretty summer frock Sally had bought for her the week before. She always brought a gift when she visited—sometimes simply a box of chocolates.

This week she had book on Greek Mythology she had found in a secondhand bookstore. It was a real find as it was a very old copy, printed in 1850, with wonderful illustrations.

She gave her mum the book, and she was delighted, but her smile faded a little when Sally told her her husband was not coming. Sally tried to make it better by explaining about his new boss, saying that she had actually met him at her dad's office, and that seemed to satisfy her.

Later Sally suggested they take a walk in the garden as it was such a perfect afternoon. Her mum agreed, and she spent a pleasant hour pushing the wheelchair around the extensive grounds.

Sally sighed as she entered the studio apartment gifted to her by her parents and closed the door behind her. She sagged against it. It had been another beautiful summer day, but she felt hot, sticky and tired.

The weekend had been bittersweet. She had not left her mum until late last night. The outing in the garden had tired her, and Sally had helped the nurse put her to bed and then sat with her for the rest of the afternoon and Saturday evening. She had done the same on Sunday, and it had been after midnight when she'd finally arrived back in London, exhausted. But worry over her mother and the images of a tall dark man had fractured her sleep, and she had had to drag herself out of bed this morning to go to work.

She felt totally worn out, both mentally and physically, and for a moment hadn't the strength to move. Shoulders slumped, she glanced around the room with jaundiced eyes. She hated the place.

It had been her father's studio apartment for years, but after her mum's accident he had sold the family home in

Bournemouth and bought a three-bedroomed apartment in fashionable Notting Hill.

How he had persuaded her mother to sell the house in Bournemouth—the house her mum had inherited from her parents—Sally had had no idea, but she had reluctantly agreed to go and see the new apartment, supposedly the new family home. It was a top-floor conversion of a large Georgian house, and she'd swiftly realised it was unsuitable for a wheelchair—which to her mind simply confirmed that her father had no intention of ever living with his wife again.

His excuse for selling the house was the cost of keeping his wife in the nursing home. As it was he who had put her there, it did not cut much ice with Sally, but she could not deny he did pay the fees.

Then, to her dismay, she had found herself the recipient of his studio apartment. Her mother had been delighted, and told her it was time she had a place of her own. When she'd tried to refuse her mother had insisted, and told her to listen to her father—he was the accountant, and the property was a good investment. Apparently, giving the studio to Sally was a great way of avoiding death duties in the future!

Sally had then realised how he had persuaded her mum to sell, and it had confirmed in her mind what a greedy low-life he really was…

She had reluctantly moved in ten months ago, when the lease on her old apartment ran out, mainly because her mother had kept asking her when she was going to move.

But to Sally this apartment didn't feel like her home, and she knew it never could—because in her head she would always think of it as her dad's sleazy love-nest. A fact that had been brought home to her the first week she'd moved in, when she'd fielded quite a few calls from present and previously discarded mistresses. She had changed the telephone number, but she could not change the fact that a string of women other than his wife had shared the king-size bed.

As a studio apartment it was a superior example, with natural wooden floors, and it was larger than most. The kitchen and bathroom were off the small entrance hall, separate from the main living area which was split-level, with a mini-staircase leading to the bedroom area. She had thrown out every piece of furniture her father had left, including his king-size bed and the mirror over it, and bought a queen-size bed for herself.

She had redecorated completely, in neutral tones, and bought the minimum of new furniture: a sofa, an occasional table, and a television for the living area. In the bedroom she had fitted interlocking beechwood units along one wall, which included drawers and shelves where she could house her books, plus a desktop that stretched the length of one unit. It held her computer and doubled as a dressing table. The other wall had a built-in wardrobe with mirrored doors. The bed had a beechwood headboard, and all her bedlinen was plain white—easily interchangeable. She didn't need anything else, and she probably would not be there much longer.

She had mentioned to her mother a month ago that she was thinking of trying to sell the studio, telling her she would really prefer a separate bedroom. Her mum had said that would be nice, and the subject had not been mentioned again. But Sally had placed it with a local estate agent the next Monday. She had stipulated that she wanted no sign outside, as she was at work all day and away every weekend and a sign tended to encourage burglars.

She need not have bothered, as she no longer cared whether she sold it or not. Since hearing the doctor's prognosis for her mother last week she'd recognised there were a lot worse things in life than living in an apartment one didn't like.

She straightened up and headed for the kitchen, dropping her purse on the sofa on the way. A cup of coffee, a sandwich and a shower, in that order, and then bed.

Checking the water level in the kettle, she switched it on, and, opening a cupboard, reached for a jar of instant coffee just as the wall-mounted telephone rang.

Her heart leapt in panic. It must be the nursing home about her mother, was her first thought, and, lifting the receiver from the rest, she said quickly, 'Sally here—what is it?'

'Not what—who,' a deep voice corrected her with a chuckle, before continuing, unnecessarily identifying himself. 'Zac.' And she nearly dropped the phone.

'How did you get my number?' she demanded.

'Easy. Your father told me you lived in Kensington. I wasn't so obvious as to ask him for your number, but you *are* in the telephone book.'

Of course she was. Hadn't she changed the number and registered it under her own name? 'You looked through all the Paxtons in the book? You must have had to ring dozens to find me.' She couldn't believe a man of his wealth and stature would go to so much trouble.

'No. Surprisingly there are only a few, and yours was the first number I tried. I am just naturally lucky, Sally.'

He was naturally arrogant as well—and what was she doing, bothering to talk to him?

'Now, about tonight,' he continued. 'I've booked a table for eight.' He mentioned a famous Mayfair restaurant.

'Wait a damn minute,' Sally cut in angrily. 'I never agreed to go out to dinner with you. So thanks, but no thanks, I am staying in to wash my hair,' she ended sarcastically, and hung up.

Her heart pounded in her chest, and she pulled in some deep breaths to control the anger and—if she was honest—the excitement the sound of his deep-toned voice aroused so easily.

The kettle boiled, and she made a cup of coffee with a hand that was not quite steady. What was happening to her? Exhaustion—that was the problem. It had probably lowered her immune system and sent her emotions haywire. Satisfied with the explanation, she made a cheese sandwich with stale bread, but ate most of it anyway and drank her coffee.

She crossed to the bed area, slipping out of her skirt, and she hung it in the closet and headed for the bathroom. She stripped naked, and, dropping her blouse, bra and briefs into the wash basket, turned the shower on to warm. She picked up a bottle of shampoo from the vanity unit and stepped under the soothing spray.

She washed her hair and then, placing the shampoo on the chrome rack, she let her head fall back. She closed her eyes and let the water wash away the grime and hopefully the grimness of the weekend.

Her mother had been pleased to see her, and had declared she was perfectly content, but Sally knew different. No matter how good the nursing home, how great the staff were or how beautiful the gardens, it was still a nursing home. The patients were there out of necessity, because they needed constant care. She doubted anyone, given a choice, would choose it over their own home.

She shrugged off her morbid thoughts, and, switching off the shower, grabbed a large fluffy towel from the towel rail and rubbed her body dry. She towel-dried her hair, deciding not to bother with the hairdryer, and letting it hang down her back to dry naturally. She cleaned her teeth at the basin, and, taking her towelling robe off the hook on the back of the bathroom door, she slipped it on, tying the sash firmly around her waist.

The telephone rang as she walked back into the living room. Surely not Delucca again? Moving to the kitchen, she answered it with a curt, 'Yes?'

'My. Sally, who has rattled your cage?' an old familiar voice demanded.

'Al!' She laughed. 'I thought it was someone else.'

'Not the guy you were having lunch with, I hope?'

'Got it in one.'

'Sally, be careful. I mentioned I had met Delucca to my dad. According to him the man is not the type to get involved with. Apparently, he is an extremely powerful man, admired by a few, but feared by most. He is known as the takeover king and he's a brilliantly astute businessman. Delucca Holdings is one of the few companies that the recession has barely affected—mainly because he is ruthless at closing down failing companies and selling off their assets. But he's equally as clever at retaining and expanding the profitable ones. He owns mines in South America and Australia, a couple of oil companies, land and a lot more besides. As my dad pointed out, all tangible assets that, unlike stocks and shares, in the long term can't fail. As for his private life, not much is known about him except that he has dated quite a few top models.'

'I know all that—and don't worry. I refused his offer of dinner. The lunch was a one-off, never to be repeated.'

'Great. So have dinner with *me* tomorrow night? I have a table booked for nine at the new *in* place, but the girl I had high hopes of turned me down.'

'That is a back-handed invite if ever I heard one.' She laughed, but agreed, and after ten minutes of talking to Al she felt revived and almost human again.

She switched on the television, and an hour later was curled up on the sofa, watching the ending of her favourite crime programme and contemplating going to bed, when the doorbell rang.

The building had a concierge, and the intercom had not rung to announce anyone's arrival, so it had to be Miss Telford from across the hall, Sally guessed. She had met her the first week she had moved in, when the elderly spinster had locked herself out. Since then, at Miss Telford's request, Sally had kept a spare set of keys for her apartment, just in case she did it again—which she did quite frequently…

Standing up and stretching, Sally switched off the television and padded barefoot across the floor to open the door.

'Forgotten the key…? You!' The surprised exclamation left her lips before she could prevent it.

Sally was struck dumb, her incredulous gaze sweeping over the man before her. Zac Delucca was standing in the doorway, with what looked like a large cooler box in one hand and a bunch of roses in the other.

'An honest woman—you actually were washing your hair,' he drawled, eyeing the damp tousled curls falling around her shoulders. 'But washing your hair or not, Sally, I figured you still need to eat. These are for you.' He held out the roses and she took them, too shocked to refuse, and then, brushing past her, he strolled into her apartment. 'Nice place,' he opined, and set the box on the occasional table before turning round to look at her.

Still speechless, Sally let her eyes roam in helpless admiration over his impressive form. Gone was the designer suit. In its place he was wearing a white cotton shirt, and denim jeans that hung low on his lean hips and faithfully moulded his strong thighs and long legs. The designer label was a discreet signature on a side pocket.

Involuntarily her gaze was drawn back to his broad muscular chest, outlined by the obviously tailor-made shirt, the first few buttons of which were unfastened, revealing the strong column of his throat and a tantalising glimpse of black chest hair. Sally gulped, and for a moment had an overwhelming urge to run her fingers through the curling body hair. She took a step forward, the basic animal magnetism of the man, drawing her like a moth to a flame…

But the door slamming shut behind her brought her to her senses, and she ruthlessly squashed the impulse and found her voice.

'The doorman never called, so how the hell did you get in?' she demanded, and lifted her eyes to his face; now he was grinning broadly, and looked even more devastatingly attractive, Sally thought helplessly.

'I told him you were my lover and it was our one month anniversary. I said I wanted to surprise you with champagne and roses and an intimate dinner for two. The man is clearly a romantic at heart—he could not refuse. Plus the tip helped,' he added cynically.

There it was again. No one ever refused Zac Delucca. And Sally had a sinking sensation that if she was not very careful she might fall into that category too.

She went on the attack. 'Then the man is going to lose his job, because I did not invite you here. I want you to leave now—get out or I will throw you out…' She raised angry blue eyes to his and caught a golden flame of desire in the dark depths so fierce she imagined she felt the heat—before his attention was diverted from her face…

CHAPTER FIVE

LOOKING at Zac, towering over her Sally had the wild desire to laugh at her own audacity in threatening to eject him. But as the silence lengthened a desire of a different kind whipped any thought of laughter from her mind. She saw he was scrutinising her slender body with an intensity that made her feel as if he was stripping her naked.

Suddenly, tension thickened the air between them, and it became hard for Sally to breathe. She felt a ripple of heat run through her, and it had nothing to do with the heat of the day.

Zac seemed to fill the small studio with his presence, and however unwillingly she was being drawn towards him despite all her best efforts to deny the fact. His dark eyes lingered on the open lapels of her robe, and jerkily she pulled the belt tighter, remembering she actually was naked underneath…

Embarrassment and the hot flush of arousal combined to make a tide of pink stain her pale face.

He stared at her for a long moment, and she wished she had done something with her hair instead of leaving it to dry in a mess of curls—ridiculous, she knew, but he had that effect on her.

'You would not cost the man his job. I know you are not that mean-spirited, Sally,' he said with certainty. He was right, damn him. 'As for throwing me out—you haven't a chance.

But you are welcome to try.' And he walked towards her, throwing his arms wide. 'This should be interesting,' he prompted and grinned at her. Her heart missed a beat at the devilish charm of his expression. 'Give it your best shot.'

He was looming over her like some great monolith, legs slightly splayed, arms outstretched. She knew he was laughing at her, but still she had an incredible urge to walk into his arms.

'Very funny,' she snapped, and looked away. She knew when she was beaten. But as she stepped to one side an imp of mischief made her smack his forearm with the bunch of roses she still held in her hand. As a tension reliever it worked…

'That hurt!' she heard him yelp, and this time she did laugh as she dashed to the kitchen to put the somewhat battered roses in water.

She took a vase from the cupboard where she kept her glasswear, and, filling it with water, put the roses in one at a time. They were magnificent blooms—or had been, she amended, before they had met the strength of Zac's arm. And suddenly she felt a little guilty as she placed the vase on the windowsill.

'Truce?' He came up behind her, and she turned. He was too close, his big body crowding her. She caught the elusive scent of his aftershave—or was it simply him?—and her pulse began to race. She had difficulty holding his gaze.

'You have already drawn my blood.' He held up his arm.

Sally looked down, and to her horror realised she had. His bronzed, hair-dusted forearm bore a small scratch, and she saw the thin line of blood and felt even guiltier. 'I'm so sorry—let me put a plaster—'

'Not necessary.' He cut her off. 'But in recompense the least you can do is let me feed you.'

Warily, she looked up into his darkly attractive face. She didn't trust him, and worse she did not trust herself around him.

'I do mean only to feed you.'

He seemed to possess the ability to read her mind. 'Okay,' she finally said—mainly because she was thoroughly ashamed of herself. She wasn't by nature a violent person, but Zac Delucca brought out a host of violent sensations in her she had never realised she possessed. And, given that she had ripped his arm open with the roses he had bought her, it seemed the least she could do…

'Good.' And, reaching into the cupboard she had left open, he withdrew two glasses. 'I will deal with the wine and let you get the cutlery we need. Everything else is provided.'

'Fine. Do you want to eat here?' she asked, glancing at the fold-down table and two stools against one wall of the kitchen, where she usually ate, and then back to Zac. She grimaced. If he stretched his arms out again he could reach from wall to wall.

'It is a bit cramped, but it is either here or the living room.'

'The living room,' he decided, and, swinging on his heels, walked out of the kitchen.

Sally opened a drawer and withdrew knives, forks and spoons, wondering what she had let herself in for. She had let her guilt at lashing out at Zac override her common sense and agreed to him staying. Now she was not so sure. He disturbed her on so many levels. He had barged his way into her home uninvited, and yet the memory of the steamy kiss they had shared in the car still lingered. And if she was honest she would not mind repeating the experience. Anyway, what harm could it do to share a meal with him?

An hour later, licking her lips after finishing off dessert—a perfect Tiramisu—Sally was confident there had been no harm at all…

Actually, it had been a great meal. When she'd exited the

kitchen with the plates and cutlery, Zac had already filled the occasional table with an assortment of dishes: delicious pasta, fresh crusty bread and Veal Milanese, as well as salad and the dessert.

He had got the food from his favourite Italian restaurant, owned by a friend of his, he'd told her, and had made her laugh with stories of the proprietor and his family. Then he'd opened a bottle of wine and filled her glass and his, and made a toast to friendship.

Zac had been charming—a perfect gentleman. He had taken care not to so much as touch her, and there was still a foot of space between them on the sofa. Nothing like the arrogant man she had met last Friday, who had hardly kept his hands off her.

In fact, apart from Al, she could not remember ever feeling so relaxed in a man's company. But then maybe seeing her with no make-up, wet hair and wearing a tired old robe had dampened Zac's ardour, she thought with a wry grin, and told herself she was glad. But a little voice in her head whispered that it would be nice to feel his arms around her once more…

'That was wonderful,' she said, casting a sidelong glance at Zac. He was lounging back on the sofa beside her, his long legs stretched out before him, a glass of wine in his hand. His big body was at ease, and she had the fanciful notion that he looked like some great half-slumbering jungle predator.

'An apple and a stale cheese sandwich are no substitute for a good meal,' she went on, telling herself she was being ridiculous, fantasising about Zac. Picking up her glass of wine, she drained it and replaced it on the table. She raised a hand to her mouth as a yawn overtook her. Too much wine and not enough sleep, she thought, and murmured a polite, 'Thank you.'

'My pleasure,' he drawled, turning towards her, a smile

curving his hard mouth. His dark eyes met hers and she smiled lazily back, feeling strangely comfortable with Zac. Then his gaze dropped to where the soft blue fabric of her robe hugged the firm mounds of her breasts, unexpectedly making her shiver with sensual awareness.

Sally flushed and looked away. Suddenly, from being relaxed and sleepy she was wide-awake, and the sexual tension that had simmered between them when he arrived was back in full force. Her heart thudded a little faster and she had to swallow hard before she could find her voice.

'Now I think you'd better leave. I am rather tired,' she said defensively, shocked at how quickly he could arouse her with just a look.

'So thank me properly and I will,' Zac prompted softly, placing his glass on the table. He studied her pale beautiful face. Sally had actually yawned—not the effect he usually had on women. Though he noted the violet shadows under her eyes had deepened. Too much fun over the weekend…

Yet this exquisite creature had been driving him mad all evening. He had tried looking across the room, but the convenience of the bed, with its pristine white covers, had simply increased his frustration. He had thought she looked gorgeous elegantly dressed. But now, lounging on the sofa, with no make-up and wearing only a long blue bathrobe that exactly matched her eyes, with the silken mass of her glorious hair falling around her shoulders, she looked sensational.

After the first glass of wine she had unbent a little, and by the second she'd started eating and obviously enjoying the food. But had she been aware that every time she'd reached for a dish the lapels of her robe had gaped open, revealing her perfect breasts down to the dusky pink areolae? Or that when she licked her full lips she almost gave him a coronary? By accident or design he was not sure, and that yawn could have been fake… He didn't care. His patience was running out.

'A freely given kiss will be enough,' he prompted huskily, and raised his hand to the side of her elegant neck, felt the pulse beating furiously in her throat, and was encouraged to let his fingers slide through the heavy fall of her silken curls—something he had been itching to do since she answered the door to him, looking gorgeous, with damp tousled hair and ready for bed…

'Fine—as long as you realise that is all it will be, Zac.' Her voice was soft, and she met his dark eyes cautiously.

'Of course. I would not do anything you did not want me to,' he assured her, and hoped this time it would be *fine*. He had noticed she had the habit of using the word when the opposite was true.

Edging closer, her slender thigh touching his, she moved to press her soft lips against his cheek.

'You call that a kiss?' He growled his frustration just as she was about to draw back, and placing one hand behind her head, looped the other arm around her waist and tugged her against him. She gave him a startled glance and tried to shake her head, but he held her firm and kissed her with all the pent-up passion that had been riding him ever since he had set eyes on her.

She responded as he had known she would, her arms reaching up to clasp his shoulders. He deepened the kiss, the taste, the heat, the scent of her enflaming all his senses. He slid a hand inside the lapels of her robe and around her back to press her closer. Her skin felt like the softest silk, and he felt her tremble in his arms.

She groaned when he broke the kiss, her fabulous blue eyes unconsciously pleading for more as they met his. 'Trust me, Sally,' he murmured. 'It gets better.' And he turned her slender body so she was lying across his thighs, his hand moving from her back to caress one luscious breast, his thumb and finger rolling and plucking the perfect rosebud peak. She watched him with wide, almost innocent eyes, and squirmed in his arms.

'You like that?' he murmured, and delivered the same treatment to her other breast, parting her robe still further. 'Let me look at you, Sally,' he demanded huskily. 'All of you.' She was perfection, and he ached to see her completely naked.

Sally did not know what had hit her. All she knew was that the sensations swirling around inside her were new and wonderful, and the man staring down at her was responsible. His husky-toned request vibrated deep in her body, and she could feel herself becoming damp with desire. She had never been naked in front of a man before, but suddenly she'd lost all her inhibitions.

Later she would blame it on the wine and exhaustion, but at this moment she had never felt more vibrantly alive in her life.

'Yes…' she breathed, and he untied the belt at her waist and pushed the robe off her slender shoulders.

In a dreamlike trance her eyes settled on his ruggedly attractive face and she saw the dark stain spread across his high cheekbones, the gold flame of desire in his night-black eyes, as he studied her naked body with an intensity that made the blood race faster though her veins. His strong hand slowly caressed her throat, her breasts, followed the indentation of her waist, traced the curve of her hip and moved over her flat belly.

'You are perfect…more beautiful than I ever imagined,' he rasped.

Flattered, but aching with a need she had never felt before, Sally moved her hand from his shoulder to slip it beneath the open neck of his shirt, her fingers tracing the curling black hair shadowing his chest that had tempted her when he'd walked in the door earlier. She felt the fast pounding of his heart beneath her palm and gloried in the knowledge that she could do this to him.

'Oh, yes…' he groaned when she touched him.

His dark head bent and her lips parted in eager anticipation, but his head had dropped lower, and suddenly his mouth closed over one pert nipple, teeth biting gently, then lips suckling hard, as his long fingers tangled in the soft curls at the juncture of her thighs.

Sensation upon sensation sent shock waves crashing through her body, igniting a blazing heat that drove her wild, and she responded with an untutored intensity that would shock her when she recalled it later. She grasped his shirt and pulled it apart, unaware of the buttons flying off, and let her hands roam freely over his magnificent bronzed chest, glorying in the feel of his firm flesh, her fingers luxuriating in the soft mat of body hair, her nails finding and scraping over his small, pebble-like masculine nipples.

Zac growled deep in his throat, and, pulling back, he swept her up in his arms and navigated the few stairs to the bedroom area. His great body tense, he flicked the robe right off her body and laid her down on the bed.

Breathless and dizzy with an excitement she had never experienced before, Sally watched him with desire-glazed eyes. He kicked off his shoes, removed his shirt and stepped out of his pants, his dark eyes never leaving her naked body.

Sally could only gaze in awe at his magnificent golden-toned physique.

He was unashamedly and blatantly masculine, with wide shoulders and a broad, muscular chest. The body hair that so fascinated her fanned out over his masculine nipples and arrowed down over a hard flat stomach. A shocked gasp escaped her as he shed his silk boxers and she realised he was massively erect. A tide of red swept up her cheeks and she dropped her eyes, but his powerful muscled thighs and long legs did nothing to stop the blush, and for a second she was afraid.

She had a brief moment of clarity, and could not believe what she had allowed to happen. But as if sensing her reaction, Zac leant forward and placed a hand either side of her, his body not touching hers. Gently he brushed his lips across her forehead, the soft curve of her cheek, and finally closed them over her mouth, stifling any protest she might have made. And the moment was gone, lost in the magic of his kiss.

He raised his head, his smouldering black eyes sweeping over her slender frame in avid fascination. Then, as if she were a sculpture, his hands began to shape her body, his long fingers discovering every curve and crevasse, teasing her flesh in a way that made her insides shake. She stretched and turned at his bidding, and for the first time in her life she abandoned every restraint she had put on herself for years and gloried in her womanhood.

He cupped her breasts, squeezing them together and nipping the rigid tips between his long fingers. A helpless moan escaped her. She was totally overwhelmed by the power of what she was feeling, delirious with the pleasure he gave.

'You *really* like that?' He grinned.

Sally nodded her head, incapable of speech, and grasped his arm, urging him to join her on the bed. He stretched out beside her, one hand resting on her quivering stomach, the other smoothing a few silken strands of hair back from her face.

His hand curved around her waist and urged her closer to his side. The heat and the musky male scent of him tantalised her nostrils, and she felt the hard length of his arousal pressing against her thigh. Amazingly she wasn't afraid, but excited beyond reason. All she could think was that this magnificent man wanted her, and her head whirled as sensation after sensation arrowed through her body.

'Tell me what else you like, Sally,' he rasped huskily.

His hands were everywhere, and she looked at him, her whole body a quivering mass of feelings. 'You,' she said mindlessly, her brain turned to mush by sex.

His surveyed her with those smouldering eyes, one hand stroking over the flat plain of her stomach to settle at the juncture of her thighs and ease her legs apart, before his head dropped and his mouth covered a rigid nipple, suckling and tantalising yet again, until she didn't think she could bear it. Then Zac lifted his head, and his hard mouth covered her swollen lips.

Her slender arms dropped to curve around his broad back, her hands sliding down to stroke his hard buttocks before tracing up the line of his spine to curve around his broad shoulders, and finally reaching up to tangle in the thick black hair of his head.

She closed her eyes, shuddering in ecstasy at the feel of his hair-roughened chest against her acutely sensitised breasts. His tongue flicked evocatively around the outline of her lips and then thrust into her mouth as he kissed her with a hard, possessive passion, and her own tongue swirled round his in wild response.

His long fingers threaded thought the red curls at the apex of her thighs to find the velvet lips that guarded the hot, moist centre of her femininity, stroking over the tiny pleasure-point concealed there with unerring accuracy. She moaned and writhed beneath him, aching for more, her nails sinking into his flesh.

His mouth covered the pulse-point that beat frantically in her neck, and she turned her head to allow him easier access.

'You want this…' he growled against her throat.

She opened her eyes, and was just turning her head back to agree, white-hot and wanting, when she caught a glimpse of their naked bodies, erotically entwined, in the mirrored doors of the wardrobe…

To Sally it was like a douche of ice water on her overheated body, and she froze.

'No. Oh, no!' she cried, and shoved hard at Zac's shoulders, catching him by surprise.

He reared back.

'No?' he grated, and she caught the look of shock on his darkly flushed face—or was it pain?

She didn't wait to decide, and scrambled off the bed, picking up her robe. With legs that trembled she stumbled down to the living area, pulling it on. She fastened the belt around her waist so tight it hurt, her heart pounding like a sledgehammer in her chest.

The image in the mirror of naked lovers was indelibly printed on her mind. No, not lovers. A couple indulging in sex, she amended. She had barely recognised herself, wantonly splayed beneath Zac's great body. But she had been instantly reminded of where she was: her dad's old love-nest.

She was not like her dad and never would be, she vowed.

The first day she had moved in she had removed the mirror that had hung above the bed, but the mirrored wardrobe doors had been a timely reminder. How many young women had her dad seduced in the exact same place? But she wasn't about to make the same mistake with Zac Delucca…

Oh, no! In her panic she had forgotten about him for a moment, but not any more. Her body ached with the unfamiliar feeling of sexual frustration. What on earth was she going to say to him?

* * *

Painfully aroused and burning up with rage, Zac lay on his stomach and counted to a hundred—a technique he had learned in the ring. A fighter who let his anger get the better of him and lost control rarely won. That was the first piece of advice Marco, his manager at the time, had ever given him. And he knew if he lost control with his redheaded temptress he was liable to shake her until she rattled.

She had said no. Sally had actually said no. He was aware it was a woman's prerogative to change her mind, and he appreciated that, but he had never had a woman say no to him in bed before.

The little witch had been with him all the way. He could still feel the sting of her nails on his back. She had led him right to the edge and then slammed on the brakes. Pride and other darker emotions had him clenching his fists. No one got away with playing games with him. He rolled off the bed and pulled on his clothes, then descended the few steps to the living area, where the object of his fury and frustration stood, head bowed.

The footsteps on the wooden floor alerted Sally, and slowly she turned round. He was dressed—well, almost; his shirt was open to where he had tucked it in his jeans, the buttons gone. A guilty tide of red swept over her face as the memory of pulling his shirt apart flashed in her mind.

'Have you any reasonable explanation?' he asked scathingly, and, not waiting for a reply, continued, 'Or is it a habit of yours to encourage a man, tell him you want him, rip off his shirt, strip naked and get into bed with him before running from the room?' he demanded with biting sarcasm.

She raised her head. Not a muscle flickered in the hard bronzed mask of his face, but his dark eyes blazed with a violent anger. She took a step back, suddenly afraid, very afraid, as it hit her just exactly what she had done…

'No…' she murmured. The air was heavy with tension, as was the man watching her she realised, his hands clenching and unclenching at his sides.

'You have a right to look afraid,' he snarled, and stepped towards her, his tall body looming over her. He grasped her chin and tilted her head back. 'Some women like to tease, but you take it too far. Consider yourself lucky it was me you tried your trick on. The next man might not have my control, and then you will get a hell of a lot more than you bargained for.'

A tremor slithered down her spine, and he noticed.

'You were not immune. You were with me all the way. Even now you tremble.'

Catching her hand, he forced it down to his thighs. She was shocked to find he was still aroused, and to her shame involuntarily her fingers flexed on his erection.

'Not too late to change your mind—after all, it is a woman's prerogative,' he drawled derisively.

'No… No!' she cried, snatching her hand free and stepping back, her face a fiery-red. She wondered how she could have been so stupid. Such a push-over.

'One no is enough. I get the message.'

'Fine,' she said, and her casual response, the use of the damn word *fine* enraged him further. For a timeless second Zac let the mask slip, and if looks could kill, she would have breathed her last by now.

Sally knew she wasn't blameless, and he had some justification for being furious, but with exhaustion overtaking her all she wanted to do was get rid of him and forget tonight had ever happened.

Maybe she did owe him an apology. Years ago her mum

had told her the best way to defuse an argument was to say sorry. Whether you thought you were right or not did not matter, because it was very hard to continue arguing with someone who was saying sorry.

Well, Zac was bristling with anger. It was worth a try. Bravely she looked up into his hard face. 'I'm sorry for how I behaved, and I apologise if you feel you have been cheated,' she offered. 'But may I point out I did not invite you here? I told you I was tired, and I asked you to go, but you talked your way round me.' She made a futile gesture with her hands. 'You are like a tank, rolling over any sign of opposition. You are too much for me, and I want you to leave now.'

'My size intimidates you?' Zac demanded.

'No,' Sally snapped. She had told him a bit of the truth, and his continuing presence in her apartment was frustrating, so she told him the rest.

'You are just too much *everything*—too wealthy, too arrogant and too stubborn to leave when asked. And I don't like you. Apart from anything else you bought Westwold, which makes you an arms dealer, which to me is a despicable business.'

'That is rich, coming from you.' His tone was bitingly cynical. 'Daddy's little golden girl, who has never done a day's work in her life. The arms business has supported you very nicely—it paid for this apartment your father gave you, for starters. Perhaps I should have arrived with a jewellery box instead of a cool box. No doubt the outcome would have been different.'

The insult enraged Sally. It was bad enough that her father had told Zac he had given her the apartment, and she could not deny it, but he obviously had not told Zac she worked—hence his summing up of her character as an idle little rich girl. Knowing her dad, it had probably stroked his ego to come across as the generous father.

'Yes, you are right. Silly me,' she said, with a heavy irony which was wasted on Zac Delucca. She could explain, but she owed this arrogant bastard nothing. Crossing to the coffee table, she picked up the cool box. 'Now we know what we think of each other, take this and get out.'

Zac studied her for a moment, his lithe muscular body tense. 'Keep it as a gift from me,' he drawled tightly, and she noticed the way a little muscle jerked in his cheek. 'A cool box is quite appropriate for a woman who blows hot and cold like you. When you're lying in bed, burning up and remembering what you have missed, stick your beautiful head in it.'

Her brows shot up, and, holding her anger in, she said acidly, 'In your dreams—but certainly not in mine.'

His hand snaked out and tangled in her hair, jerking her towards him. 'Do you know, Miss Paxton…' his smile was chilling '…I'm minded to prove you wrong.'

She tried to pull her head away from him, but his hand tightened, and she stared up at him, her blue eyes spitting flames. Suddenly she was aware of the sexual violence emanating from every line of his powerful body.

'Don't even try,' she snapped.

He raised one dark brow. 'Big mistake, Sally,' he drawled mockingly. 'Did your mother never tell you you should never challenge an angry man?' He snaked a long arm around her waist to pull her hard against him.

'Let me go.' There was a brief silence as his eyes narrowed on her mouth. She was stiff with anger, and suddenly very afraid. 'I said let go of me.'

Zac gave her another chilling smile. 'I will, but first here is something to remember me by.'

Her eyes widened as his head bent and his mouth ravaged hers in a kiss of savage passion.

When he finally let her go she was gasping for breath and her legs were trembling. 'You… You…' she spluttered, livid with rage—and something more she refused to acknowledge.

He placed a finger over her lips. 'Save it. I am leaving and I won't be back.' He stared at her for a moment, a look of icy contempt in his hard eyes. 'Shame… It could have been good—but I am not into playing games, and you are nothing but a spoilt little tease.' He shrugged his broad shoulders and turned and walked to the door.

Sally shivered and collapsed onto the sofa. Her head fell back against the cushions, a long, sad sigh escaping her. All her emotional energy was spent worrying about her mother, and she had none to waste on Zac. A man born with a silver spoon in his mouth and accustomed to wealth and power, who expected women to simply fall at his feet, was not for her.

She did not see Zac glance back, nor the frown that creased his broad brow. She only heard the closing of the door as he left.

Zac walked into the elevator and pressed the button for the ground floor. He had caught the same expression of sadness on Sally's face just now, as he'd left, as he had when they'd first met. For a second he was tempted to go to her. Then common sense prevailed.

Over the weekend he and Raffe had discovered how her father had been robbing the company for years. Today they had added up the cost, and it was well over a million. He had told Raffe he would deal with Paxton in his own time, and had sent Raffe back to the head office in Rome—mainly because of Sally. He had behaved like a stupid lovesick teenager, soft in the head and hard everywhere else.

Well, no more… He punched the wall of the lift, and barely bruised his knuckles. Never had a woman led him on and then turned him down so callously, and he would make damn sure it never happened again.

In the morning he would face Nigel Paxton with the evidence of the man's fraud, and from now on he would stick to the sophisticated ladies who mixed in his circles and played the game by his rules. In fact, he would make a dinner date with Margot, a lawyer who had made it obvious she would be up for anything—which, ironically, was why he hadn't bothered before. But tomorrow he would, and he'd be fine…

CHAPTER SIX

THE restaurant was exclusive and very expensive and the latest fashionable place to eat. Sally looked at her companion across the table and smiled. Al was just what she needed. She had dressed carefully for their date in an effort to cheer herself up. The scarlet dress she was wearing had shoestring straps, a fitted bodice with a wide soft leather belt, and a short, gently flaring skirt. She had swept her hair up in a loose pile of curls on top of her head, mainly to keep cool in the hot weather London was experiencing. Al had taken one look at her and told her she looked fabulous, which had done a lot for her confidence, and then they had caught a taxi to the restaurant so Al could have a drink.

He had spent the last ten minutes waxing lyrical about a girl he had met last weekend at a house party given by one of his father's clients on an estate in Northumberland. Apparently, she was the owner's daughter, and it was she who had turned him down for dinner tonight.

Sally pointed out if the girl lived in Northumberland it was hardly surprising. It was the other end of England, and not everyone owned a private Piper plane like his dad. If he was keen, he should fly up north to see her again.

'Of course—why didn't I think of that?' Al laughed. 'You are so bright, Sally. Your advice is always good.'

The wine waiter arrived with an excellent bottle of Chardonnay and filled their glasses, and they drank a toast to each other. Then Al began regaling her with tall tales of his South American trip, making her laugh.

After a delicious main course they were soon waiting for their dessert, and Al reached across the table and took her hand in his, his blue eyes suddenly serious.

'Enough about me, old girl. Apart from your work, you have avoided telling me anything about what is going on in your life. What is really bothering you?'

'Not me.' She sighed. 'My mother.' It was such a relief to talk to someone who understood, and softly she told him about her mum's accident and prognosis. He lifted her hand and pressed a soft kiss on the back.

'Sorry, Sally. It must be hard. If there is anything I can do for you, anything at all, you only have to ask—you know that. You have my number, just call.'

She lifted moisture-filled eyes to his. 'I know, Al, and thanks.' She tried to smile. 'And I might take you up on that one day.'

Zac Delucca, seated in an intimate booth at the rear of the restaurant, had been enjoying his dinner with Margot, the intelligent thirty-something company lawyer he had met when negotiating on an apartment block he had bought in London a few years ago. He'd been pleasantly contemplating how the evening would end when his attention had been drawn to a couple entering the restaurant.

It was Sally Paxton, wearing a low-cut red silk dress that fitted her like a glove, emphasising her tiny waist, the curve of her hips, then flaring out provocatively as she walked. It ended a good three inches above her knees. The colour should have clashed with her hair, but didn't, and the same sexy red high-heeled sandals he had noticed the first time he saw her enhanced her shapely legs.

She was hanging onto her so-called friend Al's arm, and Zac could not keep his eyes off her.

He had watched them sit down at a table near the entrance, a simmering anger engulfing him.

He had barely listened to Margot's conversation, simply nodding his head occasionally, or slotting in a yes or a no. His whole attention was focused on the younger couple. Sally Paxton had turned him down in the most brutal way possible, and now she was smiling, laughing, holding Al's hand and looking into his eyes as though he was her soul mate.

He had seen enough, and he had changed his mind again… His interest in Margot, fleeting at best, was killed stone-dead. He signalled for the bill, paid it and got to his feet.

'You are in a rush? We have not had dessert or coffee.'

He had almost forgotten his companion, and glanced down at her.

She smiled as she stood up to join him, and clung to his arm, a blatant invitation in her eyes. 'But we can have coffee at my place.'

He gave her the briefest of smiles and said nothing. She was going to be disappointed…

Sally glanced up as the waiter arrived with their dessert, and the emotional moment was gone. 'This looks positively sinful!' She smiled, eyeing the small mountain of profiteroles covered in chocolate sauce and surrounded by cream…

'Don't look now, but a man you know who probably *is*

sinful is heading this way with a stunning woman on his arm,' Al said quietly.

'Who?' She glanced enquiringly at Al, but before he could answer, a familiar tall dark-headed man stopped at their table.

'Hello, Al—and Sally. Nice to see you again.'

Al replied sociably, but the deep, dark voice had sent every nerve in Sally's body jangling.

She looked up. Zac was standing by the table, wide-shouldered, lean-hipped and long-limbed. He was wearing a perfectly tailored grey suit, a white shirt and matching tie, and he looked fabulous.

Sally was struck dumb as his dark eyes stared down into hers, and a vivid image of herself lying naked beneath him flashed in her head. She glanced to his companion and fought back the blush that threatened. The beautiful raven-haired woman clinging to his arm was almost as impressive as Zac. Tall and slender, she wore her lime-green designer gown like a model.

She probably *was* a model, Sally thought, and her brief moment of embarrassment was gone.

She had been right to say no last night to Zac Delucca. His women were as interchangeable as his shirts, and she told herself she had had a lucky escape. But she was slightly surprised that he had bothered to stop and say hello… When he'd left her apartment his contemptuous farewell had been very final.

'Enjoying your meal, Sally?'

There it was again, the seductive voice, but it was wasted on her.

She glanced up, saw the smile on his attractive face and noted that it did not reach his hard dark eyes. 'I was,' she said, with biting sarcasm.

Zac Delucca stared at her, stunned by the implied insult. Rage such as he had never felt before swept through him, and his hard black eyes raked furiously over her. He noted her exquisite face, carefully made up, and the silken red hair piled on top of her head in a mass of curls, enhancing the long line of her neck and the low neckline of her dress, which revealed a generous glimpse of her firm white breasts No one insulted him publicly and got away with it. Very few would dare. Yet this redheaded Jezebel took delight in taking potshots at him. Well, not any more. Last night she had been naked in his arms, and she would be again, he vowed.

He had confronted Nigel Paxton this morning with his fraudulent actions, and listened to the man's paltry defence. Zac had told him he was considering police action, but he wasn't… Being tied up in a court case was not Zac's idea of fun, and admitting someone had managed to cheat him was not good for business, but he had not given Paxton his final decision nor fired him yet. He had thought to let him stew for a day or two—it was the least he deserved—and now Zac was glad he had as a much more personal solution to the problem formed in his mind.

Sally saw the fury in Zac's face for a split second and she held her breath as the silence lengthened, her heart beating faster in her breast. Maybe she had gone too far. It was not like her to be deliberately impolite.

Finally, he smiled, a humourless twist of his chiselled lips, his dark eyes clashing with hers. 'Ever the tease, Sally,' he drawled sardonically. 'Enjoy the rest of your meal.' And he was gone.

Zac's subtle reminder of last night had brought a pink tinge to her cheeks, and she heaved a sigh of relief and began to relax again as the couple left the restaurant.

'What was all that about?' Al asked. 'Delucca was furious, and I certainly wouldn't ever want to be on the receiving end of the look you just got.'

'Nothing. Now, can I enjoy my dessert in peace, please?'

'Yes, but I have warned you once about Delucca. He is really not a man to fool around with, and certainly not the type to insult.'

'Al, don't worry—I am never going to see the man again, and he certainly will not want to see me.' She grinned. 'Trust me, his ego is as big as his bank balance.'

'My point exactly,' Al cut in. 'Nobody insults a man like that and gets away with it. Take it from me as a man. I recognise the signs. He was angry, but on a primitive level he wants you badly, and I would hate to see you get hurt. So beware.'

The telephone was ringing as she entered her apartment a couple of hours later. They had finished their meal, and then, as it was such a lovely summer night, Al had walked her home.

'Yes?' she answered.

'Is he with you?'

It was Zac, and she could not believe the nerve of the man. 'No—not that it is any of your business. And do not ring this—'

'This *is* business,' he cut in. 'Have you talked to your father today?' he demanded.

'My father? No.' The question surprised her, and instead of hanging up on him she listened.

'Then I suggest you do—soon. I will be round at eight tomorrow night…'

'Now, wait a damn minute—' But this time it was Zac who hung up on her…

Sally slowly replaced the receiver, a puzzled frown creasing her brow. Why would Zac Delucca tell her to call her dad? It didn't make sense. Well, she wasn't calling her dad tonight.

It was too late, and he was probably in bed with his mistress. Given Zac's brief call, he was probably doing the same with Margot…

On Wednesday morning, after a restless night, Sally was running late. She had stripped the bed and changed the linen after Zac had left on Monday, yet for some reason she imagined she could still smell the scent of him whenever she tried to sleep. Maybe it was the pillows, she reasoned as she dashed out to go to work. She would buy two new ones, she decided, and any thought of calling her father was forgotten.

Usually Sally stayed in the museum for lunch, but today, after ringing her mum to check she was all right as she did every day, she went out shopping. She bought two pillows, and then stocked up in a grocery store with some essentials: fresh bread, milk and a few ready meals. Her weekends with her mother did not leave her with much time for shopping, and she rarely bothered to cook in the evenings any more.

She dashed into her apartment building that evening as the storm clouds that had been gathering for the past few hours finally broke in a deluge of rain.

'You just made it in time, Miss Paxton.' The doorman grinned. 'So much for the heat wave—it lasted all of two weeks.'

'This is England, remember?' Sally quipped, and headed for the elevator.

A few minutes later she entered her apartment to the sound of the telephone ringing. Her hands were full of shopping, so she placed the pillows and the groceries on the kitchen bench, and then lifted the receiver from the wall.

'Where have you been? I have been ringing you since yesterday, and you were out last night.' It was her father.

'Even I have the occasional date, and I go to work, remember? And when I'm not working I visit my mother—your wife. I have tried to call you for weeks to get you to visit her, with no success. So now you know how it feels.'

'Yes, yes, I know all that. But listen to me. This is important. Has Zac Delucca rung you?'

'Why would he ring me? I barely know the man,' she said, suddenly tense as she belatedly remembered Zac calling her last night and suggesting she speak to her father.

'You know him well enough—you had lunch with him on Friday.'

'That was a one-off and never to be repeated,' she said adamantly.

'Don't be so hasty to dismiss him, Sally, darling, because I gave him your telephone number yesterday.'

'You had no right,' she shot back, but as the hateful man had already known her number, there was no point arguing the issue.

'Never mind that now, and listen. The man is a ruthless bastard. His employees are all terrified of him—he is noted for paring the workforce to the bone whenever he takes over a company, or closing it down completely and selling the assets. So if you want me to keep my career, I need him on my side.'

'Surely you can do that yourself? In every other aspect of your life you are a waste of space, but even I accept you are good at your job,' Sally said dryly.

'I have tried, but the man trusts no one except that sidekick of his, Costa, and Costa found out I'd overlooked a rule or two and told the boss. I had an awkward meeting with Delucca yesterday, and in the process I suggested he might like to check me out through you, so promise me if he calls you will be nice to him.'

Her father was worried about something. She recognised the

blustering tone of his voice and remembered she had seen a hint of it the other day in the office, when Zac Delucca arrived.

Her dad had admitted to 'overlooking' a rule or two—probably caught with his pants down with his secretary again, she thought bitterly. Most businesses had strict rules about relationships in the workplace, and the majority of people had the sense to keep their personal lives out of the office, but her father had never made that distinction.

'I know your opinion of me, but think of your mother. I've already told Delucca she is paralysed and in a very expensive nursing home, hoping for the sympathy vote. All I want you to do is back me up if he calls you—though time is running out.' He sighed. 'I have another meeting with him tomorrow morning.'

'I'll back you up if he calls,' she said noncommittally.

She had no qualms about lying to her father, and she had no intention of telling him Delucca had already called, but suddenly she saw a way to make her beloved mother happy.

'On one condition—you give me your solemn promise to visit Mum with me at the weekend. I'll pick you up and book you into the hotel I use, and just for once you will stay the *whole* weekend.'

'It's a deal. I promise,' he said, relief evident in his tone. 'But try to remember you are a beautiful woman, and Delucca is a very eligible man. He took you out to lunch, so he must have fancied you. If you play your cards right you could do both of us a lot of good.'

'You, maybe. As for me, I think you are a despicable excuse for a man. Heaven knows why Mum loves you, because I certainly don't,' Sally said, and hung up.

Automatically she unpacked her shopping and put the food in the fridge. She carried the pillows across to the bed, and, after stripping off the pillowcases, changed the old for new. Then, taking her keys, she left the apartment and pushed the old pillows down the waste chute, at the same time wishing she could push Zac so easily from her mind.

She was going to have to talk to him. She would do anything to make her mum happy, and if that included facing Zac again and backing up her dad simply to get him to visit his wife, she would do it.

Sally returned to her apartment and closed the door. Zac had said he would be here at eight. She glanced at her watch. It was already seven. She crossed to her wardrobe, and, kicking off her shoes, placed them in the cupboard. She took out a well-washed pink velour lounging suit—the comfortable outfit she usually wore when she got home in the evening—and slipped her bare feet into flat furry pink mules; she refused to dress any differently from any other evening. She headed for the bathroom. After a quick shower she bundled her day clothes into the wash basket and slipped on clean underwear and the pink suit. Then, squaring her shoulders, she zipped up the top.

She wasn't out to impress, she told herself, and, returning to the living room, she sat down on the sofa, picking up the remote and switching on the television.

Normality was what she was striving for, but without much success. Her stomach churned with nerves, and she could not concentrate on the screen, but she did not have to for long as the intercom sounded.

She crossed to the door, hit the button and listened, then answered, 'Yes.'

She waited by the door, and when the bell rang opened it.

Zac stood like a dark avenging angel, big and tall, his black hair plastered to his head by the rain, his broad shoulders fitting perfectly beneath a dark jacket that had not fared much better. Beneath it he wore a black cotton tee shirt and dark pleated pants.

'May I come in?' he asked with icy politeness, and the eyes that met hers were hard and cold.

'Good to see you did not fib your way in this time,' she said. It was the first thing that came into her head as her heart lurched at the sight of him. She made an exaggerated gesture with one slender arm. 'Be my guest.'

He pushed past her and she caught the slightest scent of his cologne—sandalwood, maybe. Whatever it was, it had a disturbing effect on her. Her stomach fluttered as if a thousand butterflies had taken up residence, and angrily she told herself not to be so stupid.

This was business. Zac had said so, and her father had told her he would check him out with her. The female on Zac's arm last night confirmed he had certainly moved on in the sexual stakes…Sally would bet her last cent the willowy model had not said no.

'Sarcasm does not become you, Sally.'

'How would you know? You don't know me,' she snapped angrily, following him into the living room. He had removed his wet jacket and was in the process of looping it over the small stair rail, his back to her.

Slowly he turned round and stared at her with narrowed eyes, his expression unreadable.

'Maybe not completely…' His eyes narrowed further, scanning her slender body with deliberate provocation and making her remember their last encounter here. 'But I am going to—very well…' His smile was chilling.

'Not in this lifetime,' she said, her temper rising, the image of him with his latest conquest still in the forefront of her mind.

He took a step towards her. 'You have spoken to your father?' he queried, his dark eyes fixed intently on her flushed face.

The mention of her dad was enough to make her tense, and it didn't help that, minus his jacket, the black cotton tee shirt Zac wore moulded every muscle of his broad chest. She tried to ignore his much superior height and strength, but the sheer physical impact of the man was enough to make her go weak at the knees. 'Yes, of course I have,' she said bravely, holding his gaze.

'And you think you have a choice?' he demanded, with a mocking lift of one dark eyebrow.

'I don't know what you mean.' And she didn't. Simply looking at the damn man turned her brain to jelly. Gathering every shred of control she possessed, she continued. 'All I know is my father called me and told me he had given you my phone number. I didn't bother to tell him you already knew it,' she slotted in sarcastically. 'Then he told me everything.'

'Everything? And you *still* think you have a choice?' he queried, his dark eyes holding her.

'Yes,' she declared emphatically. 'Apparently, you are renowned for cutting the workforce or closing a place down altogether when you take over a company, and he is worried about his job. He may not be much of a husband, but I can assure you my mother *is* in a private nursing home and he *does* pay the fees. Whatever else my dad is, he is a good accountant. In fact, I don't know why you bothered coming here. We could just as easily have had this conversation over the telephone.'

Dark eyes full of contempt held hers for a long tense moment. 'You amaze me,' he finally drawled, and a frisson of alarm ran down her spine as his face darkened thunderously. 'You really don't give a damn.'

Pride made her face him, but inside she was shaking and her legs threatened to give way. 'If you are referring to my father…not particularly,' she responded, and she was not about to explain why. 'Now, if there is nothing more, I would like you to leave.'

Not waiting for his response, she turned and crossed to the sofa. Picking up the remote control, she switched off the television. She needed to do something to escape Zac's overpowering physical presence, and just prayed he would go—before her legs gave way beneath her and she collapsed in a heap at his feet.

'There is something more,' he said bitingly, turning his black head with chilling slowness to look at her with hard dark eyes. 'A lot more,' he added, walking towards her. 'The not inconsiderable sum of over one million pounds, stolen from the company, and how you can continue to live the way you do with your father in prison.'

CHAPTER SEVEN

PRIDE held Sally's head high, though the mention of a million pounds and prison had shocked her to the core. Her father was a fool over women, but she had never thought he was a thief. But then she had no idea to what depths he could sink in pursuit of his sybaritic lifestyle. She wouldn't put anything past him…

'Perfectly,' she answered Zac's question. 'Contrary to what you believe, my farther does not give me a penny and nor would I want him to. I can't stand him. He is everything I loathe in a man—a chauvinistic, womanising, unfaithful creep. Unfortunately, my mother loves him, and I love my mother, so I am obliged to be civil to him but that is all. I would not throw him a lifebelt if he was drowning, so whatever he has done is of no consequence to me,' she declared, letting all her anger and bitterness at her father spill out. 'I have taken care of myself for years now, and will continue to do so.'

'How?' His upper lip curled in a sneer. 'On your back?'

Her hand shot out and slapped his arrogant face. 'How dare you?' she spat, and hysterical laughter bubbled up inside her. She sounded like an outraged virgin…which she was.

His head jerked back in surprise, and before she knew

what was happening he caught her shoulders and dragged her towards him.

'No one strikes me and gets away with it,' he grated through his teeth. 'Consider yourself lucky. If you were a man I'd have knocked you cold by now.' His dark eyes leaping with barely controlled rage, he added with deadly emphasis, 'But there are alternatives.'

Sally's pulse raced and she began to panic, seeing the menace and the threat of violence in his body. Frantically, she lashed out and tried to punch him, but his hands slipped down her back, pinioning her arms at her sides. His dark head bent and his mouth caught hers to inflict its own powerful method of retaliation.

She tried to twist her head away from his ruthless searching mouth, but Zac was stronger, and he kept her trapped against him, unable to escape the vengeful dominance of his savage kiss.

When he finally stopped ravaging her mouth she was left gasping for breath, her legs like rubber. Still held against him, she could feel the heavy thud of his heart even as her own raced. Then something strange happened. Their eyes met and fused, and her heart leapt crazily at the predatory sexual awareness in his. She stared, wide-eyed, and to her shame it wasn't disgust that made her tremble but the heat of arousal curling in her pelvis.

A fierce tension arced in the air between them. How did he manage to affect her like this? His touch was like being struck by lightning, igniting a flame inside her every time he came near her. Mortified by her own weakness, with a terrific effort of will she made herself rigid in his hold. But her control was not needed. As she watched his expression changed from primitive male aggression to one of icy control…he was every inch the hard-faced captain of industry once more.

His arms dropped to his sides and she was free, but she didn't trust her legs to support her if she moved. Then he spoke.

'So, Miss Paxton, back to business. How do you intend to honour the debt of one million pounds plus that your father embezzled from Westwold?' he demanded, his cold, black eyes holding hers.

'I don't have to,' she said, breathing fast. 'It is not my debt.'

'True, but much as you seem to dislike your father, and insist you do not need his money, apparently—as you confirmed—your mother is in an expensive nursing home and she does. Unless, of course, you earn enough to keep her as well as yourself.'

He raised a brow and took a step back, his gaze raking over her from top to toe, assessing her worth as if she was a slave on the block.

'You are certainly beautiful enough on the outside, with all the attributes a man could want.' He eyed her comprehensively again. 'But you might have to work on your technique if the fiasco between us the other night was typical of your bedside manner.'

Sally stared in shock and outrage as the full import of his words sank in. Then her face paled to a deathly white as in her head flashed an image of her mother in bed, her once glorious red hair now a faded grey, her body half-paralysed. She had suffered more than any human being should have to endure, and no matter what Sally thought of her dad, she knew it would break her mother's heart completely if her husband was branded a thief and sent to prison. She could not let it happen, and she could not deprive her mother of the care and comfort of the nursing home for whatever amount of time she had left.

Sally searched Zac's harshly controlled features as if she had never seen him before. He had everything—looks, wealth and power—and he used it ruthlessly, looking down on lesser mortals like some pagan god.

Suddenly she was fed up and bristling with anger. She had always thought that a man who was dependent on the female members of his family to protect his honour didn't have much of that commodity to start with. Yet here she was, she thought furiously, an intelligent, hardworking adult female, put in this invidious position by two men: her father, a spineless jerk, and Zac Delucca, a titan among men but with a positively medieval attitude.

'For your information—' she eyed him with contempt '—I have a full-time job in a museum, and while I am quite happy with what I earn, museums are not noted for extravagant salaries. So, no, at the moment I could not pay the nursing home fees,' she told him bluntly, while silently racking her brain for a solution if her feckless father really was in deep trouble.

She had very little savings, and she spent any spare cash she had on her mother. Paying for accommodation every weekend to be near her was not cheap, but if she managed to sell her apartment she could use the money she gained to pay for her mum and rent somewhere else. So far she had received one ridiculously low offer from a property developer, which she had refused, but now she would accept it, she decided.

'But if you give me time a month or so I could afford to support my mum.' It suddenly occurred to her that her dad could do the same—sell his grandiose apartment and pay Delucca back. 'And if you drop the charges against Dad between him and I we could almost certainly pay you back.' She had to think positive. Anything else was too degrading.

'Interesting, but no. Your father has stolen from the company for years, and he has run out of time.'

For a defeated second it occurred to her that if her mother

died quickly the problem would disappear. 'Oh, my God,' she groaned, despising herself for the horrific thought.

Zac took her chin between a finger and thumb and tilted her head up to face him.

'Praying will not help you, Sally, but I might!' His heavy-lidded eyes glinted with a calculating light. 'I could be persuaded, with the right encouragement, to accept the monetary loss and refrain from charging your father with theft and so keep him out of prison.'

His hand slipped from her chin to curve around her throat, and a strong arm closed around her waist to pull her into contact with his long, hard body. There was no mistaking his meaning.

'If you are really good I will allow him to draw his present salary—in a more menial position, of course—until he reaches the retirement age of sixty, in twelve months, and I will also allow him to keep his generous pension, both of which he would forfeit if found guilty of fraud. With the money he has stolen it should be more than enough to allow him to fulfil his commitment to his wife.'

The blood drained from her face, and she was trembling with a mixture of fear and fury at his insulting proposal. 'You bastard!' Her blue eyes flashed at him.

'Such language for a lady—you do surprise me, Sally,' he mocked. 'And I am not, in the true sense of the word. My parents are long dead, but they *were* married when I was born.'

'And I am not some wh-whore to—to—to…do…' She stuttered to a stop—something she had not done since she was a child.

'I never actually said you were.' One dark brow arched sardonically, and a ruthless smile curved his sensuous mouth. 'What I am proposing is quite straightforward. In exchange for my saving your father from prison and allowing him to stay in my employ, you will become my mistress.'

She swallowed hard, her strained features reflecting her shock and confusion. Zac could not be serious…

In fact, he could be lying about her dad. But then she remembered her father's conversation earlier. He had said he had 'overlooked' a rule or two, as if it was nothing to worry about. She had assumed it was to do with his penchant for bedding his secretaries. 'Is it true? About my father stealing?' she asked in a low voice.

'I do not lie, Sally. Your father has been swindling the company regularly for years, extremely cunningly. The amounts he took were small enough to be explained away as errors before I bought the company, but over a decade or more they became big enough to add up to a considerable sum. When Raffe took charge of the London headquarters he smelt a rat, but even he was not sure, and it took both of us to track where the money had gone,' he responded with a wry twist of his lips. 'So what is it going to be, Sally? Your father disgraced and broke, or you becoming my mistress?'

It was unthinkable. But deep down inside Sally knew he was telling her the truth. She also knew that for her mother's sake she could not let her dad go to prison.

'Why me?' she murmured to herself. Didn't she have enough to suffer, watching her mum dying? And now she had no choice but to agree to Zac's outrageous demand.

She wasn't an idiot, and not for a minute did she kid herself he was doing it for anything other than revenge. A million pounds was small change to him. And she was no financial expert, but, if her dad had been stealing for years, surely technically it was the previous owner who had lost most of the money, not Zac? But the blow to his ego she had dealt him by saying no on Monday, and then insulting him in public last night, were not things a man like Zac Delucca was going to forgive and forget in a hurry.

'Look at me.' His arm tightened around her waist and the hand at her throat slipped around the nape of her neck to tilt her head up to face him. 'You know why, Sally. I want you badly, and though you try your best to ignore the sexual chemistry between us you want me. If this is the only way to have you, then so be it.'

She had not realised she had spoken out loud, and she opened her mouth to deny his assumption. But his mouth had found hers, and, unlike their previous kiss, his tongue was gently outlining her lips and then probing into the warm interior of her mouth with a persuasive eroticism that totally enthralled her.

Desire and disgust fought for supremacy in her shattered mind. Desire won as a surging tide of excitement swept though her still shaken body. She must not let him know how easily he could affect her, she told herself, but involuntarily she leant against his hard frame, her pulse beginning to beat like a drum in her throat as she surrendered to his expert seduction of her senses.

'Has that helped you to decide, *cara mia?*' His husky chuckle sounded against her ear long, passion-filled moments later.

He knew he had won, Sally thought helplessly as she forced herself to struggle out of his arms. Her legs no longer capable of supporting her, she finally collapsed onto the sofa behind her.

Zac looked down at her, and she saw the knowing smile of masculine triumph curving his mobile mouth. He knew he could elicit a sensual response from her with humiliating ease, and his eyes challenged her to deny it...

She wanted to say no. She opened her mouth to do so—and closed it. Damn him to hell, she swore under her breath, and clasped her hands in her lap to stop them shaking. She stared down at them, unconsciously gnawing on her bottom lip, while her mind spun frantically as she sought for inspiration to escape what was virtually a hopeless position. Finally she took a long resigned breath, her decision made…

She would do anything for her mother, and if that meant saving the neck of her father by sleeping with Zac, she would do it. She glanced around the room, and the irony of the situation hit her.

How appropriate… Her dad's love-nest…and now hers…

A fatalistic calm swept over her, soothing her nerves and clearing her head. She was twenty-six next month, and with her father as an example she had no intention of ever marrying. As for falling in love, she only had to look at what it had done to her mother to dismiss the idea completely. Maybe it was time she took a lover, and, being brutally honest, she had no doubt Zac Delucca would be a magnificent one. She only had to remember the time she was naked in bed with him to know that. But pride and pride alone insisted that while accepting his offer she would do her utmost to remain unresponsive in his arms. A man of his ego would soon grow tired of a reluctant mistress…

'Your argument is very persuasive,' she conceded, and raising her head she caught the flicker of surprise in his dark eyes. 'I would have to be a fool to refuse what you are offering. So, yes, I agree to be your mistress—but with a few guidelines in place.'

'Guidelines?' he queried. 'Maybe your past lovers catered to your every whim, but I am not that type of man. I expect my woman to be available whenever and wherever I want her. No rules but mine apply. After all, in your case that is what I have already paid for.'

'Sorry, not possible,' she said with a shake of her head. She could be as businesslike as he was when she had to be. 'I have a degree in Ancient History and I work as a researcher at the British museum. My hours are nine to five-thirty, sometimes later, Monday to Friday. I spend every weekend visiting my mother at her nursing home in Devon, returning late on Sunday evening. The guidelines I was referring to are that on no account must my father discover the arrangement between us, and obviously not my mother either. It will be solely between us, and that you can come here any evening except Saturday and Sunday.'

Zac looked down at her pale, determined face and was stunned. He'd had no idea she was a graduate and held down a job at a prestigious museum. When she'd said 'museum' he had thought she was probably a receptionist at some commercial tourist attraction, like a house of horrors or a toy museum—there were plenty of them scattered around most major cities.

Blinded by lust the moment he set eyes on her, he had leapt to assumptions about her lifestyle with very little evidence and had misjudged her badly. She wasn't the spoiled, attention-seeking Daddy's darling he had thought her, and her dislike of the man was obviously one hundred percent genuine.

The knowledge made Zac uneasy—more so when he realised she had actually taken his word against her father's regarding the theft with barely a quibble, and accepted his offer much more quickly than he had expected.

Then, cynically, he wondered if she was spinning him a line as he recalled the first time he'd met her, in the middle of a working day, elegant and immaculately dressed. Zac could recognise a designer gown when he saw one; he had paid for enough over the years.

'If what you say is true, Sally, then explain to me how you were free last Friday and looking as if you had just stepped out of *Vogue*,' he demanded.

'I have three designer garments for special occasions that I bought in a secondhand shop here in Kensington. All at least a couple of years out of date, and deposited there by the sort of woman you usually escort, who discard them after a season or sell them,' she said scathingly.

Zac flinched, reminded of his years in the orphanage, when the clothes he'd worn had all been secondhand, donated by the good citizens of the city.

'For months I have been researching the history of a collection of Egyptian artefacts that had been stored in the basement for years prior to the new extension of a current exhibition. It happened to preview to the press and dignitaries last Friday morning. My boss asked me to attend the opening to answer any historical queries that might arise, hence the dress. Then he gave me the afternoon off as he knew I wanted to visit my mother.'

Zac flinched again as he recognised the sadness she could not hide shimmering in her blue eyes. Then he wondered if he had imagined it as she raised her head.

Control tightened her exquisite features, and her blue gaze was cold as she continued, 'Unlike you, apparently a boss that terrifies his employees, my boss Charles is a kind, thoughtful man. The reason I was at Westwold was because I had hoped to persuade my father to come with me and visit mum that night or the next day. Unfortunately for me you arrived! Satisfied…?'

After feeling uneasy about the way he had treated her, by the time she'd finished speaking all he felt was anger. How did the little witch do it? Yet again she had managed to insult him twice, without even blinking an eye.

'Satisfied? My curiosity, yes, the rest of me, no. But I will be,' he drawled, and, reaching down, he caught her hand and drew her to her feet. 'I accept your guidelines, Sally Paxton, and now, as my mistress, you have to accept me.'

Surely he could not possibly mean that they should go to bed here and now?

A trickle of fear snaked down Sally's spine, and she went hot and cold by turns. But she refused to give in to the emotion. Instead she pulled her hand from his, straightened her shoulders, looked him squarely in the eyes, her own eyes bleak, and simply said, 'Fine.'

The *fine* got to Zac; he knew she used the word when she didn't care one way or the other. Well, he was going to make her care, he vowed.

'Good. You can start by stripping off that outfit that covers you from head to toe,' he suggested. 'Or I will—the choice is yours.'

He meant it. He actually expected her to cold-bloodedly strip naked in front of him. Not content with virtually blackmailing her into being his mistress, he wanted to humiliate her as well.

Sally's cool control finally shattered. 'If I had a choice I'd never set eyes on you again,' she told him, eyes blazing. 'I hate you.'

'Hate is better than indifference.' He shrugged his broad shoulders. 'You agreed to be my mistress, and the only choice you have left is the one I just gave you, Sally.' His voice dropped to a low, menacing drawl. 'And if you don't make up your mind quickly I will do it for you.'

Swept along on a white-hot tide of burning rage, Sally unzipped her top and shrugged it off her shoulders, then slipped the pants down her hips and stepped out of them.

His dark eyes swept over her, and the hint of a smile tilted the corners of his mouth as he noted the white cotton knickers and sports bra. 'Very virginal—and we both know you are not. Just as well, because I prefer my women experienced, and wearing silk and lace or nothing at all.'

In a second of blinding clarity Sally saw her salvation. She was not mistress material, as he would quickly discover, and given his declared tastes Zac would not hang around long. Instead of trying to resist him in bed she should encourage him. The quicker she got it over with, the quicker he would be gone.

'As you wish.' She unfastened her bra and let it fall, then hesitated. Reminding herself he had seen it all, she gathered her courage and stripped off her briefs, and in a show of bravado straightened to her full height and flung her arms wide. 'What you see is what you get,' she said, and pirouetted on her toes.

But she did not complete the circle.

Zac gathered her up in full spin and strode over to the bed. Sweeping back the embroidered cotton cover, he dropped her so hard she bounced.

CHAPTER EIGHT

HE STOOD menacingly over her, blocking out most of the daylight that was left, and suddenly the anger that had got her this far deserted her. What was she thinking of? Had she taken leave of her senses? She couldn't do this…

'Don't even think about it,' he commanded.

He had read her mind. How did he do that? she wondered, and saw him take something from his pants pocket and drop it on the bedside table before whipping his tee shirt over his head and dropping it on the floor.

Helplessly, she stared up at him, her fascinated gaze taking in the masculine perfection of his great body, and the thin line of black hair arrowing down over the strong packed band of muscles over his ribcage and then lower, as he shrugged out of the rest of his clothes.

'There is no changing your mind this time, Sally,' he drawled with implacable determination in his tone.

She swallowed hard. Totally nude and aroused he was magnificent. He was also vastly experienced, and she felt hopelessly inadequate. With that thought came another. She suddenly realised she had no guarantee he would save her father.

'But what if you change yours?' she asked. 'How do I know you will honour your side of the deal?'

He tensed, his dark eyes seeking hers. 'Because we made a deal and I gave you my word. My word is my bond.'

She didn't question why, but she believed him—not that it stopped her nerves from leaping all over the place at the thought of what was about to happen, nor her adding, 'Even if you think I am really bad?'

'I certainly hope so. I rather like bad women.' Zac gave a low, husky chuckle and slid in beside her. Leaning up on one elbow, he let his gaze sweep leisurely over her long-legged curvaceous figure. She had a body made for sex, and he wondered why he had wasted so much time with tall, stick-thin women.

'Perfection,' he husked, and began to caress her with long light strokes, from her shoulders to her breasts, her narrow waist, the curve of her hips. He felt her tense, but he did not linger in any one spot, long fingers trailing over her flat stomach and down the length of her leg, then back up her other leg to circle her belly button, and higher to graze the tips of her breasts. He watched the hardening nipples with a hunger he refused to give in to…yet… He didn't want a passive lover; he wanted a passionate lover.

He saw her blue eyes widen, and the pupils expand and darken involuntarily. He heard her breathing quicken, heard the small whimpers of delight she could not control from her lushly parted lips, felt her small hand slip around his back and tentatively stroke up his spine. He had her, she was his, but he resisted the incredible urge to kiss her.

Instead he continued to caress her throat, and down the valley between her breasts. The tight nipples were pouting for his attention while his hand slid lower to the hidden valley between her thighs. Her legs parted for him, and it took every ounce of control he possessed not to take her there and then.

He pressed the heel of his hand on her soft mound and raised his head to look down at her beautiful face, flushed with arousal, and he made a husky-voiced promise. 'I am going to pleasure you more than any man has ever done before, Salmacis.'

Sally stared wildly up at Zac. He was torturing her, but it was an exquisite torture. The brushing, teasing softness of his fingers was driving her insane. She was hot and aching, and with a bravado she hadn't thought she was capable of she let her free hand sweep down over his chest and then lower, to touch his erection. She heard him groan, 'No…' and an impish smile curved her kiss-starved lips.

'Do you mean that?' she asked breathlessly, and with one finger traced the smooth, silken tip. Fascinated, she let her hand curl around the hard, pulsing length of him. Her fingers would not meet around the girth, but that did not stop her stroking down to the base and slowly retracing the path back up again.

'No…yes…' he groaned again, and, grasping her wrist, he pulled her hand up his body. 'Always the tease,' he breathed against her lips, and then, rearing up, he grasped her hands and pushed them above her head, to anchor them there with one of his as his mouth came crashing down on hers in a kiss of awesome passion.

She was pinned beneath him, and he took full advantage of her helpless state. With lips and tongue he teased and tantalised, sucking on the pulse beating madly in her throat and then moving lower to draw a rigid nipple into his mouth and suckle some more. Her back arched and she tried to free her wrists. But his clasp tightened as he kissed, nipped, stroked and licked every throbbing inch of her. His long fingers finally slipped between her thighs to dip into her moist core, finding and toying with the sensitive nub hiding there to devastating effect.

Crazy with excitement, she writhed beneath him as an incredible tension built and built inside her. Just when she thought she could take no more he let her hands free, and she moaned out loud as for a moment she quivered on the brink of some wondrous place she could barely imagine.

He reached across to the table, then grasped her hips and lifted her off the bed. She felt the tip of his shaft slide between her thighs. Involuntarily she wrapped her legs around his waist and her slender arms around his neck, to pull him to her, and her mouth opened beneath his with a white-hot hungry need her body recognised as he plunged into her.

She cried out with a pain she had not expected, and his great body stilled.

He looked into her eyes, his own black and burning like living coals of fire. 'You're a virgin.'

'Was…' she murmured distractedly, the acute stab of pain easing and the promise of exquisite pleasure returning as her body adjusted to the rigid fullness of him. She wriggled her hips and clasped her arms a little tighter around his neck.

'What are you doing?' Zac demanded, about to pull back, but she wrapped her legs even tighter around his waist.

'I don't know—I thought you did.' She gave him a wicked smile.

Zac grinned, then grimaced in an effort to still his raging body. He looked into her incredible eyes, the pupils big and dark with sensual hunger, and yet humour lurked.

Something squeezed in his chest at the same time as her inner muscles clenched around him. He had never felt anything like it in his life. He caught her husky moans of pleasure in his mouth and began to move slowly. She was so tight he was afraid of hurting her, and, hanging on to his control by a thread, he pushed inch by inch into her sleek silken sheath and then slowly withdrew. Again and again he stroked into the honeyed depths, and only when he felt her whole body begin to convulse in the ultimate pleasure, and heard her keening cry, did his iron control break free. Helpless in the throes of a sensual storm, he plunged hard and fast to join her in an earth-shattering climax.

He rolled on to his back, carrying Sally with him, and held her close against his heaving chest. He had never known a woman like her. Her fabulous body was sinfully sexy, and so instantly responsive to his slightest touch. Usually for Zac sex was a relaxing exercise, with a like-minded woman, during which the sole aim was to make the right moves and lead to a satisfactory conclusion for both.

But with Sally it was a sensual feast—and fun… He couldn't believe she had been a virgin. He had never made love to a virgin in his life. He had always steered well clear of the innocent type. But now, in a totally proprietorial way, he found enormous satisfaction in knowing he had initiated the lovely Salmacis into the joys of sex, and also oddly protective.

'Are you all right, Sally?' he rasped a long moment later, when his breathing had slowed, and he smoothed the hair from her forehead with a hand that was not quite steady. She hadn't said a word—maybe he had hurt her. He had lost control at the end, and he was a big man with everything in proportion.

Suddenly it occurred to him why she had said no the other night. She had not been teasing; it had been a totally justifiable virginal fear of the unknown, which somehow made him feel a lot better, and yet worse at the same time. He had come on to her like a ton of bricks because he'd thought she was an experienced woman, and nothing could have been further from the truth.

Sally lay against Zac's chest and listened to his rapid

heartbeat beneath her cheek. She heard his question, felt his hand on her head, but didn't look up. She couldn't...she was still throbbing internally in the aftermath of the most amazing experience of her life. Her body felt heavy, but paradoxically she was light-headed with the wonder at what had happened.

Never in her wildest dreams had she imagined sex to be so all-consuming—an intensely erotic ride on a one-way ticket to the stars. Zac wasn't just a magnificent lover, he was the absolute perfect lover, she was sure. But as the tremors finally subsided, and she relaxed into a lazy lethargy with his great body beneath her and the musky scent of sex all around them, she slowly began to recall her own eager, almost brazen actions, and she was embarrassed by them.

'Sally?' He tugged lightly on her hair. 'I asked you if you are okay.'

She had to face him some time, and, pressing her hands against his chest, she slipped down to lie at his side, casting him a sidelong glance. 'I'm fine,' she murmured, feeling inexplicably shy.

Zac rolled off the bed. 'I need the bathroom,' he grated.

'In the hall, opposite the kitchen,' Sally murmured, but he was already striding across the room, totally at ease with his naked state. Sally watched his progress, secretly admiring his tight bum and broad back. Tall, lithe and golden, he moved like a sleek jungle cat—all hard-packed muscle and sinew, with not a trace of fat on his massive frame. He was her lover, and a delicious little shiver stirred her sated body.

He had worn a condom—hence the bathroom, she suddenly realised. Good, she told herself, but the unbidden thought entered her head, that while she had been lost in mindless ecstasy Zac had still had all his wits about him, and had taken no chances with his bachelor state.

Zac stood in the bathroom, his hands clasping either side of the basin, his head bowed. The best sex of his life, and he had been damned with '*fine*'. Not wonderful, not awesome, not even good. No, he'd got *fine*. On top of which he felt slightly ashamed—not an emotion he usually suffered from—because he had given her no choice but to sleep with him.

Sally had the ability to confuse and confound him like no other woman he had known, and for the first time in his adult life he actually doubted his sexual prowess. But only for a second.

He lifted his head and ran his hands through his hair. Sally had been with him all the way. She could not have faked her response. She had been like a living flame in his arms. It was her first time, so perhaps she was simply lost for words? And he should not have left her so abruptly—in his experience women liked to be cuddled after sex.

Having analysed her reaction to his own satisfaction, he dismissed the niggling doubt he felt and left the bathroom.

He stopped by the bed and looked down at her. Her glorious red hair was spread across a pillow in a tangled mass of curls, her lips were swollen from his kisses, her exquisite body was spread across the white sheet in lax abandon, and instantly he began to harden again.

She glanced up at him. 'You're back,' she murmured, and moved to give him space. And then he saw the stain. He paused for a moment, then stretched out by her side. He swept a few strands of hair from her face, his expression sombre.

'You are sure I didn't hurt you?'

The touch of Zac's hand on her head and the warmth of his body reached out to Sally, and she lifted her eyes to his. For a moment she could have sworn she saw a look of uncertainty in the liquid depths.

'I am fine, honestly.'

'Damn it, Sally!' He scowled 'Do you have to say *fine* to everything?'

'What do you want me to say?' she asked teasingly. 'You were a magnificent lover and I only wish I had known what I was missing, then I would not have waited so long?' She tried a smile, ridiculously pleased he was back in bed with her.

'You should have told me you were a virgin.'

Zac actually sounded aggrieved, and out of nowhere Sally was reminded of all the countless times her mother had tried to appease her father in the past—anything to keep him longer at her side. And she was in danger of doing the same.

Suddenly an icy touch of reality pierced the mindless sexual cocoon that Zac had woven around her.

How like a man to make out it was the woman's fault… Then she remembered why she was there.

'What difference would it have made?' she demanded, and sat up, crossing her arms over her chest. If the coverlet had been anywhere to be seen she would have wrapped herself in it. She was here at Zac's command, because of what her father had done, and she would not forget again.

'Basically, you are paying my father for me to be your mistress.' She shot him a cold, derisory glance. 'I did try to warn you I might be bad at the job. So don't blame me if you got less than you bargained for.'

His ruggedly attractive face darkened with anger, his lips drawing back from his teeth. 'You're right,' he said tightly. 'It makes no difference at all.' His hand snaked out and caught a handful of her hair. 'As for being bad…you are a very bright lady and you will soon learn everything you need to know to please me.'

Their eyes met, and she gasped at the predatory look she saw in his, but it was not fear she felt but an atavistic desire.

He jerked her head down and her heart beat out of control as his mouth took hers in a fierce, possessive kiss. His hands dropped to her waist and he lifted her to straddle his thighs—and what followed was like nothing that had gone before…

She fell forward and put her hands out, either side of him, to stop herself ending up splayed against his chest. Her hair falling around her shoulders, she looked at him through her lashes, seeing the barely controlled hunger in his eyes.

'Stay like that.' The command was harsh, guttural, and, raising his head, he licked each pouting nipple with devastating effect. Fierce arrows of pleasure shot from her breast to her pelvis. She felt his hands running up and down her spine, his great body pressing up into her. She was amazed that he could arouse her so instantly after what they had just shared. Dropping her head, she brushed her lush, swollen lips against his and kissed him, her tongue exploring his mouth with a feverish delight that he immediately reciprocated. Suddenly he grasped her hair and pulled her head back.

'No more,' he rasped, his black eyes searing into her.

His strong hands lifted her hips and she felt the power of his erection pulsing between her thighs.

'I want to watch you—see the passion in your incredible eyes as you come for me.'

Sally closed her eyes to block out his dark, compelling gaze, a low moan escaping her as he positioned her to accept him. Her head fell back as he thrust up into her, the white-hot flames of passion growing as he lifted her, twisted her, bucked beneath her, driving her wild with the force of her need. She was oblivious to everything but his scent, his power, and the achingly exquisite pleasure, and she cried out as she shuddered helplessly, her body convulsing around him.

Still he did not stop. He reared up and without breaking contact placed her legs either side of his thighs. His hands flattened against her back, so her breasts were crushed against the hardness of his chest, and he took her mouth in deep marauding kiss that incredibly drove her higher again.

He demanded and she gave, their bodies locked together in a mutual, desperate, primitive mating. They kissed, they clawed, and finally he spun her beneath him. He paused and held her once again on the edge of ecstasy, his face a taut, dark mask of rigid control, his black eyes burning into hers.

'Please…' She groaned his name. 'Zac…'

'At last,' he growled, and thrust deeper and faster, until the fire of passion finally burned out of control, consuming them both.

For a long time the only sound in the stillness of the room was Zac's rasping breath. He lay with his head over her shoulder, his weight pinning her to the bed. Later Sally would hate him, and probably herself, but right now she hadn't the strength.

'Sorry…' he murmured, and rolled off her to lie at her side. 'I'm too heavy for you.'

And she had the oddest notion that the latter comment had been added as an afterthought. His *sorry* had been an apology for what had just exploded between them.

She didn't bother answering. She had been exhausted before Zac arrived, and now she was exhausted in a different and amazing way, her body sated and at rest. She didn't think she could even lift her head. Her heavy lids drifted over her eyes. All she wanted was sleep. She felt an arm reach around her shoulder and her eyes flew open.

'Sally, are—?'

She cut in. 'If you are going to ask me if I am okay, don't bother. I'm fine.'

But she was shocked and, yes, slightly ashamed. She didn't recognise the totally uninhibited woman she had become in response to Zac's expert lovemaking.

'You fulfilled your promise to be great in bed more than I could have possibly imagined,' she told him truthfully. After all, she had almost begged him at the last…his apologies were not necessary. 'But I really am too tired for any more tonight, so take your arm off me—you're wasting your time.'

His arm was withdrawn, and she felt strangely bereft.

'I was only going to cuddle you. Most women, I believe, like that sort of thing.'

'Well, you should know—you have had plenty of experience. Thanks, but no thanks.' She forced herself to look up at him; he was watching her, a dark, brooding expression on his hard face. 'All I want to do is sleep, so if you wouldn't mind leaving now…'

'I could run a bath for you. It will help you relax.'

'If I was any more relaxed I'd be unconscious. Please, Zac, just go. It must be late, and I have to be up for work in the morning.'

He slid off the bed and stood looking down at her. 'If you are sure I can't do anything for you?'

He'd done more than enough, Sally thought, but didn't say it. 'No—except close the door on your way out.' And she closed her eyes to block him from her view, because he actually looked and sounded as if he cared, which she knew he did not.

She listened to the muffled sounds of him dressing. She felt him place the coverlet gently over her and brush his lips against her cheek, and heard his murmured, 'Sleep well, Sally, and I'll see you tomorrow.' She didn't open her eyes. 'We have a deal, remember?'

She heard his footsteps on the wooden floor, and the door closing.

When she was sure Zac was gone Sally opened her eyes and slipped out of bed to pad along to the bathroom. She turned on the shower and stood under the soothing spray—except it did not soothe her. The events of the evening played over and over in her tired mind.

Zac and his ultimatum: become his mistress or watch her father destroyed. The amazing experience of making love—no, not love but lust. And Zac's reminder when he left that *they had a deal.*

All that and the actual reality of her life combined together to almost defeat her.

Overcome by a complex mixture of emotions, she felt the tears leak from her eyes. She cried for her mum and for herself until she had no tears left. Finally she turned off the shower, dried her eyes and her body, and walked back to bed. She withdrew a clean sheet from a cupboard in the unit, and changed the bedlinen. Then she took a cotton nightdress from a drawer, slipped it over her head and crawled into bed. She curled up into a ball and fell into a deep, blessedly dreamless sleep of sheer exhaustion.

CHAPTER NINE

SALLY blinked and opened her eyes. The brilliant rays of the morning sun shining through the window had woken her. Good, the rain from last night had stopped and the sky was a perfect blue, she noted, and stretched her limbs prior to getting out of bed. Then she remembered, as muscles she had not known she had screamed in protest.

She closed her eyes again, in a futile attempt to block out what had happened. But it was no good. A vivid image of Zac's naked body poised over hers flashed in her mind: the moment he'd possessed her, and her own avid response not once but again and again. Her nipples tightened at the memory. She had almost begged him to take her the last time… Ashamed at her own reaction, she leapt out of bed and dashed to the bathroom.

Showered and dressed in a green button-through shirt-style dress in easy-care cotton, bought from a High Street department store, she made and drank a cup of coffee and ate a bowl of cornflakes. She washed the china in the sink and stood it on the draining board. Then, taking her keys off the hook on the wall, she put them in her taupe leather shoulder bag. She slipped her feet into flat matching sandals and, flinging the chain strap of her bag over her shoulder, she headed for the door.

The ringing of the telephone stopped her in her tracks. Her heart sank. Please not my mother, she prayed, and answered the phone.

'Good morning, Sally,' a deep husky voice drawled in her ear, setting every nerve in her body on edge. Oh, no! she groaned silently. Zac.

'Good morning,' she said stiffly. 'What do you want? And make it fast—I am on my way to work.'

'You know what I want, Sally. You,' he delivered, with a deep throaty chuckle. 'But for now I will settle for knowing what time you finish work. I will pick you up.'

'That isn't necessary,' she snapped, and was glad he could not see her blush. 'I will be back here by seven-thirty at the latest.'

'Not good enough… What time, Sally?' he demanded, all humour banished from his tone.

Reluctantly she told him five-thirty, and hung up.

Zac had done his homework and discovered that the museum staff usually left by a side exit door with a short flight of steps leading down to the pavement. He parked the black Bentley Coupe on the opposite side of the road and checked the time: five minutes to go. Leaping out, he leant casually against the passenger side of the car, his legs crossed at the ankles, and waited. He was totally unaware of the admiring glances cast his way by the passing female population, his whole attention focused on the exit.

He saw Sally the moment she walked out of the door, and he swept his gaze leisurely over her even as his groin tightened in instant response at the sight of her. She was wearing a simple jade-green dress, and the evening sun glinted gold on her red hair, looped in a knot of curls on top of her head.

She was a vision in green and gold and she was all his… But not tonight. He was determined to keep his libido in check.

Sally was new to sex and she needed time to recover and to come to terms with what had happened between them. He had not been the most sensitive of lovers, certainly not the second time, and though the sex had been incredible he wasn't exactly proud of the fact.

The beginnings of a smile curled his lips but quickly turned to a frown as he realised she was not alone. A tall, blond-haired man, impeccably dressed and carrying a briefcase, was at her side. Sally stopped on the bottom step, and the man said something to her that made her laugh. He flicked a stray curl from her face and kissed her cheek, then turned and strolled away with a wave.

Sally waved goodbye to her boss and turned to step down onto the pavement. She glanced to left and right. With a bit of luck Zac would be waiting at the front of the building and she could avoid him a little longer, she thought, still smiling. Then she glanced across the road and her heart missed a beat.

Zac was leaning with negligent ease against the side of a black convertible. Tall, his olive-toned skin sun-kissed to a deep gold, his black hair dishevelled, he was wearing navy trousers and a pale blue shirt, with a cashmere sweater draped across his broad shoulders.

How was it, she wondered, that Italian men had a way with casual clothes like no other nationality? He looked every inch the Italian tycoon, and pure alpha male. He made no move to approach her, but simply lifted a hand in greeting…or was it a command? Either way, it made no difference. Her choice had been made last night, and she walked across the road and stopped in front of him.

'Hello…' Lifting her chin, she connected with his dark eyes and said inanely, 'I see you found me okay.' Suddenly she was having difficulty breathing as his virile sexuality hit her like a blow to the heart. Not twenty-four hours ago she had been naked in bed with this man, behaving in a previously unimaginable way. Her cheeks turned pink at the thought.

'Did you doubt it?' he asked, with an arrogant arch of one ebony brow.

'No, no…' she murmured, taking a step back just as a car whizzed past.

Two strong hands grasped her waist and swung her high off the ground, dropping her into the passenger seat of the convertible. 'Sit down before you get knocked down,' he said, and, crossing to the driver's side, he slid in beside her. He made no effort to start the car.

He turned to look at her, one hand on the steering wheel, the other arm draped along the back of the soft leather seat.

'So who is the blond guy?'

Sally frowned, thoroughly flustered and not sure what he was talking about. No hello, no kiss… Not that she wanted one, of course… Just a snapped question.

'I asked who was the man that kissed you goodbye.'

'Oh, you mean Charles—my boss.'

'I might have guessed. A kind, caring boss, I seem to recall you telling me. Now I know why. He wants you for himself.'

'Don't be ridiculous. He is a thoroughly decent man, and friendly with all his staff.'

'I bet he does not kiss them all,' he drawled derisively. '*Dio*, Sally, you can't be that naïve.' He shook his dark head. 'He is a man, and you are a very beautiful woman he sees every day at work. You must know he lusts after you.'

'You are totally wrong—he is a happily married man with a child.' For an instant Sally wondered if Zac was jealous…

'As is your father, and according to you it never stopped *him*.'

'That is a horrible thing to say—but coming from you it does not surprise me.'

He wasn't jealous. He was simply being his usual arrogant self, presuming every man's motives were as basic as his own.

'Charles is a happy, totally committed married man, proud of his family—and I know because I have met his wife and daughter on countless occasions. So drop this pointless conversation and drive on. You're blocking the traffic,' she snapped, oddly dispirited by his attitude.

Zac was not convinced. He knew his fellow men. Married or single, few if any would be unaware of a woman as exquisite as Sally. Even Raffe, his assistant, happily married for five years, had taken one look at her, his eyes lighting up, and declared her gorgeous.

He started the car and smoothly pulled out into the rush-hour traffic. He glanced sidelong at Sally and saw again the sadness in her expression. He could have kicked himself for being such a callous idiot.

The first time they had met he had been irritated by the way she had virtually ignored him, but now he realised that, thanks to her father's ill-conceived behaviour and her mother's illness, she unconsciously dismissed any man who showed an interest in her. If last night had taught him anything it was that Sally truly was an innocent, and naïve when it came to men—hardly surprising, given she worked for a living and spent most of her free time visiting her mother.

The silence between them stretched and stretched, and even with bustle of the city all around them Sally was beginning to get nervous. 'Where are we going?' she finally asked, as the car stopped at some traffic lights.

'I know a nice restaurant on the south coast overlooking the sea, about an hour's drive from here.'

'We are going out?'

Somehow she'd thought he would take her straight back to her apartment, but obviously not. So he could not be in that much of a hurry to get her back into bed.

'Good,' Sally murmured, and squashed the little devil voice in her brain that suggested otherwise.

'Unless, of course, you had something else in mind? I'm easy…' Zac drawled, giving her a lazy, sensuous smile that made her all too aware of what he was suggesting.

'No, the seaside sounds great. I used to live by the sea until I moved to London to work. And after mum's accident the house in Bournemouth was sold.' She frowned. 'Actually, when I think about it I have not been to the beach in over a year.'

They ate dinner on the terrace of a restaurant perched on a hilltop, overlooking a small cove where a few fishermen's cottages surrounded the beach.

Sally chose pâté as a starter, as did Zac, and he ordered lobster with salad for the main course, followed by summer pudding and coffee.

They shared a bottle of wine, and Zac quizzed her about her childhood and her days as a student. She did the same, and discovered his parents had actually died when he was one. Far from being born with a silver spoon in his mouth, as she had thought, she was amazed when he told her he had spent his early years in an orphanage and worked for every single cent he had made. Some of his stories were funny, like the one about his abortive attempt to make his own olive oil, and how he had finally called in an expert. He made her laugh, and for once she allowed herself to relax.

'More wine?' Zac asked, holding the bottle over her glass. His dark eyes, still lit with amusement, were holding hers.

'Fine.' She smiled, and he filled her glass without comment. She picked it up and took a sip.

Then Sally saw him grimace, and the humour faded from his dark eyes. Perhaps he thought she was drinking too much. It struck her that he had only had one glass all through the meal and this was her third.

'Perhaps not,' she murmured, about to replace her glass on the table.

'Yes, drink, Sally—enjoy it. It is an excellent wine, but when I am driving I only allow myself one glass with a meal.'

Enjoying the relaxed ambience of the evening gave her the confidence to ask him boldly, 'So why the grimace?'

'It is that word *fine*. When we first met I noticed you use it an awful lot when you are not bothered either way. Even last night, after we had incredible sex, you used it again. Why?'

'Oh…' She suddenly remembered him returning from the bathroom last night and sliding into bed beside her, asking her the same question. She hadn't answered him then, but now, fuelled by more wine than she was used to, she thought, why not?

'I had a terrible stutter as a child, and it is a habit I developed because for some reason I could almost always say *fine* without a problem. I quickly realised it was a very versatile word. Fine with a smile was a yes; fine with a shrug was no. It could mean good or great or simply okay. My father used to laugh when I began to stutter, but my mother took me to a speech therapist and I was eventually cured. The habit lingers.'

Zac was shocked, and disgusted with himself. Sally had

faced a huge problem as a child and beaten it, while he had behaved like a complete idiot by allowing one word to bother him. 'I'm sorry, Sally. It must have been hard for you, and it was crass of me to ask. Forgive me.'

Sally had registered the expression of disgust on Zac's face and she wasn't surprised. A supreme male like Zac expected perfection in his women, and now she had told him her secret he was obviously disappointed.

'Of course. Forget about it,' she said with a brief smile, and, turning, she looked out into the distance. The sun was slowly sinking towards the distant horizon, turning the sky to a palate of pale blue, pink, red and gold, and she had a feeling Zac's interest in her would sink just as quickly now he'd realised she wasn't quite the perfect woman he had imagined.

'How on earth did you find this restaurant?' she asked, in a deliberate change of subject, but nevertheless enchanted by the vista before her. Turning back to look at him, she added, 'I've never heard of the place, never mind the restaurant.'

'I like to drive, and I discovered it one day when I got lost,' Zac admitted with a rueful grin.

'You? Lost? That does surprise me—but I am glad you were,' she quipped. 'June is my favourite month, with the long light nights, and this view is absolutely spectacular.' Her blue eyes swept along the coastline and back out to the sea, as smooth as the proverbial millpond and reflecting the sun's rays in a band of gold.

'The view *is* incredibly beautiful,' Zac agreed, and she glanced back to find he was not looking at the view but at her, and the expression in the depths of the dark eyes that met hers sent a rush of heat careering through her slender frame.

'Yes, and the food is good as well.' She glanced down at

her plate, battling to fight back the blush that threatened. It was to no avail. Her cheeks were turning a delicate shade of pink.

'There is no need to be embarrassed because you want me, Sally,' Zac drawled throatily, a hint of satisfaction in his tone 'It is perfectly natural, and you must know after last night how desperately I want you. If I had my way I would keep you with me all the time, for as long as this passion, this hunger between us, lasts.'

The deep, dark, slightly accented drawl sent shivers down her spine, and her pink cheeks turned to a scarlet to rival the setting sun as she imagined spending all her time with Zac, sharing his bed and his life. Then she fell back to earth with a thud. For a second she had been in danger of forgetting why she was there.

'That's not possible…'

'I know—you have your mother and your work.' He reached over the table and clasped one of her slender hands in his. 'I can appreciate your mother is deserving of your time, but I am not so happy about your work since seeing your boss.'

'Not that again.' She tried to pull her hand free, but he tightened his grip.

'So long as you understand, Sally, that in a relationship I demand total exclusivity from the woman I am with and give it in return.'

'When would I have the time, even if I had the inclination?' she asked derisively.

He looked at her for a long, silent moment, and then he stood up and pulled her to her feet and into his arms. 'You have a smart mouth, Sally, and I know just the way to close it,' he said quietly, and, dipping his head, he kissed her. She collapsed against him like the proverbial pack of cards.

When he finally let her go her face was flaming with embarrassment and her eyes were dark with arousal. She couldn't begin to imagine what the other customers thought of this public display.

'That was…' she began.

'Successful. It silenced you,' he said, and after paying the bill he took her hand in his and led her out of the restaurant towards the parked car.

The evening air was a blessing to Sally's overheated skin, and she stopped and took a deep, calming breath, reluctant to get in the car. She glanced around, anywhere but at Zac, and was struck again by the beauty of the place.

'Do we have to leave straight away?' she asked. 'I have been cooped up in the basement of the museum all day, and I'd like to walk along the beach for a while.'

'Sure,' he agreed, threading his fingers through hers, and they walked down the steep hill to the small cove.

The sun was a blazing circle of gold as it slowly dipped to the horizon, and the moon was already showing in the sky over the opposite cliff, creating a magical natural picture that no artist, however brilliant, could ever aspire to.

A slight breeze from the sea made her shiver slightly, and Zac, without saying a word, took his sweater and knotted it around her shoulders.

'No, you keep it.' She tried to object. 'You are accustomed to a much hotter climate—you need it more than me.'

He laughed—a low, husky sound. 'Sally, your concern is touching but not necessary.' He placed an arm around her shoulders so she could not remove the sweater. 'I am not likely feel a chill with you by my side.' His eyes slid to hers, narrowed and unreadable. 'Here or anywhere.'

Sally stared at him for a moment, trying to read the expression on his face and failing. Then she turned her head and watched the sea, evading his eyes.

'I suppose, compared to Italy and the other places you have been, this does not look that spectacular.'

'Trust me, this is spectacular,' Zac drawled as they walked down towards the waterline and stopped just out of reach of the gently lapping waves. 'But you're right. The view of the sea and the southern Italian coastline from my home in Calabria is very beautiful.'

'Is that where you live?'

'I have a house in that area, yes, though I spend most of my time at my apartment in Rome, as the head office of my company is based there,' he told her as they strolled along the beach. 'At the moment I am staying in my apartment in London.'

'You actually have an apartment in London?' she asked, her curiosity aroused; she had thought he would be staying in some top-class hotel.

'Yes. I keep an apartment in a block I own there. I tend to do that in most of the multi-occupancy properties I buy. I have others in New York, Sydney and South America. I have decided there is a better return on apartment blocks than hotels; they take less organising, much fewer staff and a fraction of the running costs.'

'Nice…' she murmured. He sounded like the tycoon he was, and she would do well to remember that. He was an incredibly wealthy, sexy man. Not for him an assignation with his latest lady in a hotel, when he had apartments all over the world.

'I'll show you the apartment tomorrow night, if you like.'

'Fine,' she said, and stopped. 'Sorry—it just slipped out.'

'No need to apologise—now I know the reason behind your habit I think it is rather endearing.' He grinned and, pulling her close, smoothed her hair back from her face and brushed her lips with his. She shivered.

'You are cold. We are leaving,' he said, for once totally misreading her reaction—for which she was grateful.

Zac got to her with an ease that amazed her and also made her afraid. Sex was one thing, she told herself, but she didn't want to feel anything else for him. Yet it was becoming more and more difficult—especially after this evening, when he had revealed his upbringing to her.

'Sally?' She heard the deep-toned voice and slowly opened her eyes. 'We are back.'

'Oh…' She had fallen asleep, with her head resting on Zac's arm and her hand on his thigh. 'Sorry—I didn't mean to sleep,' she said, her fingers flexing on his thigh as she straightened up.

A wry smile twisted his firm lips. 'I rather enjoyed your hand stroking my thigh, but it did not do a lot for my driving skill,' he drawled in self-mockery.

'I didn't—did I?' she gasped.

He chuckled 'You will never know, Sally. Come on, you are tired. Let's get you to bed.'

And, stepping out of the car, he walked round the bonnet while Sally was trying to control her suddenly racing pulse. Was he coming to bed with her?

Zac opened the passenger door and held out a hand to her. She took it and stepped onto the pavement. She looked up into his darkly attractive face, lit by the street lamp. His expression was bland. He gave nothing away.

'Thank you for a nice evening,' she murmured politely as, fingers entwined, they walked into the foyer of her apartment block. Then, pulling her hand from his, she turned to face him. 'You do know you are illegally parked, Zac? Your car will get either ticketed or towed, so you don't need to come up with me,' she told him, trying to be assertive.

'Yes, I do need,' he drawled softly, and dipped his head and took her lips in a long, lingering kiss.

Zac had set out this evening full of good intentions to wine and dine Sally, like on a conventional date, then leave her with a kiss at her door. But as the evening had progressed his good intentions had begun to fade, and, having endured an hour-long drive with her snuggled up against him, he was having trouble remembering them at all.

'But what about your car?'

He put an arm around her shoulder and led her into the elevator. She looked up at him with big, wary eyes, but she could not disguise the awareness lurking in the smoky-blue depths.

Zac smiled at her genuine concern, and dropped a brief kiss on the top of her head. 'They can ticket it, tow it—do what they like with it. I…' He was going to say he could not do without her, but stopped. 'I insist on seeing you safely to your door,' he amended.

He had never actually needed a woman so badly that he could not do without her for a night, and it worried him. He had the troubling thought that it would take a whole lot longer to physically tire of Sally than any other woman he had ever met or was likely to.

The elevator doors opened and he paused for a moment. Maybe he should walk away now… Then he saw her standing in the hall, and she glanced over her shoulder at him, a question in her brilliant blue eyes. He put his hand on the elevator door to stop it closing and followed her.

'Give me your key.' He took it from her hand, opened the door to her apartment and ushered her inside. Before she said a word, he turned her into his arms and bent his dark head to taste her sweet, intoxicating mouth.

A long, breathless moment later, Sally stared up into Zac's dark eyes. 'Would you like a coffee?' she asked softly. Held close against him, the strength of his arousal pressing against her belly, she was achingly aware of what he wanted—and it wasn't coffee…

He smiled—a slow curl of his firm lips. 'No, I want to undress you.' And, reaching for the buttons of her dress, he began to unfasten them one by one.

Sally let him.

She told herself there was no point in resisting, but the reality was she didn't want to, as excitement fizzed in her veins like the finest champagne.

He reached her waist and unfastened the belt. Slipping his hands beneath the collar, he eased the dress down her arms to let it fall in a pool at her feet. He lowered his head and covered the pulse that beat madly in her throat, sucking gently.

'And then I want to put you to bed,' he murmured, his breath warm against her ear as he unfastened her bra and peeled it off, exposing her naked breasts to his intent gaze.

'That's better,' he said huskily, and, dipping his head, he licked each rosy peak before slipping his hands underneath the lace of her briefs and sliding them down to her hips.

A gasp of surprise escaped her as he knelt down in front of her and, lifting her feet one at a time, removed her sandals, before reaching once more for her briefs. Slowly he peeled the scrap of lace down her now trembling legs and repeated the procedure, finally removing them completely.

He looked up at her though the thick curl of his lashes. 'Exquisite…' he murmured, and before she knew what he intended his hands had grasped her waist. He kissed the flat plain of her stomach and lower, to nuzzle at the apex of her thighs.

'No!' She tried to pull back.

'You are right. You are not ready yet for what I had in mind.' Zac rose to his feet and, swinging her up in his arms, carried her to the bed. He pulled back the coverlet and laid her gently down, then pulled the cover back over her and straightened up.

She stared up at him, her luminous blue eyes reflecting her puzzlement. Surely he was going to join her? Then she remembered—he had said she was not ready…

'So I am not mistress material after all?' she murmured.

He did not answer, but looked down at her with a strange expression on his face, broodingly solemn. Then, taking his wallet from his pocket, he flipped it open and took out a card. 'These are the numbers you can contact me on any time. The last is my personal cell phone.' He dropped it on the bedside table.

'That isn't necessary. You know where to find me.' She did not fully understand what had happened from his stripping her naked to becoming the cool, aloof man before her.

'Let me be the judge of what is necessary.' And, bending over her, he kissed her slowly, tenderly. 'Go to sleep, Sally. I'll see myself out and see you tomorrow.'

The night air was cold, and Zac stopped on the pavement to put his sweater on before getting into his car. He started the engine, a tender smile curling his mouth as he thought of the look of puzzlement on Sally's face when he had tucked her up in bed. It had stretched his control to the limit to leave her instead of joining her. The image of stripping off her clothes and her standing naked in his hold flashed in his head. Not a good idea when he was driving, and he shifted uncomfortably in his seat.

He hadn't intended on having sex with Sally tonight, and strictly speaking he had not—the pain in his groin could testify to the fact. But he had not walked away as he'd intended. He hadn't been able to keep his hands off her.

A frown pleated his broad brow. He had realised when she'd murmured about not being mistress material that Sally really wasn't, and it bothered him. He wished that he had never made the distasteful deal with her, but dated her in a conventional way…

As for her guidelines… He shook his dark head. He had nothing to worry about; he was seeing her tomorrow night. She had agreed to have a look at his apartment, and once she saw it he knew her guidelines and hopefully their deal would be forgotten. The next time they had sex would be in a king-size bed, and he could hardly wait.

Sally lay where Zac had left her, her body aching with frustration, hardly able to believe he had walked out. She told herself she didn't care, that she was glad he was gone and had spared her another night of sex, but in her heart of hearts she knew she lied. Obviously to a worldly, sophisticated male like Zac she fell short of what he was used to in the bedroom stakes. She should be pleased if he had tired of her already. She knew he was a man of his word and would not renege on his deal with her father, but bizarrely the thought gave her no joy.

CHAPTER TEN

THE next evening Sally walked out of the museum and her heart leapt. Her blue eyes landed on Zac, who was standing on the bottom exit step. Immaculately dressed in a dark business suit and snowy-white shirt, he was the epitome of a sophisticated mega-tycoon, and Sally had trouble believing she had actually made love with the man. But the sudden rush of heat to her face reminded her all too swiftly.

He covered the steps between them in a few lithe strides.

'At last,' he murmured and, taking her head between his hands, he kissed her firmly on the mouth. 'You're late.'

Breathless, she stepped back—and bumped into Charles, who was following her out. His arm came round her waist to steady her.

Zac's hand caught her arm. 'Steady, *cara.*' He smiled, drawing her to his side. 'You might give the man the wrong impression.' And, glancing at an astonished-looking Charles, he continued, 'You must be Sally's boss—Charles. Sally has told me so much about you. Nice to meet you.' He held out his free hand.

Sally looked from one to the other in shocked disbelief as Charles automatically shook Zac's hand, his glance taking in the possessive arm now draped around her shoulders before he looked at her with a puzzled expression on his face.

'You are all right, Sally? You know this man?'

But before she could open her mouth Zac cut in.

'Oh, yes—she knows me intimately. Don't you, sweetheart?'

She blushed scarlet and wanted to kick him. Instead she turned to Charles. 'Zac Delucca, a recent acquaintance of mine,' she offered reluctantly.

'You English are so reserved. Acquaintance, indeed.' Zac, every inch the dominant male, gave her a blatantly sexy look before turning to Charles and adding, 'In my country we would say lover.'

'Here we would not be so blunt,' Charles responded, holding Zac's arrogant gaze. 'And it is really no concern of mine except that Sally is a valued member of my team and a dear friend. You'd better take care of her.' He glanced back at Sally and smiled. 'I hope your mother is okay, and I'll see you on Monday. Goodbye.' And with a nod of his head to Zac, he left.

Sally watched him go, and then she saw the big black limousine parked on the road directly outside the exit. It simply added to the anger she was feeling. Furious, she shook Zac's arm off her shoulders.

'What on earth are you playing at? You promised no one would know about us, and you turn up here like I don't know what.'

'Like an animal staking out his territory?' he offered helpfully, and laughed at her look of horror. 'What do you expect, Sally?' He took her elbow and urged her down the steps to the waiting limousine. The chauffeur held open the door and she got in. Zac slid in beside her and, grasping her chin, turned her head to face him.

'I only agreed to your parents being kept in ignorance of

our relationship,' he said. 'While I guard my privacy, I refuse to treat our relationship as a sordid secret. As for your boss—I know he wants you, and I am a possessive man. I keep what is mine. I was simply warning him off. The straightforward approach is usually the best, I find. You should take it as a compliment,' he declared outrageously, and shot her a wicked teasing smile.

'You are unbelievable,' she murmured, shaking her head as the chauffeur manoeuvred the car through the rush-hour traffic.

'So I have been told,' he muttered, his attention distracted by the ringing of his phone.

She glanced at him, but he had taken the phone from his jacket pocket and his dark eyes were narrowed in concentration—but not on her.

'If you don't mind, I have a few calls to make—some business to settle.' And, not waiting for her answer, he began talking in rapidfire Italian to whoever was on the other end.

Zac made her head spin. She didn't understand a word he was saying, but his deep, melodious voice sounded even more seductive in his own language. Seated next to him, with the all-male scent of him teasing her nostrils, and her lips still tingling from his kiss, she was in danger of him taking her over completely. Possessive, he had said—which she supposed *was* a compliment in a way. At least he had not added *for as long as it lasts*.

The car stopped and she looked around. 'We are in an underground car park!' she exclaimed as the chauffeur opened the door and she stepped out.

'Brilliant observation, *cara*,' Zac remarked with a smile, suddenly appearing at her side and taking her hand in his. 'I promised to show you my apartment, remember?'

Sally caught the salacious, knowing male grin on the chauffeur's face as he stepped back. Zac might as well have said *come up and see my etchings*, she thought, totally embarrassed.

But fifteen minutes later, her embarrassment forgotten, she stood in the middle of a huge bedroom, one of three he had shown her in the penthouse, and stared in amazement at a double bed the size of small state.

A brown leather headboard ran along the top and curved a few feet around either side to incorporate what passed as bedside tables, she supposed. But they were nothing like anything she had ever seen before. A bewildering array of steel buttons and switches were inset into the leather, along with screens and flashing lights. It looked like the flight deck of a jumbo jet.

From what she had seen, the whole apartment was on a massive scale. The kitchen had looked like something out of space: high-tech and unfathomable to Sally's stunned gaze. The living area was all steel, glass and black leather, and the dining room looked out over a long terrace with a fantastic view down the Thames to the Houses of Parliament and beyond.

Suddenly two hands curved around her waist from behind and pulled her back against a hard male body, and she couldn't help drawing in a sharp breath.

'So what do you think of the place?' Zac asked, nuzzling her neck, his warm breath caressing her ear.

Pride said she should at least try to resist Zac, but he pulled her tighter and the rock-hard pressure of his erection against her bottom sent her pulse-rate into overdrive.

'It is very modern—the ultimate bachelor pad,' she managed to answer, and then Zac ran his tongue up the side of her neck and traced the whorls of her ear. It was impossible for Sally to hide the way her body was suddenly trembling and she gave up trying.

His hands stroked up to cup her breasts, his thumbs gently rubbing the tender tips through the soft cotton of the top she was wearing.

'Do you like it?' he asked, his lips warm against her throat, and she wasn't sure if he meant the apartment or what he was doing to her.

But Sally said yes anyway, as he turned her around and lifted her top clear over her head and dispensed with her bra.

'You take my breath away, Sally,' Zac said huskily, his smouldering gaze sweeping over her half-naked body in almost worshipful appreciation.

He lifted his hands to caress her breasts, his long fingers teasing the tender tips into tight, ultra-sensitive arousal. A whimper of delight escaped her, and he caught it with his mouth and kissed her with a deep erotic skill that totally beguiled her.

His hands dropped to her waist and deftly removed her skirt, but she didn't notice. The same dizzying excitement and anticipation sizzled through her veins as during the first time he touched her, but now it was so much more intense as she knew the pleasure that was to follow.

Zac swept her up in his arms and eased her briefs off her legs, placing her gently in the middle of the huge bed.

'I have waited almost two days for this, and it is killing me,' he groaned, his glittering black eyes sweeping over her naked body, displayed for his delectation on the taupe coverlet.

Sally watched as he shed his clothes with a minimum of effort, and marvelled anew at his broad hair-roughened chest, at the all-male power and beauty of his naked bronzed body. He came down beside her and stroked a hand over her breast to the junction of her slender thighs. Her body bucked in response as his seeking fingers found her moist and ready.

Her hands moved over his muscular chest to curve around his broad shoulders. Her whole body shook with excitement, and instinctively she squirmed against him and drew a teasing finger down the length of his spine.

A deep shudder racked his mighty frame, and, catching her hand, he rolled over her and caught her breathlessly parted lips in a fierce kiss. Then his head dipped and his mouth found the rigid tip of her breast, suckling with an urgent need that made her groan out loud. Nudging her legs apart, he slid between them.

Sally lost all sense of time and place as Zac swept her along on a vast wave of passion that finally left her sprawled over his chest, her body still pulsing in the aftermath of his hungry, driven possession.

'I needed that,' he rasped. 'It was incredible.' His hands stroked softly down her back to her thighs and back up, to thread through the tangled mass of her hair. '*You* are incredible, my Salmacis.'

'I warned you—I do not answer to my given name,' she murmured softly, then did the opposite. 'You have no idea how embarrassing it can be when I'm introduced to people and I have to explain what it means,' she told him, with a soft, languorous smile curving her mouth. She was floating on a sea of pleasure, and she was too happy to argue.

'You answered me!' he quipped. 'But I understand it might be a problem. I won't use it in public, but I think of you as Salmacis when we make love, and by that point my first priority is rarely getting an explanation from you.' He chuckled.

'You are incorrigible.' She grinned, her blue eyes lingering on his darkly attractive face. How had she ever thought he wasn't handsome? Zac was utterly gorgeous.

'Maybe, but right now I am insatiable.' And he proceeded

to arouse her all over again, with a slow, skilful intimate exploration of her shapely body.

When his long fingers parted her thighs and found her hot and wet he rasped, 'And so, it seems, are you.'

She gave a long, shuddering groan as her body vibrated in fierce delight at the subtle stroke of his fingertips against her intimate quivering flesh. Her back arched as he moved down her body, lingering to suckle each breast before dipping his dark head lower still. His sinfully sexy mouth delivered the ultimate intimacy, the flick of his tongue teasing and tasting the tiny nub of feminine pleasure to pulsing arousal. He suddenly stopped. With every sensitised nerve screaming out for release she reached for him involuntarily, her slender fingers grasping at the black silken hair of his head.

He looked up through his thick curling lashes and murmured, 'Now you are ready for this, my sweet Salmacis.'

What followed drove her completely out of her mind as her body tensed to breaking point and she tumbled over the edge into a tumultuous release.

'What about you?' she murmured, when she was finally able to breathe again. The thick, rock-hard length of him was pressing against her still quivering stomach. 'You didn't…'

'Oh, I will.'

He covered her mouth with his own, and just when she thought she had no more to give Zac proved her wrong. Slowly he began to kiss and caress her in a deeply erotic exploration of her body, his mouth returning to her breasts to suckle on their hard, throbbing peaks.

Her whole body was suffused with sensual heat, and she quaked with need. The intensity of the pleasure he gave her was almost pain. She clung to him, her nails scoring his back as he lifted her hips and thrust into her with long, deep strokes, stretching, filling her with a power and passion that drove her once more to the pinnacle of ecstasy and held her there.

She cried out, 'Please, please, Zac—now.' Her inner muscles clenched around his throbbing hardness as he plunged deeper into her eager body and carried them both to a ferociously orgasmic climax.

Sally lay across his chest, her body sated and her breathing slowly returning to normal. How long she lay there, listening to the heavy beating of his heart gradually subside, she had no idea. Finally she raised her head and looked lovingly down at Zac's bronzed features. His heavy-lidded eyes were closed, his long black lashes curling on his high cheekbones, and somehow he looked younger, not so hard, even a little vulnerable in his sleep.

She smiled to herself, relishing the pleasure it gave her to study him in secret. She lifted a finger and tenderly stroked the line of his now shadowed jaw, and then up over his cheekbone to smooth the perfectly arched black brows. Her finger lingered on the small scar above one eyebrow and she wondered how he'd got it.

His eyes opened.

'I thought you were asleep,' she murmured.

'No, just savouring your touch. Carry on, my Salmacis.'

'How did you get this?' she asked. His huskily voiced request was oddly endearing, and the afterglow of making love encouraged her to be bold.

'In a fight when I was a teenager,' he murmured.

'That does not surprise me somehow—though I am surprised anyone managed to cut you.' She smiled, letting her gaze roam with feminine appreciation over the width of his shoulders and the muscular biceps of his strong arms. 'Who was it?' she asked.

'I can't remember his name now. I fought so many.'

Sally was intrigued. 'You mean you actually got into so many fights you can't remember what they were about? That is terrible.'

'No, I fought professionally until I was twenty. That is how I made the money to start my business empire.'

She looked at him with big, soulful eyes. He truly was a remarkable man. He had actually fought physically to enable him get where he was today. How many punches, how much pain must his magnificent body have had to suffer as a teenager? The thought of anyone hurting him horrified her.

'Zac, you are amazing.'

'Thank you,' he responded with a rogue smile. 'You are pretty amazing yourself.' And he kissed her, then let his fingers run down the length of her hair. 'I love your hair.'

Sally's heart stopped for a second. She had actually thought he was going to say *I love you*, and her mellow mood was broken. How foolish was that? They had made love for hours and it had scrambled her brain, she swiftly told herself. She didn't *want* Zac to love her. She didn't believe in love. And yet she could not dislodge the fear that assailed her…

'Thank you,' she responded in kind, and hoped Zac had not noticed her brief hesitation. She shook her head to free his hand from her hair. 'Now, what has a girl got to do to get fed around here?' she asked, with an attempt at a smile. Conveniently her stomach rumbled.

'Okay, I can take a hint.' Zac lifted her by the waist and laid her down on the bed. 'And you have already done it—quite spectacularly,' he told her with a devilish smile. 'What would you like to eat? Meat? Fish? Game? Name it and it is yours.'

'Fish—but can you actually cook?'

'Yes,' he said, turning to sit on the edge of the bed, his back to her. 'But I have no intention of doing so.'

And a moment later he was ordering a meal over the telephone—conveniently part of the stupendous headboard.

'We have forty minutes before the food arrives,' he told her, replacing the phone. 'Enough time to share a shower.' And he plucked her off the bed and carried her into the bathroom.

A lot later Sally, with her hair wringing wet, a broad smile on her face and the sound of Zac's laughter ringing in her ears, collapsed into a plastic cushioned chair that looked like something out of the fifties, a towel wrapped around her body.

Zac had slipped on jeans and a top and gone to collect the food when it arrived. Sally, on the other hand, barely had the strength to move. The man actually was insatiable, she decided…and she would not have him any other way. She loved every minute spent with him in bed—or anywhere else, for that matter.

She now freely acknowledged the disappointment she had felt and tried to deny last night, when he had left her naked and alone in bed. But he had certainly more than made up for it this evening. Not only great sex, but she felt she understood him better since he had told her about his fighting career. No wonder he appeared hard sometimes, when he had had to physically fight to survive as a teenager.

Then again, maybe it was because sex was new to her that she enjoyed it so much. she tried to reason with herself. But she knew in her innermost being it had everything to do with the man himself. She could not imagine sharing such intimacies with any man but Zac.

The huge shower, with its jets shooting out all over, had been a novel place to make love, she thought, a dreamy, reminiscent smile on her face. Zac had soaped her all over, kissed and caressed her, and she had returned the favour. She had stroked and soaped every part of his magnificent body and then, dropping to her knees, she had done what she had been longing to do but never had the confidence before.

She had let her slender fingers examine every inch of his thickened length in minute detail, in awe of the source of so much pleasure. She had felt him tense when her tongue had swept out to taste the velvet tip, and heard him groan as she'd continued further.

'No more,' he had finally grated, and, reaching under her arms, he had jerked her high in the air and thrust up into her in an explosion of need. She was convinced only a man of Zac's strength and vigour could possibly have supported her, locked to his great body, as he had driven them both to yet another mind-blowing orgasm.

Against all the odds, her own innate honesty was forcing her to admit she was halfway to falling in love with him, and strangely she was no longer so afraid—it did not worry her at all.

Carpe diem—live for the moment. That was her new motto, she decided. And there was no guarantee in life as to how many moments one had left…

With a carefree grin she got to her feet and, picking up the conveniently wall-mounted hairdryer at one side of the first of the twin white porcelain basins, she began methodically to dry her hair, running her fingers through it over and over again.

She looked at her refection in the mirrored door of the cabinet that stretched the length of the wall. Her face was flushed, her lips were swollen, and Zac's roughened jaw had left a few telltale marks. She looked what she was: a thoroughly loved-up woman, but a bit of a mess. Maybe Zac had a brush she could borrow, to try and style her wayward mass of hair into some kind of order? She could impress him with her smooth, elegant locks…

She pushed at the cabinet and a door in front of her sprang open. There was all the equipment one would expect to find in a man's bathroom, including a box of condoms, and, spying a brush, she picked it up. It was then she noticed there was also a half-used bottle of Dior perfume—definitely not male— a few black hairpins and a thick black elastic hairband.

Her carefree mood evaporated like smoke in the wind. It did not take a genius to work out that the last woman to share his bed and bathroom had been Margot, the raven-haired model from Tuesday night. Sally stumbled back in shock. Just the thought of Zac sharing with Margot the same intimacies he had shared with her was enough to make her feel sick to her stomach.

She sank back onto the plastic chair and drew in a choked breath as pain pierced like a knife in her heart. Her head fell forward, her hair forgotten as she blinked back the bitter tears that threatened. Despairingly she realised that, against her long-held belief in her immunity to love, she had done the previously unthinkable and fallen in love with the man.

No… It wasn't possible, her brain told her, but her heart didn't want to listen… Conflicting thoughts were tearing her apart. She had only known Zac a week, been intimate with him for only three days. It could not be love… She would not, could not, accept such weakness.

All her life she had watched her mother humour her father every which way to try and keep his love, to keep him at her side. Well, Sally was made of sterner stuff. She took after her maternal grandma in character, and she was nobody's fool.

Sally had fallen in lust at the hands of an expert—as many a woman had before—and to drive the lesson home she rose to her feet, straightened her shoulders and returned to the cabinet. She brushed her hair back from her face and fastened it in a ponytail with the black band left by Zac's last lover. A salutary reminder of what a naïve idiot she had been even to think of trying to impress a man who quite happily had sex with two women in the same week… No wonder he kept a whole box of condoms and never, even in the heat of passion, forgot to use one, she thought bitterly. As for loving such a man—never.

She returned to the bedroom and, gathering her scattered clothes from the floor and bed, swiftly put them on. Then, picking up her purse and slipping her feet into her sandals, she left the scene of her downfall without a second glance.

CHAPTER ELEVEN

ZAC turned as she entered the dining room. 'You have dressed. I thought you might simply grab a robe. Or at least I hoped,' he said, with a wickedly sensual smile.

'I never thought,' she murmured, and tried to smile when really she felt like cursing him to hell and back. Then, directing her attention to the dishes of food laid out on the dining table, along with two plates and glasses plus a bottle of wine in an ice bucket, she added, 'This smells delicious. I am ravenous.' Actually, the reverse was true—she had totally lost her appetite—but she was determined not to let Zac know.

Standing there, in jeans and a polo shirt, he was all arrogant male, and he would scent weakness a mile off, she knew.

'Dinner is served, my lady.' He gave her a sweeping bow and pulled out a chair for her, then waited until she'd sat down. With a flourish he opened the wine, which turned out to be champagne, and, filling her glass, gave a toast. 'To us—and long may we last!'

Reluctantly she sipped the sparkling vintage. 'To us,' she responded, and forced herself to smile again, when basically she felt like scratching his eyes out. But she could not afford to.

No matter how much she despised his morals, or lack of them, she still had to stick to their deal until Zac decided otherwise. Her mother's future happiness was at stake, short though that future might be.

Bitterly she wondered how he could almost have sex with her one night, make love to the willowy Margot the next, then have the audacity to demand Sally become his lover the following night. She wasn't jealous, she told herself, simply disgusted. For a brief space of time she had let herself become besotted by a man. Well, never again, she vowed silently…

The food looked great, but she had to make herself eat, and every morsel tasted like ash in her mouth. She refused the sweet, and his offer of more champagne, and watched him fill his glass again. Then she lifted her own to take a sip of the now flat liquid.

'I've been thinking, Sally.'

She raised her head and met his dark eyes across the table.

'We should renegotiate our arrangement and place it on a more intimate basis.'

She almost choked on the champagne. Was he crazy? She might be inexperienced, but she was pretty sure they could not possibly be more intimate than they already were.

'I know we made a deal, and you stated your guidelines, but I want to change them—for the benefit of both of us. I would like you to move in here.'

He sounded as if he was discussing some business deal in a boardroom, and she was too shocked to speak.

'You know the sex between us is incredible, but you have to admit, nice as your studio is, the bed is a little too small—especially for me.' He shrugged his broad shoulders. 'Whereas here we have plenty of space and you can enjoy every comfort money allows,' Zac offered. 'Plus, I am a very busy man. I had intended taking a few weeks' holiday, but a project I am involved in is not going as smoothly as I hoped and fixing it is going to involve quite a bit of travelling. I would feel much happier if I knew you were living here, where the security is superlative.'

Sally listened, her anger and bitterness festering as he continued.

'Think about it, Sally. All your financial needs taken care of. No more secondhand gowns, but the best money can buy.'

And then he had the nerve to slant a very male, satisfied smile her way—as if he was offering her the crown jewels when in fact he was suggesting she become his live-in lover in London. She could not help noticing he had not suggested taking her with him on his travels. He probably had other women living in his properties dotted all over the world.

Zac's arrogance was unbelievable, and his last comment had filled her with such fury that she bowed her head, so he would not see the anger blazing in her eyes.

She fought down the bile that rose in her throat and battled to control her rage. Hard to believe a short time ago she had been in danger of believing she might love him. Well, no more delusions—and no more negotiating with the vile man…

'Sally? What do you say?'

Slowly she lifted her head her and said, 'No.' Pushing back her chair, she stood up and very deliberately glanced at the thin gold watch on her wrist—a twenty-first birthday present from her mother.

'No explanation? Just no?'

Only then did Sally allow herself to look at him. The watch was a timely reminder of why she could not lose her temper with the lecherous bastard. 'Exactly. We made a deal, and I will stick by it. You said you were a man of your word, and I expect you to stand by that.'

Zac's eyes narrowed. 'Wait a minute—what just happened

here?' he demanded, and she would have laughed at the look of confusion on his face if she hadn't been so angry and—yes, she admitted it—deeply hurt…

'We have just spent hours indulging in the most incredible sex, and *no* is your immediate reaction to my generous suggestion?' He finished his drink and rose to his feet to move in front of her, his hands on her shoulders, his black brows drawing together in a frown. 'I don't see your problem with the idea. You are joking, yes?' he prompted, his accent thickening.

'No, I am not joking,' she said curtly, finding his use of the word *generous* an insult too far. Zac believed he could buy anything and anyone—well, not her… She would stick to the letter of their deal, but no more, and with that in mind she added, 'It is almost midnight, and Saturday is my time, in case you had forgotten. I need to call a cab and go home.'

His eyes narrowed with tightly controlled anger. 'No need to call a cab. The limousine will take—'

She cut him off with a bitter laugh.

'No, thank you. I saw the salacious look your driver gave me when we arrived here,' she said scathingly. 'I certainly don't need a repeat performance to remind me. A cab will do fine.'

Zac stilled, his mind running riot. He was furious at her hard-headed attitude, and he could not believe the passionate, eager lover he had held in his arms could change into the cold-eyed woman before him. He had actually imagined he felt a connection beyond the sexual with Sally—enough to confide in her the truth of his fighting past, something he had never done with any woman. Maybe that was his mistake!

He had never asked a woman to move in with him before—in fact, he had never spent more than a weekend with a woman in his life. One night, two at most, and he could count on one hand how rare an occurrence that was for him. Yet he had offered Sally more than any other woman and she had turned him down flat.

Or had she? he wondered cynically. Power and wealth attracted some women, and he had both and had learnt to recognise the type. He would be a fool if he didn't see through every hard-headed gold-digger that came along. He had put Sally in that category at first and changed his mind. Then he remembered she had said she wanted to marry—maybe she had not been teasing him, as he had thought… Was her refusal of his offer a trick to get him hungry enough for her to give her the ultimate offer: marriage? He didn't know…but he meant to find out…

Sally watched him as the silence lengthened, and when Zac finally responded, she tensed as his fingers tightened on her shoulders.

'I think I understand why you refused to move in here.' He surveyed her with dark-eyed arrogance. 'You worry about what people will think if you live in my apartment, an outdated anxiety in this day and age. As for the driver—if you don't like him he will be replaced.'

'You amaze me, Zac!' Sally exclaimed. 'You don't care a damn about anyone but yourself—as long as you get what you want, to hell with the rest of us poor mortals.' She shook her head, her eyes hating him. 'You treat people like puppets to be moved at your bidding. Well, keep your driver and keep your apartment. I am not interested in either them or you.'

'You were happy enough in my bed earlier, and eager to do my bidding,' he declared with a sardonic smile. 'I only have to touch you and you will be again. But be warned—if your refusal of my offer is simply a ploy to get what the majority of females want—a wedding ring—you are wasting your time.'

Sally's cheeks burned, and she was filled with an incredulous anger as his words sank home. He could not have chosen a better way to insult her, yet again, and he had made her hate him more by reminding her of her weakness and implying she was after a marriage proposal.

'Oh, please!' she cried. 'Don't kid yourself. I would not marry you or any man in a million years. I am here only because of my father,' she said scathingly, and wanting to hurt him, wanting to dent his ego, his arrogant pride, she continued, 'You and he are two of a kind. He actually *told* me to be nice to you, and you have to wonder what kind of man pimps his own daughter to his boss…' She sneered. 'And what kind of boss takes advantage of the fact.'

'I am nothing like your father,' he snarled, his face darkening in fury. 'And you were with me from the moment we met. You practically melted the first time we kissed—the same as I did.'

Sally's mouth hardened into a bitter, hostile line. 'I made a *deal* with my father, to back him and be nice to you when you called. In return he will come with me this weekend to visit his wife, Pamela—my mother—something he never does more than once in a blue moon. Something I was hoping to persuade him to do over lunch the first day you and I met. And we both know that didn't work,' she drawled derisively.

'I had to bargain for the presence of my father at my mother's bedside because for some reason my mother loves the man, and misses him. Heaven knows why. And that was the first reason I agreed to your deal. The second was keeping my father out of prison—again to keep my mother happy. I asked you for time to raise the money, and hopefully with the damn man's help I'd pay you back, but you would not give me time. Well, now I am not wasting what is technically *my time* on you. I am leaving. I am picking my father up at nine in the morning to make sure he keeps his side of the bargain. As for you and I…' she drawled, her blue eyes reflecting her contempt. 'You know when and where I'm available, as agreed under the terms of our deal.'

Sally felt the tension in every bone in her body as Zac stared at her in a bitter, hostile silence, and it took every inch of will-power she could muster to hold on to her self-control. She avoided his eyes, but she could feel his gaze burning into her.

Suddenly his hands fell from her shoulders and she was free. Surprised, she glanced up at him. His face was suffused with anger, a thin white line circled his tight mouth, and his eyes rested coldly on her like chips of ice. And yet she could not look away, could not move. The continuing silence hung between them like a great black thunder cloud, and neither one seemed able to break it.

Then, as if a veil had fallen over his face, his expression changed to one of hard indifference. He turned and crossed the room, picked up the phone and called a cab.

'As you so succinctly pointed out, it is almost Saturday,' he drawled as he sauntered back towards her.

Sally saw how close he was, and knew she should step back, but she refused to let him intimidate her.

'The cab will be here in five minutes,' he informed her, his hand reaching out to grasp her hair, sliding off the band constraining it, his long fingers tangling in the glossy red locks. 'You are an intelligent woman, Sally. But you have met your match with me,' he told her chillingly.

His dark head bent and his arm slid round her, pressing her against his long body while his hard mouth moved ruthlessly on hers. Her pulse leapt, and she fought an internal battle to resist the seductive power of his kiss, but his fingers bit into her waist and she lost… Helplessly she arched against him, her hands of their own volition curving over his broad shoulders and clinging in shaming response.

He raised his head, his dark eyes gleaming down at her. 'You see, my Salmacis,' he drawled mockingly, 'blame your father, make all the excuses you like, but you want me as much as I want you, and some day you might admit it. When you do, you have all my numbers—call me.'

Mortified by her easy capitulation to his kiss, Sally jerked free of him and glanced up with a bitterness that belied the longing in her eyes. 'That will never happen.' Then, to her relief, the intercom rang. The cab had arrived.

Zac walked her down to the street without saying a word until he handed her into the waiting cab.

'I am going to Italy tomorrow. Maybe we will meet again some time.' He shrugged 'Your choice.' And, turning, he went back inside without a backward glance.

Sally told herself she was glad it was over between them as the cab moved off, but she had to blink away the moisture hazing her eyes.

Zac Delucca was six feet five, and right at this moment he felt about two inches tall—not a pleasant feeling, he acknowledged as he strode across to the drinks cabinet and poured whisky into a crystal glass. He downed it in one. He was furious with Sally, but more so with himself. He was man enough to know without question that she wanted him on a sexual level, but that Sally dared class him with her father had shocked him.

He was forced to take a long, hard look at himself, and he didn't much like what he saw. When had he become such a cynical bastard about the opposite sex that he had mistaken an innocent, hard-working young woman for a teasing little gold-digger out for what she could get?

He had to accept he had behaved less than honourably in demanding Sally become his mistress. It had never entered his head to do anything so outrageous before, and he definitely never would again. But Sally had the ability to get under his skin like no other woman, and blinded by lust and—yes—jealousy he had acted on impulse and completely out of character.

Zac prided himself on his honesty and fair dealing, but his pride had taken one hell of a battering when Sally had declared with brutal frankness that as far as she was concerned her dad had tried to *pimp* his own daughter to save his neck, and that Zac was just as bad for taking advantage of the fact…

He had never once considered her feelings, other than in the sexual sense, and she responded with avid delight to what he could give her in bed. But the burden she'd had to bear with her mother and father that had led her into his bed had not bothered him at all.

One of the reasons she had agreed to be his mistress was so she could make a bargain with her despised father and get the man to go and visit his wife. How sad was that…?

It was true that Sally had asked for time so she could try and pay the debt, and he had refused. Something he had completely forgotten in his determination to bed her. All of which made him as despicable in her eyes as her father, and he couldn't really blame her… She deserved much better treatment from the man in her life than he had given her.

He had behaved abominably, and Zac knew that if Sally truly believed what she had told him, he had to let her go. His confidence and his pride in himself as a man would allow him to do no less.

He poured another whisky and tried to tell himself the

world was full of beautiful women and he didn't need Sally. By the time he had downed half a bottle he was convinced!

Zac had known from the start she was going to be trouble. So far every time they had met they had ended up arguing at some point, and it was driving him crazy… He should have listened to what his head had been trying to tell him from the beginning and walked away.

A good businessman knew when to cut his losses. He was going back to Italy tomorrow and to hell with her. As for a woman, there was always Lisa on hold in Milan…

Sally opened the door of her apartment and stumbled inside. Zac had said he might see her some time, but she knew it was goodbye. It was what she wanted, an end to the affair that had been forced upon her, so why did she feel so hollow inside?

She had no answer and, stripping off her clothes, she slid naked into bed and pulled the cover up around her neck.

Tomorrow she was visiting her mother—with her father. When she had first set eyes on Zac she had been a woman on a mission… Well, now the mission was accomplished, she told herself. But it was a hollow victory, and she felt numb inside—no joy, no tears, just emptiness.

The next morning, heavy-eyed, she staggered into the bathroom and into the shower. Immediately, the memory of Zac and the shower they had shared the night before flashed in her mind. Ruthlessly, she stamped on the erotic vision and focused on the female articles Zac's previous lover had left in his bathroom.

She had done the right thing in refusing his offer to move into his apartment. They had a deal, and if he didn't want to keep it that suited her just fine. But to her horror, by the time she stepped out of the shower, stupid tears were streaming down her face.

Five hours later, the smile on her mother's face as Sally walked into her room with her dad was enough to make all the heartache worthwhile.

Sally excused herself an hour later, saying she wanted to do some shopping in the nearby city of Exeter.

But actually she could not stand to listen any longer to her father's rant about how he had been moved sideways by his new boss. Now he had to do twice as much work for the same salary, and he had decided he was definitely retiring in twelve months, so he could see a lot more of his wife.

'Oh, Nigel, it must be so difficult for you,' Pamela had offered, her love and concern for the thieving devil shining in her eyes.

Sally had wanted to scream. It was lies—all lies. Her dad knew Pamela wasn't going to last more than a year, because the doctor had contacted him after informing Sally that her mother's heart wouldn't hold out much longer, but her mum lapped it all up, like a puppy dog devoted to its master, so instead she'd left.

By the time she returned her mum was on her own and her father had gone back to the hotel—or so he had told his wife. Sally did not see him again until breakfast the next morning. It was a silent meal, except for her father stating he wanted to leave for London directly after lunch. Sally had no intention of doing so, and as they were using her car he'd have no choice. But in that she was wrong. Five minutes after entering his wife's room, he had got her mum to agree it was best they left early…

If anything was guaranteed to confirm what Sally had always thought about love and marriage, it was seeing her mother, who was dying, comforting her father, who was lying through his teeth.

CHAPTER TWELVE

RETURNING to her hated apartment on Sunday evening, Sally tried to tell herself she was glad Zac had gone back to Italy before she got in too deep. But it did not stop her checking her messages in the vain hope he might have called. How pathetic was that? she thought miserably as she climbed into bed. But it did not stop her hoping deep inside that he might turn up Monday to Friday, as per their deal and that was even worse!

Honesty forced her to admit that, blinded by jealousy, she had driven Zac away with her hateful comments. But it was for the best… She didn't love him, could not love him, she told herself, and feverishly brushed away the tears that were determined to fall. So what if she stayed in a few evenings waiting for a call that never came, and cried herself to sleep a night or two? It was a whole lot better than a lifetime of heartache.

But as a week passed with no word from Zac it became harder to dismiss him from her mind. Being alone in bed at night—the bed she had briefly shared with Zac—reminded her all too vividly of the pleasure and the passion of his exquisite lovemaking. When she did sleep invariably her dreams were haunted by his image, his touch, and she awoke hot and aching.

On Friday, two weeks to the day since Sally had last seen Zac her friend Jemma told her she looked pale and miserable and in need of cheering up. She suggested a night out—dinner and the cinema. Sally agreed, and actually managed to enjoy the film.

But the next day, when she arrived at the nursing home, the little bit of good the night out had done her was immediately cancelled as she was met by the doctor in charge of her mum's case.

He had been trying to ring her on her mobile phone for the past two hours, but Sally was in the habit of switching it off while driving so had never received his call.

Apparently her mother had suffered a massive heart attack and slipped into a coma. The staff had made her as comfortable as possible under the circumstances, and her husband had been informed but had not arrived as yet.

He finally did arrive—an hour after his wife had died…

The six days before the funeral were the worst of Sally's life—though for once her father rose to the occasion and looked after the arrangements. Devastated by her mum's death, even though it had been expected, Sally cried herself to sleep every night. Tossing and turning in bed, she remembered how Zac had once offered to cuddle her, and, oh, how she longed for the comfort and the strength of his strong arms now.

The funeral was held on a bright July day at the church in Bournemouth where her mum had been baptised, a short forty-three years earlier. The service was brief and the congregation was no more than fifty people. Her doctor and the nurse who had been her primary carer at the home came; the rest were friends and people her mum had known all her life, plus Al and his parents, and Sally was glad of their support. But in her heart of hearts she wished Zac was by her side, supporting her. A futile wish as there had been no word from him…no call…

Her father played the grieving widower, but she was too distraught with grief to care what he did.

Her mother was buried in the cemetery in a plot next to her parents, and the funeral tea was held in the hotel where Sally and her father were staying for the night.

The whole affair took barely four hours, from start to finish.

She could not face dinner with her father, but the next morning he handed Sally her mother's jewellery box with the statement, 'She left you this. You can check with the solicitor, if you like, but what money she had she left to me. As for the studio apartment, you can keep it until probate is settled and there is no danger of it being included in your mother's estate, and then I want it back.' He said this without a trace of shame, and then got into a new BMW car and drove off.

Sally had no desire to return to her apartment, but it was legally hers and she was damned sure she was not giving it back to her father. That he could suggest such a thing at her mum's funeral beggared belief. He must think she really was the silly girl he was fond of calling her, as easily manipulated as her mother had been. He was so self-centred, so blind, he didn't realise she had only ever obeyed him for her mum's sake…

Well, not any more… She was desolate with grief, and had never felt so alone in her life, but she was not a fool…

At Al's insistence she spent a few days at his parents' home. In comfort, with old friends around her, she began to come to terms with her mum's death. And with Al's encouragement she decided she was going to take a sabbatical from her job and see the world, as she had once promised herself.

She walked into her apartment a week later, full of good intentions. The first one was to have a strong cup of coffee after the long car journey. She saw the message light flashing on the telephone as she filled the kettle at the sink.

Zac, she thought, and her heart missed a beat. It was over

four long, devastatingly sad weeks since she had seen him, but she was wrong. There were two messages: in the first no one spoke—probably a wrong number—and the second message was from the estate agent who was handling the sale of her apartment, asking her to get in touch immediately. He had a cash buyer for the property at the full asking price, on condition she left the furniture and could complete and vacate within two weeks…

August in Peru, and spring was on the horizon. Sally breathed in the warm air and felt her excitement mounting as she boarded the bus outside Lima airport with the other members of her tour group, embarking on a month-long tour of the country.

She still thought of her mum every day, and the sadness would be with her always, Sally knew, but it would no longer rule her life. She thought of Zac most days as well, but she was gradually coming to terms with their one-week affair, having accepted that that was all it had ever been or could have been with a womaniser like Zac.

Today was her birthday: she was twenty-six and free to do exactly what she wanted, with no one to worry about except herself for the first time in years.

Actually, it had been surprisingly easy to leave London. The sale of her apartment had gone through without a hitch, she had sold her car, and with her clothes and the few belongings she wanted to keep she had stayed with Jemma for a week until her holiday started. Jemma was storing her things for her, and Sally now had more money than she had ever dreamt of. She would buy somewhere to live eventually—but not yet.

Her boss had agreed to her taking a year-long sabbatical, and the world was her oyster. If some nights she woke from sleep with dreams of Zac Delucca still haunting her she dismissed them from her mind—usually by making a cup of hot chocolate. It was now seven weeks since they had parted—not that she was counting!

Sally's blue eyes widened in awe as she stood high in the Andes, the ruins of Machu Picchu spread out before her. She had made it, her dream come true, and with the other members of the party she followed where the guide led.

It was everything and more that she had ever imagined, and she would have liked to spend some time to explore on her own, but when they stopped for morning coffee to her embarrassment she fainted… The youngest and probably the fittest member of the party, and yet she was the only one affected by the thin air—or so she thought…

Zac Delucca ran his hands through his hair. He could not concentrate on the papers before him, and, spinning around in his chair, he stared out of the window of his office, looking out over Rome and seeing nothing but the image of Sally. He had lost count of the times he had reached for his phone to call her and put it down again. Once he had actually let it ring and had got her answering service; he hadn't left a message. And Lisa in Milan was a lost cause, because he had no desire to bed the woman—or any woman except Sally, which was a first for him.

Salmacis, the nymph of the fountain, he thought with a wry smile. If she had been anything like her namesake Sally then poor Hermaphroditos hadn't stood a chance but to become one with her…

Finally Zac had to accept that he felt as if he had become one with Sally in a way he had never considered possible before. She had totally bewitched him. From the night she drew blood from his arm with the roses, and then lay naked in his arms, he had fallen under her spell, and now he felt as if she was drawing the life blood from his body. He couldn't concentrate on work; he couldn't think straight for any length of time. His waking and sleeping hours were filled with images of his Salmacis.

The door opened and Zac swung back. 'I ordered that I was not to be disturbed,' he growled as Raffe walked into the room and sat down in a chair facing the desk. 'I hired you to take care of things. What's gone wrong now?'

'Nothing—except you. According to Anna, your secretary, you are impossible to work with and someone has to tell you. I have been given the task. For the past four months you have travelled constantly and driven all your staff crazy—both here and in America. Not to mention the Far East, where apparently your abrupt attitude so insulted the head of the Japanese company we were in the process of buying that he has just informed me he is pulling out of the deal. What is going on with you, Zac? Woman trouble…?'

'I don't *have* women trouble,' Zac said adamantly, and knew he lied. He also knew he could not go on like this.

He had never been close to anyone in his life except maybe Raffe and Marco, his old fight manager, who now, with his wife, took care of his home in Calabria. They were as near to family as he had. He was a loner, and he had never needed anyone before, but now he needed Sally Paxton every which way there was…

He had been a coward too long. He loved Sally, and he wanted her bound to him by every law known to man—including marriage, he decided, and he was going to make it happen.

'Well, something is bugging you.' Raffe interrupted his musing. 'And the sooner you get over it the better for everyone. Anyway, back to business. I have just come back from London and everything is going smoothly and very profitably. A new contract has been signed to provide the Saudi Arabian government with the components they want.'

'Good. And Paxton? Is he behaving himself?' Zac asked, in the hope that Sally might be mentioned. Not that it mattered. His mind was made up: he was going to London to get her...

'Yes, though I never did understand why you kept him on just because his wife was in a nursing home. You are not usually so generous to a thief. Actually, it is immaterial now, as apparently his wife died a few months back. He took a couple of weeks' compassionate leave and returned to work, so there is nothing to stop you firing him now, which is no more than he deserves.'

'And his daughter?' Zac demanded, leaping to his feet. 'Sally? Has anyone been in touch with her? Offered our sympathy? Anything at all?'

'I should have guessed!' Raffe exclaimed. 'The short temper, the irritability—it all makes sense. Your problem is the very lovely daughter, and that is why you let Paxton stay. I'm right, aren't I?'

Zac gave him a quelling look. 'Shut up, Raffe, and order the jet. I'm going to London.'

Five days later Zac walked out of the British Museum, almost defeated. Sally appeared to have vanished off the face of the earth. His first shock had been the discovery that she had sold the apartment and left no forwarding address. The estate agent who had handled the sale had been no help, except to tell him the apartment had been on the market for a couple of months. Sally had never mentioned the fact, but he realised now where she had hoped to get the money from to pay him back, which made him feel even worse.

He'd had a long talk with her father, but he had no idea where she had gone and didn't care. Her boss had informed him she was on a year's sabbatical. He had not heard from her yet, but she had said she would keep in touch. Finally Zac had swallowed his pride and contacted Al, and he had told him Sally had left to go on a month-long tour of Peru. But that had been over a couple of months ago, and he had no idea where she was going afterwards.

Zac paused by the Bentley, the lines of strain etched deep in his face as he pondered on what to do next. He had called on her boss a second time in the hopes he might have heard from Sally, but no joy. A private detective was the next step, he decided, and was about to get in the car when a young woman approached him.

'Excuse me, but are you Mr Delucca?'

He was going to ignore her—until she added, 'My boss told me you were looking for my friend Sally…'

Sally didn't notice the big black car parked fifty yards further up the road as she turned her car into the drive and stopped. She slid out and picked up her shopping bag, which contained the new phone she had purchased along with other items. There was a smile on her face as she walked up the short garden path to the cottage she had rented in the seaside town of Littlehampton. Once, as a six-year-old, she had spent a weekend in a hotel here, with her mother and her grandma, and it was one of the most treasured memories she had of her childhood.

Her whole life had changed from the moment she had fainted at the ruins of Machu Picchu. Joan Adams, a retired doctor she had got to know well as they were the only single females travelling with the group, had pointed out that it was unlikely the thinness of the air had affected a fit young woman like her, and had suggested she might be pregnant. At first Sally had denied the possibility, but as the tour had continued and the morning sickness had started, Sally had had to reconsider.

She had thought long and hard on the flight back to England. Further travelling abroad was out for the foreseeable future, she'd decided, but that did not mean she had to stay in London.

Jemma had let her stay with her for the time it took Sally to buy a new car and pack up most of her belongings, and had accepted Sally's excuse that rather than travelling abroad she wanted to see more of her own country.

She had spotted a picture of the cottage in Littlehampton in the window of an estate agent in the nearby town of Worthing: for sale or to let unfurnished, with great sea views. Sally had viewed it on impulse, and taken a twelve-month lease on it the next day.

She opened the door and walked into the hall, hung up her coat and, dropping her shopping bag in the living room, she went to the kitchen to make a cup of tea. It was amazing, she thought, how life could take with one hand and give back with the other. She had lost her mum, but was soon going to *be* a mum…

She had registered with a local GP, and had her first scan at the hospital in Worthing. The baby was well, and the precious picture from the scan was in a picture frame at her bedside. If the baby was a girl she was going to call her Pamela, after her mum; if it was a boy… She hadn't decided… And she hadn't decided when she would tell Zac Delucca either.

She made a cup of tea and carried it through into the living room. She placed it on the table at the side of the nearest of the two cream soft-cushioned sofas she had bought that flanked the fireplace. She had opted for side-tables rather than a centre one, to give the illusion of space. Kicking off her shoes and sitting down, she curled her feet up on the sofa and reached for her teacup.

Sipping the hot tea, she supposed she would have to tell Zac Delucca some day—a man had a right to know he had fathered a child—but not yet… Maybe after the birth…

She wanted to savour every minute of her pregnancy in peace, and there was nothing peaceful about Zac Delucca. He went through life like a tornado, sweeping up anything he wanted and discarding the rest. Telling him could wait…

She glanced around the room. The warm, peach-painted walls, the oak ceiling beams and the polished oak floor looked sturdy and timeless, and the large peach, green and cream rug she had bought to put between the two sofas added a cosy touch. She had enjoyed choosing and purchasing the furniture for the living room and main bedroom. The second bedroom was for the baby and she had yet to start on that.

She was into nesting in a big way, she thought happily, and with a year's lease and the opportunity to buy if she wished she had left all her options open. If she decided to go back to her job in London at the end of her sabbatical she could. Or she could stay here. In the meantime all she had to concentrate on was her baby. With a contented sigh she reached for her shopping and withdrew the box containing her new phone and put it to one side. Then she took out the package containing the baby garments she had bought. She laid the tiny yellow booties and matching hat and jacket on the table, a soft smile curving her lips. It turned into a frown as the doorbell sounded. Reluctantly she got to her feet, padded into the small hall and opened the door…

CHAPTER THIRTEEN

SALLY'S mouth fell open, her eyes widening in stunned disbelief on the man standing before her. It couldn't be… It wasn't possible… But it was Zac Delucca…

She grasped the doorjamb, her legs suddenly weak and her heartbeat thundering in her breast, and she could not stop the heated rush of awareness flooding through her body as she looked up into his darkly handsome face. She had convinced herself she was over the hateful man, and she had certainly never *loved* him. That had been a momentary aberration brought about by sex, nothing more. She was content with her new life—and yet just the sight of him made a mockery of her hard-won serenity.

No, she would not allow herself to think that way. She straightened up, squaring her slender shoulders; it was probably her hormones running riot—something her doctor had warned her about—nothing more…

'Hello, Sally.' Zac could barely speak as he drank in the sight of Sally with hungry eyes. She stood in the doorway, her glorious red curls falling around her shoulders, her surprise evident in the shocked expression on her face, and emotion clogged his throat.

He looked and looked again. He would not have thought it possible, but she was even more beautiful than he remembered. The almost constant hint of sadness in her brilliant eyes and the faint shadows underneath them had faded away. Her beautiful face was free of make-up and her silken skin glowed with health.

She was wearing a fine blue sweater that clung lovingly to her full breasts, and a hip-hugging, gently flaring skirt that stopped just below her knees, showing a tempting glimpse of her fabulous legs. Her bare feet with pink-tipped toes were almost his undoing, and he had to battle to control his surging flesh. Sally was the most overtly feminine woman he had ever known. He had never seen her wear a pair of jeans or trousers, like the majority of women her age. Apart from the pink velvet lounging suit… No. He didn't dare go there. The memory of her removing it and what had followed was too vivid, and he would not be able to stop himself reaching for her.

'Zac—what are you doing here?'

Her voice was just the same: slightly husky, with a low timbre, her pronunciation precise—probably a result of losing her stutter, he realised. And it was corny, but true; it was music to his ears.

'A concerned friend of yours, Jemma, asked me to look you up.'

'Jemma?' Sally had phoned Jemma twice since she had left London, the last time just after she had booked into a hotel outside Littlehampton, but not since—mainly because she had only replaced her lost phone today.

'But she can't have known my new address, so how did you find me?' Wondering what evil trick of fate had brought him here, she was trying valiantly to remain calm while her heart was still pounding like a drum in her chest.

'It is cold out here. Ask me in—I need a drink,' Zac commanded, ignoring her question. Surprisingly, he was more afraid than he had ever been in his life. He could hardly blurt out that he had tracked her down because he loved her and wanted her back—not after the way he had treated her before… She would never believe him. He had made enough mistakes with Sally, and this time he was determined to do it right. Romance her, date her, grovel if he had to. And sex could wait until she came to him of her own free will.

Sally swallowed hard. Slowly recovering from the shock of seeing Zac, and her own instant reaction to him, she began to note the change in him. His face was thinner, the grooves from nose to mouth more deeply etched, and the lines of strain around his eyes were plainly discernible. The cashmere overcoat he wore appeared to hang loosely on his broad frame. Realising she was staring, she stepped nervously back and indicated with her hand that he should enter, taking care that he did not touch her as he moved into the hall.

'The kitchen is this way…' she began, but she was too late. He had already walked into the living room.

Swiftly she followed him as she realised what he might see. She reached for the baby clothes she had left on the table, but again she was too late. He had picked up the tiny yellow jacket…

'Give that to me.' She held out her hand, her face burning. 'I'll put this stuff away and make you a cup of coffee. You said you were cold. October can be chilly…' She was babbling, she knew, but she didn't seem able to stop.

'Enough, Sally,' he snapped, catching her hand. 'Baby clothes? Who for? You?' he queried, his eyes narrowed on her scarlet face.

'So what if they are?' she snapped back. She would not lie and deny her baby. Pulling her hand free, she gathered the garments up and shoved them back in the bag. 'It is none of your business.'

Her reply ignited a furious anger in Zac as it hit him that she must be pregnant—and the child could not be his; he had always used protection. No wonder he had thought she looked glowing. While he had spent months aching for her, Sally must have gone straight from his bed into the arms of another man.

The thought of Sally with another man cut him to the bone. She had responded to him in spite of the disgust she felt at his tactics, in spite of her declared hatred of him. In his arrogant conceit he had thought her responsive body was enough for him, and too late he had realised differently.

He had taken her innocence, made her aware of the pleasures of the flesh and left. In fact, he scathingly reminded himself, he had let guilt get the better of him and decided it was the right thing to do—for her sake. What an idiot... He should have taken his fill of her and to hell with his conscience...

He let his gaze sweep contemptuously over her and noted the subtle changes to her body. Her waist was not so clearly defined, and her high, firm breasts appeared fuller. His attention returned to her face. She was watching him with wide, wary eyes, and she had a right to be afraid at this moment. He felt like wringing her slender neck.

'So who is the father?' he sneered. 'Or don't you know? As I recall you were a very eager pupil, but I thought I had taught you better. You should have remembered protection. I always did—even when you were gagging for it.'

Sally saw red. Her hand flew out and connected with his face, knocking his head sideways. 'You sanctimonious bastard! Mister bloody perfect,' she swore—something she never did. 'Well, you are not that clever. My baby was conceived on the nineteenth of June, so work it out for yourself and get out.'

His cheek stinging, Zac raised his hand to catch hers—and dropped it as the import of her words sank into his head. That was the date of the first night he had made love to her. He knew because it was burnt like a brand into his mind for all time. Recalling that night now, he remembered that the second time he had made love to her had initially been in an anger-driven passion because of that word.

'Fine…' he murmured, and all the colour drained from his face. She was right—he had forgotten to use protection. Sally was pregnant with his child. He was going to be a father and it was one hell of a shock. But Zac, being the man he was, although reeling from the knowledge, did not stop considering all the options, and swiftly he realised Sally's pregnancy solved all his problems. He could not have planned it better if he had tried.

He wanted Sally any way he could get her, and this would cut out any need to grovel—not something he had ever done before. Now he would not have to. In fact, she would probably be delighted and grateful when he told her he was prepared to marry her, and the idea of having a baby was growing on him by the minute… A son and heir…

'Good. I'm glad we agree. So go.' She was walking back into the hall, but he reached out and caught her shoulder, spinning her around to face him.

'You misunderstood, Sally. I am not going anywhere, *cara.*' He smiled. 'Obviously you and I need to talk. Discovering you are pregnant with my baby has come as quite a shock. My first reaction was less than gallant, I admit, but the thought of you with another man did nothing for my temper. I want you to know I accept totally the child you are carrying is mine, and naturally I will marry you as quickly as it can be arranged.'

If Zac had expected her grateful acceptance, that was not what he got.

Stunned, Sally looked at him. He was smiling. Zac was actually smiling, and confidently expecting her to accept his magnanimous offer. With a terrific effort of self-control she resisted the temptation to slap the grin off his face.

'I think I may have told you this once before,' she said, with no trace of the anger and the turmoil he had caused visible in the cool blue eyes she lifted to his. 'But I'll say it again so there can be no doubt in your mind. I wouldn't marry you in a million years,' she drawled sarcastically.

Zac had gone pale when she'd said the baby was his, but now his face flushed dark with anger. True to form, then… They always ended up fighting, and she didn't need the hassle in her present state. Shrugging his hands from her shoulders, she took a few steps back.

'If I had not turned up today were you ever going to tell me you were pregnant?' he demanded harshly.

'I hadn't given it much thought.'

'I don't believe you. Any woman who discovers she is pregnant is naturally going to think of the father and what genes her child might inherit.'

He was right—but then Zac always thought he was right. It infuriated Sally, and she told him the truth.

'I wanted to enjoy my pregnancy, relaxed and free of stress, and as you are the least restful person I know I decided on balance it was better to put off telling you straight away. But I would have told you eventually. I was thinking probably after my baby is born.'

'After?' His rapier-like glance raked her from head to toe, as though he had never seen her before, and in one stride he was towering over her. 'You were *thinking* about telling me *after* my child was born?' he prompted incredulously. 'How long after? One year? Two? Ten?' he drawled, and, reaching for her, he hauled her hard against him.

Her eyes widened at the icy anger in his tone. His dark gaze caught and held hers and she was powerless to break the contact.

'Well, listen to me now, Sally Paxton. I am doing the thinking for both of us from now on. No child of mine will be born out of wedlock. You *will* marry me, and our child *will* have two parents.'

'No,' she bit out between clenched teeth. 'I won't marry you. But I will allow you visiting rights,' she conceded determined to hang onto her temper and stay calm and reasonable. But she was equally determined not to allow Zac to walk all over her.

'If anyone gets visiting rights it will be you, because I fully intend for my child to live with *me*. I will file for custody the second it leaves your womb.'

'You won't get it,' she shot back. 'This is England—the mother almost always gets custody.'

'Not quite right. Britain is part of the European community, and I will tie you up in the courts here and in Europe for years. Is that what you want for our child?'

'You would do that?' Sally asked, and saw the implacable determination in his dark eyes. Suddenly she was more afraid than angry.

'Yes.' His hands slipped from her shoulders, but before she could move his arms wrapped around her, one hand splayed across the base of her spine, bringing her into close contact with his large body. 'But it does not have to be that way, Sally.'

Her breasts tightened against the soft wool of her sweater in agitation—or so she told herself. But to her shame the pressure of his strong thighs against her was arousing other more basic emotions. She curled her hands on his forearms in an attempt to keep some space between them, but it didn't help…

'Be reasonable, Sally.' He glanced down to where her swollen nipples were clearly outlined by the fine wool of her jumper, then back to her face. 'Sexually we are more than compatible—we are totally combustible,' he said wryly. 'And all marriages are a money-based transaction and I have a limitless amount. Whether I spend a fortune fighting you in court, or you marry me and gain the benefit of unlimited wealth for yourself and our child, it is up to you to decide, but either way I will win in the end. I always do.'

Sally looked searchingly at him. The tension in the room was palpable. Her decision, he had said… She either married him or consigned her as yet unborn child to growing up in the midst of a battle between two warring parents. A far from ideal scenario, she knew, but the idea of marriage terrified her. She was only four months pregnant, and no matter what Zac threatened she had plenty of time to make a decision.

'Then I will see you in court,' she answered spitefully.

She saw the surprise and anger in his eyes, and his arms fell to his sides and she was free.

'Now I want you to leave.'

'Not before you give me the coffee you promised… I am frozen in shock, and it is the least you can do seeing as I have given you a child,' he drawled mockingly.

Torn between good manners and a desire to be rid of him, she hesitated. Good manners won as he added, 'Please…'

'Have a seat.' She indicated the sofa. 'I'll make you a coffee and then you can leave.' And, turning, she entered the kitchen.

Sally switched on the kettle and put her hands flat on the worktop, her head bent. She had managed to hold her own with Zac, but only just… Being in his company, talking to him—mostly arguing, she amended—had brought a host of painfully suppressed emotions bubbling to the surface, and being held in his arms had almost been her undoing.

She lifted her head and stared out of the window at the garden and the rolling fields beyond. She took a few deep, steadying breaths, striving to calm her fast-beating heart and slowly rising temper. That he had the gall to turn up out of the blue and then demand she marry him was unbelievable.

But stress was not good for the baby, and she continued to breathe deeply.

She had half expected Zac to follow her to the kitchen—she wasn't blind; he was as mad as hell beneath that mocking exterior—but surprisingly he didn't. The kettle boiled, and she made a mug of instant coffee for him, and a cup of tea for herself. She placed a few biscuits on a plate and put the lot on a tray. But she was reluctant to face Zac again.

A deep, shuddering sigh escaped her. She couldn't hide in the kitchen much longer, and Zac was right in a way: they *would* have to talk eventually. Her baby deserved to know its father. But then, thinking of her own father, she was not absolutely convinced that was true, and on that thought she walked back into the living room.

CHAPTER FOURTEEN

SALLY walked straight past Zac to place the tray on the opposite side table. She picked up the coffee mug and turned to look at him, and her hand froze in mid-air.

He had removed his overcoat and was wearing a black sweater and matching pants. Sitting on the sofa with his shoulders hunched, his elbows resting on his knees and holding his head in his hands, the arrogant Zac Delucca looked utterly exhausted. As she stared he lifted his head and ran his hands distractedly through his now over-long hair.

'Are you all right?' she asked, concerned though she did not want to be. She had never seen him look anything other than vibrant and totally in control until now. At her query he raised his eyes, and she saw uncertainty and pain mingled in the black depths as they met hers.

'No, not really, Sally,' he admitted surprisingly. 'I have been sitting here thinking of our past relationship and the mess I made of it while you were in the kitchen.'

'Your coffee,' she said swiftly, and handed him the china mug. She didn't want to talk about their brief affair; it hurt too much…

'Thank you.' His long fingers brushed hers as he took the mug, setting off an unwanted frisson of awareness through her body, and swiftly she stepped back.

'Instant, I'm afraid,' she told him, and sat on the sofa opposite. 'I ran out of the real stuff some time ago, and as I don't drink coffee any more…' she trailed off.

'It will do.' She watched as he lifted the mug to his lips and took a swallow. 'Maybe not.' He grimaced, replacing the mug on the table. Glancing across at her, he added, 'Have you anything stronger? Whisky? Wine, perhaps?'

'No. I don't drink because of the baby.'

'Ah, yes…our baby,' he remarked softly.

Sally recognised his anger had abated, but she had a sneaking suspicion a low-voiced Zac was a lot more dangerous.

'You must really hate me, Sally, if you are prepared to fight me in court for our child. I would never have done it, but my temper got the better of me. The perceived wisdom is that two parents are the ideal, but, being brought up in an orphanage, I would have thanked my lucky stars to have even one loving parent.'

Zac could say that now, and perhaps he meant it, but she didn't trust him and she didn't bother responding. Instead she picked up her cup of tea to take a drink. Actually, she had no intention of fighting him over the baby; she just needed breathing space to think of an acceptable alternative—preferably another five months… But she saw no reason to tell Zac. Let him suffer… After all, she had suffered enough at his hands… *Liar,* a tiny devil in her head whispered. *You loved his hands all over you.*

Abruptly she replaced the cup on the saucer and smoothed the fabric of her skirt down her thighs in a nervous gesture. As the silence stretched between them the room suddenly seemed very small, the air heavy with tension. Sally was still shocked Zac had actually turned up here, and then she realised he had never answered her question as to how he knew where she lived.

'How did you find me? You never said,' she prompted.

'I was in London and I called at your apartment, thinking to offer you my condolences on the death of your mother. Belatedly, I know, but Raffe had only just informed me of the fact. I know more than most how much you did for your mother,' he said with a self-deprecating grimace. 'I know how much you loved her, and I am truly sorry for your loss.'

'Thank you,' Sally responded. 'But you still have not answered my question. How did you get my address?'

'When I called at your apartment building I was surprised to discover you had sold the place, and your father had no idea where you had gone. I called at the museum to see if your boss knew, and your friend Jemma accosted me as I left, and told me she was worried about you. Apparently, on your return from Peru you had stayed with her just long enough to buy a new car and take off on your travels around Britain. You had said you would call her every week, but apart from a couple of calls, the last from a hotel near here, she had heard nothing more and she had been unable to contact you for over a month.'

'I lost my phone—or it was stolen. I only replaced it today,' Sally interjected.

He glanced at the box on the table. 'So it would seem. Anyway, I told Jemma I would help her find you. A call to a detective agency with the name of the hotel you stayed at and I had your address within twenty-four hours.'

'Oh.'

'Oh? Is that all you have to say?' he asked quietly, his dark eyes holding hers. 'Aren't you in the least curious as to why I came instead of Jemma?'

'I never really gave you much thought.'

'I can't say I blame you.' He shook his dark head. 'I never gave you any consideration when I forced you into an affair, and for that I am truly sorry.'

Zac? Apologizing? What was wrong with the man? 'Forget it. I have,' she lied. This soft-spoken, caring Zac was doing strange things to her heart-rate.

'Damn it, Sally.' He got to his feet. 'I can't forget.' And he paced the length of the room, which for him was about six steps, looking strangely agitated. Then he dropped down beside her. She tried to get up, but he looped an arm around her waist and urged her back down. His contrite attitude hadn't lasted long, Sally thought, squirming to break free.

'Please, Sally, sit still and listen,' he demanded. 'I deserve that much, surely?'

She stopped struggling. He didn't deserve anything in her book, but he was too big to fight, and to be honest she was curious.

'I missed you like hell when we parted, Sally, and I realised I did not want to forget you—could not forget you.' His dark, serious eyes sought hers. 'Not then, not now, not ever.'

She looked away. 'If this is a trick to sweet-talk me into marrying you for the baby, forget it. My mum is dead. I owe you nothing,' she said bluntly. But with his hand curving around her waist, his long fingers resting on the side of her now rounded stomach and the warmth of his body against hers, he was arousing a host of old, familiar emotions.

'It is no trick, I swear. I had made up my mind to go to London and ask you to forgive me for being such an arrogant, overbearing idiot even before Raffe told me your mother had died. I used her death as an excuse when you asked me because I am no good at revealing my emotions. Not that I had many until I met you,' he said dryly. 'The moment I saw you enter Westwold that day, I wanted you with a passion I had never felt before. I smiled at you, and you didn't notice me.' He gave her a droll look. 'And I am quite large to overlook…'

'Dented your ego…?' she quipped, and met his eyes—which was a mistake. The warmth and the hint of vulnerability in the dark depths made her breath catch in her throat. Maybe, just maybe, he was telling the truth. A tiny flicker of hope ignited inside her. He no longer seemed quite the hard, overbearing Zac she had known, and though she did not want to marry him, they could perhaps come to some suitable arrangement.

'Yes. That and more. It was a salutary experience, and probably long overdue,' he admitted ruefully.

He sounded sincere, but Sally still didn't quite trust him—though she did give him an explanation. 'I was too worried about Mum to notice anything much that day. Her doctor had told me the weekend before she had not long left.'

Zac's arm tightened around her. 'Now I feel even worse.' He grimaced. 'I coerced you into being my lover at a really low point in your life, and I can only say sorry again, Sally. But I would be lying if I said I was sorry for making love to you. I think I fell in love with you on sight. My first thought was that you looked bridal… Maybe my subconscious was trying to tell me something even then.'

Sally drew in a deep, shocked breath. Maybe once she would have been ecstatic to hear Zac mention the *L* word, but now she was doubtful.

'From day one you confused me. I found myself changing my mind about you over and over again. But from our first kiss in the limousine I knew I had to make you mine.' He stopped and was silent for a while. 'The night I came to your apartment—the night you left me aching and frustrated and I stormed out—I was determined to have nothing more to do with you.'

'I gathered that,' Sally shot back smartly. 'I think it was you telling me to stick my head in the cooler box that convinced me.'

Zac's lips twitched in the beginnings of a smile. 'Not one of my better moments, Sally, and the only excuse I have is I was out of my mind with frustration. I wanted you so badly.' He caught her hand and curled it in his own. 'But later, when we did make love, I realised why you stopped me. It was the understandable nerves of an innocent.'

Nerves of a not so innocent sort tightened at the warmth of the hand holding hers. Zac was getting to her, making her remember things she had tried to forget, and she tugged free.

'Wrong. I caught sight of the two of us in the mirrored wardrobe and was reminded of where I was. My dad's old love-nest. He graciously gave it to me at my mum's instigation, after persuading her to sell the family home so he could buy himself a much grander apartment in Notting Hill. Mum agreed because the insensitive swine actually told her it would help with death duties.'

It still enraged her even now when she thought about it, and once she'd got started Sally could not stop.

'I hated that apartment. The first week I moved in the phone never stopped ringing with women trying to contact him. I changed the number in the end, and painted the whole place, replaced his furniture with my own. But nothing could change what that studio was in my eyes. The only reason I set the guidelines on our deal to that apartment was because it never failed to remind me of the faithlessness of men, and was therefore entirely appropriate for what you had in mind.'

Sally had said too much. But digging over the past had aroused emotions she did not want to face. She just wanted Zac to leave, and she tried to rise.

'Dio!' Zac exclaimed. 'This just gets worse and worse. But

they say confession is good for the soul, and you *are* going to let me finish, Sally.'

His arm tightened around her waist, the expression on his face one of grim determination.

'I had no intention of seeing you again after that night, but when you and Al walked into that restaurant the next night, I saw red. I was crazy with jealousy—a first for me… I was frantic. I wanted to walk over and rip his head off.'

There was no humour in his tone, but Sally had to bite back the laugh that bubbled up in her throat at his outrageous statement. She didn't think he would appreciate being laughed at.

'Instead I was sociable and polite, and you ignored me, then deliberately insulted me.'

'What did you expect? A medal?' Sally slotted in.

'Don't be facetious, Sally. I am serious. I was furious to the point of mindless rage with you, which was why I decided to use your father's dishonesty against you. I knew you responded to me, and I didn't care how I got you as long as I did. I behaved disgracefully, and I am thoroughly ashamed of my actions. But I can't be ashamed of the result. And, though I bitterly regret any hurt I caused you, I will never regret making love to you. It was the most amazing, memorable experience of my life and always will be. What I am trying to say, Sally, is that I love you, and I want to marry you, and I did long before I knew about the baby.'

Sally frowned, her blue eyes wide and wary, searching his face, looking for some sign that would convince her he was telling the truth. But with her parents as an example she had spent too long mistrusting love, and was too cynical about most men to immediately believe Zac.

'Humph!' she snorted 'You could have fooled me. You walked in here, and when you realised I was pregnant you insulted me, and then demanded I marry you. Why should I believe a word you say now? I remember our first limousine ride as well. When you told me you were not into commitment, and had no intention of ever marrying, but were up for an affair with no strings attached. So you will excuse me for believing your transformation from arrogant, commitment-shy ex-lover to soft-talking want-to-be husband is just a tad too convenient.'

'You don't believe me, and I deserve that. But Sally, if you will just give me another chance to let me prove how much I love you… I won't pressure you into making love as I did before, though it will be hell waiting. I need you, want you so much. You get under my skin like no other woman has ever done.'

At his mention of other woman Sally was brought back to reality with a thud. Margot's image loomed large in her mind. She reached for her cup and took a sip of tea to control her nerves before she responded.

'As for being the only woman to get under your skin—that is no great accolade, given how many get into your bed. Margot for one. You must take me for an idiot, Zac. You tried to seduce me on the Monday, took her to your bed on Tuesday, and blackmailed me into sex the following night.'

Sally watched his reaction and saw the effect her words had on him. His great body tensed and all the colour drained from his face, leaving him grey and looking older than his years.

'You really think so little of me that you believe I am capable of such deplorable behaviour?'

'I know so,' she said bluntly.

'I have never had sex with Margot in my life. In fact, you are the only woman I have made love to in well over a year,' he declared outrageously.

He actually sounded sincere, Sally thought bitterly. Going by her own limited experience with Zac, he was a highly sexed, three or four times a night man. Zac celibate for over a year was a joke… Why was she wasting her time listening to him?

'I found her black hairband, clips and perfume in the cabinet in your bathroom. So don't bother to lie.'

For a moment he was silent, his brows drawn together in a frown. That had stopped his fairy tale of love and marriage, Sally thought cynically.

Then suddenly he threw his head back, a broad grin lighting his face. 'So that is why the last night we were together you changed from my Salmacis, my dream lover, to a cold-eyed witch,' he declared. Taking her cup from her hand, he placed it on the table, and with his other around her waist tugged her towards him.

'What…?' was as far as Sally got as he kissed her with a hungry, driven passion that knocked the breath from her body. The suddenness of his action gave her no time to build a defence, and she reacted with helpless hunger to the pressure of his mouth, welcomed the thrust of his tongue with her own.

Her instinctive response was all the encouragement he needed to continue, with a heady sensuality that drove her almost mindless. He groaned and lifted her bodily onto his lap, his arms like steel bands around her. The swiftness of his action, the tightness of his hold, the sudden awareness of his intensely aroused body, brought her back to her senses, and she flung back her head.

'Stop it, Zac,' she gasped, pushing at his chest. 'Let go of me.'

'Never,' he said.

But surprisingly, he did slacken his hold on her, and jerkily Sally slid back onto the sofa. But one arm remained gently yet firmly around her waist, preventing her moving any further away.

Breathless, she brushed the hair out of her eyes and glared angrily at him. 'What did you do that for?'

'I had to.' He grinned: a broad smile, revealing his perfect white teeth. 'Because you gave me the first glimmer of hope I have had in months,' he said, totally unrepentant.

'Me?' She was confused, and still shaken from the assault on her senses.

'Yes. I realised you were crazy jealous because you thought I had made love to Margot.'

'Don't flatter yourself,' she huffed, but without much force.

'I wouldn't dare with you,' he said dryly. 'You have the ability to chop me off at the knees with a glance. But I was telling you the truth before, Sally. And as for the stuff you found in the bathroom cabinet, Raffe and his very attractive black-haired wife were using the apartment while he worked on the transition at Westwold. After I arrived he went back to Italy on the Monday, and I moved in. It is a company apartment—not only for my use.'

'Oh.' Sally felt a fool. 'I didn't know Raffe Costa was married.'

'He has been for five years, and they are desperate for a child.' This time his smile was rueful. 'I think he will be pleased for us, but hardly ecstatic given the circumstances.'

'There is no us,' she said automatically, but now she wasn't quite so adamant. If she had known what she knew now that night in the apartment, would she have been so nasty to Zac?

'Oh, yes, there is, Sally,' Zac assured her in a husky tone. And, turning towards her, he ran his long fingers through the silken fall of her hair to cup the back of her head in his strong hand. 'And you *are* going to marry me,' Zac told her in a firm voice. 'After we parted I spent the most miserable few months of my life, worrying about what you were doing and who you were with. I had the most dreadful nightmares. I'd wake up in the night sweating, imagining you with another man. Or I'd dream you were in my arms and wake up devastated to be without you… I am not going through that again, and I am not going anywhere until you promise to marry me.'

Sally looked at him uncertainly. Had he really suffered so much without her? She saw the strain in his face and lifted a finger to trace the deep groove from his nose to his mouth. She looked into his eyes and saw he was deadly serious.

'You once told me you wanted three children while you were young enough to enjoy them. Think about it, Sally. Do you want this baby to be an only child, like you and I were, or to have a few siblings to play with?'

'I did not mean that. I was only trying to put you off.'

'You didn't succeed.' And, taking his arm from her waist, he tilted her head back against the soft cushion. He withdrew his hand and stood up. He stared down at her, as though searching for words, and then slipped his hand into his pants pocket.

'I know you, Sally, and I'd bet my life it never occurred to you to get rid of this baby—though plenty of women would.'

'You'd win that bet.'

'I also know that with your father as an example marriage might scare you.' To her utter amazement he dropped down on one knee and, taking her hand in his other hand, he produced a small square box. 'Sally, my Salmacis, please, will you marry me? I love you, and I swear I will never betray you.'

He opened the box to reveal a brilliant sapphire and diamond ring.

'I am not asking you to love me, but to let me love you, as your husband, and who knows…?'

Sally looked into his eyes and saw the glimmer of moisture that could not dim the blaze of love and sincerity in the dark depths. Suddenly the defences she had built around her heart for years cracked wide-open, a flood of emotion pouring out, and she said, 'Yes.'

With an Italian sound of exultation, Zac grasped her hand and slipped the ring on her finger, then pulled her down beside him and kissed her with deep, profound tenderness and a love that touched her soul.

Sally's new rug was very convenient, as were the cushions from the sofa. With gentle, shaking hands he undressed her and shed his own clothes. He kissed her again, his hands cupping and caressing the fullness of her breasts and then stroking lower to cradle the still small mound of her tummy. She looked at him and saw the wonder, the awe in his eyes, before he bent his head to press a kiss on her stomach and his child.

He lifted his head, his dark eyes seeking hers. 'I won't hurt you or the baby, will I?' he asked.

Sally smiled softly. For once her magnificent, arrogant man did not have all the answers. She responded by reaching for him, her hands curving around his broad shoulders and pulling him down to her. 'No. I am past the first trimester—it is *fine…*' She accentuated the last word and smiled.

With a shout of joy mingled with relief Zac began to make love to her, with a gentle but tender and passionate intensity that surpassed anything that had gone before. Sally gave herself eagerly, and when Zac finally claimed her as his once more, she arched up to meet him, and they became one in a sunburst of love and life…

EPILOGUE

SIXTEEN months later Sally stood in the nursery of their home in Calabria, looking into the cot where Francesco, their son, was finally sleeping after an exciting day.

She had married Zac in a quiet Christmas wedding at the small church in Villa San Giovanni, the nearest town to his home in the countryside. Zac had insisted she wear white, despite her swelling belly, and the guest list on her side had been Jemma, and Charles and his wife and family, but not her father. Zac had had Raffe and his wife, who had just discovered she was pregnant, Marco and his wife, and a few local friends and employees.

Francesco had arrived on a beautiful spring day in March, just like today, and was a joy to behold. Sally reached down into the cot and stroked his black curly hair with a gentle hand. He was the image of his father, and just looking at him was enough to make her heart overflow with love and happiness. Today had been his first birthday, and they had thrown a party for a dozen children, from the ages of a few months to ten years old.

Zac had supposedly been in control of the party. But he had been a bigger hit than the troupe of clowns and jugglers he had hired to entertain the children. Francesco had ridden around on his shoulders, and so had most of the other children. And a riotous game of football, beloved of all Italians, had mostly consisted of Zac running after the ball as the youngsters kicked anywhere and everywhere. Now he was lying in the huge bath in their en suite bathroom, trying to ease his aching bones.

It seemed incredible to her now that she had ever doubted Zac or been afraid of marriage. He was a wonderful husband, and a devoted father who adored his son. Totally the opposite of her own father, who had married a woman thirty-five years younger than himself within six months of her mum's death and retired to Spain. Who said crime didn't pay? she thought, but without the anger and bitterness that had plagued her before. She had accepted that he had never been cut out to be a father, or faithful, and if anything she pitied his new wife…

Zac had told her about her father at the same time as he told her he had sold Westwold Components, because he knew she did not approve of the arms business. He had also added that the office gossip was the woman had married her dad for his money, and would leave him just as quickly when the cash ran out… What goes around comes around, Sally thought, and she didn't care any more.

She had her own family, and sometimes Sally could hardly believe how blessed she was. Zac had cut back on his workload and they spent most of their time here in Calabria. She had fallen in love with the house the moment she had seen it.

The original two-hundred-year-old farmhouse was only part of one wing now. If Zac wanted something he got it, and he had used the same approach to the house. It was a great rambling home now, with a gym and a swimming pool, six en suite bedrooms and an amazing master bedroom that had panoramic views across the Strait of Messina to Sicily and the toe of Italy. The building had evolved over the years to sit perfectly in the surrounding landscape of olive groves, cliffs and sea, though it would probably never win any prizes for architectural beauty.

She loved the house, and she loved Zac—but, strange as it seemed, she had never actually said the words. Maybe it was time she did…

Sally bent down to drop a kiss on Francesco's head.

Straightening, she felt two arms close around her waist.

'Is he asleep?' Zac murmured, looking over her head at his son sleeping in the cot. 'He looks like an angel. *Dio,* don't you just love him?'

Sally turned in his arms and linked hers around his neck. He was wearing only a towel slung around his lean hips and a smile to warm her heart—and quite a few other parts of her anatomy.

'Yes. And if you have recovered from the party, I thought I would take you to bed and show you how much I love *you*, Zac.'

His dark eyes flared with a luminous light, and he groaned as he pulled her against him, his sensuous mouth kissing every one of her delicate features before claiming her mouth in a deep, loving kiss.

'Thank you for that, *cara mia*,' he murmured, holding her close. 'I was beginning to worry you would never say the words I longed to hear, even though I know you feel them.'

'Conceited devil.' She grinned 'But I do love you.'

'No, not conceited—just a man who loves you to distraction. Now, what were you saying about taking me to bed…?' And, curving an arm around her waist, he led her quietly out of the nursery.

'I was thinking today,' he said as they walked towards their suite. 'If you agree, maybe it is time we started trying for the second of those three children you insisted you wanted when we met.'

'You are never going to let me forget that, Zac.'

They both laughed.

And then they wandered off to make a start on extending their family.

THE ITALIAN'S BLACKMAILED MISTRESS

JACQUELINE BAIRD

CHAPTER ONE

MAXIMILIAN ANDREA QUINTANO—Max to his friends—walked out of the bathroom wearing only a pair of navy silk boxer shorts. Just the effort of bending to pull them on had made his head spin. He needed air and, walking out onto the balcony that ran the length of the suite, he willed the pain behind his eyes to vanish. It was his own fault. It had been his thirty-first birthday two days ago, and although Max owned a penthouse in Rome and a house in Venice, he had done what was expected of him and spent the day at the family estate in Tuscany with his father, stepmother, Lisa, and other family members.

But on his return to Rome yesterday, after he had taken his yearly medical exam for insurance purposes, he'd met up with his best friend Franco and a few others from his university days for lunch. The party that had ensued had ended up with Franco belatedly remembering his wife was expecting him home in Sicily. Max, due to fly there the next day anyway, had agreed to accompany Franco to the island to carry on the party there.

Finally, at four-thirty in the morning and feeling much the worse for wear, Max had got a taxi to the Quintano

Hotel, the hotel he was scheduled to arrive at that same afternoon in place of his father.

Ever since Max's grandfather had built his first hotel on the island, before relocating the family to Tuscany, it had become a tradition for the Quintano family to holiday at the Sicilian hotel during the month of August. For the last decade Max had rarely visited, leaving it to his brother Paulo and the rest of the family to carry on the tradition.

A deep frown suddenly creased Max's broad brow as he thought of his older brother's tragic death in a car accident just four months ago. When Paulo had enthusiastically entered the family business and become a top hotelier, Max had been given the freedom to pursue his own interests, and he knew he owed his brother a lot.

An adventurer at heart, Max had left university with a degree in geology, boundless energy and a rapier-sharp brain. He had headed to South America, where on his arrival, he'd acquired an emerald mine in a game of poker. Max had made the mine a success and started the MAQ Mining Corporation, which over the last nine years had expanded to include mines in Africa, Australia and Russia. The MAQ Corporation was now global, and Max was a multimillionaire in his own right. But, as he had been forcibly reminded a few months ago, all the money in the world could not solve every problem.

Deeply shocked and saddened by Paulo's death, Max had offered to help his father in any way he could with the hotel business. His father had asked him if he would check the running of the hotel in Sicily and stay a while to keep the tradition going. The loss of Paulo was too fresh for

Paulo's widow Anna and their young daughters to go, so of course Max had agreed.

Max rubbed his aching temples with his fingertips. The way he felt at the moment he was glad he had agreed to his father's request—he desperately needed the break. *Dios!* Never again, he vowed. By some miracle, when he'd arrived at the hotel just before dawn he had retained enough sense to instruct the night porter to keep his early arrival quiet. Nothing and no one was to disturb him....

Max stepped from the balcony into the sitting room. He needed coffee—black, strong and fast. He stopped dead.

For a moment he wondered if he was hallucinating.

A tall, feminine figure with a mass of flowers in her arms seemed to glide across the room towards him. Her hair was pale blond, and swept back into a long ponytail to reveal a face ethereal in its beauty. Her breasts he could only imagine, but her waist was emphasised by a black leather belt neatly holding a straight black skirt, which ended a few inches above her knees. The simple skirt revealed the seductive curve of her hips, and as for her legs... A sudden stirring in his groin said it all. She was gorgeous. '*Ciao, bella ragazza,*' he husked.

Sent up by the hotel manager to deposit the flowers and check the suite before the arrival of its illustrious owner, Sophie Rutherford was startled by the sound of the deep, masculine voice. She jerked her head towards the open French doors, the flowers falling from her hands at the sight of the huge man standing before her.

Frozen in shock, she swept her green gaze over him. Thick black hair fell over a broad brow, and dark, heavy-lidded eyes were set in a square-jawed, ruggedly handsome face. His bronzed muscular body was wide shouldered, with a broad chest lightly dusted with black hair that arrowed down over a flat stomach and disappeared beneath his dark shorts. His legs were long and splayed. He looked like some great colossus, she thought fancifully, and her green eyes widened in awe at so much masculine power.

Then he stepped towards her…. 'Oh, my God!' she cried, suddenly remembering where she was and belatedly realising he had no right to be there. 'Don't move! I'm calling Security.'

The scream echoed though Max's head like a razor on the bone. He closed his eyes for a second. The last thing he needed was someone calling the deity down on him. Then his less than sharp mind finally registered that her words had been spoken in English.

Max slowly opened his eyes, but before he could make a response she was disappearing out of the door. He heard the turn of the key in the lock behind her and could not believe it; the crazy girl had locked him in his own suite….

Shaking his head in amazement, he picked up the telephone and revealed his presence to Alex, the hotel manager. The he ordered some much needed coffee, and strode back into the bedroom to dress. Once he had shaved and dressed he returned to the sitting room, to find a maid cleaning away the flowers and Alex placing a coffee tray on the table. There was no mistaking the barely contained amusement in Alex's eyes as he greeted his old friend.

'Max, it's good to see you. I guessed you were the undesirable *giant* about to rob the place,' Alex said and he burst out laughing.

'Very funny, Alex. It's good to see you, too. Now, tell me, who the hell is the crazy girl?' Max asked, pouring himself a cup of coffee and downing it in one go, before collapsing onto one of the sofas.

'Sophie Rutherford,' Alex answered, joining Max on the sofa. 'Her father, Nigel Rutherford, is the owner of the Elite Agency in London. They handle the arrangements for a lot of our European clients, and Nigel asked me if his daughter could work here for a couple of months during her university vacation to improve her language skills. She is studying Russian and Chinese, but she also has a good grasp of Italian, French and Spanish. I thought, given the international clientele we attract, she could be very useful. She has certainly proved her worth already in the month she has been here. She is happy to work anywhere, and nothing is too much trouble for her.'

'If she is as good as you say, then I trust your judgement.' Max grinned at the older man. 'But my guess is the fact she is so beautiful might also have affected your decision,' he mocked.

'You would say that.' Alex grinned back. 'But, unlike you, it takes more than a pretty face to influence me—especially at my age.'

'Liar,' Max drawled, a knowing, sensual smile curving his hard mouth as the image of the young woman flashed up in his mind. 'Any man with breath in his body can see she is gorgeous, and I for one would like to get to know her a whole lot better.'

'Sophie is not for you, Max,' Alex said suddenly

serious. 'She is only nineteen, and in the absence of her father she is under my protection. Much as I like you, I do not think she is your kind of woman. She is serious about her studies and not the type of girl to have an affair—she is more the marrying kind.'

Max could have been insulted, but he wasn't. Alex was like an honorary uncle to him, and knew him well. As much as Max loved women, and they loved him, he had no intention of marrying for years—if ever. Since Paulo's death his father had begun to hint that it was time he married, constantly reminding Max that if he didn't there would be no male to carry on the great name of Quintano. But Max didn't want to settle down. He wanted to travel the world, doing what he loved. And with more money than he knew what to do with, Max was quite happy for Paulo's family to inherit their rightful share of his father's estate—as they naturally would have done if Paulo had lived. The last thing Max felt he needed was a wife.

'That's a shame.' His firm lips twisted wryly. 'She is delectable. But have no fear, old man, I promise not to seduce her. Now, shall we get down to business?'

Later that afternoon Max walked through the semicircle of trees that fringed the secure hotel beach and scrambled over the rocky headland to the small cove he had first discovered as a boy. He loved to dive from the rocks, and it was here that he had first become interested in geology. Today, however, the only rocks that concerned him were the ones in his skull, and he knew a swim would clear his head and cool him down.

Just then, a flash of pale gold against the backdrop of dark stone captured his attention. His dark eyes narrowed intently as he realised it was the girl from this morning. As he watched she flicked the shimmering mass of her hair over one shoulder and stretched herself out on a towel.

Silently Max moved towards her, his body reacting with instant masculine enthusiasm as his dark gaze swept over her. The pink bikini she was wearing was quite modest, compared to some he had seen, but the figure it graced was the ultimate in feminine allure. Her eyes were closed, and her glorious hair lay in a silken stream over one high firm breast. He had been right about her legs—they were long, slender and very sexy—and her skin was as smooth as silk, with just the shimmer of a tan. Max couldn't take his eyes off her, and he was instantly regretting his promise to Alex to leave her alone.

As he moved closer his shadow fell over her and she opened her eyes.

'Sophie Rutherford, I believe?' he drawled smoothly, and held out his hand. 'I am Max Quintano.' Max watched as she shot to her feet as though electrified. 'This morning did not seem to be quite the right time to introduce myself. Please forgive me for any embarrassment I may have caused you.' He smiled.

'Sophie, yes…' She blushed and took his hand. 'It is nice to meet you, Mr Quintano, but I think it is I who should apologise to you, for locking you in your room.'

Max felt the slight tremble in her hand and looked into her gorgeous green eyes. There he saw embarrassment, but also the feminine interest she could not hide—and miraculously his hangover vanished. 'Please, call me Max. There is no need to apologise—it was my fault—I must have startled you. Anyway, it is much too hot to argue, and as it happens you are occupying my favourite beach.' He smiled again. 'I wouldn't want to chase you away—I have already done that once today—please stay and allow me to show you that my apology is genuine and I am not some *giant* burglar.'

Sophie pulled her suddenly tingling hand from his and almost groaned. 'Did Alex tell you I said that? How embarrassing.'

Never before had she felt such instant and overwhelming attraction for a man. She had taken one look at him this morning and, shocked witless, had behaved like a terrified child.

Now, desperate to improve his impression of her, she added with a wry smile, 'But, in my defence, you really *are* very tall.'

'I'm six foot five—and there is no need for embarrassment, Sophie. I can assure you I am not in the least embarrassed by it. However, you do look rather red in the face—how about a swim to cool off?' Max suggested. Not giving her time to answer, he added, 'Race you to the water!'

Of course Sophie followed him. He hadn't doubted for a moment that she would; women had chased him all his adult life.

Wading into the water, Max turned and splashed her, and saw her smile broaden to light up her whole face. He also saw the gleam of mischief in her eyes just before she bent down and splashed him back.

The horseplay that followed did nothing to cool Max's suddenly rampant libido. Had she any idea that when she bent forward her lush breasts were bobbing up and down and almost out of her top? he wondered.

Eventually Max could stand it no longer, and he scooped her up into his arms. 'Trying to splash me, are you? You're going to pay for that, lady,' he declared, and waded farther out until the water lapped at his thighs.

'Don't you dare!' she cried, wrapping her arms firmly around Max's neck, her green eyes sparkling with laughter.

'There is nothing I wouldn't do to have you in my arms, Sophie,' Max teased, his dark gaze clashing with hers.

For a long moment their eyes locked, and the teasing stopped as desire, fierce and primitive, raced between them.

Sophie's green eyes darkened as for the first time in her life she felt the sudden rush of sexual desire for a man. She was intensely aware of Max's arm under her thighs, his other across her back and under her arm, the pressure of his long fingers splayed against the side of her breast. Her stomach churned and her pulse raced as the rest of the world seemed to stop. She simply stared into his eyes as though hypnotized, and the air between them grew heavy and shimmered with sexual tension.

Her gaze fell to his wide, firm mouth, and instinctively her lips parted as she imagined how his lips, his kiss, would feel.

The next second Sophie was under the water, swallowing what felt like half the ocean. Spluttering and gasping, she stood up and wiped the water from her eyes, to find Max watching her with a strange, almost regretful look on his face.

'I think we both need to cool off a little. I'm going to swim to the headland—see you later, Sophie.' And, like a sleek dolphin, Max dived out to sea, his strong brown arms cleaving the surface without so much as a ripple in the water.

Only later would she realise that a shark would have been a more appropriate metaphor….

Sophie watched him, helpless to do otherwise. Nothing in her nineteen years had prepared her for a man like Max Quintano.

After the death of her mother, when she was eleven, she had been sent to a girls' boarding school by her father. By the time she had reached the age of thirteen she had sprouted up like a beanpole to five feet nine and had become terribly self-conscious. She'd had few friends, and had spent the school holidays at home in Surrey, with Meg the housekeeper, while her father had worked.

A late developer, only in the past year at university had she felt her confidence grow in leaps and bounds. She'd been delighted to discover that being tall was no deterrent to making friends of both sexes, and she had even dated a few boys.

But never had she felt anything like the stomach-flipping, spine-tingling excitement Max Quintano's teasing smile and playful touch aroused in her.

A dreamy smile curved her wide mouth as she walked back up the beach and sat down on her towel, her besotted gaze focusing on his dark head, which was now a distant dot in the water. She could still feel the imprint of his arms as he had lifted her, the touch of his fingers against her breast on her heated skin…. Was this love or just fascination? she mused, unable to take her eyes off him.

Max turned in the water and struck back towards the shore, his tumescent flesh finally quietened by his strenuous swim. He had not had a woman since returning to Italy from Australia at the news of Paulo's death. He had endured four months of celibacy and was certain that this was the reason for his extreme reaction to the lovely Sophie.

Holding her in his arms, he had known she wanted him to kiss her—and he had certainly been aching to taste her lips and a lot more. But he had done the right thing and had left her alone, as Alex had requested. Alex was right. She was too young.

Feeling quite self-righteous, Max strode out of the water and flicked the hair from his eyes. He could see that she was still there on the beach, and as he approached she sat up and smiled. All his good intentions vanished. He was going to be in Sicily for a while, so what was wrong with a little flirtation with a beautiful girl?

'Come on, Sophie.' He reached a hand out to her. 'You have had too much sun. I'll walk you back to the hotel.' As she rose to her feet Max pressed a swift, soft kiss on the curve of her cheek. He heard the sharp intake of her breath, saw the sudden darkening of her incredible eyes his kiss had provoked, and before he made a complete fool of himself added, 'I'll show you the secret of the maze.'

As one week slipped into two Sophie didn't know if she was on her head or her heels. She was hopelessly in love for the first time in her life. Just the sight of Max Quintano set her heart aflutter, and when he spoke to her she was breathless. He treated her with a teasing friendliness, but his casual invitations to join him for a swim or a walk when she was off duty were enough to send her into seventh heaven. Of course she agreed like an eager puppy, and though they were not really dates they were both an agony and an ecstasy to her foolish heart. Max was the perfect gentleman at all times, and as much as Sophie wanted him to he never progressed past a kiss on her cheek.

Two weeks after first meeting Max, Sophie walked out of her bedroom and into the sitting room of the chalet she shared with her friend Marnie, the head receptionist of the hotel. Sophie was sure that tonight would be the night all her dreams would be fulfilled. Max had asked her out to dinner at a restaurant in Palermo—at last, a proper date!

'So what do you think, Marnie?' Sophie asked as she made a quick twirl. She had bought the sophisticated green silk designer gown from the hotel boutique that afternoon, hoping to impress Max.

'Let me guess—you are meeting Max Quintano?' Marnie quipped.

'Yes.' Sophie beamed. 'But do I look okay?'

'You look stunning! Max will be knocked for six. But are you sure you know what you are doing?' Marnie asked with a frown. 'I've warned you before about Max and his women. I even showed you a magazine article, remember? I can understand how you feel, but he is a lot older than you, and a sophisticated, experienced man. You're young, with your education to complete. Don't throw it all away on a brief affair—because that is all it can ever be.'

Sophie stiffened. 'I know, and I've heard all the rumours, but I'm sure those stories are vastly exaggerated.'

'Believe what you like—teenagers usually do,' Marnie said dryly. 'All I am saying is be careful. Max is a multimillionaire with a matching lifestyle. He rarely stays here for more than the odd weekend. The only reason he is here now is to fill in for his father and his family after the death of his brother. But that is about to change, because I heard today the rest of the family are coming soon—and when they do, Max will not hang around for long.'

'You don't know that for sure,' Sophie said, her heart plummeting in her breast at the thought of Max leaving.

'No, I don't. But Max and his father do not have the closest relationship in the world. I understand that although he gets on well with his extended family, the person he cares the most about is his stepsister, Gina. It's well known that they have had an on-off relationship for years. Some say she tolerates his other women because she is dedicated to her career as a doctor and not interested in marriage. But rumour has it that Old Man Quintano told Max ages ago he would not countenance such a relationship. As far as he is concerned they are brother and sister, and anything else between them is unthinkable. But circumstances change, and Max is very much his own master, and if and when he does decide to marry I wouldn't be surprised if Gina was his bride. So be warned, Sophie, and don't do anything foolish.'

Sophie was saved from responding by the ringing of the doorbell, but her happiness of five minutes ago had vanished. However, it returned the moment she opened the door and saw Max, starkly handsome and elegantly clad in an immaculately tailored suit. His tall figure oozed sex appeal, and Sophie's already pounding heart leapt in her breast.

Max turned a smiling face towards the open door and looked at Sophie. For a moment he was struck dumb. Her mass of blond hair was swept up in an intricate knot on top of her head. Her exquisite face was delicately made up to enhance her superb bone structure and fabulous green eyes. As for what she was wearing—the mid-thigh-length sheath of emerald-green silk outlined every feminine curve and lay straight across her high firm breasts. Damn it, he was getting aroused just looking at her.

'You look amazing—and remarkably you're ready,' he said, thinking that she wasn't the only one—he could have quite happily ravished her there and then.

'Yes.'

She smiled at him and the breath left his body. Max had to remind himself once again that he had promised Alex he wouldn't seduce her—but the trouble was, Sophie intrigued him on every level. She made him laugh, she was clever beyond her years and she was a great companion. As for her physical appearance—he only had to look at her to want her. He should never have asked her out tonight, he realised, because he did not trust himself to keep his hands off her.

Sophie sensed none of Max's doubts, either during the short car ride or as he took her arm and led her into the restaurant—she was simply too excited.

Max ordered champagne, and when their glasses were filled he raised his and said, 'To a beautiful girl and a beautiful night.'

Sophie's face heated at his mention of night. Did he mean what she hoped he meant? Was he at last going to move their relationship to the next level? Kiss her and then make love to her? Yes, she decided as his deep, dark eyes smiled into hers and they touched glasses. With that simple exchange, the mood had been set for the evening.

Sophie let Max order for her, and as course followed course and the champagne flowed freely she fell ever deeper under his spell. They talked about everything and nothing, and Max punctuated their conversation with a smile or the touch of his hand on hers. He fed her morsels of food she had never tried before, watching her every reaction with amusement and something more. By the end of the meal Sophie knew she was totally in love with Max.

'That was a perfect meal.' She sighed happily as Max paid the bill.

Perfect food, maybe, Max thought. But pure torture for him. He was white-knuckled with the strain of keeping his hands off her. He must have been mad to think he could have just a mild flirtation with Sophie, and when he slipped an arm around her waist and led her out of the crowded restaurant it was nearly his undoing. She was tall, and when she leant into his side they were a perfect fit, her hip moving sexily against his thigh.

'I am so glad you brought me here.' She turned her head to smile up into his face. Her teeth were even and brilliant white against the light golden tan of her skin and he felt his body tighten another notch.

He was no masochist. This had to stop or he was in real danger of losing control—not something he ever did. Dropping his arm from her waist, Max opened the car door for her—but it did not stop his heart hammering in his chest. She looked so utterly exquisite and so damn naïve she hadn't the sense to hide her feelings.

'My pleasure,' he said, and abruptly slammed the door.

By the time he slid behind the wheel and started the car he had his body under control. As he manoeuvred the vehicle along the winding road back to the hotel he glanced at Sophie and realised he had no right to be angry with her. It wasn't her fault she had the looks and the body of a temptress and stopped men in their tracks, he thought dryly as he brought the car to a halt outside her chalet.

After their laughter and intimacy over the dinner table Sophie sensed Max's mood had inexplicably changed, and when the engine stopped she glanced up at him and wondered what she had done wrong.

'Home again,' she said inanely, and blushed as she realised she was way out of his league in the sophistication stakes. But in the next moment he proved her wrong.

'Ah, Sophie,' he drawled huskily. 'What am I going to do with you?'

She saw the sensual smile that curved his firm lips as he reached to slide his arm around her waist and pull her close to the hard wall of his chest. He growled something softly, something she did not understand, and then his mouth covered hers and she didn't care.

It was as though a starburst exploded in her brain, sending shock waves to every nerve-ending in her body. He slid his tongue seductively between her softly parted lips, exploring the sweet, moist interior, and her hands involuntarily reached up to clasp around his neck. His kiss was more than she could ever have imagined, and Sophie closed her eyes and gave herself up to the wonder of his embrace. She felt his hand stroke up to cup her breast, and as his thumb grazed the silk-covered, suddenly taut peak, a fiery wave of desire scorched through her veins.

'*Dio!* How I want you,' Max groaned.

Sophie's fingers were tangled in the sleek dark hair of

his head, and her tongue—at first tentatively and then tenaciously—duelled with his as an ever-increasing hunger consumed her.

Max heard her moan when he finally lifted his head, and saw the passion in her dazzling green eyes. He knew she was his for the taking. He almost succumbed—after all, he was not made of stone, and denying his body was not something he was used to. But he had made a promise to Alex, so he had to rein in his carnal impulses.

Gently he pushed her back against the seat, and got out of the car, drawing in a few deep, steadying breaths as he walked around to open her door. 'Come on, *cara*.'

Hazy-eyed, Sophie glanced at the hand Max held out. It took an enormous effort on her part to still the shaking in her own hand and take the help he was offering, and step out of the car.

She looked at the staff chalet and back at Max, her body still strumming with excitement, not sure what to do, what to say.

Sensing her uncertainty, Max curved an arm around her waist and led her to the door. Once there, he turned her in his arms and narrowed his dark eyes on her bemused face—he would make it easy for her.

'Thank you for a lovely evening, Sophie. I won't come in. I have some international calls to make—different time zones, you understand.' He brushed his lips against her brow and said regretfully, 'I am leaving tomorrow, but maybe we will dine out again the next time I am here?'

Max wanted her, but he had a growing suspicion that once with Sophie would never be enough. He didn't believe in love, but he was astute enough to recognise that what he felt for Sophie and how he lost control around her could very easily become dangerous to his peace of mind.

'Thank you—I would like that,' she murmured.

Max saw the naked adoration and the hurt in her eyes, and much as he wanted Sophie he knew Alex was right—she wasn't for him. He had watched her with the guests, the staff and with the children she quite happily looked after whenever she was asked. She was so caring and everyone adored her. Sophie deserved the very best, and he was far too much of a cynic to believe in love and happy ever after—whilst she was too young and too much of a romantic for the kind of affair he enjoyed. The timing wasn't right. Maybe in a few years, when she had completed her studies, and if she was still single…who knew…?

'Good night, sweet Sophie.' Because he couldn't resist touching her one last time, he lifted a finger and traced the outline of her lips, saw her smile. 'That's better. A young girl like you should always be smiling,' he drawled softly, his dark eyes enigmatic on her beautiful face.

He opened the chalet door, and with a hand at her back urged her inside with a wry twist of his lips. She was temptation on legs, and far too responsive and eager for her own good—not every man had his self-control.

'And be careful,' Max warned her as frustration rose up in him. He spun on his heel and left. His decision was made. He would take a flying visit to Russia, to iron out a few problems with the manager of his Russian operation. As he recalled, the company's receptionist, Nikita, was a very inventive lover. With the arrogant confidence of a wealthy man in his prime, he told himself the world was full of beautiful women more than willing to share his bed. He didn't need Sophie, and he would dismiss her from his mind.

Sophie watched Max walk away, wishing he would at least look back and give her some sign that he cared. But it was in vain.

Later that night, when Marnie found her curled up on the sofa, red-eyed from weeping and looking miserable, she gave Sophie the benefit of her opinion.

'What did you expect after one dinner date? An avowal of love? Cheer up, girl. Max Quintano can have any woman he wants and he knows it. You were a pleasant diversion while he was here.' She shrugged. 'Who knows? If he returns he might take you out again, and if he does just remember what I told you before: a brief affair is the best any woman can hope for from him.'

Marnie's words didn't help, but at least they made Sophie face up to reality. Her first ever crush on a man and it had to be on Max Quintano—a much older, super-rich mining tycoon, and a womaniser by all accounts. Where had her brain been? He was as far out of her reach as the moon. Her mistake had been in mistaking a teenage crush for true love, she told herself flatly, and she had to get over it. At least she hadn't slept with him….

But somehow that thought gave her no comfort at all.

CHAPTER TWO

Seven years later

ON SATURDAY afternoon Sophie parked her ancient car on the drive and, taking her suitcase from the back she breathed a sigh of relief as she entered her old home. Timothy, her brother, ran down the hall to meet her and, dropping her suitcase, she swept him up in her arms and kissed him.

'Hello, darling,' she said as she carried him into the elegant living room to find his mother and their father.

Sophie looked at her stepmother, Margot, and then at her father. Immediately she sensed the tension in the atmosphere and wondered what was wrong.

'Oh, good you have arrived,' Margot said.

No, *Hello—how are you*? Sophie thought dryly, and sat down on the sofa, still holding Tim.

'I suppose we should be honoured you can spare the time to visit your brother with your jet-setting lifestyle. Where is it this time?'

'Venice, for a three-day international conference on global resources. But I don't have to leave until tomorrow night, so I have more than enough time to babysit this little man.' Sophie hugged Timothy closer on her knee and added, 'Why don't you and Dad make a night of it and stay at the hotel until tomorrow? I don't mind.' That should put a smile on Margot's face, she thought.

Two hours later Sophie was sitting in the stainless steel kitchen of the house she had been born in, feeding Tim his favourite tea of fish fingers and mulling over how her life had changed.

Five years ago, when she had graduated from university, Sophie had taken a year off to go backpacking around the world. On her return she had discovered that her father's new secretary was also his pregnant girlfriend. Marriage had followed, and Meg the housekeeper had departed at Margot's request—much to Sophie's disgust. And four months later her adorable young brother had arrived.

Sophie had been besotted with Tim ever since, and if she was honest he was the main reason she tended to go along with whatever Margot wanted. He was why she had agreed to Margot's last-minute request for a babysitter so they could attend a glamorous charity ball at a top London hotel.

Sophie glanced around the ultra-modern kitchen. The family home in Surrey had been totally renovated by Margot, and she barely recognised the interior any more. But at least, with the help of a small legacy from her mother, Sophie had her own apartment, overlooking the sea in Hove. The commute into London was not something she would like to do every day, but then she didn't have to. She was a brilliant linguist, and her work as a freelance translator took her all over the world. She had built up an impressive list of corporate and private clients.

She had spent the last eight weeks with a trade delegation, travelling around China, and before that six weeks working in South America. This weekend was the first time she had been home in months. It wasn't that she disliked Margot—after all, she was only two years older than Sophie—in fact they should have had a lot in common, but unfortunately they didn't. Margot was a social animal who loved the high life—the best restaurants and the right places to go and see and be seen. But to give her her due Margot, for all her love of society and designer clothes, was a good mother and would not leave Tim with anyone she didn't know.

Much as she loved her brother, it was with a sense of relief that Sophie left the next afternoon to catch her flight to Venice. She wasn't imagining it—the atmosphere between her dad and Margot really had been no better when they'd returned at lunchtime than it had when they'd left the evening before. Something was not right in their relationship. But as long as it didn't affect Tim, she wasn't going to worry.

She had enough to worry about going to Italy again for the first time in seven years. The very thought brought back a host of unwanted memories of her one and only love affair—and of what a complete and utter idiot she had been. She had fallen for Max Quintano like a ton of bricks, and when he had left the hotel in Sicily where she worked, she had been hurt. But when he had returned a week later she had fallen into his bed without a moment's hesitation. After he had taken her innocence she had leapt at his proposal of marriage, and had even agreed to keep it a secret until he could meet her father.

For all of two days she had been deliriously happy—that was until she had discovered the kind of open marriage he had in mind….

A cynical smile twisted her lush lips. Still, she had learnt a valuable lesson from the experience—men were not to be trusted. That lesson had been reinforced over the years as she'd seen how a lot of them behaved as soon as they arrived at a conference well away from wife and family. Sophie had lost count of the number of times married men had hit on her, and she had developed an icy stare and a cool put-down to perfection.

The following Tuesday evening Sophie walked into the ballroom of a top Venetian hotel on the arm of Abe Asamov. Abe was a fifty-something, barrel-chested and bald-headed Russian who barely reached her shoulder. She had been delighted to see him arrive at the hotel this morning, for the second day of the conference, because his was a friendly face amongst a sea of strangers.

Abe was witty, and took great delight in fostering a ruthless reputation. Only Sophie knew he was devoted to his wife and family. In her last year at university she had spent her summer vacation in Russia, teaching his four grandchildren English.

When Abe had asked her to be his partner at this gala dinner-dance, she had agreed. The company she was temporarily contracted to had been overjoyed, because Abe Asamov was a billionaire oilman and owned a great deal of Russia's resources. Sophie wasn't sure she believed Abe's claim that he spoke only Russian, but she didn't care because she was glad of his company.

'You realise, Sophie, that they will all think you are my lady-friend.' Abe said in his native Russian, grinning up at her as the waiter showed them to their table. 'No ordinary man could look at a beautiful blonde like you and imagine you have a brain.' He chuckled. 'I think I will enjoy fooling people tonight.'

'Watch it, Abe.' She grinned, knowing he was no threat to her. 'Remember you are a married man—and if that was meant to be a compliment it was a bit of a backhanded one.'

'You sound just like my wife.' Abe grinned back, and they both laughed as they took their seats.

Seated comfortably and with a glass of champagne in her hand, Sophie glanced around the room, taking in the other guests there that evening. Many she knew through her work. There was the ambassador, Peter, and his wife Helen, and next to them a couple who worked for the Italian government—Aldo and his wife Tina. There were also two Spanish men—Felipe and Cesare—whom Sophie was seated next to. Very pleasant company, she decided, and, taking a sip of her drink, she began to relax and look at her surroundings.

The dinner tables were set around a small dance floor, and at one end on a raised dais a jazz band played background music. The evening was a glittering showcase of the powerful elite of Europe. The men looked immaculate in dinner suits, and the women were dressed in designer gowns and jewels worth millions. But Sophie did not feel intimidated. Over the years she had worked and mingled with some of the richest people from all around the world—even crowned heads of countries. As a result, she had acquired the social skills and sophistication needed in such company.

At home, jeans and a sweater were her favoured form of dress, but she had amassed what she called her 'business wardrobe'. The black satin Dior gown she wore tonight was one of her favourites, as were the crystal necklace and earrings. She knew she looked good and could hold her own in any crowd.

Feeling relaxed, Sophie glanced across the dance floor as a group of late arrivals took their seats and her green eyes widened in appalled recognition…Max Quintano and his stepsister Gina. Her shocked gaze skimmed over his hard, handsome profile and moved swiftly away. She was almost sure he hadn't seen her.

With her heart pounding, Sophie manoeuvred her chair so she could turn her back slightly towards his table and hopefully remain unnoticed.

She turned to Cesare, seated on her left, and asked in Spanish, 'So, what do you do?' On hearing his response she focused all her attention on him. 'An earth scientist? How interesting.'

Fool that she was, Sophie could not believe she hadn't made the connection between global resources and Max Quintano before now.

Across the other side of the room Max Quintano smiled at something Gina said, not having registered a word. He had recognised Sophie Rutherford the minute he had entered the room. Her blond head was unmistakable, with the fabulous hair swept up in an elegant pleat, revealing her long neck and the perfect set of her bare shoulders. The cut of her gown displayed the silken smoothness of her back and the slight indentation of her spine. A spine he had once trailed kisses down. His body tightened at the memory.

He saw the exact moment when she recognised him, and watched as the cold-hearted bitch turned away in fright. He had despised her with a depth of passion he had not known he was capable off when they had parted, and the way he had dealt with it had been to ruthlessly blot her out of his mind for many years. Then, on the death of his father four months ago, due to a massive heart attack, the name of Rutherford had reared its ugly head again in the shape of Nigel Rutherford. Surprisingly, two months later on a brief trip to South America, Sophie Rutherford had been the object of much speculation. Twice in as many months he had been confronted with the very name he had tried to forget.

As executor of his father's estate, and with his stepmother distraught at her husband's death and in no fit state to concentrate on the running of Quintano Hotels, naturally Max had stepped in to help. An audit of the family's business had disclosed that it was running at a very healthy profit, but there were one or two bad debts outstanding. The largest one was the Elite Agency, London—Nigel Rutherford's firm. Max had soon discovered that they were not just slow at paying their clients' accommodation bills, they had not paid at all for almost a year.

How it had been overlooked Max could only surmise. Maybe his father had been in failing health for some time without believing it. He could relate to that feeling, because he had done the same thing seven years ago. When Max had been told he might have cancer he hadn't wanted to believe it, and a couple of nights in the lovely Sophie's bed had fed his illusion of invincibility. How wrong he had been.... So he could not blame his father for doing the same.

On further investigation into the bad debt he had discovered that Quintano Hotels was not the only firm owed massive amounts of money by Nigel Rutherford. Max had joined with the rest in calling for a creditors' meeting, which was to be held next Monday in London. However, Max had no intention of going—he was leaving it to the lawyers and accountants to take care of. He could not care less if the Elite Agency went under, along with its owner, as long as Quintano Hotels got paid.

But now, with the beautiful but shallow daughter only thirty feet away, sipping a glass of champagne and smiling as if she hadn't a care in the world, a different scenario sprang to mind. If *he* attended the meeting in London he knew he would have no trouble convincing the other creditors to bankrupt her father's firm; he was a very persuasive man.

Sophie was occupied at the moment, but next week he would make it plain to Nigel Rutherford that he wanted to meet his daughter *again*! He had already waited years, so a week or two longer wouldn't matter. With ruthless cynicism Max decided it would be interesting to watch Sophie squirm when she realised who was responsible for her father's downfall, and very satisfying to see how far she would go to save him.

Sophie Rutherford was the only woman who had ever walked out on him, and it had taken him a long time to get over the insult. Now fate had once again put her back in his life—and in his power, if he wanted to use it. With his body hardening at the mere sight of her he knew he did, and the iniquitous plan took root in his mind.

* * *

It had been an appalling trick of fate that had sent Max dashing back to Sicily and Sophie seven years ago. He had returned from five days in Russia to his apartment in Rome still celibate, and still resolved to stay away from Sophie. He had called an old girlfriend and arranged to have dinner that night, and also arranged to have lunch with Gina the following day—Friday.

His date had not been a success, and he had gone to his office early the next morning and finally caught up with the personal items of mail his PA had not opened. A casual glance at the report from the medical he had taken a couple of weeks earlier had told him there was a query about one of his results and that he would need to contact a Dr Foscari.

Two hours later Max had been sitting numb with shock as Dr Foscari informed him that his urine test had revealed irregularities in his testosterone levels—a sign of testicular cancer. The doctor had gone on to explain that it was the most prevalent form of cancer in males between the ages of twenty and forty-four, but was easily treated. He'd told Max not to worry, because the test wasn't certain, but as a precaution he had made an appointment with a top consultant at the best hospital in Rome for the following week.

Max had walked out of the clinic with fear clawing at his gut. But he had been furious at the mere suggestion he could be ill, and had determined to seek a second opinion. Gina was an oncologist; she would know the leading specialist in the field. He would talk to her over lunch, tell her his fears, knowing she would keep his confidence.

By the time lunch had been over Max had known more

than he'd ever wanted to know about his suspected illness. Gina, in her forthright manner, had immediately called Dr Foscari, and after speaking to him had told Max not to panic. She had explained that there might be other causes for the irregular testosterone levels, and that anyway there was now a ninety-five per cent success rate in the treatment of testicular cancer. At Max's insistence she had gone on to outline the worst-case scenario if it *was* cancer. She had asked him if he had noticed any little lumps, if he was feeling unusually tired or suffering any loss of libido—all of which he had vehemently denied.

When she had then begun to explain in detail the treatment and the side effects—the possible loss of virility, the freezing of sperm as a precaution against infertility—Max had actually felt sick. To reassure him, Gina had offered to contact a colleague at a clinic in America who was a renowned specialist in the field, in case a second opinion was needed.

He had suggested flying straight to America, but she had told him not to be so impulsive and added that as nothing was going to happen in the next few days he should try to have a relaxing weekend.

Max hadn't been able to ignore Gina's opinion because he trusted her completely. He had done since their parents had married, when he was four and she was five, and they had instantly become as close as biological siblings, with a genuine liking for each other that had lasted into adulthood. She had supported him in his ambition to be a geologist, and he had done the same for her in her medical ambition and in her personal life.

'Max? Max!'

The sound of his name intruded on unpleasant memories of the past. He looked across the table at Gina, and the other two people in their party—Rosa and her husband Ted.

Gina and Rosa were lovers, and had been for years. Ted had his own reasons for keeping the secret—Rosa was the mother of his two children, and Max knew he had a long-term mistress. As for Max, he kept the secret because Gina wanted him to. She was convinced that their parents would be horrified if they knew the truth, and that the potential scandal of the relationship might harm her career prospects.

'Sorry, Gina.' He smiled. Personally, he thought Gina was wrong, and believed that not many people were bothered about a person's sexual preference in the twenty-first century, but it wasn't his secret to reveal.

'You have seen her? Sophie Rutherford?' Gina prompted. 'Are you okay?'

'Yes, fine.' He saw the concern in her eyes and added, 'I can't say I am impressed by her choice of partner.' He cast a glance at the blond-headed Venus in question, his mouth curling in a cynical smile. 'But I'm not surprised.'

Always a man of action, Max was not given to moods of reflection. But now, as he ate the food put before him, he found it hard to concentrate on the present when the woman responsible for so many painful memories of his past was seated just a few yards away. Seeing Sophie again had brought to mind in every vivid detail perhaps the worst episode in his life all those years ago….

Max had left Gina outside the restaurant, his mind in flux, and slowly walked back in the direction of his office.

For a self-confident man who prided himself on always being in control, a man who made business decisions involving millions on a daily basis and never doubted his course of action, it had been sobering to realise he was just as susceptible as the next man to the unfamiliar emotions of doubt and fear. He enjoyed his work, was very successful and very wealthy, and he had gone his own way for years with very little thought to the future. But now he'd been forced to face the fact he might not have one, and suddenly everything he had achieved didn't amount to much.

If he dropped dead tomorrow his family and a couple of friends might grieve for a while, but eventually it would be as though he'd never existed.

A few days before Max had thought he had all the time in the world, that marriage and children were something he wouldn't have to consider for years. He had thought in his arrogance that the *timing* had not been right for an *affair* with Sophie—that he didn't need her. But with the threat of serious illness hanging over him *time* had suddenly become vitally important.

Impulsively he had called his pilot, and an hour later had been flying back to Sicily—and Sophie. Alex be damned! He needed Sophie's uncomplicated company, her open adoration, her stunning body, and he wasn't going to wait. He was going to have her—and she might just be the last woman he had in this life.

Max had glanced around the familiar view of the hotel gardens. His dark eyes had narrowed on a group of three young boys in the swimming pool, playing water polo with a girl. The girl had been Sophie, and as he'd watched she had hauled herself out of the water and flopped down on a sunbed, the young boys sprawling on the ground around her.

The mere sight of her in the familiar pink bikini had knocked any lingering doubt from his brain and he'd felt his body stir and strode towards her.

'Hello, Sophie. Still playing around, I see,' he drawled mockingly, and tugged lightly on the long wet braid of her hair falling down her back.

Her head turned and her green eyes widened to their fullest extent. 'Max—you're back! I didn't know.' And the rush of colour and the welcoming smile on her face were all Max could have hoped for and more.

'Dare I ask if you are free for the evening?' Of course her answer would be yes. He never doubted it for a moment. And the events of the morning in Rome were pushed to the back of his mind as his dark gaze lingered over her scantily clad form. 'I thought a drive along the coast, and a picnic, perhaps?' He wondered why he had denied his own desire the day he met her, three weeks ago.

'I'd love it,' she said, a smile curving her luscious mouth, and he couldn't resist pulling her into his arms and kissing her.

Lifting his head, his brown eyes dark with need, he searched her lovely face. *Dio!* How he wanted this woman. There was certainly nothing wrong with his testosterone levels. In fact, if he didn't get away fast the rest of the guests around the pool would be well aware of that, too.

He sucked in a deep, steadying breath and gently pulled her away from him. 'I'll pick you up at eight.' And he turned and walked away.

Sophie watched Max's departure, her eyes drifting

lovingly over him, the misery and doubt of the last week forgotten in her euphoria at seeing Max again.

Later that evening Max helped her out of the car and, lifting a hamper from the back, he took her hand firmly in his.

'Where are we?' Sophie asked. He had stopped the car at the harbour of a small town, and she glanced around her with pleasure. Coloured lights danced in the darkness, following the curve of the harbour that had a dozen yachts bobbing in gently lapping water.

'La Porto Piccolo,' he said, looking down at her with a reminiscent smile on his starkly handsome face. 'It was a favourite haunt of my friend Franco and I when we were younger. We bought our first yacht together when we were nineteen and hoping to impress the girls. We have always kept it here, away from our families' prying eyes. It is small, but we had some great times.' Taking her hand, he helped her on board.

Sophie wasn't sure she liked the implication in his words. Was this some kind of love boat? And just how many girls had Max entertained on board? But then she spotted a table and two chairs set out on the polished wood deck. 'We are eating here?' she asked.

'Yes.' He placed the hamper on the table and drew her gently into his arms. 'It is a beautiful night, and I thought you would appreciate dining on the deck.' He brushed his lips against her hair. 'You have no idea how much I want to please you, in every way.' His lips lowered to brush gently against her mouth and she was stunned by the gentleness in his gaze.

Max cared, he really cared for her, and involuntarily

Sophie raised her hand to rest on his broad chest. 'You already do,' she said with blunt honesty. 'I missed you so much when you were away. I missed your unruly black hair, your teasing smile…' She flicked a silken lock from his brow. 'I'm glad you are back.'

'You can show me how much later.' Max covered her hand on his chest with his own and bent his dark head so that his mouth lightly nuzzled her neck. Sophie shuddered when she felt the flick of his tongue against her sensitive skin. 'But first a tour of the yacht, and then food,' he prompted.

With his arm around her waist, his fingers splayed across the soft skin of her midriff, Sophie was too aware of the magic of his touch to notice the boat. She had a fleeting view of one small cabin, and heard Max's comment about 'two berths', and then he was opening a door into the only other cabin.

'Duck your head,' he instructed, ushering her inside and closing the door behind them. The cabin was tiny, and lit only by the lights of the harbour, which were casting flickering shadows on the double bunk that almost filled the space. 'It is only for sleeping,' he murmured, his breath warm against her brow.

Sophie had never felt less like sleeping. And when Max's hand tightened on her waist and turned her to face him all she felt was breathless. She looked up, every nerve-ending tingling at the close proximity of his great body, and stared as if mesmerised by his glittering dark eyes, any thought of caution vanished.

Then his mouth found hers, his tongue moving within it with a deeply erotic passion, and Sophie was lost to everything but the incredible sensations shooting through her body.

He lifted his head and looked searchingly down at her.

'You want this?' he prompted huskily, his voice barely audible as he gently brushed a strand of silken hair from her cheek.

'Yes,' she gasped, and in moments they were naked on the bed.

A long time later Sophie lay collapsed on top of him, breathless and shaking—she had never known such pleasure existed. Max gently lifted her chin with his index finger. 'You should have told me I was your first.'

'And my only,' she sighed. 'I love you so much.'

'Oh, Sophie, I adore you. You are truly priceless—don't ever change,' he drawled softly.

'I am changed now, thanks to you,' she whispered.

'I know.' Max kissed her swollen lips again—he couldn't help himself. 'But it is I who should be thanking you. You have given me something precious and worth much more than you can ever imagine.'

Never before had he made love to a virgin, and never before had he met with such a wild reciprocal passion. He had lost touch with everything but the incredible agonising pleasure he had felt as he came inside her.

But that was the problem. He had done just that—forgotten protection. He looked into her happy love-lit eyes, about to tell her, but couldn't bring himself to spoil the moment. Instead he heard himself say, 'Marry me.' And realised he meant it.... Whatever the future held, Sophie was to be his and his alone....

With anger simmering just below the surface, Max cast a hard, cold glance at the catalyst of his trip down memory lane. With the benefit of hindsight he realised his proposal had probably been a simple gut reaction to the massive blow his male ego had suffered at the thought of testicular cancer. But at the time, after having sex with her, he had deluded himself into believing it was something more and asked her to marry him.

Max glanced across at Sophie again, and this time his gaze lingered, his dark eyes narrowing as he saw her smiling and charming the men either side of her. He saw Abe Asamov stroke her cheek with one finger, and his mouth curled in a bitter, cynical smile—a smile that was strained to the limit as she got up to dance with the man. The easy familiarity between Sophie and Abe was unmistakable.

Dio! Sophie was certainly sleeping with him, and it could only be for one reason—money. Disgust churned his gut. When he saw them leave the dance floor, and watched her kiss the fat Russian on the cheek, he dismissed any notion of waiting a week or two to speak to her. In fact another minute was too long, and he changed his plan accordingly.

It was said that revenge was best taken cold, and Max told himself he felt nothing but ice-cold anger for the beautiful Sophie and what she had become. He rose to his feet and excused himself. He had once thought the timing wasn't right for an affair with Sophie, and then changed his mind. Two days later he had been dumped unceremoniously by the heartless witch. Now he had changed it back again, and this time he would be the one to walk away. But not until he had sated himself in her gorgeous body….

CHAPTER THREE

EVERY SELF-PROTECTIVE instinct Sophie possessed was telling her to turn and run. She'd known coming back to Italy was not a good idea, and seeing Max confirmed it. But she knew she had to get through this dinner—if only to prove that she was a true professional and Max Quintano meant nothing, in fact less than nothing, to her.

Luckily for Sophie, Abe had asked her to interpret Cesare's conversation and she readily agreed; if she kept her eyes on Cesare and Abe she could almost pretend that Max and Gina didn't exist.

Back at university, after her brief affair with Max, it had been hard—but with the help of her friends and by throwing herself into work she had finally got over him and convinced herself she didn't care. Now it was galling to have to admit that it still hurt to see Max with Gina.

For the next hour Sophie ate, drank and smiled in all the right places, but she was intensely conscious of Max Quintano's powerful presence. She felt as though his eyes were on her, and that made the hair on the back of her neck stand on end. It took every bit of will-power she had to chat normally and avoid glancing back at the hateful man. The realisation that just the sight of him could upset her so much after all this time gnawed away at her. To compensate she sparkled all the brighter with the clearly admiring Cesare, so much so that Abe picked up on her distress.

He raised a finger to her cheek and stroked her jawline. 'Sophie?' She looked into his shrewd blue eyes. 'You are trying too hard—whoever it is you are trying to avoid, my dear,' he murmured, 'use me, not young Cesare. You could hurt him. But I have broad shoulders, and I don't mind playing the game.'

'You see too much,' Sophie sighed, and when Abe asked her to dance she managed an almost natural smile and rose to her feet, going gracefully into his arms.

Surprisingly, for all his bulk, Abe was a good dancer, and Sophie relaxed into the music, her tall, graceful body drawing the eye of many appreciative males—and one in particular.

'You're a very beautiful woman, as I've told you before,' Abe said as the music ended and with a guiding hand around her waist he led her back towards the table. 'Whoever he was, he was a fool, and he didn't deserve you in the first place. You are worth the best, and don't you forget it.'

She looked at Abe's hard face and realised that not only was he an extremely nice man, but also extremely astute—no wonder he was a billionaire oil mogul.

'You're right.' She smiled and kissed his cheek. 'Thank you.' Why was she wasting her time getting upset all because she had had one disastrous love affair with a womanising bastard? It was time she moved on with her life, she thought determinedly.

'Excuse me,' a deep, dark voice drawled mockingly,

and Max Quintano appeared in front of them. 'May I claim your partner for the next dance?'

Abe looked up at Max, not in the least intimidated by his great height, and slowly let his eyes inspect the man, before quirking an enquiring brow at Sophie and demanding in his own language to know what had been said. She was too shocked by Max's sudden interruption and request to think of lying, and she told Abe.

'Ah.' He looked back at Max. 'You want my woman?' he managed in English, and his blue eyes danced with a wicked light.

Sophie knew Abe was enjoying himself, and she glanced up at Max through the thick veil of her lashes. The look of cynical contempt on his harshly handsome face infuriated her. Abe had implied that she was his lover, and it was obvious Max believed him. He had a nerve to sneer at her, when *he* was the one with a legion of lovers and his long-term lover sitting at the other side of the dance floor. So why was he insisting on dancing with her given his obvious distain?

'I hope you will allow me the pleasure of dancing with your charming companion. Sophie and I are old friends.' His dark eyes narrowed challengingly on Abe.

Abe let go of her waist and threw up his hands in a theatrical gesture. 'I am not her keeper—ask her.' Abe suddenly seemed to know a lot more English than anyone had given him credit for—Sophie included.

Max's dark head turned and his gaze captured hers. 'May I have this dance, Sophie? Your partner does not seem to mind,' he opined, with a sardonic curl of his firm lips.

'Max—what a surprise,' she said coldly. Words couldn't begin to describe the anger that had swelled up inside her as the two men talked over her as if she wasn't there. 'I didn't know you could dance. Did Gina teach you?' she asked pointedly. The two-timing toad had the nerve to take a dig at her in front of everyone, and still demand that she dance with him.

'As a matter of fact she did. Amongst other things,' he said, grinning.

Shock kept her silent for a moment, his brazen reply adding insult to injury. Then, realising that standing in silence, sandwiched between two men on the edge of the dance floor, was arousing the antennae of the company around them, she said sweetly 'I'm sure she did. And, given she is your companion for the evening, shouldn't you be dancing with her?'

'No, Gina has other things on her mind,' he replied with an amused glance across at his table.

His callous indifference amazed her, and she allowed her gaze to rake angrily over him. He hadn't changed much. His black hair was cut shorter, and liberally sprinkled with grey, and the lines bracketing his mouth were slightly more pronounced. There was a hard edge about him, which was in direct contrast to the laughing, teasing man she had known, but he was still strikingly attractive.

'I'm surprised you want to dance with me,' she finally said bluntly.

Max moved closer and held out his hand. 'You shouldn't be, Sophie. After all, we were once *extremely* close friends.' His glittering eyes mocked her, and for a moment she hesitated. But she didn't trust him not to blurt out something even more compromising if she refused, and the gossip it would cause was not something she wanted.

'I'd be delighted to dance with you, Mr Quintano,' she said with a coldly polite social smile, and put her hand in his.

Max sensed she hated the idea but was too polite to say so, and he deliberately linked his fingers through hers and felt the slight tremble in her hand. 'Now, that wasn't so hard,' he said, dipping his dark head to murmur in her ear as he led her onto the dance floor. He had won the first battle without her putting up much of a fight

As he stopped, he caught her other hand and deliberately held her at arm's length. 'You are looking well.' He allowed his dark gaze to sweep insolently over her. She was. Sophie Rutherford had turned into an exquisitely elegant lady—even if she did have the morals of an alley cat. 'More beautiful than ever, in fact. But I've been watching you, and some things never change. You are still as eager as ever where men are concerned—and Abe Asamov is quite some catch! You do realise he is a married man?' Max prompted cynically, and did what he had been aching to do since he'd first set eyes on her tonight. He pulled her close against his hard body and guided her expertly around the floor to the slow music.

The brush of his long legs against hers, the familiar warmth and scent of him, sent a tremor of what Sophie hoped was revulsion down her spine. His callous reference to her pathetic eagerness with him so long ago was making her squirm inside at how naïve she had been. A lamb led to the slaughter sprang to mind... But she didn't let it show. That girl was long gone. She was now a confident, sophisticated woman who could hold her own in any situation.

'So?' she said, with a casual shrug of one shoulder, even whilst tensing against the inevitable close body contact. 'I'm not looking for a husband.'

'No,' Max drawled, glancing down at her with hooded eyes. 'I more than most should know that you want wealth and pleasure. But the stress and strain of marriage, of caring for a husband—' he gave a wry grimace '—is certainly not for you.'

'You know me so well,' she said sweetly, and felt his strong hand stroke up her naked back and press her closer, until she was in contact with his broad chest. Much to her dismay, she was helpless to control the sudden tightening of her nipples, or the leap in her pulse-rate.

'You've got that right.' He slanted a glance down at the soft curve of her breasts revealed by the low-cut neckline and a sardonic smile twisted his firm lips. 'And I wouldn't mind getting to know you all over again. What do you say, Sophie?' he queried arrogantly. 'Me instead of the ape Abe? You know we were good together, and they do say a woman never forgets her first lover.'

With a supreme effort she hid her shock at his statement. Max was certainly direct, if not downright crude, and it seemed impossible to her now that she had ever thought she loved this man.

'You're disgusting,' she finally said bluntly, attempting to lean back from him. Being so close to him was playing havoc with her nervous system. Age hadn't dimmed his powerful animal magnetism, and even though she despised him she was drawn to him like a moth to a flame. She felt exactly the same as the first time she had set eyes on him, and she hated the powerless feeling he ignited in her.

'Maybe.' She felt his lips brush against the top of her head. 'But you haven't answered my question.'

'It isn't deserving of an answer.' She looked up into his hard face, her green eyes turbulent with the mixed emotions of fear and anger—at her own weakness almost as much as with him. 'I don't know why you even asked me to dance, given when we parted you never wanted to set eyes on me again. Or why I allowed good manners to influence me to agree, because *you* certainly have none.'

That Max thought she was capable of having an affair with Abe was bad enough, but that he actually had the nerve to suggest she swap lovers! 'I have not seen you in seven years, and if I don't see you again in seven times seven years it would still be too soon.'

'My, Sophie, what a shrew you have turned into—and here I was, trying to be kind,' he said silkily. 'I may not be quite as wealthy as Abe, but I can certainly keep you in the manner to which you have become accustomed. The gown is Dior, but your lover has short-changed you. As my mistress you would be wearing diamonds, not crystal, I promise you,' he ended mockingly.

'Why, you…' Words failed her. She didn't have to put up with this, she wasn't a star-struck nineteen-year-old any more, even if her traitorous body was still excited by the man. That he should endow her with his own despicable morality was the last straw, and she attempted to wriggle out of his grasp.

'Stop it,' Max warned, and his hand moved up her back

to hold her firmly against him, his long fingers splayed just below her shoulder blades. 'For your sake more than mine, I would prefer us to reach a mutual beneficial agreement without the avid interest of this crowd.'

'Agreement! What the hell are you talking about?' she demanded, beginning to feel like Alice in Wonderland when she fell down the rabbit hole.... No, more like the Mad Hatter, she amended.

When the music thankfully stopped, Sophie placed her hands on his chest to push him away, but his other arm tightened about her and she was unable to move.

She looked bitterly up at him, saw the flare of raw anger that hardened his eyes and watched his dark head lower. He wouldn't dare kiss her in public, she thought—just before his mouth brushed over hers in a brief, hard kiss. She was too surprised to resist, and her hard-won icy control shattered into a million pieces as the awareness she had been trying to deny from the moment she saw him again heated her blood and coloured her face.

When he lifted his head her hands were resting on his chest. She didn't know how they had got there, but she was humiliatingly aware that to anyone watching it must look as if she had consented to his kiss. 'God! You have no scruples at all, you bastard.'

'Where you are concerned, no. And now maybe Abe will have got the message. You were mine before you were his, and you will be mine again.'

'Have you lost your mind?' Sophie asked, but with her head spinning from the dizzying effect of his kiss it was her own mind she was worried about. 'I wouldn't have you gift-wrapped with bells on.'

'Yes, you will.' He disentangled his arms and laid a hand on her waist. 'Your reaction told me all I needed to know,' he said as he led her back to her table, his head bent solicitously towards her as he continued talking. 'I have heard glowing reports about you from a friend of mine in South America. Apparently, your career has really taken off. It seems you are in great demand—and not just for your language skills,' he drawled sardonically.

'You've heard?' She was horrified to think Max Quintano might know some of the people she worked for, but suddenly she realised how blind she had been. Of course he moved in the same sphere as a lot of her clients—why wouldn't he?

'The Chilean ambassador's son—a fantastic polo player—was quite besotted with you. Apparently when you arrived at his last cup match he couldn't take his eyes off you, and as a result he fell off his horse and broke a leg. But needless to say you didn't rush to his side.'

Sophie remembered the incident, and the gossip it had caused—which had shocked her because she barely knew the man in question. But she shrugged off his comment with a terse, 'So what?'

'I also heard your father is married again and you have a little brother.'

'Yes,' she answered mechanically. It was taking all of her will-power simply to walk beside him, when all she really wanted to do was run and hide. Away from him—and the curious eyes that were watching them.

'If you value their security, you will meet me tomorrow for lunch to discuss it. I will call at your hotel at noon,' he commanded, as they reached the table.

'We have nothing to discuss,' she muttered, as he pulled out a chair for her to sit down. She looked up into his taut, cynical face and wondered why on earth he wanted to see her again when he had the doting Gina—and what it had to do with her family.

'Be there,' he said with a silky smile. 'And thank you for the dance. It was very illuminating.' But the smile never reached his eyes and she watched numbly as he turned and said, 'Thank you, Abe,' his narrowed eyes glittering with triumph as they met the older man's.

Abe took a long time to answer, his cool blue gaze holding Max's, and then he shook his bald head. 'I do not need the thanks,' he said dryly. 'You have my…' He turned to Sophie and asked for the word for sympathy. She told him and he repeated it. 'My sympathy.'

'What do you mean by offering Quintano your sympathy?' Sophie asked Abe as soon as Max had walked away. 'I thought you were my friend. I can't stand the man, and I'm certainly not having lunch with the arrogant devil.'

'The Ice Queen cracks.' Abe grinned. 'And if you don't know why I offered the man sympathy, then maybe I am wrong and all is not lost,' he answered cryptically. 'In which case Quintano does not need my sympathy and we shall continue the game.' He called the waiter and ordered more champagne, toasting Sophie and teasing her with, 'My wife will be delighted when I tell her the story. We have been waiting for this for a long time—you are far too lovely to be alone.'

Sophie denied she had *any* interest in Max Quintano, and tried her best to appear unaffected by her encounter with him, but it was an uphill struggle. She sipped the champagne and joined in the conversation, but her emotions were all over the place.

She felt angry with Max for intruding into her life again and deliberately humiliating her by kissing her in front of a crowd of people—but also angry at herself for letting him. He was still with Gina, and if he had been serious about propositioning her then he was also still a womaniser and beneath contempt. But then she already knew that, and the only thing to do was to dismiss him from her mind. As for his demand that she should have lunch with him—in his dreams!

She drained her champagne, and when Abe suggested coffee she agreed. They left shortly after.

Max watched them leave, his dark eyes burning with an unholy light. Abe Asamov would never get another chance with Sophie, he decided with ruthless implacability. He had the power to make sure she was his again for as long as he wanted her delectable body, and he was going to use it.

CHAPTER FOUR

BACK AT THE HOTEL Sophie stripped off her clothes and headed for the bathroom. She washed, then removed her make-up, and after brushing and braiding her hair pulled on a cotton nightshirt and slipped into bed. She was weary beyond belief and, sighing, she closed her eyes and snuggled under the covers.

But sleep was elusive. She moved restlessly, turning onto her stomach and burying her face in the pillow, trying to block out the image of Max from her brain—but it was no good. Meeting him tonight had stirred up a host of memories that she had tried her damnedest to forget.

From the first day she had met Max she had been totally besotted with him, and when he'd left the hotel two weeks later, after their one and only dinner date, she had been devastated. But with Marnie's help she had almost convinced herself it was for the best. Max Quintano was streets ahead of her in every way. As a mega-rich mining tycoon he was too old, too worldly and too wealthy to be tempted by an innocent young student, and she had begun to recognise that she had been extremely foolish to imagine otherwise.

That was until he had returned unexpectedly a week later. All her doubts and reservations had vanished like smoke in the wind when he'd asked her out again.

Much later, when trying to account for what had happened next, Sophie would realise she had been set up and seduced by an expert. But when he'd taken her to his yacht—a boat he'd actually told her had been more or less bought for the purpose—she had made no complaint. When he'd led her to the cabin, stripped her naked and laid her on the bed she had made no protest. Naked before a man for the first time in her life, she should have been nervous—but with Max she hadn't been. And when he'd joined her and begun to kiss her face, her eyelids, the soft curve of her cheek, she had reached for him.

Sophie could see his smile in her mind's eye even now, all these years later. His heavy-lidded eyes molten with desire as he took her mouth in a deeply passionate, hungry kiss—then her breasts, her stomach, everything else, until she was moaning and writhing, her whole body shaking. She had never felt such pleasure, and he'd taken her into realms of sensuality she had never known existed.

When he had discovered she was a virgin he had stilled for a moment, then moved again slowly. With erotic caresses from his hands and mouth he had driven her ever wilder, and thrust even deeper, until they'd moved together in perfect rhythm. Finally, with more powerful strokes, he had filled her to the hilt and driven her over the edge into a delirious climax, and, crying out, had joined her.

Stifling a moan, Sophie squirmed in the bed. Whatever else Max was, there was no denying he was a magnificent, considerate lover. She doubted that any woman had ever had a more incredibly satisfying initiation into sex—one that had been topped off with a proposal of marriage. Delirious with happiness, she had accepted immediately, and agreed that their engagement would remain secret until he had spoken to their respective fathers.

Wryly, she conceded that at the time she would have accepted black was white if Max had said so. But her state of euphoria had lasted just one more night, and their final day was etched into her brain for all time....

Eyes closed, she could picture Max perfectly as he had walked out of the hotel dining room after lunch on the Sunday afternoon.

Casually elegant in pale chinos and a loose cotton shirt, Max had moved with a lazy grace to lean against the reception desk, where Sophie had been helping out for a few hours, his gleaming dark eyes holding hers and a sensual smile playing around his lips.

'I was hoping we could enjoy a siesta,' he said, his long, tanned fingers closing over hers on the desktop Even after two nights of Max's incredible lovemaking and their secret engagement she still reddened. 'No need to blush, Sophie.' He chuckled. 'It is what all engaged couples do—in fact it is a tradition here in Sicily. And you would not want to upset the locals,' he teased, tongue in cheek.

'You are insatiable, sir,' she teased back. 'And I am not off duty until four.'

He glanced at his wristwatch, and then his knowledgeable eyes met hers again, a wealth of tenderness in their depths. 'Two hours—I suppose I can wait that long, but it will be hard,' he said, with a tilt of one ebony brow and a wicked grin, and Sophie burst out laughing.

But Sophie's laughter faded as someone distracted him by calling his name. He spun around, and she watched in surprise as Max dashed to the small, gamine-looking woman with close-cropped black hair approaching the desk, swept her up in his arms and kissed her on both cheeks. A tirade of Italian followed for the next five minutes, interspersed with much hand waving, before Max turned to walk back to the desk with his arm firmly around the other woman.

'Sophie, I want you to meet my sister Gina,' he declared. 'She decided to make a surprise visit.' And, smiling down at the other woman, he said, 'This is my friend Sophie.'

Sophie smiled shyly at Gina and held out her hand to the woman who would be her future sister-in-law. 'Pleased to meet you.'

Gina acknowledged her with a bright smile. 'The pleasure is all mine. You're very lovely.' She shook her hand, then immediately turned back to Max. 'Staying true to form, I see. It would take a bulldozer to flatten you!' She laughed, and although Sophie didn't get the joke, she thought to herself that Gina seemed friendly enough.

'Sophie, be a dear and order a light lunch and coffee to be sent up to my suite. Gina hasn't eaten yet, and we have a lot to discuss. I'll catch you later.'

Sophie watched Max walk away and enter the elevator with his arm still around Gina—and without a second glance for her. Slightly disturbed by his offhand manner, she felt her happy mood sink a little as she rang through to inform the kitchen of Max's requirements. Only after she had replaced the receiver did Marnie's warning come back to haunt her.

Gina wasn't his sister but his *step*sister—and the woman it was rumoured that Max had been having an affair with for years. Suddenly Sophie's shining confidence in her lover, her *fiancé*, took a nasty knock.

It didn't help when Marnie came in at four to take over from her. When she told her that Gina had arrived unexpectedly, the sudden pity in her friend's dark eyes simply increased Sophie's doubts. Feeling dejected and suspicious, she returned to the staff chalet and stripped off her uniform and took a shower. Grasping a big fluffy towel, she dried her body—and grimaced at the telltale stain.

Maybe it was the time of the month that was making her feel jealous and moody, she thought as she walked back into the bedroom and dressed casually in Capri pants and tee shirt. It also meant no lovemaking for a few days, which lowered her mood still further.

Too restless to settle, she prowled around the chalet, her eyes constantly drawn back to the telephone. Surely Max would ring soon, stepsister or no stepsister. He knew she was off duty at four.

When it got to five she could not stand to be cooped up inside any longer, so she decided to go for a walk around the gardens to the maze where Max had taken her the first day they met.

Sophie rolled over onto her back and squeezed her eyes tight to hold back the tears that threatened, even now, after all these years. She could hear their voices as clear as if it had been yesterday.

'Max, you have to tell the girl, if you really do intend

to marry her. Young women are much worldlier nowadays; she might handle the situation without so much as batting an eyelid.' Sophie recognised Gina's voice, and the urgency in it, and slowed her pace a little.

'Do you think so? I'm not so sure. She is very young, and not very worldly at all—unlike most women I know.'

What situation? Sophie wondered, all her earlier feelings of jealousy and doubt flooding back as she walked slowly towards the end of the hedge—and, if she had but known, towards the end of her dreams…

'In that case, why are you even contemplating marrying her?'

'Because, among other things, I was careless and didn't use any protection. She could be pregnant.'

Sophie heard his response and froze in her tracks. So bewitched had she been by the wonder of his lovemaking, his proposal, it had never crossed her mind she might get pregnant. How could she have been so dumb and blind? It was obvious Max had realised the implication of unprotected sex straight away. Was that why he'd asked her to marry him? Was that the real reason for their secret engagement, which obviously wasn't secret where Gina was concerned? He had told Gina he had asked Sophie to marry him, and mentioned the words *careless* and *pregnant*, but the word *love*, the most important reason for marriage, had never passed his lips.

Sophie's heart squeezed in her chest and she had trouble breathing as pain sharp as a knife sliced through her. Max had told her he *adored* her, he had said she was *priceless*—but, sickeningly, she realised he had never once mentioned *love.*

Was the secrecy he had insisted upon less to do with informing her father and more to do with Max keeping her sweet until he discovered if she was pregnant?

'I might have guessed.' Gina's scornful voice cut through her tormented thoughts. 'I warned you not to do anything impulsive, but no. You reacted like most men do at the sight of a willing woman. Well, whatever happens, you can't marry her without telling her. She hardly knows you, and in my opinion she is far too young to marry anyway. She hasn't even finished her education. And she has the right to choose whether she wants to be involved in this situation. So if you don't tell her, I will.'

To Sophie, it was another nail in the coffin of all of her hopes, and that Max should submit to such a scolding from a woman without any comment stunned her. He thought very highly of Gina, that much was obvious, and she had to be very sure of her standing in his life to lecture him in such a way.

'Sophie might be dumb enough to fall into bed with you—what girl wouldn't? Even I can't keep count of the number. I've given up trying,' Gina drawled angrily. 'But from what you have told me about her academic achievements she cannot be that stupid. She would soon guess something was wrong if her new husband kept disappearing from the marital home on a regular basis, probably overnight, and then when he did return did not have the energy to make love—which we both know is almost inevitable.'

'I will tell her—I will,' Max declared. 'But not yet. It has only been a couple of days.'

'Ah, Max, I do love you. But you are a typical man—impossible!' Gina replied.

'I know,' he chuckled, 'and I love you. I don't know what I would do without you. But look on the bright side—with any luck I may not need to tell Sophie anything at all.'

Suddenly, with blinding clarity, Sophie saw it all.

Marnie had been right. Max and Gina were lovers, and the only reason Max had proposed marriage to Sophie was because he might have made her pregnant. He had never even mentioned the possibility to *her*, his so-called fiancée, and tellingly she realised he had been careful to use protection every other time. What did he intend to do? She answered her own question—wait and see. And if she wasn't pregnant he would use her, then drop her like he did all the other women in his life.

If she *was* pregnant the pair of them were discussing how Sophie might handle their ongoing love affair as the pregnant wife left at home. She couldn't even blame Gina. She was all for telling the truth; it was Max who was the devious, lying one of the pair.

Pain and anger such as she had never felt in her life before consumed her. Tears pressed against the backs of her eyes, but she refused to let them fall. She wanted to rage and scream at the man who had seduced her so completely, stolen her heart and her innocence. How could she have thought he loved her? She was as dumb as Gina had said she was for falling for Max's charm, and the knowledge was soul destroying.

It took every bit of will-power she possessed to carry on walking to the entrance of the clearing. Maybe, just maybe, she was mistaken and there was some other explanation, her foolish heart cried. But the sight that met her eyes was the death of any hope that she might be wrong.

They were sitting on the bench, their arms around each other, their whole body language screaming long-term intimacy, and her heart turned to stone in her chest.

From somewhere she got the strength to move forward, and it was pride and pride alone that allowed her to declare, 'You are right, Max—you don't need to say a word. I heard everything, and—' *You don't need to marry me.* But she never got the chance to say it as Max cut her off.

'You heard everything?' He jumped to his feet. 'I'm sorry. I should have told you the truth. I didn't mean you to find out this way.' He walked towards her, a regretful, almost shameful smile on his handsome face. But she held up a hand to ward him off.

'No need to be sorry.... Gina's right. I am far too young to marry, and your situation does not appeal to me at all. I am leaving at the end of the week anyway, as my two months are up, so I'll say goodbye now. And wish you luck.'

'No, Sophie, you can't mean that!' he said, reaching for her. She took a step back; she couldn't bear for him to touch her. 'It is not as bad as it seems. Come and sit down, and we can talk it over with Gina. '

Not as bad! Disgust curled her mouth. It probably *wasn't* that bad in their sophisticated, decadent world, and that realisation was enough to numb all feeling in Sophie. 'No.' She shook her head, her green eyes glistening with anger, sliding contemptuously over him from head to toe. Her hero...her lover... The conniving, lying rat actually had the gall to suggest she sit down with him and his lover and discuss—what? A three-way relationship? Career woman or not, parental disapproval...whatever! Why Gina put up with him she had no idea.

'I have heard it all and there is nothing more to say. It was an interesting experience, but under the circumstances not one I wish to continue. I am not in the least interested in the kind of future you have mapped out, and luckily for me I discovered today there is no chance I am pregnant, so you have nothing to worry about except yourself.' She almost added *as usual.*

Max had never really cared about her. Even his love for Gina was not something Sophie recognised as true love. And she finally realised Max was the most arrogant, manipulative, selfish man she had ever had the misfortune to meet.

Sophie saw him straighten his massive shoulders and tense. For a second she imagined she saw a flash of raw pain in his dark eyes, but she must have been mistaken because when he looked at her his handsome face was a taut, expressionless mask.

'You are not the girl I thought you were. And you're right, there is nothing more to say—except there is no need for you to stay until the end of the week. Please oblige me by packing as soon as possible. I will square it with Alex and have your flight tickets waiting at the desk. I never want to set eyes on you again.'

Thinking about their parting now, Sophie saw again the hostility in Gina's eyes, and the hard, cold anger in Max's, and wondered why she had let the memory bother her for so long. They deserved each other, and she was well out of it. As for meeting Max for lunch—not likely… And on that defiant thought she finally fell asleep.

But the next day, at the end of the morning conference, as she was deep in conversation with the organiser, Tony

Slater, her defiance dipped when Max Quintano suddenly appeared in the foyer.

'Sophie.' He nodded his head in her direction and held out his hand to Tony Slater. 'Good to see you again, Tony. Sorry I could only make the dinner and not the meeting, but I hear the conference has been a great success. I believe that some very positive ideas have been formulated, which may be put into practice in the future. Maybe we can get together and discuss it further?'

Sophie's mouth fell open in shock. She could not believe the nerve of the man, interrupting their conversation, but if the expression on Tony's face was anything to go by *he* could not believe his luck—the great Max Quintano, suggesting a one-to-one, with *him!*

'Yes, that would be great.' Tony beamed, much to Sophie's disgust.

Max's dark triumphant eyes flicked mockingly over her and he chuckled softly as he addressed Tony again. 'Sophie and I are old friends and I am taking her out for lunch. I believe there are only closing speeches this afternoon, so please do me a favour and make Sophie's apologies to any interested parties for her early exit from the conference. I would like to show her something of Venice before she leaves tomorrow.' Withdrawing a card from his pocket, Max added, 'This is my number. Give me a call in the morning and we can arrange a meeting.'

Sophie tried to object; she had to fulfil her contract, and that meant staying until the end. But with the organiser of the conference declaring it was not necessary, that he would square it with her clients, before Sophie knew what had happened Max's hand was at her elbow and he was leading her out of the hotel. A male conspiracy if ever there was one, Sophie thought bitterly, with the sound of Tony's eager suggestion to enjoy her lunch ringing in her ears.

She shrugged off Max's hand as soon as they made the pavement and spun around to face him. 'I suppose you think you're clever, manipulating Tony Slater into excusing my absence? Where do you get off, interfering in my work?' she snarled, so angry she wanted to hit him.

He was staring down at her from his great height, all arrogance and powerfully male. The autumn sun was gleaming on his black hair and highlighting his chiselled features. Clad all in black—black jeans and a black cashmere sweater—he looked like the devil himself, she thought. But she was too mad to be frightened of him.

'Well, I have news for you, Quintano: I am *not* having lunch with you. Not today, not ever.' And, pulling her shoulder bag a little tighter over her shoulder, she added facetiously, 'But, hey, thanks for the day off.' And, swinging on her heel, she walked away.

Max let her go, because she was moving in the right direction. His motor launch was tied up fifty yards along the canal, and, although he was quite prepared to drag her kicking and screaming onto the launch, watching Sophie stride along was a lot more interesting. Her hair was loosely pinned with a mother-of-pearl clip at the nape of her neck and flowed like a curtain of pale silk down her back. Her pert bottom in a slim-fitting, short navy wool skirt was a pleasure to watch, and her legs—covered, he guessed, in silk stockings—were a pure joy.

Sophie didn't look back—she didn't dare! She was marching along the side of the canal, congratulating herself on her easy escape, when suddenly an arm snaked round her waist and she was lifted bodily into the air. She let out a surprised yell and began to struggle—only to be dumped unceremoniously onto a leather seat in the back of a boat. Before she could rise fully to her feet Max started the engine and cast off, which sent her crashing into the bottom of the vessel.

'You're crazy,' she yelled at Max's broad back. 'Stop this boat this minute, or I will have you arrested for kidnapping!' And to her utter astonishment, he did. She heard the engine die and, lifting her head, saw that Max had turned around and was leaning against the wheel, gazing down at her, his handsome face hard.

'If anyone is to be arrested it will be your father, Nigel Rutherford, for fraud.'

What the hell was he talking about now? Sophie thought furiously, tilting back her head to face him. A frisson of fear slid down her spine at the implacable intent in the cold black depths of the eyes that clashed with hers as he added, 'Unless you do exactly as I say.'

'You're mad! You can't threaten me or my father,' she blustered. Suddenly she recalled Max's comment last night about her family. She had thought nothing of it at the time, but now she wasn't so sure. Unease stirred inside her—how did he know her father was married again and had a son?

'I don't have to,' he responded calmly.

'Then why?' she asked, and stopped. She could read nothing in his austere features, but she knew for a fact that her father did not know Max. When she'd returned from Italy seven years ago her father had asked her if she'd enjoyed the break. In the conversation that followed he had revealed he had only met the owner, Andrea Quintano once, but he knew Alex. She supposed Alex might have mentioned her father's marital state. She had to wonder what else Alex might have mentioned.

Did Max know something about her dad's business? Was there something wrong? The tension between Margot and her father had been glaringly obvious at the weekend. Worriedly, she gnawed at her bottom lip—maybe they had money problems she knew nothing about. Dear heaven, the way Margot spent money it was certainly possible.

She was beautiful, Max acknowledged. With her skirt riding up around her thighs, her long legs splayed out in front of her, he saw he'd been right about the stockings—he could see the ribbons of her garter belt. The jacket of her suit was open, and the white silk blouse she wore underneath fitted over the high, firm curve of her breasts, revealing an enticing glimpse of cleavage that encouraged the eye to linger.

Reluctantly he raised his eyes to her face and saw the exact moment when she realised he was not joking. The angry glitter faded from her incredible eyes and her small white teeth nibbled at her full bottom lip. His body tightened—very soon *he* was going to nibble on her lush lips, and a lot more, and he did not intend to wait much longer.

'Because the law will, when his creditors get together next week,' he drawled sardonically. 'Unless I help you, of course—and that comes at a cost.'

'His creditors? And what do you mean—help *me*?' Suddenly realising she was at a distinct disadvantage sprawled at his feet, she struggled to sit up on the leather seat.

'I think you know. If you don't, have a guess,' he said with mocking cynicism, 'while I take us to lunch.' And with that he turned his back on her and started the engine.

For a moment Sophie stared at his back and wished she could stick a dagger in it, but it wasn't an option. Instead she ran their conversation over and over again in her head, and the more she thought the more worried and angry she became. But she did not dare argue with Max—not yet—not until she knew exactly what was going on.

Sitting on the edge of her seat, incapable of relaxing, she tried to focus on the beauty of her surroundings rather than the oppressive presence of Max at the wheel.

Venice in mid-October, cooler and with the worst crush of summer tourists gone, was a magical place. The sun-washed buildings edging the canals, the various crafts skimming through the water, the intricate bridges arching over the smaller canals—she should have been fascinated. And in any other circumstances she would have been. But she was too tense and too aware of Max to concentrate on anything.

CHAPTER FIVE

SOPHIE heard the tone of the engine change and, lifting her head, realised they were approaching a landing stage. She glanced up and saw a large, elegant pale-pink-washed house with a massive stone stairway leading up to it from two sides. She saw the huge double doors open and a man run down one side of the steps to catch the rope Max threw to him. Within seconds the launch was tied up.

She began to rise to her feet, and Max took her hand to help. She tried to pull free, but his fingers tightened. For a moment his eyes flared with anger, and when he spoke his voice was dangerously soft. 'Sophie, behave. I will not have you embarrassing me in front of my staff—understand?'

Glittering green eyes lifted to his. 'I don't want to be here. So we can solve both our problems if you just let me go,' she drawled facetiously. He had the nerve to laugh.

'Nice try, but no.' A moment later, with Max's arm firmly around her shoulders, she'd been introduced to Diego, his factotum, the man who had tied up the launch, and was walking up the steps to the impressive entrance doors, Diego leading the way.

The house was incredible; Sophie stood in the great entrance hall and simply stared.

The floor was a magnificent marble mosaic in cream and earthy tones, the walls magnolia, with elegant gold mouldings and works of art tastefully displayed all around. Marble columns formed a framework for the huge reception hall, an open door between two of them revealing a long dining table laid for lunch. She tilted her head back to look up at the ceiling and gasped at the centre dome, painted to rival the Sistine Chapel, and the huge chandelier that had to be Murano crystal. It took her breath away. The impressive steps outside were mirrored, and outclassed only by the fabulous marble staircase inside, which swept up to a central landing and divided again to a vast gallery that she presumed led to the bedrooms.

'Welcome to my home, Sophie.'

Awestruck, she glanced at Max. 'It's amazing!' she exclaimed. 'But I never knew you lived in Venice.' The Quintano family had been a constant source of gossip in the hotel when she'd worked there. She knew Max had an apartment in Rome, but no one had ever mentioned Venice. If she had known she would never have set foot in the city.

'When we first met I had just bought this place. It was a rundown *palazzo,* and I had it faithfully restored to its original style. Do you like it?'

'Like it? You are joking—it's fabulous.' She smiled, forgetting her animosity towards him for the moment, but she was brutally reminded of it two seconds later.

'Good. Then you will have no problem with living here for a while,' he said smoothly.

'Wait just a damn minute. I—' She never got the chance

to reiterate that she didn't even want to stay for lunch, because he pulled her possessively into his arms.

His dark eyes glittered golden with some fierce emotion, and his mouth settled on hers with a passionate intensity that caught her completely off guard. She flattened her hands against his chest, trying to push him away, but he simply pulled her tighter against him so she could not move. It was a kiss like nothing she had experienced before—a ravaging, possessive exploration that horrified her even as she shuddered at the fierce sensations he awakened.

Sophie closed her eyes and tried to will her body not to respond. As the kiss went on and on and he plundered her mouth, one hand swept feverishly up and down her spine, urging her into ever closer contact with his hard thighs. His other hand dipped below the neckline of her blouse to cup her breast, long fingers slipping beneath the lace of her bra to stroke a burgeoning nipple. An ache started low in her stomach and snaked down to her loins as a long-forgotten passion ran like wildfire through her veins.

When he finally allowed her to breathe, she was gasping for air, shaking all over with the shock of her arousal. He didn't give her time to recover but began to trail kisses down her throat, sucking on the vulnerable hollow where her pulse beat madly.

She never heard the discreet cough, only felt Max's head lifting and glanced up to see anger and desire mingling beneath his heavy-lidded eyes as he told Diego they'd be there in a few minutes.

'What do you think you are playing at?' she demanded, fighting for breath and trying to move out of his arms without much success.

'Tasting the merchandise,' Max said with brutal honesty. 'If I am going to bail your father out of debt, then I need to know it will be worth my while.'

Finally the penny dropped, and she realised his *living here* comment made horrible sense. Sophie looked at him with wide, appalled eyes. 'You actually imagine I will stay with you to get my father out of a fix?' she murmured. 'That is what all this is about?' She shook her head as if to clear it, fury rising inside her to give her eyes a wild glitter. 'Sorry to disappoint you, but my father is a grown man. If he is in any trouble—which I very much doubt—he is old enough to get out of it on his own,' she said with bitter sarcasm, hating Max with a depth of feeling that was almost frightening.

'He is your father. You should know.' He set her free and she took an unsteady step back, relieved he had given up on his demeaning proposition. But her relief was short lived. 'Maybe being bankrupted will do him good—though how it will affect your young brother remains to be seen.' He shrugged. 'But you probably know that better than I.'

'You bastard.' Sophie was goaded to retaliate at the mention of Timothy. 'You make me sick. If my father needs money I will willingly give him all I have, even borrow for him—there are plenty of ways of doing it. But take money from you? Never.'

His dark eyes narrowed cynically on her flushed furious face. 'Never is a long time, and your father only has a few days until the creditors' meeting. You should also know I got a call a couple of hours ago from your friend Abe. He knew I was having lunch with you and he asked me to say goodbye for him and told me to look after you. Of course

I said I would. Apparently he's flying to the Caribbean to join his wife and family on his yacht. So if you're counting on running to him for money, forget it.'

She swallowed the sudden lump that rose in her throat. How like Abe to put his mischievous oar in. She wouldn't mind betting he was laughing all the way across the Atlantic. But *she* wasn't laughing. Anger raged inside her that Max had had the arrogance to tell Abe he would look after her—as though she was a parcel to be passed around. But with the fury came an underlying sadness that Max, whom she had once thought she loved, could happily live in such a moral vacuum.

'Nothing to say?' he asked smugly.

She shook her head in disgust. 'I take it you're not married yet?' He couldn't be. Surely not even Max would have the gall to bring her here if he was? 'But, just out of curiosity, what would Gina say if I did agree to your disgraceful proposition?'

'There is nothing she can say—though obviously she won't be very happy, after last time. But as my mistress you won't need to meet her.'

She almost pitied Gina. Max's callousness appalled her. For one wild moment she considered walking out of his house, taking a water taxi to her hotel and then the next flight back to England, back to sanity. But the thought of Timothy held her back.

Max Quintano was not the sort of man to make mistakes—at least not in business. Much as she would like to, it would be foolhardy to just assume he was wrong about her father and dismiss the man. She needed to know the facts.

Max saw the indecision on her beautiful face and knew what she was thinking. 'If you don't believe me, call your father and ask him.' He indicated the telephone on a console table. 'Be my guest.'

He wanted Sophie more than any other woman he had ever known, and he had finally faced that fact when fate had put her in his path again last night. It had made his blood boil to see her with Abe Asamov, to see what she had become. The idea of the fat Russian enjoying her body—a body that *he* had initiated into sex—had sent a totally alien streak of possessively charged sexual desire raging through him.

Sophie was the only woman he had ever asked to marry him, but luckily he had discovered in time that she was the type to be economical with her wedding vows. As he recalled, the old English vow was *With all my worldly goods I thee endow.* She was obviously all for that but when it came to *in sickness and in health* she didn't want to know. She had dropped him like a shot when she'd heard he might have cancer.

It had taken him a while to recover from the cancer, and it had taught him to be a lot more circumspect in his sex life. But it hadn't stopped him wanting Sophie in the most basic way the minute he had set eyes on her again. Sexual desire took no account of the character, or lack of it, in the object of desire. It was simply there, twisting his gut.

He had denied it for seven years, because seven years ago he'd had more to worry about than her betrayal, but now he was damned if he was going to let her get away with deserting him unscathed. Now he was going to indulge his passion until the desire faded and he could look at her with nothing but the contempt she deserved.

Sophie looked at him standing before her, overpowering and arrogantly male, with an aura of silent, deadly strength that was decidedly threatening. 'I'll use my cellphone,' she said, determined to exert what little bit of control she had left over the situation. 'And I would like some privacy.'

'I will wait for you in the dining room,' Max drawled, and she watched him turn before she retrieved her cellphone from her bag.

Sophie switched off her phone and switched off her life, as she knew it, for the foreseeable future.

Surprisingly, she had contacted her father easily at home. When she'd told him she had bumped into Max Quintano at dinner last night, and he had told her there were rumours in the hotel trade that his company was in trouble, her dad had been amazingly frank. A group of creditors *were* due to meet next Monday, varying from airlines to hoteliers. Apparently he had delayed payment of clients' money and spent it.

He'd been sure he could put it right if he sold the house and rented something small until he had a chance to straighten out his business, but Margot hadn't accepted the fact so he had been trying to raise money from the banks. Last week Margot had finally accepted the house had to be sold, but she wasn't happy about it. The reason he was at home in the middle of the day was because he was expecting the estate agent.

Hence the atmosphere last weekend, Sophie thought bitterly, moving reluctantly towards the dining room. Her father's last comment was ringing in her head: 'I'm sure

I can convince the creditors to hold off until I sell up, but whatever you do, don't upset Max Quintano. His father died a few months ago, and it was only when he looked into the family business that the discrepancies in payment came to light. If he had left his mother, who ran it with her husband for the last few years, in sole charge then this would not have happened so fast.'

Her father had never had a high opinion of women in the business world. Being such a chauvinist, it was surprising he allowed Margot to push him around.

She entered the dining room. Max was sitting at the top of a long table, with the light from the window catching the silver streaks in the gleaming blackness of his neatly styled hair. No sign of the errant locks that used to fall over his brow, or the teasing brilliant smile that had haunted her dreams long after she'd left him.

He had changed; he was leaner, harder, more aloof. But he could still make her pulse race just by looking at her. Sophie's stomach muscles clenched into a tight knot of tension as she stared down the length of the table at him.

'Did you speak to your father?' he asked.

'Yes.' She made herself walk forward until she reached the place-setting Diego had laid on Max's right. 'And you are correct.' She watched as he rose and pulled out the chair for her, ever the gentleman. She almost laughed at the hypocrisy of the man; why treat her like a lady when he was intent on turning her into little better than a prostitute? But she said nothing and sat down.

'I usually am,' he drawled, arrogantly resuming his seat, and at that moment Diego entered with a champagne bucket and placed it beside Max. 'Thank you, Diego. I will do the honours.' Taking the bottle, he uncorked it expertly and filled the two fluted glasses on the table. He held one out to Sophie.

'Take it, Sophie. A toast to old friends and renewed lovers,' he said sardonically.

'I haven't agreed to anything,' Sophie protested, but it was a weak protest and he knew it.

'Your very presence at this table tells me you have agreed,' he declared, his eyes lit with mocking amusement 'Otherwise you would have been out of this house in a heartbeat.'

He was right, damn him! Hot, angry bitterness swept through her, but she was not prepared to give up without a fight. 'My father is putting the family home on the market as we speak. Given time, he can clear his debts,' she said defiantly. But deep down she knew she wasn't going to see her little brother homeless and her father ruined.

'He does not have time,' Max asserted softly, his firm mouth twisting with cynical derision. 'I made sure of that this morning.'

'You… But how?' Sophie demanded tensely, green eyes flaring across the table at him.

'I had a very productive morning and bought out your father's creditors. I am now his sole creditor, and as such his fate is in my hands.' An ebony brow arched sardonically. 'Or yours…'

'You swine!' she exclaimed. 'You really expect me to sleep with you to pay my father's debt?'

'Sleep is not what I have in mind,' he said with silken emphasis. 'And outraged virtue ill becomes you when I know Abe Asamov was the most recent in no doubt a long line of lovers.' Dark, insolent eyes mocked her fierce tension, and he lifted the glass again. 'Take this. You look like you need it.'

Sophie could feel angry colour rising in her cheeks at his casual destruction of her character. But with her father's warning ringing in her head she fought back the fury that threatened to engulf her and took the glass he offered from his outstretched hand. The slight graze of his fingers on hers made her flinch, and her skin tingled with a multitude of sensual yearnings that shamed and inflamed her. She raised the glass to her lips and took a large swallow of the sparkling liquid—she *did* need it!

Max was so damn arrogant, so confident in his ability to get what he wanted in business and in his private life. Look at the way Gina still clung to him. Yet he must have hurt her a thousand times with his decadent lifestyle—a lifestyle he was intent on dragging Sophie into.

'No argument, Sophie?' he queried, leaning back in his chair, the trace of a satisfied smile quirking his wide mouth.

She affected a casual shrug, but inside she was seething with a mixture of emotions—the uppermost a burning desire to knock the smug look off his face. 'I don't believe in fighting. A reasoned debate is more my style,' she said coolly.

'So sensible, Sophie,' Max opined mockingly. 'But are you able to pay your father's debt by next Monday?' he demanded, his challenging gaze capturing hers.

Tension crackled in the air, and suddenly Sophie felt seriously threatened. He quoted a figure slightly over a million, and she stared at him in mute horror. The amount was nothing to a man of his wealth, but a fortune to most people—herself included. The house in Surrey had been the family home for thirty years and, given the astronomical rise in property prices in London and the home counties recently, the sale might fetch that much, but her father would be left with next to nothing.

Minutes earlier she had been determined to play it cool, but now every vestige of colour drained from her beautiful face.

'I take your silence as a no. And, that being the case, you will agree to be my lover until such time as I tire of you or your father repays me.'

'Not if...*when,*' Sophie asserted vehemently, but a chill was invading her body, and with it the growing certainty that she had no escape. How long would it take to sell the house in Surrey? she wondered. Set in an acre of garden, it was a highly desirable residence, with five bedrooms and five bathrooms, thanks to Margot's expensive modernization. The irony of the situation didn't escape her. It was an easy commute to London, and it should sell quickly.

How hard could it be to have Max as a lover for a month or two, maybe three? Millions of women would leap at the chance.... If she could get over the fact she despised the man it might even cure her of her helpless physical reaction to him. Then afterwards she could move on with her life and maybe meet and marry a decent man, have a family....

'Then we are agreed?'

Reluctantly she nodded her head, just as Diego arrived with a silver platter and proceeded to serve the meal.

She picked at the mushroom risotto, her stomach churning in sickening protest at the bits she tried to swallow. The veal cutlet that followed she ignored, while Max tucked in to everything with obvious enjoyment. The only words spoken were a few conventional comments on the food. On the inside Sophie was almost overwhelmed with a sense of frustrated anger at her situation, and her hatred of Max was building with every passing minute.

'More wine? Or would you prefer coffee?' Max asked. 'Then we can get down to business.'

She glanced at her half-empty glass, realising she had drunk too much already on a near empty stomach, and clipped back, 'Nothing, thank you.'

'I must say, Sophie, you have surprised me,' he said, subjecting her to a long, lingering scrutiny that roamed over her face and then down, to pause over the proud thrust of her breasts. 'I didn't think you would accept my proposition quite so quickly.'

The arrogant devil knew damn well that she'd had to. With her nipples hardening simply at his glance, she was shamed and furious at the same time.

She had dated and kissed a few other men over the years, but none had aroused her enough to want to do anything more. Yet with just a look this man could make her body react like the dumb teenager she had once been. It wasn't fair.... But then life wasn't fair, she thought bitterly, or she wouldn't be here now. She glanced at him, big, dark and dangerous. A couple of hours in close proximity to Max had strained her nerves to the limit, but he was so arrogantly sure of himself that she decided to strike back.

'Well, as you said, Abe has left for the Caribbean, and my father tells me time is of the essence.' She smiled slightly and deliberately let her eyes roam slowly over him before adding, 'You're not a bad alternative, I suppose.' She drained her glass. 'Now, as you said, we should get down to the nitty-gritty.' Filled with Dutch courage, she continued, 'As well as settling my father's money problems, I would like to know how much you are going to pay *me.* I have a well-paid job, and I stand to lose a lot if I have to hang around with you. I'm not sure of the going rate for a mistress, so I will have to trust your wealth of knowledge on the subject.' She saw his thunderous frown and warmed to her theme. 'Do I have to stay here, or do I get my own apartment? I need to know all these things, and obviously I need it in writing.'

CHAPTER SIX

BAITING a man like Max Quintano was a stupid idea, Sophie realised almost immediately. To say her response had infuriated him was an understatement. He leapt to his feet, grabbed her wrist and hauled her to hers, then spun her around to face him in one fluid movement.

'*Dio*! You would tempt the devil himself with that smart mouth,' he grated, his dark eyes glittering with inimitable anger. 'You obviously need some training in how to be a mistress. For a start it is bad form to mention past lovers. My study—now.'

Sophie took a deep, steadying breath as he almost dragged her from the room and into another that was obviously his domain. Books lined one wall, and a state-of-the-art computer set-up stretched along another. There were armchairs either side of a large fireplace, and in front of the window there was a massive desk with a winged-back chair behind it.

His hand tightened briefly on her wrist, and then with a muffled oath he thrust her into an armchair. 'Stay there and don't move.' She cringed at the force of his barely leashed fury as he strode over to the desk and flung himself down in the hide chair. 'You want it all legal? Then that is what you shall have,' he declared, and picked up the telephone.

An hour later he dropped a document on her lap, but Sophie was past caring. She was thoroughly disgusted with the whole affair. She had always known Max was a ruthless man, but she had never realised quite how brutally blunt he could be.

He had called his lawyer and the man had appeared within fifteen minutes. The following conversation had been the most shaming in her life. Max, as her father's only creditor, had agreed not to demand payment of the debt and bankrupt the company if in return Sophie would live with him until he decided to end the arrangement. At that point the debt would be wiped out. In other words, Sophie was the collateral for her father's debt. At her insistence, a clause had been added to say that she was free to go immediately if her father repaid the debt. This clause was unnecessary, according to the lawyer, but she didn't trust Max an inch.

She had tried to brazen it out, and had suggested again that men usually provided a mistress with an apartment, and did not have her living in their own home. Only to have Max respond that with her track record he didn't trust her out of his sight. She had shut up after that.

The lawyer had presented the finished document and signed it, and witnessed her total humiliation along with Max. But she had signed it, so what did that make her?

'Satisfied?' a laconic voice drawled, and she looked up to see Max towering over her like some great avenging angel.

Getting to her feet, she picked up her shoulder bag. 'Yes, you have made my position perfectly clear. Now, if you don't mind, I need to go back to the hotel and consult my diary, make some calls and rearrange my schedule for a week or two. I'll get back to you tomorrow,' she informed him coldly.

'No. You can do that from here. Now it is time for *my* satisfaction.' Without another word he swung her into his arms and carried her up the stairs, oblivious to the blows she landed on his broad chest.

'Put me down,' she snapped. 'I am quite capable of walking.'

'You're not getting the chance,' he asserted as he shouldered open a door and lowered her slowly down the long length of his body until her feet touched the floor. 'Because your first lesson as my live-in lover starts here,' he declared, his dark gaze hard and chilling in its intent as he closed the door behind him. 'A mistress is always ready and willing for her man.' He reached for her, his hands catching her shoulders. 'And she never strikes him.' He paused. 'Unless asked to in the pursuit of pleasure of course,' he mocked.

In that moment the enormity of what she had agreed to finally hit her. She glanced wildly around the luxuriously appointed room, her eyes widening in fear at the enormous bed. 'Oh, my God. What have I done?' she groaned, her gaze lifting to the man holding her.

'Nothing, so far.' His sensuous lips curved in a sardonic smile. 'But that is about to change.' He pushed her further into the room and stopped by the bed. 'Take off your jacket,' he demanded, his hands sliding down her shoulders to the curve of her hips. 'And the rest—except for the garter belt. I rather like the idea of removing that myself.'

'How do you know—?' But he cut her off with a finger to her lips.

'Sprawled in the boat. But no more questions now.' He moved back and sat down on the edge of the bed. 'I want to inspect the goods and see if you are worth what I am paying.'

He wanted to humiliate her—as if he hadn't done that enough already. But for the first time in hours Sophie began to think clearly and wonder why. She let her gaze roam over him. He was aggressively male, with a fantastic physique and rugged good looks; he could have any woman he wanted. So why blackmail her into his bed? Because basically that was what he had done, by using her love for her family against her. Why was he so mad about it?

They had parted years ago. She supposed technically she had jilted him, but under the circumstances he had nothing to complain about. Yet she could sense the latent anger lying beneath his apparent casual control and she could see no reason for it—unless it was some dubious desire for revenge. Maybe she had bruised his ego by walking out on him—not many women would, if any—but why bother after seven years?

'Did you plan this? Did you know I was going to be in Venice?' She asked the questions she should have done at the beginning, her gaze lifting to his, searching for the truth.

'No,' he said smoothly, and the expression in the eyes that held hers was contemplative. 'The first time we met, my brother had died four months earlier. This time my father died four months ago. The Japanese consider the number four unlucky—the devil's number. I am not superstitious, but you seem to have a knack of appearing in my life after a tragedy.' He shrugged his broad shoulders. 'Fate or sheer chance—take your pick. I saw you with Asamov, looking more beautiful than ever and obviously more experienced, and—knowing the state of Nigel Rutherford's finances—I decided to have you.'

'And that is why you are doing this?' She drew a deep, unsteady breath, a snippet of conversation from years ago coming back to her.

Gina had told him she'd warned him not to do anything impulsive when he had revealed he might have got Sophie pregnant. Max obviously hadn't changed that much—he still took what he wanted on a whim. Suddenly she felt heart sick, because the really sad thing was that deep down, in the sensual part of her being, a part she had denied for years, was a secret longing to be back in his arms…and even now she didn't want to believe he was as cruelly amoral as he appeared.

Max saw the puzzlement in her eyes, noted the pallor of her face and grimaced. She looked like some virgin being led to the sacrificial altar. Hell! She was doing it to him again—tricking him with her aura of innocence when underneath she had the heart of a bitch.

A cynical smile twisted his lips. 'I'm not doing anything. I am waiting for you to perform.'

Who was she trying to kid? Max had no finer feelings. Well, if he wanted a whore he could have one.

Fuelled by anger, she shrugged off her jacket and slipped the blouse from her shoulders. She unzipped her skirt and shimmied out of it, and stood hands on hips brazenly before him. 'Do you like what you see?' she prompted scathingly. He could look, but she was damned if she was going to lie down and surrender without a fight.

Max more than liked it… Her lush breasts were cradled in gossamer white lace, high-cut white lace shorts—so much more sexy than a common thong—enhanced her incredibly long legs, and the matching garter belt was all he had imagined and more.

He lifted his gaze to her face. 'So far, I do.' She looked sinfully sexy, her green eyes glittering with defiance, and slowly he rose to his feet. 'Except the picture is not quite right. The rest has to go—but first…' he reached for her shoulders and curved one hand around her neck '…*this* has to go.' Deftly he unfastened the clip that held her hair and ran his fingers through the pale silken mass. 'I prefer your hair loose.' He pulled the soft strands down over one shoulder and traced the length over her breast. 'Try to remember that.'

A shiver snaked down Sophie's spine and she tensed, her moment of bravado over, suddenly fiercely aware of his hand on her bare shoulder, the knuckles of his long fingers grazing her breast. 'Yes,' she murmured, lowering her eyes from his intense gaze, appalled at the ease with which her body responded to his slightest touch.

'*Yes* is good.' He drew her closer. 'You're learning fast,' and Max was fast losing what little control he had left.

She felt his fingers gripping her shoulders and glanced up through the shield of her lashes to his mobile mouth. She knew he was going to kiss her.

She wouldn't respond. She would *not,* Sophie silently vowed, her hands curling into fists at her sides. But when his lips found hers her resolve was strained to the limit. His kiss was hungry, punishing, and passionate. She didn't struggle, but neither did she respond. He lifted his head, his hands dispensing with her bra, and she stifled a groan as he palmed her breast.

'There is no escape now, Sophie. You will only delay the inevitable and hurt yourself in the process if you try to deny me.'

His voice was implacable, and a shiver ran through her. Max saw this and snaked an arm around her waist. He drew her against him, his mouth finding hers again, and he kissed her with such power that it made her senses swirl. Together, the caress of his hand against her bare breast and the demanding power of his mouth conspired to defeat her resistance, and helplessly her traitorous body surrendered to the heat of arousal surging through her.

A whimpering cry escaped as his mouth left hers to bite the curve of her neck, his hand stroking over her full breast, cupping the firm flesh with his fingers, teasing the sensitive peaks into aching buds of need. He lifted his head, his dark eyes burning down at her, and she grabbed his shoulders, afraid she would fall as her bones turned to water. But the arm around her waist held her firm, his fingers edging beneath her lace briefs.

'I swore I would make you strip, make you squirm,' he rasped. 'But somehow it does not seem important any more.'

She saw the savagery in his glittering gaze and for a second she was afraid. But with a low groan Max captured a rigid rosy nipple in his mouth and she was past all conscious thought. He licked and suckled with tormenting tender bites that sent quivering arrows of need cascading through her body.

'Yes, tremble for me,' Max grated and, lifting her off her feet, he swung her onto the bed and wrenched her briefs down her long legs. 'This is how I pictured you,' he growled, his eyes devouring her. The white lace garter belt and silk stockings were her only covering, and her glorious hair tumbled around her shoulders. Desire raged through him, and swiftly he dragged off his clothes, all the time feasting his eyes on the sensual splendour of her spread out before him.

Breathless and lying on her back, Sophie widened her eyes in helpless fascination on his tall tanned body. He was totally aroused—all hard, urgent male, and she wanted him with the same passion, the same eagerness, as the first time they'd made love. She knew later she would hate him again, but now she was not even embarrassed by their nudity.

'Look all you like,' Max said, with a low, husky laugh of masculine pleasure as he knelt on the bed beside her. He reached to brush her hair from her shoulders, and somehow his words hit a nerve—was she still so obvious to him?

'I will—and don't forget protection,' she said, in an attempt to reassert some control, remembering the first time she'd been with him and the awful aftermath. 'I want no repercussions from this sordid affair.'

'I'm not that careless. I don't know where you have been,' he lashed back. For a second his hands tightened on her shoulders, his dark eyes blazing down at her with a contempt he did not try to hide. He felt a primitive determination to drain every ounce of satisfaction from her exquisite body, to imprint his mastery over her so all her past lovers faded into oblivion. But first he reached for the bedside table and protection.

'Be my guest,' he drawled, sinking back on his knees and holding it out to her.

'I...' She stretched out her hand and then dropped it. 'No...you.' And the heat that coloured her skin was not so much sexual as a total body blush.

He offered her a mocking smile and leant over her to brush the hair away from her brow. He saw the tumult in her green eyes. 'Not so forward now.' Actually, Max was amazed she could still blush—but it didn't make any difference to the need pounding away in his blood, the need to dominate and captivate this sexy siren who had haunted his dreams for far too long. With that in mind, he dipped his head to claim her mouth, all of her...

At the touch of his lips on hers Sophie was once again swept away on a wave of sensuality. His tongue tasted her mouth, and when the need to breathe moved him his lips brushed down her throat and bit gently on the madly beating pulse he found there, then moved lower to her taut breasts.

She touched him then, letting her hands slide over his shoulders to feel the tension in his mighty body. She stroked her fingers down his back, lost in the wonder of him, of his satin-smooth skin beneath the pads of her fingers. His tongue licked her breast and she groaned, her fingers digging into his skin as he took the aching bud into his mouth and suckled with fierce pleasure, first one and then the other. The feel of his tongue, hot and wet, sent a renewed explosion of passion though every part of her.

Max lifted his head and knelt back, so her hands fell

from his body. He stared down at her, his heavy-lidded eyes glinting with fiercely leashed desire.

'Patience, *bella mia.*' His hands stroked tantalisingly slowly up from her ankles over her silk-clad legs to settle on her thighs. He parted them and moved between her legs, bending his dark head to kiss the band of naked skin above her stockings, and she groaned out loud, her thighs quivering at the subtle caress. She needed to touch him and tried to rise, but Max placed a hand on her stomach and pushed her back down. 'Not yet.'

Helplessly Sophie watched him gaze down at her naked thighs, at the golden curls guarding her femininity, with dark, intense eyes. His fingers slipped beneath the two white suspenders, flicking them open with hands that were not quite steady, then very slowly he peeled the stockings down her legs. And then just as slowly, with hands and mouth, he stroked and kissed his way back up, until she was a trembling mass of mindless sensation.

She gasped as his fingers reached the short golden curls to part the soft velvet folds beneath. His head dipped again, and she cried out as his teeth grazed the nub of her sex, then lost all control and gave herself up to the wondrous torment of his lips and tongue.

Her hands stretched out to clutch at his shoulders, her fingers feverishly stroking up into his thick black hair. She felt him tense and pull back.

'*Dio!* The taste of you is so sweet,' Max groaned, and slipped his hands beneath her thighs, kissing his way up her quivering flesh to her stomach, her breasts and finally her lips.

As his tongue plunged deep into her mouth he parted

her thighs wider and in one smooth thrust entered the hot, pulsing centre of her. Sophie winced at the slight pain—he was hard and thick, and it had been so long—but her legs and arms instinctively locked around him. And when he moved inside her time stopped. There was only the rapture, the ecstasy, of his awesome body possessing her.

She cried out as he moved in her with ever deeper powerful strokes, until she was sobbing his name over and over again. Her inner muscles clenched around his throbbing length as she was swept into a violent climax, and before her orgasm had time to subside he joined her, his great body shuddering uncontrollably with the powerful force of his release.

Max lay over her, his head on the pillow beside her, and Sophie held him, her slender hands stroking down his broad back, glorying in the weight, the scent of him, the heavy thud of his heart against her breast. For a while the real reason for her presence in his bed was completely forgotten. But she got a rude awakening when Max rolled over and slid off the bed.

Unashamedly naked, he stared down at her, his black eyes glinting with pure male satisfaction. 'The chemistry is still there—you still want me. That wasn't bad to begin with,' he drawled, in a deep, dark voice, and a chill invaded Sophie's bones at the mocking tone. 'But I never did get to take off your garter belt. Stay where you are until I get rid of this, and then we can continue.'

She watched him walk across to a door on the far side of the room—the bathroom, she guessed. The afternoon sun shone through the windows, gleaming on his big bronzed body, and stupid tears burnt the back of her eyes.

What had she expected? Tenderness? Caring…?

Blinking hard, she slid her legs off the bed and stood up. No way was she going to wait for him like some besotted fool. Been there, done that….

CHAPTER SEVEN

THE NEXT MORNING Sophie opened her eyes and yawned, and for a moment she was blissfully unaware of her surroundings and her situation. She stretched languorously and flinched, as muscles she hadn't known she had ached, reminding her of the humiliating truth. She had given herself to Max as she had done when she was nineteen—but it had been very different.

Because after seven years of celibacy, and with Max presuming she was vastly more experienced than she really was, he had subjected her to a lesson in eroticism and introduced things she had never imagined were possible. Worse still was the knowledge that she had responded with an eager mindless sexuality that she had no control over. She glanced across the huge bed. The only sign that Max had been there was an indentation in the pillow, and the lingering scent of him on the bedlinen and her body.

She drew in a deep, steadying breath and sat up, pulling the sheet around her neck. The clock on the bedside table said eight. She glanced warily around, as if she expected him to leap out at her at any moment.

She couldn't face him…not yet. Slowly she swung her legs off the bed and stumbled to the bathroom. She stepped into the huge circular shower stall and turned on the water, flinching as a dozen powerful jets pounded her body. She let her head fall back and closed her eyes—and a kaleidoscopic picture of the last twenty-four hours whirled in her head….

Max returning from the bathroom, his tautly muscled body still totally naked… The ease with which he had changed her mind and removed the garter belt… Her breasts swelled at the memory.

The tender lovemaking of her youth hadn't prepared her for the full force of Max's sexual expertise—or the wild woman she had become in his arms. She didn't know herself any more…. Turning off the shower, she stepped out and wrapped a bathsheet sarong-style around herself, and a smaller towel around her hair, then padded back into the bedroom.

She didn't want to think—to remember the humiliation when later Max had accompanied her back to the hotel to collect her belongings, or his brooding silence over dinner. When she had tried to speak, tried to assert some independence and insist she had to return to England to make arrangements for her apartment to be taken care of, he had coldly dismissed her suggestion and taken her back to the bed that was the scene of her earlier downfall.

At one point, buried deep inside her, driving her mad with a torturous pleasure, he had stopped. Sophie had begged him to continue, arching up, her nails digging desperately into his firm flesh, but he had resisted her every effort. And she had opened her eyes and registered the triumph in his molten black gaze, his taut features, as he'd grated, 'Did Abe make you feel like this?'

She'd given him the 'no' he wanted, and seen the glitter of masculine supremacy in his eyes as he took her over the edge.

Glancing at the rumpled bed now, she twisted her lips wryly as she recalled Max pointing out, as he'd left, that this was *her* bedroom. Where his was she had no idea. At least she didn't have to actually *sleep* with him, she thought, determined to try and be positive about their arrangement. But oddly the thought was not as much comfort as it should be.

Bending her head, she began to ferociously towel-dry her hair, in the hope of knocking every image of her shameful capitulation of him out of her mind.

'Here—let me do that.'

She jerked upright in surprise at the sound of his voice. 'Where did you come from?' she demanded. Six feet plus of arrogant male was standing in front of her, dressed casually in navy pants, a navy shirt and leather jacket. But to her shame the instant picture in her mind's eye was of the same body naked. His dark gaze met hers, and the gleam of sensual knowledge in his send a red tide of embarrassment over her pale face.

'I'm sure you would like to think I had sprung up from hell,' he drawled sardonically. 'But nothing so dramatic. This is the master suite. We share the bathroom and dressing room. I'm surprised you did not notice the connecting doors.'

Of course she had—the same way she'd seen the up-to-the-minute bathroom, all white and steel, with two vanity basins and a massive circular pedestal bath. But it had not registered. In fact, nothing much had registered in her head since yesterday afternoon, except the dynamic, powerful presence of the man standing before her, and it had to stop.

But, before she could formulate a cutting response, Max took her unresisting hands from her head to slide them gently down her sides. Catching her shoulders, he pulled her close, and to her amazement began drying her hair.

For an instant she was tempted to rest her head on his broad chest and let him continue. But what little pride and self-respect she had left after her helpless surrender to him in the physical sense would not let her. Planting her hands on his chest, she pushed him away and he was left holding the towel.

'There is no need for that. I can use a hairdryer.'

His hooded eyes ran slowly over her wild tumbling hair, and lower, to the towel that slanted across her breasts. 'Need—maybe not. But want—well, *want* is a very compelling emotion.' To her surprise he chuckled, making a deep, sexy sound. 'And with that towel threatening to fall at any second, it is one emotion I am becoming very aware of.'

'What?' She glanced down and saw the towel sliding, and grabbed it up around her breasts as his arms captured her. His mouth came down to cover her own. She couldn't struggle, not without losing her only covering, and as his tongue stroked over hers she didn't want to. Her body melted against him as though tuned to his touch, and the familiar heat flared up inside her.

'Much as I would like to continue,' Max murmured, taking his mouth from hers, 'we have a flight to catch at ten.'

'A flight?' she exclaimed in confusion.

'Yes.' His hands fell from her. 'We have an appointment with your father for lunch. I arranged it last night, before dinner.' He looked at her stunned face with a gleam of mockery visible in his dark eyes. 'You have kept your part of the bargain more than adequately so far. Now I have to keep mine. But I want to meet the family who drove you to be so—obliging,' he said in a deep, cynical voice. Stepping back, he turned and walked over to the door, opened it, then stopped to fling over his shoulder, 'I'll see you downstairs in forty-five minutes. Don't keep me waiting,' and then left.

Sophie found the dressing room, and her few clothes neatly hanging in a wardrobe. It took her less than thirty minutes to get ready, she was so angry. After refusing her request yesterday, to return home to sort out her apartment, he had some nerve arranging to meet her family. But why was he doing it? To humiliate her further?

She gave a quick glance at her reflection in the mirror. Her hair was tied back with a red scarf, she'd applied minimum make-up and was wearing the same navy suit as yesterday. Someone had obviously pressed it, and, teamed with a red cotton top and flat red loafers, it gave a more casual effect. Her choice reflected her new status as a scarlet woman, she thought wryly—but she hadn't much choice. She had packed sparingly for her trip: a business suit, an evening dress and a selection of tops. The only casual item she had with her was a tracksuit she wore to run, or to lounge around in. Somehow she couldn't see the sophisticated Max appreciating his mistress in a track-suit. She tensed at the thought. When had her mind accepted she *was* his mistress?

She remembered reading the definition of the word in her mother's dictionary years ago, when Meg had mentioned her father's latest mistress. By definition a female *paramour*—a woman *courted* and beloved. If only, she grimaced. It certainly wasn't the connotation most people put on the word today—*kept and paid for* was the common assumption, and unfortunately in her case it was the truth.

Telling herself she didn't care, she straightened her shoulders and, with a defiant tilt to her chin, walked downstairs.

Max was waiting for her, and though she had told herself she would be perfectly composed, her stomach somersaulted as he let his gaze rake blatantly over her.

'A punctual woman.' His sensual mouth twisted with amusement. 'Or were you just keen to see me?' he mocked.

'No,' she said grimly. 'But I *am* keen to know why on earth you would want to meet my father with me in tow. Surely it's enough you will see him at the meeting next week? Even *you* can't be such a bastard as to tell him the truth about our arrangement.'

He shot out a powerful arm and yanked her against him. 'I've warned you before about your smart mouth.'

Sophie was trapped by the savage brilliance in his dark eyes. Her heart raced as his head dipped, taking her mouth in a deep, powerful kiss that was meant as a punishment.

She wanted to pull away, but the familiar musky scent of him teased her nostrils. Her toes curled with pleasure and with a will of their own her hands lifted to curl around his neck. She kissed him back, hungry for the taste of him. Then, without warning, he pushed her away.

'Call me all the names you want, but you *do* want me,' Max drawled, his dark eyes scanning her flushed face with cruel amusement. 'You worry too much.' He didn't bother to hide the derision in his tone as he added, 'Given the circumstances, your father will be delighted to see you, I have no doubt.'

'But what—?'

'What am I going to tell your father?' he said, reading her mind. 'The truth, of course.'

'Are you crazy?' she declared, eyeing him in horror. 'You can't possibly do that! He may not be the greatest dad in the world, but I *am* his daughter. He'd probably kill you!'

To her amazement, he laughed in her face. 'Ah, Sophie.' He shook his dark head. 'When I said the truth, I meant *my* version of it.' He reached an arm around her waist, and once again his dark head bent to take her mouth with his.

She shuddered beneath the brief, forceful passion of his kiss, and it took her a while to register what he was saying after he took his mouth from hers.

'We met and became *friends* years ago, in Sicily, and again in South America, and then again in Venice. For want of a better word—you are now my girlfriend, and as such I can't see you upset over your father when I can help…'

'You're definitely crazy. My father is not likely to believe that.' But bitterly she realised that Max was smart; there was just enough truth in his words to make them plausible.

'Yes, he is—because he will want to. I understand that as a widower he was quite a ladies' man, and spent generously on his woman. According to my information, his present wife costs him a fortune. I think we can safely say he will swallow the story whole, as long as you give me your full co-operation.'

Max was right about her father. In the years after her mother's death she would have had to be blind not to notice his penchant for the ladies. She had tried not to let it bother her, and mostly she had succeeded. How Max knew, she had no idea—and she wasn't sure she wanted to find out. In a way, they were two of a kind, she thought bitterly.

Letting none of her feelings show, she glanced coldly up at him and asked, 'What exactly do you mean by that?'

He grasped her chin between his fingers and looked deep into her eyes. 'You shall play the part of the eager and besotted lover—you did it once before to great effect, so you shouldn't find it too difficult. Especially after last night.' He pressed one last brief, punishing kiss on her mouth before, with her firmly held to his side, they walked out to where Diego waited with the launch.

An hour later Sophie, tense and trying to marshal her turbulent thoughts, sat in his private Citation X jet. According to Max, his enthusiasm evident, it was the world's fastest business jet, and could fly close to the speed of sound. It allowed up to eight people to travel the world and hammer out business deals at the same time. Talk about toys for the boys—multimillion pound toys, in this case, she thought dryly as the jet winged its way to London.

She glanced at Max in the seat next to her. He was wearing glasses and all his attention was on the papers he had withdrawn from a large briefcase—and had been since they took off, over an hour ago. Nervously she chewed on her bottom lip; they would be landing in another hour, and she still wasn't convinced the story Max had outlined to tell her father would work.

'Max,' she said beginning to panic, 'my father is not a fool—though he behaves like one at times,' she amended with feeling, still not able to fully grasp the ramifications of her dire situation. 'Are you sure…?'

His dark head turned towards her, and he slipped the glasses from his nose and rubbed his eyes.

'I never knew you wore glasses,' she said, diverted by his action.

'There is a lot you don't know about me, Sophie.' His mouth twisted cynically. 'But you have plenty of time to learn. As for your father, he will believe what we have already discussed. He is an experienced man with eyes in his head.' Curving a hand around her nape, he captured her mouth with his in a deep kiss. 'And you, Sophie, have the glow of a *satisfied* woman,' he drawled with silken satisfaction.

Did it show? Sophie wondered, flushing as she remembered last night. His last sentence effectively silenced her—as did the habit he seemed to have developed of kissing her without a second thought.

Seated to the left of her father, with Timothy beside her, Sophie tried her best to appear happy. But with Max and Margot opposite she was fast losing the will to live….

From the moment they had arrived from the airport by chauffeured limousine, and seen the 'For Sale' sign at the entrance to the drive, Sophie had been walking on eggshells. She'd had a brief respite when Timothy had demanded a ride in the limousine, and Sophie had gone with him while Max spoke privately with her father. She had shown the chauffeur the way to the village pub and back again, but when they had returned so had her tension.

Apparently Max had boldly announced to her father that he wanted to help him out of his present difficulties because he could not bear to see Sophie worried about her family, and a deal had been made.

Everyone was happy—especially Margot, who had taken one look at Max and started to flirt shamelessly. Max had cleverly fielded her innuendos and played the ardent suitor to perfection, keeping Sophie pinned to his side, and only letting her go when Margot had told them where to sit at the table.

Before the main course was finished, and after far too many personal questions from Margot, Max smoothly explained that he had had a soft spot for Sophie ever since he had first met her, when she was nineteen. He went to explain that they had met up again, purely by chance, in South America a few months ago—which wasn't strictly true. They *had* both been there; they'd just never met up.

Sophie could almost marvel at the way he avoided telling a direct lie, and when he said that their relationship had become serious in Venice, he turned his shining brown eyes to hers to add, 'Isn't that right, *cara*?'

'Yes.' What else could she say? She blushed scarlet at the gleam of mockery only she could see in Max's gaze, and that blush confirmed the story for her father.

It got worse when Margot asked her to help with coffee and cornered her in the kitchen.

'My goodness, you *are* a dark horse. I can't believe you've pulled a man like Max Quintano—but thank heaven you have. Play your cards right and he might even marry you. You want children, so get pregnant. That way even if he won't tie the knot you will be made for life.'

Sophie had often wondered if Margot had got pregnant deliberately, and now she knew—but she couldn't be angry because she loved Timothy so very much.

Sophie began to say, *I am quite happy with my life as it is*, but stopped, realising it would be a lie. She had only been happy until she had met Max again.

Margot shook her head and loaded the coffee tray. 'At least we get to keep the house. Whatever you do, don't upset the man until your father's debts are settled.'

'No, Margot, you don't understand. The house still has to be sold.'

'Don't be ridiculous. You're as bad as your father. Even if the house *is* sold, after the mortgage is paid off it won't make a fraction of what is owed. But for some reason Max fancies you—maybe you are good in bed.' She cast Sophie a brief doubting glance. 'I have heard he is a great lover. Maybe the attraction is in teaching you... But, whatever it is, one word from you and he will not see your family home sold to strangers. So start talking, quit worrying and pass me the cream and sugar.'

Trailing behind Margot back into the dining room, Sophie barely glanced at the others as she resumed her seat. She drank the coffee Margot poured without lifting her head. From the couple of months she had envisaged as being Max's mistress, her sentence seemed to have become open-ended. She knew that on the death of her mother the mortgage on the house had automatically been paid off by joint insurance—her father had told her so. It had never entered her head that he would remortgage it. How stupid was that? But with a young and expensive wife like Margot it was inevitable, and she supposed she should have guessed.

Barely two minutes after serving the coffee, Margot was leaning towards Max. 'More coffee, Max?' Her avid eyes were almost eating him alive. 'Let me fill you up—or perhaps you would prefer something else?' she prompted with an arch look, before adding, 'A cognac, or champagne to celebrate?'

Sophie could stand it no longer; she pushed back her chair and dragged Timothy out of his. 'Come on, Tim, you have sat still long enough. We will leave the adults to their drinks and go for a walk.' And she was out of the dining room and into the kitchen like a shot.

Opening the back door with Tim's hand in hers, she walked out into the crisp autumnal air. She took a few deep breaths, trying to cleanse her mind and her body from the shame she felt about what she had done and what was happening inside.

Tim tugged at her hand. 'Can we climb to the tree house?' he asked eagerly.

Looking down into his happy, innocent face, her heart swelled with love and she knew she had made the right decision. She would do anything to keep her brother in a happy home, with both parents, and if that meant saving her dad from bankruptcy, so be it….

Margot was young, attractive. Sophie didn't see her as the type to stay with a much older husband who was broke. Cynical, she knew, but realistic.

She smiled at Tim. 'Yes, of course, darling.' They set off down the path that wound round sculptured flowerbeds and manicured lawns to where a box hedge half hid the lower garden of fruit trees and pasture. A well-used child's swing and a slide stood in a clearing among the apple trees, and at the bottom was a hawthorn hedge with a large beech tree at the end. It had been Sophie's favourite place as a child. She had an abiding memory of her mother, pushing her high in the air on the swing, and sweeping her up in her arms as she careened to the foot of the slide.

Moisture hazed her eyes as they approached the beech tree and the rickety platform built across a fork in the trunk that Tim euphemistically called the tree house. Sophie had built it with her mother's help when she was eight. She had reinforced it last year. Now, giving Timothy a hand up, she climbed up behind him. Memories, she thought wistfully, looking at Tim's happy and excited face. They had no price. She knew she had done the right thing in accepting Max's dishonourable proposition.

'Really, Sophie, what must poor Max think? Climbing trees at your age.' Margot's tinkling laughter brought Sophie's attention down to the ground where Margot, clinging to Max's arm, was leading him down the path and smiling up into his face. 'I swear sometimes Sophie is more a child than Timothy, and I've told her over and over again not to let him climb.' She shrugged her elegant shoulders as they stopped beneath the tree. 'But she takes no notice of me.' She flicked a glance up at Sophie. 'Come down this minute.'

Seeing Sophie, her hair spiked with a few autumn leaves, tumbling free from the scarf that fought to contain the silken mass, her skirt around her thighs, didn't make Max think of her as a child—quite the opposite. She had the little boy firmly in her hold, and the two of them looked very similar, he realised. Sophie also looked childishly guilty.

'You heard what your mother said, Sophie,' Max prompted, tongue in cheek, his dark eyes glinting with amusement.

'I'm not her mother,' Margot said indignantly, and Sophie had to stifle a laugh.

Max ignored Margot and tipped his head back, his eyes taking in Sophie's lovely face and the humour twitching her lips. 'Come down this minute,' he commanded sternly, his gaze flickering over her slender body on the precarious perch, before lingering on her thighs, straddling the planks. 'Better still—hand me Timothy.' He held out his hands and glanced up, a brilliant smile slashing across his face. 'Then I will come and get you.'

His smile was so natural and so unexpected that Sophie laughed and handed Timothy into his arms. Before Tim was on his feet Sophie had swung out of the tree and was standing firmly on the ground.

Sliding a casual arm around her waist, Max pulled her into his side. 'You are a strange mixture, Sophia.' He drawled the Italian version of her name as he scanned her exquisite features. 'A beautiful, elegant woman—and yet you can act like a child.' His dark gaze held hers with compelling intensity. 'I have settled with your father—you have nothing to worry about. After seeing you with Timothy, I understand you a little better.'

Sophie very much doubted that—he thought she'd had

a host of lovers, for a start—but with his arm around her waist she felt oddly protected, and she wasn't about to argue with him.

But she *did* argue with him when her stepmother suggested they stay for dinner and the night and Max accepted.

'No—we can't possibly.' She shot Max a vitriolic look. He was seated on the sofa next to Margot in the drawing room, his long legs stretched out casually before him, looking perfectly at home, with a glass of brandy in his hand. 'I have to check on my apartment and make sure everything is okay with my neighbour.' Stiffly she rose from the armchair, and crossed the room to stare down at Max. 'If that is okay with you, Max?' she said, with a brief attempt at a smile.

It was a novel experience for Max to be looking up at Sophie. A Sophie who was actually asking his opinion instead of spitting defiance at him. For a moment he was tempted to deny her request just for devilment. But as his gaze slid appreciatively over her, and his body responded predictably, something stopped him. His tall, beautiful lover looked positively fragile. He saw the tension in her slender shoulders, the strain on her lovely face, and realised she was near breaking point.

'Yes. Of course.' He rose to his feet and read the flicker of relief in her guarded green eyes as she stepped back a little. He moved to slip a protective arm around her waist and took his cellphone from his pocket. 'I'll call the driver.' She glanced up at him and he felt her relax slightly. 'Ten minutes and we'll leave…okay?'

'Thank you,' she said softly. 'I'll just go and freshen up.'

She slipped from his hold. He watched her walk to the door, saw the effort she made to straighten her shoulders and hold her head high as Margot objected.

'Really, Sophie, we hardly ever see you. And that little apartment of yours can look after itself, for heaven's sake. You and Max *must* stay.'

He saw her head turn. 'No, I'm sorry, Margot. We must go.' She carried on out of the door, and for the first time since he had set eyes on Sophie again Max questioned what he was doing.

He looked at her so-called parents, and realised that two more self-centred people would be hard to find. He recalled Sophie telling him that her mother had died when she was eleven and she had gone to boarding school. Her father cared for her, but not enough to disrupt his lifestyle, and he was quite happy to take Max's offer to save his skin without so much as a private word with his daughter to ascertain how she really felt.

Max flicked open his cellphone and made the call, the realisation that he had behaved in just as cavalier a fashion—if not worse—making him feel as guilty as hell. Not an emotion he appreciated.

Sophie didn't go back downstairs until she saw the car arrive, and their goodbyes were mercifully brief. Her father kissed her cheek and Margot kissed air. Only Timothy was really sorry to see her go. She lifted her brother up and hugged him, smothering his little face in kisses and promising him he could come and stay with her again by the sea next summer, as he had before. She then slid into the back seat of the car.

'Are you okay?' Max asked, noting the moisture in her

eyes as he slid in beside her, after telling the driver to make for Hove.

She brushed a stray tear from her cheek, before looking bleakly at him. 'Of course. You have solved my father's problem in a day—I couldn't be happier. What do you expect me to say?' she prompted, with a negative shake of her head. And, not expecting an answer, she looked away.

Max had never seen her look more disgusted or more defeated, and unexpectedly his conscience bothered him. He had bulldozed his way into her life and into her bed without a second thought. He had taken one look at her with Abe Asamov and a red-hot tide of primitive possessiveness had blinded him to everything except a burning desire for revenge on the only woman who had ever walked out on him. But now he wasn't so sure…

'*Thank you* would be good, but not necessary.' Max caught her chin and made her face him. 'But I consider it not beyond the bounds of possibility that you might be happy with our arrangement.' He watched her green eyes widen in disbelief. 'Our sexual chemistry is great—' the slight colour rising beneath her skin encouraged him to continue '—and, contrary to the impression I might have given in the last day or two, I'm not an ogre. And with a bit of goodwill on both sides we could rub along very nicely.' Bending his dark head, he took her mouth in a quick, hard kiss. 'Think about it during the journey, while I get on with some work.' Parting his legs slightly, he lifted his briefcase to his lap, extracted the latest mining report on a new excavation in Ecuador and began to read.

Rub along very nicely—was he for real? she asked herself, her lips still tingling from his kiss. The only thing rubbing around here was his thigh against hers, with the motion of the car, and *nicely* was not an adjective she would use—*naughty*, more like. She cast a sidelong glance at his granite profile; he was so cool, so calm, so in control. How did he do that? she wondered. He was far too ruthless, too lethally male to ever be associated with the word *nice*, and she was surprised it was even in his vocabulary.

As for goodwill on both sides! She edged along the seat to put some space between them. She could just imagine how *that* would play out. An all-powerful, arrogant male like Max would consider his will good for both of them…. He certainly had so far.

Yawning, she closed her eyes. She had barely slept for two nights, and she was bone-weary and tired of thinking.

CHAPTER EIGHT

'SOPHIE...SOPHIE, wake up.' She heard the deep voice from a distance and slowly opened her eyes—to find herself with her head on Max's chest. Her arm was burrowed under his jacket and her fingers grasped the back of his shirt, while his arm was looped across her shoulders and under her other arm.

She jerked her head up. 'I fell asleep,' she murmured, stating the obvious and blushing scarlet.

'With you plastered to my chest, I did notice,' he quipped, his eyes smiling down into hers. 'But we have arrived.'

Pushing on his chest, she scrambled back to a sitting position and ran her fingers through her hair, straightening her skirt over her legs. 'I am sorry. I must have stopped you working,' she said, too embarrassed to look at him.

'Don't be. It was my pleasure,' he chuckled, and stepped out of the car.

Her apartment was on the first floor of a double-fronted detached Victorian house on a main road overlooking the beach and the sea.

'Great view,' Max remarked, glancing around as he took her hand and helped her from the car.

Standing on the pavement, it suddenly struck Sophie that she didn't want Max in her apartment. It was her private sanctuary, and when this affair was over she wanted no spectre of Max hanging around her home.

'There is no need for you to come in.' She slanted a smile at him that faded slightly as she met with intense dark eyes, studying her curiously from beneath lush black lashes. He really was incredibly attractive, and for a moment her intention wavered as she enjoyed looking at him.

She blinked rapidly and continued fighting back the blush that threatened. 'Why don't you have the driver show you around the area? He can't park here anyway, and Brighton is just along the road and very interesting,' she pointed out, with admirable cool. 'It won't take me long to pack a few things, and I have to visit my neighbour. You would be bored.' She tried to casually free her hand from his.

An ebony brow arched sardonically. 'You cannot be serious, Sophie.' In an aside he quietly dismissed the driver for the night and tightened his grip on her hand. 'I have had enough of driving around for one day.'

Sophie fitted her key into her front door lock and walked into the elegant wood-panelled foyer.

'I live on the first floor,' she murmured, and was very aware of Max's eyes on her as she walked in front of him up the enclosed staircase, and unlocked the door at the top that led into her hallway.

'Not quite up to your standards,' she said bluntly, as she led him into the sitting room. Without thought, she heeled off her shoes, dropped her bag on the usual sofa table and turned to face him. 'But I like it.'

Max gaze skimmed over her. She was bristling with defiance, and he knew she did not want him here. 'I'm sure you do,' he said smoothly, glancing around the room. 'It is charming.'

It had a sophisticated elegance, with its high ceiling and light oak floor. A grey marble fireplace housed an open fire, and a deep wide bay window that overlooked the sea was fitted with a comfortable window seat. The décor was mostly neutral, with a touch of colour in the rug and the sofas, and on one wall a waist-high long mahogany bookcase was filled with books. Above it a group of paintings were displayed.

'Would you like coffee, or a glass of wine?' Sophie asked, uncomfortable with the growing silence.

'Wine, please. Your English coffee is terrible.' Max strolled across the room and, shrugging off his jacket, draped it on the arm of the sofa and sat down.

'I left a bottle of South African chardonnay in the fridge, but I can't guarantee it will be better than the coffee,' she responded dryly.

The sight of him sprawled at ease in her home, looking as if he belonged there, confirmed Sophie's worst fears. She'd never get the image of him out of her head, she just knew it, and she was glad to escape to the kitchen-diner off the main hall.

She took off her jacket and hung it over the back of a pine chair. Taking the bottle from the fridge, she opened it and filled two large crystal glasses. She took her time, sipping a little of the wine, feeling reluctant to face him, and then realised her mistake—the quicker she got him out of here the better. She drained her glass and replaced the bottle in the fridge.

Moments later she walked back into the sitting room and placed the crystal glass on the table. 'Enjoy—the bottle is in the fridge if you want a refill. I'll just go and pack—it won't take me long. A quick call to my neighbour and we can be gone.' She knew she was babbling, but he made her nervous.

A strong hand wrapped around her wrist, and with a jerk he pulled her down beside him.

'What did you do that for?' she demanded, struggling to sit up. Another tug pulled her back, a strong arm clamping around her shoulders.

His dark eyes made a sweeping survey of her mutinous face, and he just grinned. 'Relax, Sophie; you have a lovely home—unwind and enjoy it. We are not going anywhere tonight. When you decided after lunch that you had to come here, I gave my pilot the rest of the day off—he started at ten, and he is only allowed to work twelve hours.'

His hand was warm through the fabric of her top, his thumb and fingers idly kneading her collarbone, making her achingly aware of the dangerous sensuality of his touch. Her breath caught and she had difficulty speaking for a moment. She swallowed hard, determined not to give in to his overpowering sexual attraction. She glanced at the clock on the mantelpiece. They'd left Italy at ten, and they could be back by ten if they hurried.

'It…it's just six.' She couldn't help the stammer, but carried on urgently. 'I can pack, and we can be at the airport by seven if we hurry. It is only a two and a half hour flight—we can be there by nine-thirty.'

'I'm flattered you are eager to return to my home, and your mathematical attempt on my behalf is quite impressive. Unfortunately, *cara*, you haven't allowed for continental time being an hour ahead.' Max looked at her mockingly. 'So it is not possible.'

'You can't sleep here.' Her eyes widened on his in appalled comprehension—it was her own stupid fault he was here at all. It was bad enough having him in her sitting room, but it would be a hundred times worse having him in her bedroom.

'Would you mind telling me why not?' Max enquired smoothly, his hand stroking up the side of her neck and his long fingers wrapping around her loosely tied hair.

His wide shoulders were angled towards her, and she was strikingly aware of the virile male body, the glimpse of golden skin beneath the open-necked blue shirt. She blurted out the first thing that came into her head. 'You have no clothes.'

'You are wrong. Surely you know that I am always prepared? Not that it matters—remaining naked with you will do just fine.' He grinned. 'Come on, Sophie, we both know the game is over and I won.' He tugged on her hair and tilted her head back, his glinting dark eyes capturing hers. 'Cut out the pretence. You're mine for as long as I want you—here or anywhere.'

'Only until the house is—' She tried rather futilely to deny his assumption, and was silenced by his abrupt bark of laughter.

'After meeting Nigel and Margot, I know that is never going to happen unless I make them. And I won't.'

That he had seen so easily through Margot didn't surprise her, but, forcing herself to hold his gaze, she said, 'You're probably right. But it does not alter the fact I'd rather we didn't stay here. A hotel…'

'A hotel?' His brow pleated in a frown. 'Afraid I will discover signs of your last lover in your bedroom?' His amusement vanished.

'No, of course not,' she shot back, incensed, and then wished she hadn't as his expression became strangely contemplative.

'So something else is bothering you?' His piercing black eyes narrowed shrewdly on her face and suddenly she was afraid.

'I've been away since Saturday—there is no food in the house,' she said, swiftly tearing her gaze from his, frightened he would see more in her expression than she wanted him to know.

'Is that all?' She sensed rather than saw the smile an instant before his lips brushed hers. 'I am a big man, and I need my food, but there must be a restaurant around here. We won't starve.'

Her green eyes focused on his starkly handsome face, saw his mouth curved in a sexy smile, and for a moment she was transported back in time, to the laughing, teasing Max of her youth. She felt again the heavy beat of her heart, as though it would burst from her chest, the incredible lurch in her stomach that accompanied her every sight of him, and it terrified her.

'You're right.' She forced a smile to her lips. 'Drink your wine. I need to shower and change,' she managed to say steadily. 'Climbing trees is a messy exercise.' She indicated the TV remote control on the table. 'Watch the television, if you like. I might be a while.'

Intense dark eyes skimmed over her face and lingered for a moment, then he calmly lounged back on the sofa as she rose unhindered to her feet. 'I'd rather share your shower,' he prompted softly.

'It isn't big enough,' she said without turning around and she walked slowly out of the room, closing the door behind her.

She leant against the wall, physically and emotionally drained. It had hit her like a thunderbolt when she had mentioned Saturday and made the excuse about food. Five days—it had only been five days, and her life had changed for ever. His easy dismissal of her excuse about food and her reaction had shocked her to her soul. Suddenly she realised the futility of trying to keep him out of her bedroom. It wouldn't matter where or whom she was with; the image of Max would always be in her mind.

Making herself move, she walked down the hall and into the bathroom. She stripped off her clothes and felt a chill down her spine as she realised with a sense of inevitability that she was in very real danger of becoming addicted to Max's undoubted sexual charisma all over again. She refused to call it love....

Turning on the shower, she pulled on a shower cap and stepped under the spray, her thoughts in turmoil. She had tried to dismiss her feelings for Max as a teenage crush the first time they'd been together, and had convinced herself—until last night. Now her mind was at war with her body, and the internal battle was tearing her apart. That she was Max's mistress was a huge blow to her pride, her self-respect, but the pleasure she had felt at the touch of his lips, his hands on her body, the wonder of his possession she could not deny. She could not fool herself anymore—she wanted him with a ferocity that frightened her, and he must never find out. Because if he did that would surely destroy what little self-respect she had left.

Stepping out of the shower, she dried and dressed, wondering all the time how was it possible to lust after someone when she hated the kind of man he was—and certainly didn't trust him.

Dressed in jeans and a sweater, Sophie was still asking herself the same question when, forty minutes later, she walked back into the sitting room. Max was still seated on the sofa, his briefcase open beside him and some papers in his hands. He looked up as she entered.

'Quite a transformation.'

'Not really. I always dress like this when I am at home.' She flicked a cold green glance his way. 'If there is a dress code for a mistress you should have told me.'

Max knew she was angry with him for forcing her into this situation, and in a way he didn't blame her, but on another more cynical level he didn't see what she had to complain about. She was no longer a starry-eyed virgin, not by a long way.

'Not that I am aware of. An *un*dress code, yes. Any time I say so,' he stated bluntly, his dark gaze skimming over her. She looked stunning—her long shapely legs were covered in close-fitting blue denim, and a deeper blue sweater clung to the firm thrust of her breasts. The pale blond hair was swept back into one long braid and reminded him forcibly of the teenager he had first known—and of the reason they'd parted.

He reached for her, his hands palming each side of her head, and looked deep into her angry, resentful eyes. Infuriated, he took the lush mouth with his own in a bitter, possessive kiss. If anyone had a right to be angry it was he; she had walked out on him without a second thought, at the lowest point in his life.

He felt her fingers link around his neck, the softening of her gorgeous body against his, the response she could not deny. And, disgusted with himself as much as her, he lifted his head and pushed her away. 'Where is the bathroom? I need a wash.'

As rejections went, it was a bad one, and Sophie learnt a valuable lesson. Sucking in a deep breath of air, she forced her chin up, her face expressionless. If she was to get through the next weeks or months she had to be as cool and emotionless as Max. 'First door on the right along the hall,' she replied.

Max heard the laughter as he approached the sitting room door minutes later. Light and sexy, it ripped open a Pandora's box of memories he could do without. For a moment he stood in the open door, watching her. She was sitting in the window seat, her lovely face wreathed in smiles.

'Oh, Sam, you are impossible.'

At the name Sam, Max stiffened and stepped into the room. He must have made a sound, because she turned her head towards him and the smile vanished from her face.

'Look, I can't talk now, but I promise I will try my best to get back in time. Okay?' She put the telephone down and rose to her feet.

'Sam is a friend of yours, I take it?' he prompted, and sat down on the sofa, swallowing the bitter taste that rose in his throat. How many men had sampled Sophie's luscious charms? he wondered. It was not something that had ever bothered him with his other women, and the anger surging through him felt suspiciously like jealousy.

'Yes. We spent a year backpacking together when we finished university.'

'How nice.'

Sophie glanced at him. So the word *nice* was in his vocabulary—but by the tone of his voice and the way he used it it was anything but. 'Yes, it was brilliant,' she said defiantly. Letting him know she hadn't pined for him was a good idea. 'Now, if you're ready, it is quite a pleasant night. I thought we could walk along the seafront to my favourite Italian restaurant. It is probably not in your class, but the food is great.'

'I'm relieved to hear you appreciate something about Italy,' Max grated, rising to his feet.

With him looming over her, big and threatening, she bit back the comment that sprang to mind. *It was only Max she didn't like*. Instead she said, 'If you don't mind, I'll call on my neighbour on the way out to tell her my change of plan. It won't take a moment.'

He raised an ebony brow mockingly. 'Lead on. I am in your hands.'

It was after eleven when they left the restaurant, and Sophie was feeling quite relaxed for the first time in days—though it might have had something to do with the three glasses of wine she had consumed with the meal.

Max took her hand and tucked it under his arm. 'Are you okay to walk, or shall I get a cab?'

'You should be so lucky.' She grinned up at him. 'The

pubs close at eleven—this is the rush hour for cabs. If you haven't booked one you have no chance.'

Of course he proved her wrong, by flagging one down two seconds later.

'You were right about the food—it was good. And I have never had such fast and efficient service in my life. Though I think that had more to do with your presence than mine,' Max said dryly, looping an arm around her shoulder in the back seat of the cab. 'You seem to know the family very well; you must go there a lot.'

'Oh, I do—two or three times a week when I'm at home.'

'The owner's two sons, Benito and Rocco, seem to be very friendly with you.' *Friendly* wasn't the word he really wanted to use. Fixated would be more appropriate. The two young men were clearly completely besotted with her, and, as he glanced down at her now, it wasn't hard to see why. It had been an eye-opening experience for Max.

Ironically, Max had been cross-examined by the owner as if he was Sophie's father—something Nigel Rutherford should have done earlier, but hadn't. As for the two sons, they had virtually ignored him except to shoot dagger glances at him when Sophie wasn't looking. They were much the same age as Sophie, and entirely too familiar with her for Max's liking.

'Yes, we are great pals. Sam and I met them when we were in Australia on our world travels, and they linked up with us for the last six months of our tour. We all came back to England together, and we have stayed in touch ever since.'

Dio! She had a trail of men lusting after her; they might have already had her for all he knew. 'That does not surprise me,' he snarled, his hand tightening on her shoulder at the unpalatable thought. He saw the surprise in her eyes, and with a terrific effort of will he reined in his temper. But he couldn't resist touching her, and he tilted her chin, slid a hand around the nape of her neck to hold her head.

She was a beautiful, vibrant young woman, and he had introduced her to sex—unlocked her passionate nature in what had turned out to be the most sensually exciting experience of his life, he had to admit. It was only natural she had taken other lovers after they'd parted; she wasn't cut out to be celibate.

The Abe Asamovs of this world he could deal with, but seeing her tonight, with two young men of her own peer group, so obviously relaxed and at ease with them, he'd been forcibly reminded of how much older he was than Sophie. He realised he should be thanking his lucky stars he had got her at all—she truly was priceless.

He caught her lips beneath his and explored her mouth with long, leisurely passion, before trailing a teasing path down to the beating pulse in her throat.

The cab stopping halted any further exploration, but Max kept an arm around her waist as they walked up the stairs and into her apartment. As soon as the door closed behind them he turned her in his arms.

'Your bedroom, Sophie,' he demanded, and saw the hectic flush of arousal in her face. He nipped playfully on her lower lip. 'Quickly would be good, *cara*.'

He stared down at her and, held against his big, taut body, Sophie realised that what was to follow was as inevitable as night following day. With every cell in her body crying out for what he was offering—why fight it? And, easing out of his arms, she reached for his hand and linked her fingers with his, leading him along the hall to the door opposite the sitting room and opening it.

Max laughed out loud, a rich, dark sound in the stillness of the utterly feminine room. The carpet was a soft ivory, and along the wall furthest from the door was a four-poster bed, draped in yards and yards of white muslin tied with pink satin bows. A delicate dresser and matching wardrobes in antique white, delicately painted with roses, plus a matching chaise longue were arranged around the other walls. But it was the big bay window that amused him.

'How on earth do you sleep with all those eyes watching you?' The window seat was lined with a startling array of dolls in every form of dress, and on the floor in the bay was a Georgian-style dolls' house.

'Very well, as it happens,' Sophie declared, abruptly recovering from the sensual daze he had evoked in her. Pulling her hand from his, she said, 'And what has it got to do with you, anyway?' He was never going to come here again, if she could help it.

Dark eyes glinting with amusement sought hers, and a predatory smile revealed brilliant white teeth. 'I'm intrigued as to why a woman of your intelligence and sophistication would have a bedroom like this.'

'The dolls' house was my mother's, and as for the dolls—some I have had for years, and I've got into the habit of collecting others from every country I visit,' she said defensively. 'I do have another bedroom you can use. I'll show you.' She grasped the chance and turned to leave.

But he stopped her, his arm snaking around her waist to keep her clamped against him.

'No, Sophie, this will do just fine,' he informed her softly, and he bent his head just enough to brush his lips against her own.

She jerked her head back in rejection. 'In Venice you have your own bedroom. At least let me keep the same distinction in *my* home,' she demanded.

'Remember our deal—sex anywhere, any time, my choice,' he drawled, and he caught her mouth again and this time didn't stop.

Helplessly her eyelids fluttered down, and she raised her slender arms to wrap them around his shoulders, her body arching into his. Her tongue traced the roof of his mouth and curled with his, her blood flowing like liquid heat in her veins. His hands were all over her; his long fingers finding the snap of her jeans and sweeping up her spine under her sweater to open her bra, then sweeping around to find the thrusting swell of her breasts.

Her hand darted down to tear at his shirt, and she whimpered when his mouth left hers. Her eyes still closed, her slender body shaking with need, he lifted her onto the frilly white coverlet and with a deftness that underlined his experience she was soon naked.

At the touch of cool air on her skin her eyes opened, and her gaze fixed on the masculine perfection of Max standing by the bed. Big and formidable, his muscular, hair-roughened chest was rising not quite steadily, and his lean hips and hard thighs framed the great dynamic power of his sex.

How often had she lain in this bed with the image of a

naked Max haunting her dreams? The erotic fantasies she had built in her mind of him appearing and declaring his undying love while she drove him mad with desire had left her sleepless and frustrated.

'Max,' she murmured throatily, her fantasy now a reality, and her green eyes darkened as with a slow, seductive smile she lifted her arms to him.

He chuckled a deep, sexy sound that vibrated across her nerve-endings and, leaning over her, curved his hand around her throat. He looked deep into her eyes. 'Yes, Sophie—say my name.'

His hand slid down over her breast and her stomach to settle between her legs. He held her gaze as a finger slipped between the soft folds and stroked once, twice, and she shuddered, groaned out her frustration when he stopped. Then he was beside her on the bed, his dark head dropping, his mouth taking the groan from her throat as his tongue stroked hers in a wicked dance of desire.

Lost between fantasy and reality, Sophie reached for him, her slender hand curving eagerly around his neck and raking into the silken hair of his head. Her other hand stroked down over his broad chest, her subtle fingers grazing a pebble-like nipple on their descent down his sleek, muscled body to his flat belly. She touched him where she had never touched him before, her hand closing around the long, hard length of his erection, a finger stroking the velvet tip. She felt his great body jerk in response, heard his groan and gloried in it as her hand moved inquisitively down to the root of his male essence. Then abruptly he caught her straying hands and, rearing back, placed them on either side of her body.

'Now you want to play?' he growled, his dark gaze sweeping over her body, lingering on the perfect rose-tipped breasts, and lower, to the soft blond curls at the apex of her thighs, then dropping to her spectacular long legs and moving back to her face. '*Dio*, you are exquisite.'

His compliment fed her fantasy as his avid glance seared her flesh. Sophie was on fire for him, liquid heat pooling between her thighs. She reached for him again, her hands stroking over his wide shoulders.

He looked down at her, his sultry smile a sensual promise, and parted her thighs to move between them. He took her mouth once more in a fiercely passionate kiss, his hand cupping her where she wanted him, his long fingers easing again between the sensitive folds.

She clung to him, the tantalising movement of his clever fingers driving her wild with want, and when his mouth dipped lower, to draw on her straining nipples, she cried out. 'Please, Max, please,' her whole body quivering with need.

At her cry, Max groaned hoarsely and lifted his head. Her green eyes glazed with passion, she was *so* wet and *so* ready. Lifting her hips, his great body taut with strain, his breathing harsh, he plunged into her. She was tight and hot, and, using all his skill and self-control, he moved—sometimes with shallow strokes, and then more intensely, with long, full strokes ever deeper. He wanted to make this last. He wanted to blot out every other lover from her mind.

Sophie had never known such almost painful pleasure existed as he swept her along in an ever-increasing ferocious tidal wave of tense, torturous desire.

Max rolled onto his back and lifted her above him, his

strong hands firm on her waist, crazy with need as she hovered on the brink and stared down into his dark face. He was watching her with a feral light in his night-black eyes, and he stilled for a second whilst she rushed headlong towards her climax. She cried out at the tug of his mouth on her rigid nipples, and at the same time the power of him filling her to the hilt with ever more powerful strokes sent her over the edge into a delirious climax. She was wanton in her ecstasy, pushing down hard on him with every increasing spasm. She felt his great body buck and shudder, and he called her name once in a voice that was close to pain as he joined her in a cosmic explosion of raw, passionate release that was completely beyond their control.

Sophie collapsed on top of him, breathless and shaking, burying her head in the soft curls of his broad chest. She had never known such intense sensations were possible. For a few blissful moments while she lay in the circle of her arms she could almost believe it was love: the familiar scent of him, the weight of him, the pounding of their hearts almost in unison. Then he moved her over onto her back and flopped down beside her, and the fantasy vanished as the silence lengthened.

Suddenly she felt cold; there was no love, only a primitive lust. Of course it was great…Max was an expert at sex, and so he should be…he'd had plenty of practice, by all accounts, she reminded herself. She clenched her fists at her sides, to prevent her weaker self reaching for him again.

The movement of the mattress told her he had stood up, but she didn't look; she couldn't, in case he saw the hurt in her eyes. She heard the door open, and moved to slip beneath the covers, a shiver of revulsion assailing her at what he had made her. A willing slave to her sexuality, nothing more….

She pulled the lace-covered duvet up around her chin and buried her head in the pillow. She heard the door close, and then nothing…. He had probably found the spare bedroom. It was no more than she expected, and she had to learn to live with it….

'Sophie.' He drawled her name softly and she turned, her eyes widening in surprise. He was standing by the bed stark naked, with two wine glasses in one hand and the half-full bottle of wine in the other.

'A nightcap? Or perhaps a drink before the second round?' he prompted with a wicked grin. And she couldn't help it—she grinned back.

Sophie yawned and opened her eyes. She blinked at the sunlight streaming through the window, and then blinked again as a dark head blotted out the sun.

'Max,' she murmured, and she was intensely aware of his long body against her own. 'You stayed all night.'

'I had nowhere else to go.' He dropped a swift kiss on her softly parted lips. 'Unfortunately I do now.' His hand curved around to cup her breast and she sighed. 'I know,' he said, and his thumb grazed her rosy nipple. 'Unfortunately we haven't any time. My pilot has a take-off slot in eighty minutes.' Withdrawing his hand, he rolled off the bed. 'Come on—the car will be here any moment now.'

Twenty minutes later, washed and dressed in a short red and black kilt-style skirt, with a soft black mohair sweater pulled hastily over her head and her feet pushed into red pumps, Sophie slid into the limousine.

She was still trying to make sense of this new, relaxed Max when they boarded his jet and a steward served breakfast.

CHAPTER NINE

DIEGO WAS WAITING with the launch as they exited the airport at noon, and their return to the *palazzo* was swift. Entering the elegant hall, Sophie was shocked to see a group of six smiling adults lined up to meet them. She was surprised to discover as Max made the introductions that Diego did not run the house on his own. Maria, his wife, was the cook, Tessa, their married daughter, was the maid and her husband Luke was the gardener…quite the family affair.

'I didn't know you had a garden,' Sophie said as the staff dispersed.

'Obviously you need a tour. Diego will take your luggage upstairs while I show you around.' Max waved around the ground floor. 'Dining room, study and morning room and grand salon. Beneath is the kitchen, utility room and Diego's apartment, and beneath that the cellars.'

Of course—the massive steps to the entrance concealed the fact this was actually the first floor, and not the ground, she realised as he led her around the back of the staircase and opened a large double door. To her surprise inside there was a fully equipped games room and gym, with a swimming pool half in and half out of the house. The exterior part had glass walls and a roof that opened to the sky. Steps led down into a walled garden.

'Feel free to use this whenever you like.' Striding back to the reception hall, he added, 'I have some work to catch up on, so I will leave you to your own devices—but remember lunch is at one-thirty.'

She saluted. 'Yes, oh master.' But he was not amused. The Max of last night, who'd drunk wine in her bed, was gone, and the autocratic tyrant was back.

'That is exactly what I am, and don't you forget,' he replied stiffly, and without another word disappeared into his study.

Sophie made her way upstairs to her bedroom just as the young maid Tessa was disappearing through the open door of the dressing room with the smallest case in her hand. 'No—please, I can unpack myself,' Sophie said with a smile. From what she had seen so far there was precious little else for her to do around here—except await her master's bidding.

But she was too late. After Tessa had left she occupied her time by placing a few personal items—her make-up, jewellery box and perfume—on the small, ornate antique dressing table. It was just for show, however, because she had no intention of using the dressing room for anything other than storing clothes now that she knew she shared it with Max. And at that moment he appeared.

'I forgot to give you these,' he said as he walked towards her. Stopping at her side, he dropped something on the dressing table. 'I have opened an Italian bank account for you, as agreed, and that is your credit card.' He glanced at her. 'After lunch we are going out, and much as I like that short, flirty skirt I don't want you wearing it in public. Get changed.' And, swinging on his heel, he left as abruptly as he had arrived.

What did he *want* her to wear? Sackcloth and ashes? Sophie fumed as she stripped off and headed for the shower. She had lived on her own and been her own boss for years. Kowtowing to a man was not in her nature—especially not to an arrogant, ruthless man like Max.

She frowned as she stood under the soothing spray. Sophie knew herself well. She was not cut out to be a mistress; she was far too independent. But the trouble was, until her father's business was secure she had no choice.

Deep in thought, she walked back out of the bathroom and into the dressing room. What she needed was a strategy for living with Max that would not leave her an emotional wreck when they parted. Inexperienced as she was, she knew Max was right: they *were* sexually compatible, dangerously so, and it would be very easy for her to become addicted to the man. She had to guard against that at all costs.

Slipping into white briefs and a matching bra, she opened the wardrobe door, her hand reaching for a pair of denim jeans, and stopped. She wasn't at home; this *palazzo* would never be her home. Max had told her that a mistress agreed with her man at all times, and an inkling of an idea occurred to her.

She entered the dining room half an hour later, dressed in a sage-green double-breasted jacket with only a bra beneath, and a matching slim-fitting skirt that ended just above her knees. She had scraped two swathes of hair back and fastened them in a loop at the back of her head. The rest she had left loose, to fall down her back. Her make-up was perfect, but a lot more than she would usually use, and on her feet she was wearing three-inch-heeled stilettos.

Max was standing by the drinks trolley, a glass in his hand, and turned as she walked in. His hard, dark eyes swept slowly over her from head to toe, lingering on the plunging V of her jacket and even longer on her legs. He was examining her like some a master in a slave market. She could feel angry colour rising in her cheeks, but she fought it down.

'You have taken my advice, I see. Would you like a drink?'

'Yes, please.' Her temper rising at his arrogant certainty that she would do as she was told, she had almost said no. But, mindful of the part she had decided to play as she had dressed, she agreed. Hadn't Max told her a mistress always said yes? The beginnings of a smile twitched her lips. This might even be fun.

'Do you always eat in here?' she asked, and smiled up at him as she took the glass of wine he offered her. It was a large, elegant room, but her preference would be to eat somewhere less formal.

'Yes, when I am here. Which is not that often.'

'Well, if you don't mind, when I am on my own would it be all right for me to eat somewhere smaller—the kitchen, perhaps?' she asked.

'If you like.' Max pulled out her chair for her as Diego entered with the first course, then took his own seat.

As the meal progressed Max grew puzzled. Sophie had changed from the tiny skirt into an elegant suit, as he had suggested, but it did not help him much. Because although her legs were halfway covered, he could see her cleavage—and he was pretty sure she wore nothing under the jacket. She had left her gorgeous hair loose, and she was smiling and talking perfectly politely, agreeing to everything he said. So why did he get the feeling something was wrong?

'So, where are you taking me this afternoon?' Sophie asked as she took a sip of coffee, the meal over.

Max knew where he wanted to take her—straight to bed. But he reined in his baser impulse; there was something different about her and it infuriated him because he could not pinpoint the change. 'I am taking you to the jewellers to fulfil my side of the bargain,' he said, shoving back his chair and standing up. 'I promised you diamonds instead of crystal.'

'Oh, yes. I forgot.' Sophie stood up as well. She didn't want his damn diamonds, but in her new role she had to agree. 'But there is no hurry,' she couldn't help adding.

'I'm a busy man, and I am never usually here on a Friday. As I am here, I want to get the matter settled now.'

Sophie bit down hard on her bottom lip. 'Yes, of course,' she replied and headed for the door before she lost her cool and landed him a slap in the face. He was talking to her as if she was some blond bimbo. But then that was what he *thought* she was….

'Sophie?' Her skin prickled at the way he drawled her name, and a long arm slipped around her waist, halting her progress. 'We don't *have* to go out….'

She glanced up at him, saw the intention in his dark eyes. The warmth of his arm around her waist was making her temperature rise—and with it her temper.

'Yes, we do,' she said sweetly, and her plan to say *yes* to everything suddenly seemed very easy.

Half an hour later, when they walked into the jewellers, it was not quite so easy. The jeweller saw them seated and then presented a staggering array of diamond necklaces, earrings and bracelets for their perusal.

'Do you like this set?' Max indicated a stunning waterfall of diamonds.

'Yes,' she said, and continued to say yes to everything he suggested.

'Oh, for heaven's sake, chose one,' Max snarled, finally losing his patience, and he saw her luscious lips curve in a secretive smile.

She turned wide, innocent green eyes up to him. 'You choose, Max. After all, you are paying for it so it has to please you.'

Then it hit him. The little witch had been saying yes to everything, agreeing with everything he said, since the moment she'd come down to lunch. It was every man's fantasy to have a lover who said yes to everything, so why did it feel so damn irritating?

Indicating the waterfall set, he bought and paid for it, ignoring Sophie, and then, taking her arm, he pulled her to her feet and they left the shop.

'I am on to you, lady,' he drawled, turning her into his arms, his dark eyes gleaming down into hers. 'Will you jump into the canal for me, Sophie?' He felt her stiffen in his arms. 'Or kiss me, here and now?' And he saw the guilt in her green eyes. She knew she had been found out. God, she was a stubborn creature—but beautiful with it. He made it easy for her. 'Say yes to the latter. You know you have to,' he chuckled.

The broad grin and the laughter in his eyes were Sophie's undoing. 'Yes,' she laughed, and he bent his head, taking advantage of her open mouth to slip his tongue between her parted lips. Her hands slipped up around his neck—and that was how Gina found them.

'Max? Max—what on earth are you doing?'

Max lifted his head but kept an arm around Sophie's waist. 'Gina.' He grinned. 'You're a doctor—and you don't know?' He felt the sudden tension in Sophie and tightened his grip. She had to face his sister some time—the one witness to her brutal dismissal of him years ago. 'I didn't know you had stayed in Venice.'

'Even doctors are entitled to a holiday. But I am surprised *you* are still here. Though I can see why,' she said drolly, with the lift of a delicate brow in Sophie's direction.

Sophie looked at the small dark woman and her companion, another slightly older woman, and wished the ground would open up and swallow her whole. To be caught kissing in broad daylight was bad enough, but to be caught by Gina, his ex-lover—or maybe not ex—was doubly embarrassing.

'You know Sophie, of course,' Max said suavely, and glanced down at her. 'And you remember Gina, *cara*?'

As if she could forget. 'Yes,' she said slowly, and gave Gina a polite smile. 'Nice to see you again.' Why on earth had she said that? She couldn't give a damn if she never saw either her or Max ever again.

'Nice to see you, too,' Gina agreed. 'This is my friend Rosa.' She made the introduction. 'We thought we would do some shopping, then stop for a coffee at Florian. What are you and Max up to?'

'The same.' Max answered for her. 'Except we have finished our shopping.'

'My God, Sophie, I don't believe it—you actually got the world's worst chauvinist to take you shopping!' Gina laughed. 'If you hang around longer this time he might even become halfway human.'

Confused by Gina's obviously genuine laughter, and the lack of malice in her tone, Sophie gave a wry smile. 'I doubt it.'

A husky chuckle greeted her words and Max glanced at his stepsister. 'Watch it, Gina. I don't want you frightening Sophie off with your biased view of me.' He drew Sophie closer to his side.

'So it would seem,' Gina said, slanting an amused look at the pair of them. 'It is to be hoped—'

'Are we going for coffee or what?' Rosa intervened. 'I need my caffeine fix.'

'Yes—sure. Why don't you and Sophie join us, Max?' Gina asked.

An hour later, when they left the coffee shop, Sophie was none the wiser about Max and Gina's real relationship. On the launch going back to the house she replayed the meeting in her mind. Surprisingly, the conversation had been easy. Rosa, she had discovered, was married with two boys—who sounded like holy terrors from the anecdotes she had shared with them. It was obvious Max and Gina were close, and totally at ease with each other, but whether it was sexual Sophie didn't know. She had sensed under their apparently friendly conversation and laughter a kind of tension—and it wasn't just the tension *she* always felt around Max. It was something more, but she couldn't put her finger on it.

'Rosa was funny—and Gina was quite pleasant,' she said slowly as they entered the house.

'Were you surprised?' Max asked with a sardonic lift of an ebony brow. 'You shouldn't be—she almost always is.'

'Yes, if you say so,' she murmured.

With his finger and thumb he tilted her chin. 'Have I missed something?' he demanded. His dark eyes narrowed intently on her upturned face. 'Or are we back to the yes game again, I wonder?' His astute gazed dropped to the lush curve of her mouth and his hand tightened slightly.

She knew his intention, felt it in the sudden tension between them.

'No to both,' she said hurriedly, and lowered her lashes to mask her own reaction.

'You look tired. Have a rest before dinner.'

'I know your kind of rest,' she said with biting sarcasm, and, shrugging off his hand, she headed for the stairs.

But she didn't escape completely.

She was standing in front of the dressing table, having kicked off her shoes and shrugged off her jacket, and was about to remove her make-up when Max walked in.

'You forgot this.' He strolled over and dropped the jewellers box on the table, his cold dark eyes meeting hers in the mirror. 'The deal is finalised. I always keep my word—just make sure you keep yours.'

Over breakfast the next morning Sophie could barely look at him. He had come to her bed last night and made her wear the diamonds while he made love to her—no, *had sex* with her. And she had never felt so demeaned in her life.

'I am going to the family estate this morning,' he informed her coldly, rising from the table. 'Since the death of my father I need to help out with the running of the Quintano hotels. I'll be back Sunday night. In the meantime, if you want to go out you are not to go alone. Diego will accompany you at all times—understood?'

It was a very different Sophie who, six weeks later, looked in the same dressing table mirror and slipped a diamond drop earring into her earlobe. They were going to a charity dinner, and she could hear Max moving around in the dressing room. He had returned an hour earlier, from a week-long trip to Ecuador, and they were in danger of being late because he had joined her in the shower....

Max was an incredible and determined lover, and she had long since given up on trying to resist him. He was also very generous—her lips twisted at her reflection in the glass. The Versace emerald-green evening gown revealed more than it concealed, a pair of designer green satin shoes were on her feet, and the large diamond Van Cleef earrings with matching necklace completed the look. Yes—she looked what she was: a rich man's mistress.

In bed, she had no defence, and only a strong sense of self-protection stopped her revealing her ever-deepening feelings for Max. But paradoxically her image in the mirror satisfied her, because it made it easier to play the part of a cool sophisticate around him.

Surprisingly, it seemed to work, and they did—to use

Max's words—*rub along* quite well. Every night he was in Venice he came to her bed and aroused her with a slow, deliberate eroticism, aware of every nuance of her response until she cried out for release and he tipped her over the edge into ecstasy. Sometimes he came with her, and sometimes he followed her. Either way, they ended up breathless and spent—but also silent. Sophie didn't dare speak, and she guessed Max had no reason to; he had got what he wanted. As often as not he stayed till the morning and they made love again. And sometimes when she was locked in his embrace she almost believed it was love instead of lust….

Over the weeks she had developed her own routine to make life bearable, and the kitchen had become her favourite room in the house. She got along well with Maria, Tessa and her three children, and she took great pleasure in teaching the young ones English—the adults benefited as well.

She had quickly realised Max worked incredibly long hours. Sometimes he was here, in his study, but he was just as likely to fly halfway around the world for a couple of days. When he was at home he spent at least two or three days a week—always including Friday—at his head office in Rome.

Sophie had travelled to Rome with him only once, about a month ago. He had worked all day, taken her shopping in the evening, then to dinner in an intimate little restaurant, and finally to bed in his penthouse apartment. She had thoroughly enjoyed the experience; somehow in Rome she had not felt like a mistress.

But the following morning, after Max had left for the office she had again. She'd taken a shower and, looking in the bathroom cabinet, hoping to find a toothbrush, had discovered a bottle of perfume and various other female toiletries—plus a large black hairslide and a bottle of prescription medicine in Gina's name. The slide she knew could *not* be Gina's—the woman had close-cut hair.

The next time Max asked her to accompany him to Rome she refused, with the excuse that it was the wrong time of the month.

Sophie frowned now, as she clipped on the other earring. He had dismissed her excuse as irrelevant—saying there were many routes to sexual pleasure—and it had only been when she'd insisted she felt ill that he had given in. She had seen in his sardonic smile as he'd said, 'Have it your way,' that he didn't believe her.

Sophie knew from Maria that she was the only woman Max had brought to live in the *palazzo.* To the romantic but conservative Maria that meant they would marry, and Sophie didn't like to disillusion her. Sophie now accepted that Max shared her bed—honesty forced her to admit she couldn't resist him—but she couldn't accept sharing his bed in Rome. Not when he had all his other lovers.

Sophie spent quite a lot of time on her own. Max, she presumed, continued to go and visit the family estate—though he had never told her so since that first time—or perhaps he stayed in Rome. The fact that he never asked her to accompany him again didn't bother her. At least that was what she told herself. And when he telephoned her occasionally she never asked him where he was; she was afraid to show too much interest.

She enjoyed the freedom to explore Venice—not that she was entirely free; Diego had strict instructions to accompany her when she went out. But, on the upside, Diego was a fount of information. She had visited St Mark's and sat outside the Café Florian, sipping coffee and watching the world go by. They had visited the Guggenheim and the Accademia, and many more smaller art galleries, which she would never have known existed without Diego, plus countless churches filled with stunning masterpieces that one would not normally expect to see outside a museum.

The city itself was probably the most beautiful and romantic in the world—but how much better it would have been to explore the tiny alleys and hidden *piazzas,* to linger in the small cafés with someone she loved, she thought sadly. Someone like Max....

If she was honest she missed him when he was away—she kept telling herself she hated him and it was just sex, but it was becoming harder and harder to do. He occupied her thoughts all the time. Like now, she realised, her forehead pleating in a frown.

'Why the frown?' a deep, dark voice drawled.

Sophie turned her head to see that Max had emerged from the dressing room and was watching her with a look of genuine concern in his eyes. Her heart squeezed in her chest. He had his dinner jacket in one hand and was wearing black trousers and a white evening shirt that contrasted brilliantly with his tanned complexion. He looked staggeringly attractive. But then he always did to her. And it was in that moment she knew she loved him. She could fool herself no longer. She loved him, probably always had and always would, and the knowledge terrified her.

Sophie looked back at her reflection in the mirror, to give herself time to get over the shock of realising how she truly felt about Max and to try and compose herself. 'I was wondering if these earrings were too much,' she finally answered, turning back to him with her face a sophisticated calm mask—she hoped.

'Not a bit—you look exquisite,' he declared, dropping his jacket on the bed, His gaze swept appreciatively over her. A slight smile quirked the corners of his sensual mouth and she saw the gleam of gold in his dark eyes and recognised that look. Given it was no more than half an hour since they had indulged, and given the scary knowledge that she loved him, she resented the ease with which he aroused an answering response in her own body.

She lifted her chin—an angry sparkle in her green eyes. 'You paid for it,' she snapped, and his eyes narrowed fractionally at her sudden outburst.

'True,' Max said, and stepped towards her. 'I also pay for your services.' He stretched out his arm.

'We haven't time,' she gasped, taking a step back.

'Oh, Sophie, you really do have a one-track mind—not that I am complaining,' he mocked. And, grasping her hand, he dropped a platinum cufflink in her palm. 'Fasten this for me.' He shook his outstretched arm, amusement dancing in his dark eyes. 'I can never manage the right as easily as the left.'

Her lips twitched. 'You, Max Quintano, can and do manage *everything*,' she said, but fixed the cufflink, admiring the fine dark hair on his wrist as she did so.

'And that is what irks you, my beauty.' Slipping an arm around her bare shoulders, he brought her into close contact with his hard body. His mouth closed over hers in a long deep kiss. 'How about we skip this party and stay here? I have been away too long, and I have not had nearly enough of you yet.'

'You're actually asking my opinion?' she prompted, with the delicate arch of a fine brow. 'Now, that *is* a first. You usually do as you like.'

'True,' he said, all arrogant virile male, his hand sliding down over her bottom. 'But you also like.' He smiled as he felt her shiver.

'Maybe.' She recognised the sensual amusement in his dark gaze. 'But you're crazy if you think I got all dressed up like this just for you to undress me.'

'Crazy about you—yes,' he said, with a wry smile that completely stunned her. It was the closest he had ever got to hinting that he cared, and a tiny seed of hope lodged in her heart. He moved his hand to curve it around her waist and added, 'But I promised to attend this charity dinner, so the undressing will have to wait until we return.' He ushered her towards the door. 'Though maybe we can fool around in the launch on the way. What do you think?' he asked, with roguish lift of his black eyebrows.

He looked like a swashbuckling pirate, Sophie thought, and, shaking her head, she laughed. She couldn't help it. At moments like this she could almost believe they were a happy normal couple.

The dinner-dance was a select affair held at Hotel Cypriani, and with Max's hand linked in hers she walked into the elegant room. The first person she saw was Gina, in a group of half a dozen distinguished-looking people. She turned her head and laughed at something that had been said, then caught sight of Max and came rushing over.

'Max, *caro.*' She grabbed his arm and stood on tiptoe,

her body pressed against his side, to give him a kiss full on his lips. Still clinging to his arm, she turned to Sophie.

'Sophie, I'm surprised to see *you* here. I didn't think this was your thing. But we do need all the support we can get,' she said with a smile, and turned back to Max. 'It's weeks since I've seen you. I am so glad you could make it.'

Gina could not have made it plainer that it was Max who interested her and she only tolerated Sophie's presence at his side, Sophie thought, her new-found love making her hypersensitive as jealousy, swift and painful, sliced through her. When had the conventional public kiss on both cheeks developed to a full-blown kiss on the mouth?

Then, out of the blue, a distant memory hit her like a punch in the stomach. Old Man Quintano had strongly disapproved of Max and Gina's relationship, but now he was dead there was no one to object to them marrying.

Suddenly Max's desire to have her as his mistress made more sense, and the blood turned to ice in her veins as the reality of the situation sank in. Max was a highly sexed man—as Sophie knew all too well. One woman would probably never be enough for him. As a teenager *she* had been the prospective bride, because she might be pregnant, and Gina the lover; now the situation was reversed, and *she* was cast in that role.

'You're right—this isn't my thing.' And Sophie didn't mean the dinner. She meant Max and Gina's relationship. 'In fact, I will quite happily leave.' Sophie saw no reason to pretend any more. A ménage à trois had never been and never would be for her, and she tried to pull her hand from Max's.

Max's jaw tightened in anger. Enjoying Sophie's exquisite body, he had almost dismissed the reason she had left him, excusing her behaviour by telling himself that she had been young and naturally frightened of the prospect of tying herself to a sick man. Now he knew better—she didn't give a damn about anything but her own pleasure. What kind of man did that make him? Lusting after a heartless woman who had quite happily been Abe Asamov's mistress and heaven knew how many more?

He gave her a hard look, saw the beautiful, expressionless face and the cold green eyes, and said with chilling emphasis, 'This is Gina's night—her cancer charity.' He smiled coldly and twisted Sophie's hand around her back to pull her against him in what looked like a loving gesture. 'You will stay and be civil to everyone,' he murmured against her ear. 'You will act the part of my loving consort—something I know you are good at. After all, that *is* what I pay you for,' he reminded her with sibilant softness. He felt her tense, and simply tightened his grip.

Then he turned his attention to Gina. 'I am sure your night is going to be a great success. Don't mind Sophie. She did not mean to offend you. Did you, *cara*?' His hard black eyes turned on her.

'No, it was a joke,' Sophie said feebly. But the joke was on her. She had finally recognised in her heart and mind that she loved Max, only to find out half an hour later nothing had changed.

Sophie sank into the seat Max held out for her, glad to be finally free of his restraining hold. But it was only in memory of her mother that she sat down at all. She was sick to her stomach and simmering with anger. From the teasing lover of an hour ago, he was once more the ruthless, autocratic swine who had forced her to be his mistress. She hadn't missed the threat in his words, and he couldn't have spelt out more clearly exactly where his loyalty lay. And with that knowledge the faint seed of hope she had nurtured earlier of something more than sex between them died a bitter death.

She straightened the slim-fitting skirt of her gown over her thighs, fighting to retain her composure, and when she did lift her head her lips twisted cynically as she noted the seating arrangement. Gina was seated on Max's left and she was seated on his right—now, why didn't that surprise her?

She forced a smile to her lips as introductions were made all round, and realised they were mostly medical professionals. She accepted the wine offered and did her best to ignore Max. It wasn't hard, as Gina engaged him in conversation—for which Sophie was truly grateful.

As course followed course and the wine flowed, the conversation became more animated. But Sophie took very little part. These people were probably all very good and clever, but she was in no mood for talking.

Beside her, Max wore the mantle of dominant and sophisticated male with ease, his input into the conversation witty and astute. His occasional comments to Sophie were smoothly made with a smile, and to any onlooker he appeared a caring partner, with a touch on her arm, an offer to fill her glass. Only she could see the restrained anger in his gaze, and it took all her will-power simply to respond to him civilly. The way she felt right now, she couldn't care less if she never spoke to him again.

She'd got over him once and she would again, Sophie

vowed. But although she tried to ignore it, the pain in her heart refused to go away.

For the rest of the meal she avoided his glance, with her head bent down, concentrating on her food, although she had never felt less like eating in her life.

It was when coffee was served that the conversation really became boisterous. Sophie gathered the discussion was about ways of raising money for cancer research and involving patients at the same time. But she wasn't paying much attention; it was taking every atom of self-control she possessed simply to stay seated at the table with Gina and Max. Her mind was reeling at the thought of them together—and heaven knew how many other women had shared the pleasure of his sexual expertise.

'Why not have an auction, with the beautiful Sophie selling kisses?' a voice declared loudly, and at the sound of her name Sophie raised her head. A man sitting opposite her, whom she had noticed earlier staring at her cleavage and ignored, was ogling her again. 'The patients could buy them as well. I know if I was seriously ill a kiss from a gorgeous woman would do me good.' Everyone laughed, and all eyes were on her.

'That would never work.' Gina chuckled. 'Sophie is a beautiful, decorative woman, but not cut out to visit the sick. She'd probably give them a heart attack. Isn't that right, Sophie?' Gina quipped, and everyone laughed.

It was a hurtful thing to say, and for a moment Sophie was struck dumb. Gina knew nothing at all about her—and yet she felt able to pass comment on her. She glanced around the table; nobody here really knew her, she thought, so why bother to argue?

'If you say so,' she murmured.

'I wouldn't allow her to anyway,' Max drawled, and reached for her hand.

But she avoided his hand *and* his glittering gaze by picking up her glass and draining it before she put it back down. She wished she was anywhere in the world but here.

A veined hand patted hers on the table. 'It was just a joke. We medical people *en masse* tend to lose our sensitivity a little—don't take it to heart.' It was the professor seated next to her who spoke, quietly seeing what no one else had noticed.

Sophie was touched and grateful for his intervention, as it allowed her to turn her back on Max and look up with moisture-filled eyes into the old man's face.

'Thank you,' she said, trying to smile. 'But it is an emotive subject for me,' she explained quietly. 'My mother died of breast cancer when I was eleven. For two years before that I did my best to nurse her, but I was still a child and obviously not up to these people's standards.' She attempted to joke.

'Forget it, and do me the honour of this dance.' The professor stood up. 'If you do not mind, Signor Quintano?' he asked Max over the top of Sophie's head.

Max glanced at him, and sharply at Sophie. Her body was angled towards the professor, all her attention on the older man. The witch had the nerve to ignore him and then captivate the eminent Professor Manta, right before his eyes. The old fool was grinning all over his face as if he had discovered the cure for cancer. How the hell did she do it?

'Be my guest.' He couldn't do much else with Gina tugging on his arm again. Since when had his sister become such a chatty type? he wondered in exasperation as he watched Sophie and the professor take to the dance floor.

'Feel better now?' the professor asked Sophie, his brown eyes twinkling into hers.

'Yes—yes, I do.' She relaxed in his formal hold. 'I am not usually so emotional, but the comment about me not being cut out to visit the sick caught me on the raw and I didn't see the joke. You see, the anniversary of my mother's death was the twenty-fifth of November—three days ago.' And also she had realised she loved a man who didn't deserve to be loved.

'You are a lovely, emotional little woman—and that is nothing to be ashamed of,' he reassured her gently.

Sophie did smile at that. 'Hardly little.'

'Maybe not, but you are extremely feminine. Something, I am afraid, that in my experience can sometimes get knocked out of female doctors over the years.'

'Feminine I like,' she chuckled, appreciating the distinguished-looking man more by the minute—even if he was a bit of a chauvinist.

'Good. Now, a change of subject is called for, so tell me about you. Are you on holiday here? And what do you normally do when not visiting our fair city?'

Whether he knew of her connection with Max or not she didn't care. Because she instinctively knew the professor was a gentleman.

'I am visiting a friend for a while, but I'm a linguist and I work as a translator. Sometimes I teach, but at the minute all I do is teach English to the cook's grandchildren.'

With his next words, much to Sophie's surprise, Professor Manta was offering her a job. Apparently he was on the board of governors at the private school that his grandchildren attended, and they were looking for a language teacher—someone to fill in for the rest of the term, as the present teacher was on extended sick leave.

'I'm flattered, though I'm not sure it will be possible,' she said, but she took the card the professor offered and promised to ring him tomorrow, to let him know one way or the other.

Max couldn't believe it. He saw her take the card from the old goat as they approached the table and he had had enough. He rose to his feet and, with a stiff smile for the grinning professor, wrapped his arm tightly around Sophie's waist.

'It is time we left now.'

Sophie felt his proprietorial arm around her and tensed, but refused to look at him. Instead she said good night to the professor, and a general good night to the rest of the company. Gina she ignored. But Max's prolonged goodbye to his stepsister more than made up for Sophie's lapse in manners.

CHAPTER TEN

'YOU are very quiet, *cara.*' He dipped his head towards her as they exited the room. 'Upset that I took you away from your latest conquest?'

His words were soft, but she heard the angry edge in his tone, and when she tilted her head back she saw his eyes glittering hard as jet.

'The professor is not a conquest but a gentleman,' she snapped. 'Something you would know nothing about.'

'Maybe not,' he said, his smile cruel. 'But I *do* know you're no lady. The fact is you are available to the highest bidder, and at the moment it happens to be me. So hand over the card he gave you—he is not for you.'

'God! Your mind never lifts above the gutter!'

She stared at him. His face was a mask of barely contained anger, and for a fleeting moment she wondered if he was jealous. No…for that he would have to care, and all he cared about was getting his money's worth. He had just said so.

'It just so happens that Professor Manta offered me a job. Not everyone sees me as just a body. That distinction appears to be a peculiar trait of you and Gina.'

'A job?' he sneered. 'We both know as what. But I hate to tell you, *cara*, distinguished as he is, he cannot afford you.'

She was about to snap back with the truth, but they had reached the foyer and a member of staff arrived with their coats.

What the hell? Why bother to explain? It wouldn't make a blind bit of difference to the way Max felt about her. He saw her as an experienced woman with dozens of lovers, thanks to Abe, and tonight there was no longer any point in telling him the truth. Because she no longer cared.

She looked at him, tall, dark and stony-faced, as he held out the rich sable coat—another one of his presents she really didn't appreciate. He had dismissed her arguments on wearing real fur in his usual autocratic manner. Venetian women in winter *all* wore fur. Maybe he was right, and she had actually seen children in fur coats, but it didn't make her like it—or him, she thought as he helped her to slip it on, keeping his arm around her shoulders.

It was a miserable night—a thick fog had descended, along with drizzling rain. Luckily the launch was waiting, and she stepped on board, shrugging off Max's restraining arm, and walked down into the small cabin and sat down.

She heard Max talking to Diego and hoped he would stay on deck. Sophie let her head fall back and closed her eyes; she could feel the beginnings of a tension headache—hardly surprising, under the circumstances. It was impossible to believe she had left the house with a smile on her face a few short hours ago, confident she could handle her relationship with Max, fooling herself that they got along well and he was genuinely beginning to care for her. Only for the evening to turn out an unmitigated disaster. It had opened her eyes to a reality she didn't want, couldn't accept, and made her realise she had been in danger of succumbing to living in a fool's paradise. Well, no more….

Rising from the seat, she exited the cabin. Max was leaning against the roof, with Diego at the wheel. Diego's head turned. 'Well timed, Signorina Sophie.' He grinned at her as he swung the boat in to the landing stage.

She smiled back, ignoring the looming figure of Max. It was Diego's hand she took as she stepped off the boat, and she didn't wait but ran up the steps and into the house. She slipped the sable from her shoulders, not caring where it fell, and she didn't stop until she reached her bedroom and closed the door behind her. She kicked off the killer heels and, withdrawing her earrings, walked to the dressing table and dropped them in a box. The necklace quickly followed. She stepped out of her dress and slipped on a towelling robe. With the outward signs of Max's ownership gone, she heaved a deep sigh of relief.

She picked up a sliver of lace that in Max's opinion passed for a nightgown and, walking into the bathroom, locked both doors. Now all she had to worry about were the inward signs of his ownership, and she had a nasty suspicion they would be a lot more difficult to deal with. She pulled on a shower cap, had a quick shower, twisted her hair into one long braid over her shoulder and slipped on her nightgown and robe again. Unlocking both doors, she walked back into her bedroom—only to find Max standing there, a glass of whisky in his hand.

'Running scared, Sophie?' Max fixed her with an unwavering glare. 'Or an act of defiance?'

'Neither,' she said flatly, ignoring the angry tensing of his jaw as she met his gaze. 'Just an overwhelming desire to be clean after an evening spent with you and Gina.'

'What the hell do you mean by that?' he demanded, and she shivered, her stomach muscles knotting at the anger evident in his dark eyes.

Max saw her tremble, and for a moment the fury inside him subsided, his eyes narrowing astutely on her flushed but stern face. Thinking back, he recalled other times when Sophie had made remarks about Gina. Given that Sophie had only met her a couple of times, it made no sense. He drained the glass of whisky and crossed to put it on the bedside table before walking back to stare down at her.

'Tonight you made your distaste plain the moment we arrived. I can understand that the thought of cancer scares you—I know it does a lot of people,' he prompted. 'But what have you got against Gina?'

Sophie paled. Good, Max thought savagely, he was on the right track. 'I want the truth, and I am in no mood for any more of your sly innuendos.'

Pale with fury at his sanctimonious comment about understanding her fear of illness, Sophie threw him a venomous glance—the only sly person around here was Max, and she had had enough.

'Oh, please,' she drawled, her eyes spitting fury. 'What do you take me for? An idiot? You and your sainted stepsister Gina have been having an affair on and off for years and everyone knows it.' A short laugh of derision left her lips. 'My God, she flung herself into your arms tonight and the pair of you kissed like long-lost lovers. It was disgusting.'

'*Basta*,' he roared, and she took an involuntary step backward. But it was futile. In one lithe stride Max had narrowed the space between them. Steely hands caught hold of her arms and hauled her hard against him, his dark gaze sweeping over her swift and savage.

'Oh, no, you don't,' he grated, and his eyes narrowed as she began to struggle. 'Stop!' he commanded furiously, and his fingers bit into her soft flesh.

'You're hurting me.'

'Right at this moment I don't damn well care,' he swore. 'I would flatten *any* other person without the slightest hesitation for even *implying* what you have just said,' he revealed harshly.

Sophie stared at him defiantly. 'You can't face the truth, that's your trouble.'

Max saw the determination and conviction in her eyes and realised she actually believed what she was saying. For once he was speechless. He heaved in a strangled breath. 'You actually believe I…' He couldn't say it, and with a shake of his head he shoved her away. 'That is some sick opinion you have of me.'

'Not an opinion. Fact.'

'Fact—Gina is my stepsister, period. She kissed me because she was pleased to see me—a quite common occurrence in my culture. As for anything more, that is only in your head.' He looked at her lovely face, saw the childish braid over her breast rise and fall as she took a deep breath and wondered how anyone so beautiful could harbour such evil thoughts. Maybe it was jealousy. For some reason that did not seem so bad, if a bit extreme. 'If you're jealous—'

'Jealous?' Sophie cut him off. 'Don't flatter yourself—

and don't bother lying.' She swallowed nervously. 'I was there, remember? Seven years ago. The stupid teenager with the enormous crush on you. Marnie warned me about you. She told me about your legion of women and I refused to listen. She even showed me a magazine article about you, with photographs of some of them. Finally she told me about your affair with Gina, *and* the fact that your father didn't approve of the relationship. But I still refused to believe what kind of man you were. I was the dumb kid you seduced and asked to marry because you thought I might be pregnant.'

Her eyes filled with anger. 'The idiot who believed you—until I walked through the maze and heard you and Gina talking about me. To give Gina her due, at least *she* said you had to tell me about her if you really intended marrying me. I heard you both discussing whether I was worldly enough to accept the situation—and you call *me* sick?'

Sophie didn't see the colour drain from his face; she was swamped by memories she had tried to suppress. But no longer. 'What a joke!' She laughed—a raw sound. 'And when Gina asked why you were marrying me your response was a real eye-opener—*because you were careless and I might be pregnant*. Then came her descriptive account of how life would be for the pregnant bride, with a husband who took off at regular intervals to stay overnight with his lover and then came back too tired to make love to his dumb wife.

'My God, it was a revelation,' she spat at him. 'And how could I ever forget your comment that it had only been a couple of days, and with luck you wouldn't have to tell me anything at all. Well, you got lucky,' she mocked bitterly. 'I wasn't pregnant. And I had no intention of joining a three-way relationship then and I haven't now. So don't try and fob me off with Italian culture or any other excuse.

'As I walked round into the centre of the maze I heard you say you loved each other, and I found you in each other's arms. Last month in Rome I found her medicine in the en suite bathroom cabinet, along with signs of your other women.' She paused, then added with a shake of her head, 'The only thing that amazes me is why Gina puts up with you. I have no choice—as you so often remind me. You are a despicable excuse—' She raised her eyes, and for a heart-stopping moment she thought he was about to strike her. His face was contorted with rage, and she shivered at the cold black fury in his piercing gaze.

'Shut up—just shut up.'

Max had listened with a mounting horror that had quickly turned to red-hot rage. He wanted to grab hold of her and shake her. He couldn't believe that Sophie, the woman he had made love to for weeks, had all the time been harbouring these cancerous thoughts about him. No pun intended, he thought blackly. And that stopped him. His brain rerunning what she had just said, recalling the conversation, the circumstances at the time, he could begin to see why, fed by gossip, she had jumped to the wrong conclusion.

'Dio mio!' Max curved a hand around her neck. He could feel the rapid beating of her pulse against his fingertips, and he looped an arm around her waist and hauled her hard against him. 'You actually believed that rubbish?' he snarled, his dark eyes sparking with outrage. 'You crazy fool! You listened to gossip and believed the worst of me.'

'The magazines didn't lie.'

'I was over thirty—of course I had slept with a few women.' His hand tightened on her throat. 'But as for the rest—you got it all wrong in your stupid juvenile mind.'

'I heard you, remember?' Sophie shot back, refusing to be intimidated by the towering proximity of his great body bristling with outraged fury.

'You said you heard everything, but you didn't.'

'I'm—'

'Shut up and listen,' he roared, his hand moving higher to grasp her chin, turning her face to his, forcing her to meet his eyes. 'The day you overheard me talking to Gina we were *not* talking about a three-way relationship. I have never had one in my life. Nor have I ever had anything other than a brother and sister relationship with Gina. Her preference is for her own sex, as it happens—Rosa is her partner. You should have had more sense than to listen to the idle gossip of a middle-aged woman like Marnie.'

'She said it was common knowledge,' Sophie defended, but the revelation that Gina was gay and Rosa her partner...well, it made sense of the odd tension she had felt when they'd all had coffee together. Her voice lacked a little of her earlier conviction as she added, 'She had no reason to lie.'

'In her dreams,' he grated. 'What you *actually* overheard was Gina comforting me as a sister should—because two days earlier I had been told I probably had testicular cancer. At the same time she was advising me, as a doctor, that I couldn't marry you without telling you the truth, because you would be bound to find out when I went for treatment. Is that plain enough for you?'

He studied her face closely and then smiled mirthlessly. 'The reason she is a little restrained around you is because, as a caring professional, she believed from what you said that you wanted no part of me as a sick man or—in your words—the future I had mapped out. She is a serious woman, and she thinks you are beautiful but too superficial. You can't blame her. Her joke tonight at dinner was perhaps a little crass, but from her past experience perfectly valid.'

At the word *cancer* her stomach had plunged, and shock held her rigid. His dark eyes were cold and hard on hers, but she couldn't look away as a dozen conflicting thoughts whirled in her brain. The overriding one being that surely no man, and certainly not such an arrogantly masculine man as Max, would lie about testicular cancer.

But then again it was still hard to believe, given he'd had no problem making love to her years ago. And his sexual prowess in the bedroom certainly had not diminished over the years—quite the reverse.

'Are you sure you were ill?' She stared at him. 'You seemed remarkably fit to me.'

'Yes, I was.' He met her gaze with sardonic challenge and continued. 'But don't worry—I got over it, and I'm fine now.'

She eyed him uncertainly, remembering that conversation on the fatal day *verbatim.* Dear heaven, she had run it through her head over and over again after they'd parted, to remind herself what a bastard he was in the hope it would cure the hopeless love she felt for him. Could she have been mistaken? Max's explanation made a horrible kind of sense. And if Gina was gay, as he said… She saw again Max reaching his hand to her at the end, when she'd told him she was leaving.

'When you asked me to talk with you and Gina, you meant about your illness?'

'Correct. It was that one-track mind of yours that thought otherwise.'

Appalled, she looked at the face only inches from her own. 'You really *did* have testicular cancer?' she murmured.

'Yes,' he said, a curious blankness in his dark eyes, as though he looked through and beyond her to some bad memory.

'Oh, my God!' All the blood drained from her face. 'I'm sorry—so sorry. What must you both have thought of me?' No wonder Gina was offhand with her. And as for Max, the anger she had sensed in him since they'd met again was now easily explained. He wanted her body, but he thought she was heartless. 'If only I had realised…' Green eyes full of compassion fixed on his. She wanted, needed to tell him—what? That she would never have left him? That she loved him? No, she didn't dare. 'If I'd known you were ill I would—' But he cut her off.

'It would have made no difference,' he said flatly. 'It was caught very early, quickly treated, and I've been clear for years. I don't need your pity.' Drawing her closer to him, he slowly ran his hand down from her throat to lightly cup her breast. 'Only your body. That hasn't changed.' For interminable seconds he stared down at her in total silence, then gave a mocking laugh. 'And before you go beating yourself up over it—you were right. I *did* set out to seduce you. I heard the bad news in the morning and took you to bed in the evening to reaffirm my manhood. Apparently it's a common impulsive reaction with most men, according to Gina.'

'Thanks for that,' she snapped. 'Glad to be of service.' From feeling heartsick and sorry, she was suddenly angry—and yet aroused as his hand slipped inside her robe.

'My pleasure,' Max said sardonically. 'So we both made a mistake years ago? It doesn't matter—I much prefer what we have now.'

She stared at him with huge pained eyes. She knew exactly what he meant; he had never wanted a teenage wife—or any other kind—he much preferred a mistress. Nothing had changed…including her devastating physical awareness of him. But it wasn't enough, would never be enough for her….

As if he knew what she was thinking, he gave her a slight arrogant smile, his head lowering.

'No…' she murmured. 'No,' she said more forcibly, and, shoving hard at his chest, she twisted. But he quieted her by capturing her hands in his and folding his arms around her.

'Yes,' he mocked.

She flung her head from side to side, but he backed her to the bed, and then she was falling.

His impressive body came over her and his mouth covered hers. She tried to keep her lips sealed, but he circled them with his tongue and bit gently, until with a helpless sigh she opened for him. He clasped her head in his hands and kissed her with a deep, possessive passion that stole the breath from her body.

'Forget the past,' he murmured, and stripped off her robe, his dark gaze skimming over her thinly covered slender body. 'The present is all I am concerned about.'

'But—' she started, but he bent his head and kissed her again and again, until she groaned with pleasure. And when he left her for a moment, to strip off his clothes, she simply watched with dazed, hungry eyes. He came back to her and divested her body of the scrap of lace to cover it with his own.

Much later, lying in his arms as the aftermath of passion subsided, Sophie hugged him close and stroked her hands up his chest, her earlier burst of defiance forgotten as she thought of what he must have gone through. Her heart filled with love and compassion for what he must have suffered.

She murmured, 'I am truly sorry you were ill, Max.'

A barely stifled oath left his lips, and abruptly he rolled off her and the bed. 'I told you—I don't need your mawkish sympathy,' he said coldly. 'I never did.' And he left.

CHAPTER ELEVEN

SOPHIE GOT OUT OF BED late the next morning after a restless night, and felt sick. Hardly surprising: the enormity of her mistake about Max and Gina haunted her. Dear heaven, what a fool she had been at nineteen—and she wasn't much better now. Because, being brutally honest, last night, with the original cause of mistrust between them resolved, she had nursed a secret hope that he might grow to love her as she loved him. Well, he had certainly disabused her of that notion. When was she going to learn?

He was a giant of a man in every way—enormously rich, successful and supremely confident in his abilities to defeat anything or anyone who stood in the way of what he wanted. A silent laugh escaped her. Given his stamina in the bedroom, not even cancer had dared dent his virile power. But he had not stayed in her bedroom last night, and that said it all....

It was Friday; he had probably left for Rome. It crossed her mind to wonder whether he would tell Gina the truth, and realised bitterly it didn't really matter. She was still the mistress and would never be anything more.

She dressed and went down to the kitchen, and poured

herself a cup of coffee from the pot on the stove. She took a sip as Maria came bustling in through the back door.

'That is my job. You should have rung,' Maria scolded her. 'Now, what would you like for breakfast?' And she told her to sit down.

Sophie pulled out a chair and sat down, a bitter smile curving her lips. Everyone had a job but her, and being a lady of leisure was really not her scene. Even the coffee tasted bitter, she thought, but drained it down to the dregs. Unless she did something about the sybaritic lifestyle Max had ordained for her, she was in danger of becoming bitter through and through.

She picked up a banana from the fruit bowl in the centre of the table and rose to her feet. 'Don't bother, Maria, this will do,' she said, and left the kitchen to run back up to her bedroom.

She found the card Professor Manta had given her….

The revelations of last night had changed nothing—except now she knew what Max had really thought of her when they had met up again. Not only had he seen her as a promiscuous woman with a string of lovers, but also as the kind of heartless girl who would walk away from sickness. Her heart ached to think of him suffering, but he had told her quite bluntly he didn't want her sympathy. More chilling, he had also told her what deep down inside she had always known: he had deliberately seduced her years ago, simply to confirm his masculinity when it was threatened.

He didn't want her caring or her compassion. There was nothing more to do except play out the charade of being his mistress until he tired of the sex. And, going on his past record, that shouldn't be long.

But in the meantime she had had enough of bowing to his every order. She sat on the end of the bed and took out her cellphone to dial Professor Manta's number. When she rang off, she had made an appointment to meet him outside the school.

Much to Diego's annoyance, she flatly refused to use the launch, insisting she was going out on her own and wanted to try the *vaporetto,* the public transport. Before he could stop her she left.

The sense of freedom was exhilarating. She met Professor Manta, and after a short interview with the principal of the school accepted the job of teaching two mornings a week until Christmas.

Professor Manta insisted on buying her a coffee at Florian before he had to leave for his hospital clinic, and that was where Max found her….

Last night Max had been furious when he'd discovered the depths of depravity Sophie thought him capable of. But, rather than discuss the rage and resentment burning inside him, he had swept her into bed and made passionate love to her—the only sure way he knew they could communicate.

Even in his wildest days he had never kept two women at the same time. He had demanded fidelity in his relationships for however long they lasted. His affair with Berenice at university had taught him that, after he'd discovered she had slept with half of his friends as well as him.

But this morning, in the early light of dawn, his anger fading, he had finally begun to think straight. He had walked back into Sophie's bedroom, determined to talk to her, but she'd been sound asleep. He'd clasped the sheet and pulled it down, intending to wake her, but had stopped. She'd looked so precious, with her knees tucked up like a baby to her stomach, the childish braid falling over her shoulder and across her breast, and he hadn't had the heart to waken her.

He'd watched her for a long time and realised he had no right to be angry with her. She had been young and innocent. Because of his wealth and lifestyle he'd always been the subject of gossip. It had never bothered him, but to an impressionable young girl it must have been a cause for insecurity. A half-heard conversation and she had leapt to a conclusion based on that gossip. But he was older and wiser, and should have known better. He should have insisted on telling her the truth, made her listen, but instead, because of his own problem, uppermost in his mind, he had told her he never wanted to set eyes on her again.

His perception of her as heartless had coloured the way he had treated her over the last few weeks, and he wasn't proud of his behaviour. He had left her sleeping this morning with one thought in his head—to try and make it up to her.

With that in mind he had given Maria strict instructions that she wasn't to be disturbed, and had spent two hours in his study, clearing up some work. He'd called Rome, and the hospice he helped out at every Friday, and told them he couldn't make it. Then he'd made an appointment with his lawyer for lunch, intent on having the humiliating agreement Sophie had signed destroyed. That done, he hoped maybe they could start again. Finally he had hot-footed it to the jewellers. He wanted to buy her a present; he wanted to surprise her....

But it was he who was surprised. Max stood in the shadow of the buildings for a while and simply watched. She was sitting outside the coffee house sipping coffee and smiling at Professor Manta. Elegant in a mulberry-coloured trouser suit, her silken hair loosely tied back with a velvet ribbon, her face delicately made-up, she looked relaxed and happy.

His hand turned over the small velvet box in his pocket. He was going to surprise her all right. Not with a gift, but with his presence. He had been an idiot to think differently of her, but that did not mean he was going to give up what he had got. She was *his* very sexy mistress, and at the minute a disobedient one. He was damn sure he wasn't going to lose her to some old professor. Straightening up, a look of grim determination on his face, he walked across the square.

'Sophie. I didn't expect to see you here this morning.' He saw her head lift and a guarded look come into her eyes.

'Max what a surprise. I thought you had gone to Rome. You always do on a Friday.'

He barely had his temper under control after the shock of seeing her with the professor. But he saw she was nervous, her hands clenched and twisted in her lap, and he thought, *You have a damn good right to be.*

'Obviously not,' he drawled. 'I have a luncheon appointment with my lawyer.' He turned to Professor Manta. '*Buongiorno, Professore*,' he said, and, indicating a chair, '*Permesso*?'

'*Prego*,' the professor said, and stood up. 'How is the hospice going these days? Still expanding?' he asked Max.

'Yes,' Max said shortly.

'Good work.' Patting Max on the back, he added, 'I have to leave now. I'll give you the pleasure of escorting Sophie home. You're a very lucky man. I can't tell you how grateful San Bartolomeo is to have secured her services. *Arrivederci.*'

Max looked at Sophie for a long, silent moment. 'Explain.'

Sophie drew in a shaky breath. Dressed in a charcoal-grey business suit, and a paler grey shirt and tie, he looked tall, dark and austere—and decidedly dangerous. He was staring at her with cold dark eyes, but she refused to be intimidated.

'I told you. Professor Manta asked me if I was interested in a job.' She gave him a sweetly cynical smile. 'Teaching languages at his grandsons' school—San Bartolomeo. They need someone to fill in for a language teacher who is on extended sick leave until Christmas.' She picked up her coffee and drained the cup. 'I called him this morning and said I was interested. We have just been to see the principal. I start work next week, Tuesdays and Thursdays. Is that okay with you, oh lord and master?' she mocked.

He was taken aback by her vehemence, but he couldn't really blame her after what he had implied last night about the professor. The man actually had offered her a job. He wondered what else he had got wrong about her. But he wasn't about to let her get away with openly defying him. 'Where was Diego while all this was going on? I told you not to leave the house without him. You deliberately disobeyed my orders.'

She pushed back her chair and stood up. 'He is probably at your house, where I left him. As for your orders—I forgot,' she said lightly. 'Now, I am going to catch the *vaporetto* and return—if *that* is okay with you?'

His face grim, he got to his feet and grasped her arm. 'Such meekness. But I will escort you back, and we will discuss your idea of working later.'

'There is nothing to discuss. I have accepted the job at San Bartolomeo.'

'You already have a job. Me,' he reminded her succinctly. 'You also have credit cards and a generous allowance.'

'A salary, don't you mean?' Sophie heard herself snipe, very conscious of Max's steely grip on her arm as they walked to the landing stage.

'Call it what you like, but spend the damn money. Shop, lunch, do what other women do. You don't have to teach a bunch of kids.'

'But I love children—and I hate shopping.'

Max hand tightened on her arm. 'In my experience *every* woman likes shopping with unlimited money. Try it and see,' he drawled cynically.

'Your kind of woman, yes, but not me.' Her head lifted fractionally, and her voice was remarkably calm as she met his dark gaze. 'You really don't know me at all, Max.' The *vaporetto* had arrived and people were disembarking. 'Contrary to what you and Gina think for whatever mistaken reason, I *do* care about people. The only reason I stayed at that dinner last night after being the butt of Gina's so-called joke was not because you threatened me but for my mother. She died of breast cancer, and for two years Meg and I nursed her. The only reason I am here now is because I care for my brother Timothy. If you had the least interest in me in any way other than sexual you might have realised that.'

His hand fell from her arm and she saw a muscle jerk in his cheek. He didn't like that, but she was sick of pandering to what Max liked.

'I finally realised last night exactly how you see me. In your mind I am an experienced woman of the world, out for what I can get from any man and without a caring bone in my body. And do you know what really sickens me? Even believing that, you still had no scruples about enjoying my body. So what does that make you?'

Not waiting for a response, she walked on board the *vaporetto*, went inside the cabin and sat down.

A few moments later a stony-faced Max sat down beside her, the warmth of his hard thigh seeping into hers.

'I thought you had a lunch appointment,' she gibed, trying to move along the seat, but she was pressed up against the window already.

'*Non importante*,' he said, with a wave of his hand. 'You and I need to talk.'

'I know your idea of talking. A few brief commands that usually involve me being horizontal,' she said bluntly. 'But you're wasting your time today. Every Friday afternoon Tessa brings her children over. I give them an English lesson and we all have dinner together. My life does not stop when you're not around.'

She looked at him. His starkly handsome face was dark and taut, and she could feel the tension in the long muscular body so close to hers. 'And if you are going to tell me I can't accept the job at San Bartolomeo, forget it. The way I feel at the minute, the thought of working is the only thing keeping me sane. For two pins I would say to hell with you *and* my father and get back to my own life. So don't push it.'

'No, I don't mind you working at San Bartolomeo at all,' Max said swiftly. The very idea of her leaving him was not something he could bear to contemplate.

'Just as well,' she muttered, the wind taken out of her sails. Maybe Max was getting tired of her. That was her next thought. She turned her head and looked out of the window, for some inexplicable reason moisture glazing her eyes.

'This is our stop.' He took her arm and led her off the boat.

'Are you sure?' she glanced around. 'This is not where I caught the *vaporetto*.'

His hand tightened momentarily. 'This is quicker.' And, holding her arm like a vice, he strode forward. She stumbled to keep up with him. He never once slackened his pace, and he almost pulled her up the steps to the house.

'Where is the fire? she asked breathlessly, trying to shake off his hand as they entered the hall.

He stood looking down at her for a moment, towering over her, his eyes glittering with some fierce emotion. 'In me,' she thought she heard him say. But at that moment Diego came dashing from the kitchen.

'*Signor*, you are back.'

'Yes, and I want a word with you.'

With Max's attention diverted, Sophie slipped upstairs to her room. She kicked off her shoes as usual, took off her suit and replaced it with the pink tracksuit she favoured for visiting the gym and hanging around the kitchen with Tessa and the children.

Her stomach rumbled and she realised she was starving;

she had eaten only a banana at breakfast. She had her hand on the door to go back downstairs when suddenly it was flung open. Instinctively she put her other hand to her face and went staggering back against the wall.

'Sophie!' She watched with eyes that were watering as Max dashed into the room.

'You could have broken my nose, you great oaf.' Blinking, she shoved the door back. 'As it is, my knuckles will be black and blue for weeks. Are you raving mad? Have you never heard of knocking?' she yelled, straightening up and rubbing her bruised hand with the other.

She was not aware of the fierce tension affecting Max's tall frame. She was too busy checking out her own; her back wasn't feeling too great after its sudden contact with the wall.

'Yes, I *am* mad—about you,' Max said fiercely, and suddenly he was in front of her, his hands reaching for her, roaming gently over her head and her shoulders, down her arms. '*Dio!* If I've hurt you I will never forgive myself.'

Wide-eyed, Sophie stared up at him and saw such pain, such passion in his dark eyes, her breath caught in her throat. She couldn't believe what she was hearing—what she was seeing.

'I'll call the doctor,' he declared, his hands moving feverishly over her. 'My love, I couldn't bear it if I lost you.'

'What did you say?' she asked, stunned.

The austere, sophisticated mask Max usually presented to the world had cracked wide open, and he looked absolutely frantic.

'The doctor. I'll call the doctor.'

'No—after that,' she prompted, a tiny ray of hope

lighting her heart as she saw his slight confusion. 'Tell me again.' She needed to hear him say *my love* so she could start believing it might be possible.

His hands stopped their urgent search and settled on her waist, his dark eyes holding hers. 'I couldn't bear it if I lost you,' he said, in a voice husky with emotion.

Sophie saw the vulnerability in his eyes and was amazed that Max, her handsome, arrogant lover, could be so unsure of himself.

'I did once, and I never want to make the same mistake again.'

'And why is that?' she asked, hardly daring to breathe, the ray of hope growing bigger and brighter by the second.

Max tensed, his hands tightening on her waist, a flush of colour burning under his skin as he looked at her. 'Oh, I think you know, Sophie.' Even now he had difficulty saying the words. Even when he knew his happiness, his life, depended on convincing the woman in his arms to stay with him. 'My love.'

He had said *my love* again; she had not imagined it. Sophie was suddenly conscious of the erratic pounding of her heart, and it took every shred of courage she possessed to ask the next question. 'Am I really your love, Max?

'Yes.' Max gulped, his eyes burning into hers. 'I love you, Sophie. I know I have given you no cause to believe me, but it is the truth. I love you.' From not being able to say the words, Max suddenly had no trouble repeating them. In fact he would tell her a million times over if he thought it would convince her to stay with him.

It was the answer she had prayed for, and Sophie drew a shaky breath. Only then did she raise her hands to touch him. She ran her fingers through his hair and cradled his head in her palms. 'You love me?' She paused, saw the answer he made no attempt to hide in his dark luminous gaze, and added, 'As I love *you*, Max.'

She finally told him the truth she had held in her heart for years. Because the impossible had happened; Max loved her. Tears of emotion misted her vision, a smile of pure joy that reflected her inner radiance lighting her beautiful face.

'You love me? You really mean that, after all I have done?' he asked roughly, and his doubt squeezed her heart.

'I fell in love with you the first moment I saw you. I still love you and always will.'

Max saw the truth in the glittering green eyes that met his intense gaze.

'Ah, Sophie. I don't deserve you,' he groaned, and kissed her with a deep tender passion. She clung to him and returned the kiss with all the love in her heart. His arms tightened around her and he lifted her off her feet to lay her gently in the middle of the bed. Quickly he shed his clothes, but Sophie was almost as quick pulling off her tracksuit and panties.

Max groaned, falling down beside her and scooping her into his arms. Their limbs entwined, she glimpsed the deep, throbbing desire in the depths of his smouldering eyes as his mouth met hers. She gloried in the hungry passion of his kiss and reciprocated with a wondrous abandon. He loved her, and she cried out his name as his mouth found her breasts, his caressing hands arousing and exploring until her every nerve was taut with quivering, aching desire—and more. Love had freed the hungry yearning inside her. Urgently her hands roamed over his hard muscled body, from his wide shoulders down to lean hips.

'Sophie,' he groaned, and he slid his hands under her back. Frantically she locked her legs around him as he surged into her with a primitive and powerful force that reached to her very core. In a wild wonderful ride, their mingled cries echoed a mutual pleasure of cosmic intensity as they reached nirvana, that joining of the souls with creation as one.

They lay, a tangle of welded bodies, breathless, shuddering and speechless, until Max raised his head to say, 'Sophie, my love,' and kissed her with a tenderness so profound her eyes filled with tears of happiness.

Eventually, as their breathing grew steadier, he withdrew from her, then wrapped her in his arms to cuddle her into his side.

'I thought the first time I made love to you was the most intense sexual experience of my life,' Max said thickly, staring down into her flushed face. 'But now…' He was lost for words. '*Dio*, how I love you.' He gave up and kissed her love-swollen lips, slowly, gently and with aching tenderness. He swept a damp tendril of hair from her brow. 'I know I have treated you abominably in the past, and I also know that if I apologise to my dying day it will not be enough.'

'Shh…it doesn't matter,' Sophie murmured, placing a finger on his lips. 'As long as I know you love me now, that is all that matters.'

'No.' Max took her hand and saw the red knuckles, gently brushed them with his lips. 'You're hurt, and I know

I have hurt you in other ways. I need to talk—to explain.' He dropped her hand and she stroked it teasingly up his chest.

'You're sure about that?'

'I need to talk. And I am not going to give in to temptation again until I have,' he said with a wry smile, and recaptured her hand.

'Spoilsport,' Sophie teased

'Maybe.' He grinned and lay back, his deep, husky voice serious. 'But for too long I have used sex as the only way to communicate with you. Now I am determined to tell you the truth.'

'That sounds ominous.' Sophie pushed up on her elbow to stare down at him and threw her other arm over his broad chest, her fingers stroking through his curling chest hair. 'Are you sure you wouldn't rather do something else?'

'Witch.' He grinned again. 'I know what you're trying to do, but I refuse to be sidetracked.'

'Pity!'

He clasped her hand on his chest. 'I am serious, Sophie.' The determination and the intensity of his dark gaze kept her silent. 'From the minute I first set eyes on you in Sicily I wanted you. But Alex warned me off you; you were too young and under his protection. I accepted that, as up until then I'd preferred mature women who knew the score, not dewy-eyed romantic teenagers.' Sophie stiffened. 'Please don't be offended—I am trying to tell you the truth as I saw it at the time.'

'Okay,' she murmured. She was not pleased to think that

Alex had warned Max off, but it *did* explain Max refusing to touch her at first, and she had to admire his restraint.

'I very quickly realised I couldn't keep away from you. I told myself there was no harm in having a light flirtation with a beautiful girl, and I had no intention of taking it any further. I liked my freewheeling lifestyle. But that night when I took you out to dinner, in the car after, I very nearly… Well, suffice it to say it took every bit of willpower I possessed and then some not to follow you into the chalet and make love to you. I left the next day, determined not to see you again.

'In my conceit, I thought there were plenty of willing ladies around without getting embroiled with a teenager. I even convinced myself that the time wasn't right, but if I bumped into you a few years later it would be okay.'

'That was some conceit,' Sophie could not help saying.

'Yes, I know. But a few days later I was already weakening,' he said with a wry smile. 'I went to Russia intending to get rid of my sexual frustration with a lady there. But I didn't. I returned to Rome and made a date with an old flame for that night. I left her at her door, still frustrated.'

'I'm not sure I like such determination,' Sophie murmured.

'Nothing happened, I swear,' Max said quickly. 'On the Friday morning I went though my personal mail in the office and there was a letter informing me to get in touch with the clinic I had attended earlier for a medical. There was some doubt about a sample I had given. I made the appointment the same morning, and it was then I discovered I might have cancer. I'd already arranged to meet Gina for lunch, and she filled me in on the facts. It was easily treatable, with a very high success rate, and did not necessarily affect a man's virility. But as a precaution I should freeze some sperm just in case I couldn't father a child naturally.'

'Oh, my God! You must have felt terrible!' Sophie said, blinking back the tears pricking at her eyes and squeezing his hand. But he let her hand go. He still wasn't prepared to accept her sympathy, she realised sadly.

'No, what I felt was furious—and scared. I couldn't believe it was happening. From thinking I had all the time in the world, I was wondering if I had any. It seems selfish now, but the one thought in my head was that if I was going to die I was going to make damn sure I had you first. And I ordered the plane to take me to Sicily.'

How like her impulsive, arrogant, but adorable Max, Sophie thought, a husky chuckle escaping her.

'It wasn't funny,' Max chided her. 'When I saw you by the pool all I could think of was making love to you. I suppose I did deliberately seduce you. But when we made love it was the most wonderful experience in my life. Until now.'

Max reached up and tenderly outlined her lips with one long finger, his dark eyes burning into hers. 'I would like to say I knew I loved you then, but I have to admit that afterwards I did wonder if it was a subconscious reaction at the thought of having cancer—a need to prove there was nothing wrong with me as a man. All I do know is that when you lay asleep in my arms I thought I wouldn't mind if you were pregnant. And when I asked you to marry me I did mean it. Later, of course, when Gina arrived, it all fell apart. And now we know why.'

Sophie could understand his uncertainty, but she chose

to believe he had loved her from the start. Raising her hand, she gently stroked his cheek, her green eyes gleaming with love. 'That was my fault. I should have listened to you.'

'No. No, it was mine. I was older and should have explained. Instead I dismissed you as a heartless young girl. I was determined to put you out of my mind and concentrate on getting better. The latter I succeeded in doing quite easily. But forgetting you was not so easy.'

'Good, I'm glad.' She let her hand stroke over his shoulder and moved closer, to stretch one long leg over his thighs.

'Yes, well… I am trying to confess here, Sophie, and you are trying to do something else.' His mobile mouth quirked at the corners. 'And it is not going to work. At least not yet.'

She responded by slumping on top of him, her breasts against his chest. 'Okay, go on.' She wriggled, and he laughed.

'When I saw you again at that dinner, looking so beautiful with Abe Asamov, I saw red.'

'I was never *with* Abe, the way you mean. I spent a summer vacation from university in Russia with his wife and children, teaching them English. He is just a friend,' she explained quickly. 'I hadn't seen him for ages, and he just acted like that for fun.'

'Yes, well, it doesn't matter now.' Max believed her—he had to, for his own peace of mind. 'But at the time I think I went a little crazy. I had been helping out with the hotel business, and your father's name had come up—as you know.' He grimaced. 'I decided it was fate. I should never have forced you into being my mistress, but once I had, and you were so responsive in my arms, I told myself that was all I wanted. Until last night. I stormed from this bed because I didn't want your sympathy. But I came back and watched you sleeping, and knew then that I loved you quite desperately. Because I wanted so much more. I wanted back the love you once said you felt for me.'

'You should have wakened me, then,' Sophie said softly

He smoothed a hand over her cheek and swept back the long swathe of her hair, his dark eyes holding hers. 'No. I was determined not to make mistakes this time. I arranged to meet my lawyer for lunch, to cancel that demeaning contract I made you sign, and then I went out to buy you a present—to surprise you, to ask if we could start again. But you surprised me. I saw you with Professor Manta and I was mad with jealousy.' His lips curved in a self-deprecatory smile.

'But it got worse. I discovered he really had offered you a job teaching, and then came your revelation about your mother, your flat refusal to spend your time and my money shopping, like all the other women I have known.'

She didn't like *all the other women*, but she let it pass. He was hers now.

'I had misjudged you over and over again. You were right when you said I didn't know you at all. I stood for a moment, paralysed with fear, and watched you board the *vaporetto*, certain I was going to lose you. I followed you on board determined to make it my life's work to remedy that and keep you at any cost.'

'You've succeeded,' Sophie said, her voice husky with emotion. That Max, her arrogant, magnificent lover, should bare his heart to her had convinced her beyond a shred of doubt that he really did love her. She looped an arm around his neck. 'If you've finished talking…' she smiled, a slow, sensuous curve of her lips '…can I do what I want now?' And she pressed her lips against his throat, then to the hollow of his shoulder blade, whilst her slender fingers traced his silky chest hair and she teased a hard male nipple.

'It depends what you want,' Max said, on a strangled groan.

Pushing on his chest, Sophie sat up, straddling him. Tossing her head back, her green eyes gleaming, she said, 'I want to make love to you. I always want to; it is just what you do to me.'

Max had never heard, felt or seen anything more seductive in his life. Her beautiful face was flushed pink, her glorious hair falling in a tumbling mass around her shoulders, playing peek-a-boo with her lush breasts, and as for her thighs gripping him…

'Feel free,' he murmured.

In the silence of the afternoon, with the sun pouring through the window, Sophie did just that. She was like a child in a candy shop as she kissed and licked her way down his great torso, tracing his belly button and lower, stroking his thighs, and by the time she was kneeling between them he was painfully aroused. Fascinated, she stroked her hands up his inner thighs.

'I never knew a man could be so…beautiful,' she said, glancing up at his taut, dark face. She grinned a broad, beautiful smile. 'You are perfect.'

For a long moment Max stared at her with the strangest look in his eyes, and then said, 'What about Sam?'

Sophie frowned in confusion. 'What about Sam? I'm going to be her bridesmaid in February,' she murmured.

'*Her* bridesmaid—Sam is a *woman*?' he choked. 'Tell me, Sophie, how many lovers have you had?'

'Well…' She pretended to think as it dawned on her that Max was very definitely jealous, and had been from the minute they'd met again. First Abe, and now Sam. 'Let me see, including you—one.'

He pulled her down to take her lips with his in a fierce, possessive kiss, and then, grasping her thighs, he thrust up into her sleek wet heat in a paroxysm of passion.

Sophie collapsed on top of him, her heart pounding fit to burst as she felt the lingering spasms of their mutual climax in every nerve-ending of her body. With his arm wrapped securely around her, his hand gently stroking her hair, calming her down, she closed her eyes.

'Are you all right?' Max asked.

She heard his huskily voiced question and opened her eyes, looking up at him, a languorous smile curving her full lips. 'Surprised, but never better,' she sighed.

'Surprised… *Surprise*!' he exclaimed, and pushed her away. He leapt off the bed and picked up his trousers.

It *was* time they surfaced, she supposed. Heaven knew what the staff must think. And she swung her legs off the bed—only to see him drop his trousers again.

'Max?' she queried, and to her amazement he fell to his knees and grasped her left hand.

'I almost forgot your surprise.' He opened a velvet box and held up a magnificent emerald and diamond ring.

'Will you marry me? I swear I will love and cherish you to my dying day.'

His starkly handsome face, taut with strain, filled her vision, and tears of emotion flooded her eyes. 'This was my surprise?'

She swallowed the sob in her throat. He wanted to marry her—he had already bought the ring.

'Yes,' he said, and, taking her hand, slipped the ring on her finger. He stood up, pulling her with him. 'Now, all you have to do is say yes.'

'Yes,' she cried, and their lips and hearts met in a kiss like no other—a kiss that was an avowal of love and a promise for the future.

'Are you sure about this?'

Sophie fingered the pearls at her throat, her wedding gift from Max, and glanced up at him with a wealth of love and laughter in her sparkling green eyes. Today was her wedding day, and with her family and friends from England, and Max's family and friends in attendance, they had married, in a moving church service in Venice.

Sam and Gina had been her bridesmaids, and Timothy a pageboy. Gina, on learning of the gossip and the trouble caused by her hiding her sexuality, had come out, and her mother had accepted the fact.

The wedding breakfast had been held in an elegant restaurant near the church, and now they were going home by gondola, to change and adopt a more modern form of transport to fly to Paris for a short honeymoon.

'Trust me,' Max said huskily. He had never seen Sophie look more exquisite, in a long white velvet gown, her magnificent hair loose, entwined with a crown of rosebuds, and a velvet muff decorated with the same flowers on one wrist. She looked like some fey medieval princess and she took his breath away. She already had his heart.

He caught her hand and helped her into the gondola. Sitting down, he drew her to his side. 'It is a tradition that Venetians travel in a gondola on their wedding day.'

'You're not Venetian,' she pointed out teasingly, and a great cry went up from the crowd gathered at the landing stage as the vessel, covered in garlands of flowers, began to move.

'True—but we would never hear the end of it from Diego and Maria if we didn't,' Max offered, looking down at his beautiful blushing bride.

'You're such a pussycat, really, Max Quintano.' Sophie laughed.

'And you, Sophie, are my wife—Signora Quintano,' he said, with pride and heartfelt satisfaction. And he couldn't resist; the kiss in church had not been nearly enough. Closing his arms around her, he kissed her again.

The gondola rocked and the crowd cheered again, but the two locked together heard nothing but the pounding of their two hearts as one.

Much later that evening, after they had consummated their marriage, they lay with their limbs entwined in the huge bed of the bridal suite in a luxurious Parisian hotel, and Sophie gave Max her wedding gift.

'You know you told me Gina insisted you freeze your sperm just in case you couldn't father a child?' She felt him tense and kissed his jaw. 'Well, there was no need. I'm pregnant.'

He grasped her hand and their eyes met, and she was sure she saw moisture in the luminous depths of Max's. 'That's incredible—a miracle. But are you sure? How? When?'

'Well…' She linked her fingers through his and cuddled up to him, secure in his love for her. 'A certain guy walked into my bedroom and laughed at my dolls, and then he made love to me and left for a while. Then later he returned, with a bottle of wine and two glasses and nothing else, and he made love to me again.' She knew the exact moment, and as he remembered his mouth curled in a broad smile.

Max chuckled, and the grip on her hand tightened. 'It must have been all those eyes watching me that made me forget protection.' He drew her to him, the look in his eyes one she knew very well.

'Or maybe I should have mentioned that a couple of the dolls I collected on my travels are fertility symbols.'

He threw back his dark head and laughed out loud. 'Ah, Sophie, *amore mia*, you are truly priceless and all mine—now and for ever.' And he proceeded to show her what he meant, with her enthusiastic co-operation.